THE BEST AMERICAN

NONREQUIRED
READING

2016

THE BEST AMERICAN

NONREQUIRED
READING™
2016

∎

EDITED BY

RACHEL KUSHNER

AND THE STUDENTS OF

826 NATIONAL

MANAGING EDITOR
DANIEL GUMBINER

A MARINER ORIGINAL
HOUGHTON MIFFLIN HARCOURT
BOSTON ▪ NEW YORK
2016

ISSN: 1539-316x
ISBN: 978-0-544-81211-6

Printed in the United States of America
DOC 10 9 8 7 6 5 4 3 2 1

CONTENTS

Editors' Note

THIS SPRING, the *Best American Nonrequired Reading* (*BANR*) committee was invited to watch its editor, the celebrated novelist Rachel Kushner, interview another celebrated novelist, Don DeLillo. We arrived way too early for the interview so we walked across the street, to a café called The Grove, where we ordered breakfast sandwiches, because all the normal sandwiches seemed too expensive. After this we walked over to the theater to retrieve our tickets at will call. Because our tickets were complementary, they had to be retrieved from a different pile. This made us feel sort of like celebrities and less like people who couldn't afford a sandwich.

The stage at the Nourse Theater was spare: just two chairs and a table with a bowl of apples. The theater itself was cavernous and full of people who like books.

"Do you think they will eat any of the apples?" one of our committee members asked.

"We will have to wait and see," another committee member replied.

They did not eat any of the apples. Mr. DeLillo discussed his latest novel, *Zero K*, as well as his past work. At one point, he told a story about the book *Libra*, his bestselling novel, which takes as its subject the Kennedy assassination and Lee Harvey Oswald. People often asked him, Mr. DeLillo explained, if he knew the book would be a bestseller. He always had a hard time responding honestly to this question, because he was afraid that no one would believe him if he told the truth. The truth was this:

Throughout the whole process of writing the novel, Mr. DeLillo had kept a photo of Lee Harvey Oswald propped up on his writing desk and then, as he was typing the final sentence of the book, the picture began to slide off the shelf. Mr. DeLillo paused to catch the falling photo.

"God damn it," he said to himself. "It's a bestseller."

For three years that photo had stayed propped up on his writing desk as he worked on the novel. It's the type of story that is too perfect to believe, too poetic. We're still not sure we believe it ourselves and yet, here we are, including it in our editors' note. Why are we doing this? Because we want an opportunity to complain about the price of sandwiches at The Grove? Partially, yes. Like most sandwiches in San Francisco, they are much too expensive. Because we want to brag about the fact that we got to see Rachel Kushner interview Don DeLillo? This as well. It was a great interview. But mostly because Mr. DeLillo's story speaks to something that our committee frequently discusses, and that is: What makes a story convincing?

If you drew a graph that documented drama and credibility, it would show that drama increases as credibility decreases. Or at least many suspect it would. At the time of this printing, science is not yet advanced enough to produce such a graph. We have tried to draw several of these graphs ourselves and they never come out right. Somehow the lines always end up all squiggly and sideways. Once we ended up with a Venn diagram, which was useful to no one at all. The point is that things tend to be dramatic because they seem both fantastic and true, but when things become too fantastic, our brains decide that they are not credible, and then they cease to be very dramatic. Most of the time.

The high school students on our committee come from all over the Bay Area. Some of them go to private school and some of them go to public school. Some are sophomores and others are seniors. Together, we meet on Monday nights at McSweeney's Publishing in San Francisco to read through all of the magazines and literary journals published in a given year. During each meeting we discuss at least two texts that have been nominated for inclusion in the book. We talk about what they had to teach us and we explore their merits and deficiencies. In the end, after much deliberation, we select the work that gets published in this anthology.

In this book you will find a modern history of the Black Lives Matter movement and a short story about Bulgaria. There will be poems and investigative journalism and an interview with our president. There will be one book review. We have selected these texts under the guidance of Rachel Kushner, our brilliant editor and a graduate of San Francisco public schools herself. Together, we have looked for texts that say something about what it means to be alive in 2016. We have tried to find work that moves us, work that is captivating and dynamic and honest. In many cases, we have asked ourselves: Is this work true to life? It's often a difficult question to answer. Sometimes, highly fantastical things feel true to life. Other times, ostensibly realistic things don't feel true at all. This is why the graph always gets messed up.

Our committee in San Francisco is aided by another committee of high school students in Ann Arbor, who work out of a robot supply and repair shop. They are excellent readers and have provided us with a good deal of help, although we cannot speak to their ability to repair robots because, in the past year, we have not needed to repair any of our robots. Thank you to everyone on their committee. Thanks also to the great Ali Kucukgocmen, whose work was vital to the production of this book. We tip our caps to you, Ali. And, lastly, we would like to extend our thanks to you, amiable reader. We hope you enjoy the book and we'll see you again next year. Same place, same time.

DANIEL GUMBINER and the *BANR* Committee
San Francisco, June 2016

INTRODUCTION

THEY SAID do you want to be the guest editor and I said what does it entail and they said not much because high school students actually pick the work. The student editors of the *Best American Nonrequired Reading* are mostly from San Francisco, and I immediately wanted to know where they go to school, which was a loaded question, because what I really wanted to know was if any attend public schools, as I did. "They are a mix," Daniel Gumbiner, a former student-editor and now the grown up and very talented managing editor of the anthology, told me, "and so partly yes."

Two of *BANR*'s student editors, it turned out, were even enrolled at my own alma mater, George Washington, a large high school in the Richmond District that a reporter for Pacific News Service, in 1981, the year before I began attending, described as looking "like it has been hit by a series of bombs and nobody ever bothered to clean up the mess." That is not how I remember it, though this reporter goes on to savor her descriptions of our trashed and garbage-strewn school, where she says the windows are all broken and the lockers graffitied and smashed. Maybe it was like that and I didn't know any better, or maybe this reporter was sheltered and had never been to a big city high school and had to compensate for her fears with hyperbole. She conveniently didn't mention the beautiful view of the Golden Gate Bridge, and she portrayed our race and ethnic diversity as a violent mish-mash of warring groups, rather than as something positive. "Almost as if out of the rubble," she wrote, groups of teenagers emerged, "each with its own style of dressing, its music, drugs, cars, militant rhetoric—and weapons." This, I'll admit, was basically true (except for the militant rhetoric, unless she simply meant the puffed-up talk of teenagers who want to seem tough). Washington had a fully outfitted auto shop. Customizing cars was a major activity and indeed, the aesthetics hewed to race affiliation. She said we had race conflicts. Also true. It was a school of three thousand, a world where people of different racializations and ethnicities were forced to actually mix, to deal with one another, and the effect of that on the students was incredibly complicated, and also lasting.

In the early 1980s, when I went there, Washington High School was about 10 percent white, very few of whom were middle class. Now, Washington is almost 8 percent white. Middle class and more affluent whites in the city still send their kids to private school. When I went there, the school had twice the number of African-American students it does now, the drop mapping the decline in population of African-Americans in San Francisco, itself mapping the lack of affordable housing, and the skyrocketing cost of living there. San Francisco has changed a lot, as everyone knows: tech boom, rich people, housing crunch, Google bus—you've heard about it. One thing that hasn't changed is a dramatic wealth disparity, which overlaps and interlinks with a race divide. Almost 80 percent of white students in San Francisco go to private school, while a higher overall percentage of students in San Francisco are enrolled in private school than in any other major city in America. The public school system has changed from the time when I was a student. Since 2001, when the city was legally mandated to no longer use race and ethnicity in efforts to desegregate, there is a "choice" lottery, instead of district schools. White students typically try for the same few schools, where they concentrate. And regardless of race, middle class kids have parents with time and resources to navigate the lottery. Students end up cordoned by class and race, just as they have all through the city's various efforts at integration, starting in 1971, with mandatory busing. Despite several desegregation decrees over the last forty years, San Francisco is as far now, or possibly farther, from the objectives of *Brown vs. the Board of Education* as it was when the ruling was made, in 1954.

You might say the situation I depict is similar everywhere in America, but I'm not from everywhere, I am from San Francisco, where the differences have always seemed extreme. I did not even realize how extreme until I went to college, across the Bay (in an era when a UC education was almost free). In college I met people who were from my city, but from worlds I had not known existed. My brother and one other friend were the only people I knew in high school who went to four-year colleges upon graduating, but I'll confess that may have had something to do with my choice in friends, many of whom had already dropped out by the time I graduated. Those who didn't, eventually transferred to schools like John O'Connell, where they could learn trades, or Independent Learning Center, where less than half graduated, or Downtown High, which was the last stop in the school district for students with disciplinary problems. What propelled me, unlike them, toward college is obvious: I had educated parents. We were living on their modest salaries as post-doctoral researchers in biology laboratories. They could never have afforded private school tuition, but class in this country is not determined merely by income. It reproduces itself in deeper and more insidious ways, and education is one of them. But also, I was lucky enough to have a wonderful English teacher at Washington, Mr. Williams, whose lectures on *Moby Dick*, on *Hamlet*, on *The Great Gatsby* I still remember in vivid detail. When my first novel came out, my mother tracked down Mr. Williams, by then retired, and invited him to a reading I gave. He was impressed I'd become a published novelist, said I was the only one, so far as he knew, of all his students over the thirty-something years he taught at Washington. But he also confessed that he had no recollection of me whatsoever, though he remembered my older brother quite well. This seems appropriate and fine: His purpose was to form and mold the students, and not the other way around. From what I hear, Washington is now a better school than it used to be. According to city data, 57 percent of its graduates go on to four-year colleges. I feel confident the English teachers there will have students who become published authors. And this year alone, they have two who have already become published editors.

If a great teacher can be found at any school, what can't often be found is an opportunity for students of various backgrounds, social class, outlook, to blend. This is part of what makes 826 Valencia such a special organization, one to be revered and supported. Among its many incredible programs is Best American Nonrequired Reading, where students can work together, read together, debate, and discuss, and they are from different environments and neighborhoods and schools—public and private, religious and secular. The esteemed and brilliant 2016 editorial board at *BANR* are a truly diverse group of people whose commonality was reading carefully, with empathy and humility. I only wish I could have attended their meetings every week, but since I do not live in San Francisco, I made a single guest appearance. We worked long distance. I suggested some things, but most of their selections they discovered as a group, by reading broadly. When I was at their meeting, it was clear to me, and to the group, that part of our objective was to encompass some of the critical themes and events of the past year, aside from the more general project of choosing excellent and hopefully timeless texts.

The unit of the year suggests the arc of its news cycle, and behind that cycle, the real fluctuations, the rhythms and ruptures, of historical time. But inside of a year, there is also the dynamic potential for poetic transcendence, where a person is only a reader, a mind, and can go wherever a writer takes them: out of their own era, their own limits, into something remarkable.

RACHEL KUSHNER

Rachel Kushner *is the author of two novels,* The Flamethrowers, *a finalist for the National Book Award, and* Telex from Cuba, *also a finalist for the National Book Award, as well as* The Strange Case of Rachel K, *a collection of short prose. She is a Guggenheim Fellow and winner of the Harold D. Vursell Award from the American Academy of Arts and Letters. Her fiction has appeared in* The New Yorker, Harper's Magazine, *and the* Paris Review.

THE BEST AMERICAN

NONREQUIRED
READING
2016

ANTHONY MARRA

■

The Grozny Tourist Bureau

FROM *Zoetrope*

THE OILMEN HAVE arrived from Beijing for a ceremonial signing over of drilling rights. "It's a holiday for them," their translator told me, last night, at the Grozny Eternity Hotel, which is both the only five-star hotel and the only hotel in the republic. I nodded solemnly; he needn't explain. I came of age in the reign of Brezhnev, when young men would enter civil service academies hardy and robust, only to leave two years later anemic and stooped, cured forever of the inclination to be civil or of service to anyone. Still, Beijing must be grim if they're vacationing in Chechnya.

"We'll reach Grozny in ten minutes," I announce to them in English. The translator sits in the passenger seat. He's a stalk-thin man with a head of hair so black and lustrous it looks sculpted from shoe polish. I feel a shared camaraderie with translators—as I do with deputies and underlings of all stripes—and as he speaks in slow, measured Mandarin, I hear the resigned and familiar tone of a man who knows he is more intelligent than his superiors.

The road winds over what was once a roof. A verdigris-encrusted arm rises from the debris, its forefinger raised skyward. The Lenin statue had stood in the square outside this school, arm upthrust, rallying the schoolchildren to glorious revolution, but now, buried to his chin like a cowboy sentenced to death beneath the desert sun, Vladimir Ilyich waves only for help. We drive onward, passing brass bandoliers and olive flak jackets, red bandannas and golden epaulettes, the whole palette of Russian invasion painted across a thunderstorm of wreckage. Upon seeing the 02 Interior Ministry plate dangling below the Mercedes's hood, the spies, soldiers, policemen, and armed thugs wave us through without hesitation. The streets become more navigable. Trucks can't make it from the cement works to the holes in the ground without being hijacked by one or another shade of our Technicolor occupation and sold to Russian construction companies north of the border, so road crews salvage office doors from collapsed administration buildings and lay them across the craters. Affixed to the doors are the names and titles of those who once worked behind them. *Mansur Khalidov: Head of Oncology; City Hospital Number Six. Yakha Sagaipova: Assistant Director of Production; Ministry of Oil and Gas Industry.* Perhaps my name is written over a gash in some shabby side street, supporting the weight of a stranger who glances at the placard reading *Ruslan Dokurov: Deputy Director; Grozny Museum of Regional Art* and wonders if such a person is still alive.

"A large mass grave was recently discovered outside Grozny, no?" the translator asks.

"Yes, an exciting discovery. It will be a major tourist attraction for archaeology enthusiasts."

The translator frowns. "Isn't it a crime scene?"

"Don't be ridiculous. It's millions of years old."

"But weren't the bodies found shot execution-style?" he insists.

I shrug him off. Who am I to answer for the barbarities of prehistoric man?

The translator nods to a small mountain range of rubble bulldozed just over the city limits. "What's that?"

"Suburbs," I say.

We pass backhoes, dump trucks, and jackhammers through the metallic dissonance of reconstruction—a welcome song after months of screaming shells. The cranes are the tallest man-made structures I've ever seen in person. We reach the central square, once the hub of municipal government, now a brown field debossed with earthmover tracks. Nadya once lived just down the road. The oilmen climb out and frown at each other, then at the translator, and finally at me.

Turning to the northeast, I point at a strip of blue sky wedged between two fat cumuli. "That was Hotel Kavkaz. ABBA stayed two nights. I carried their guitars when I worked there one summer. Next to that, picture an apartment block. Before '91, only party members lived there; and after '91, only criminals. No one moved in or out."

None of the oilmen smiles. The translator leans to me and whispers, "You are aware, of course, that these three gentlemen are esteemed members of the Communist Party of China."

"It's OK. I'm a limo driver."

The translator stares blankly.

"Lloyd from *Dumb and Dumber*?"

Nothing.

"Jim Carrey. A brilliant actor who embodies the senselessness of our era," I explain.

The translator doesn't bother translating. I continue to draw a map of the square by narration, but the oilmen can't see what I see. They observe only a barren expanse demolished by bomb and bulldozer.

"Come, comrades, use your imagination," I urge, but they return to the Mercedes, and I am talking solely to the translator, and then he returns to the Mercedes, and I am talking solely to myself.

Three months ago, the interior minister told me his idea. The proposition was ludicrous, but I listened with the impassive complacency I'd perfected throughout my twenty-three years as a public servant.

"The United Nations has named Grozny the most devastated city on earth," the minister explained between bites of moist trout.

I wasn't sure of the proper response, so offered my lukewarm congratulations.

"Yes, well, always nice to receive recognition, I suppose. But as you might imagine, we have an image problem."

He loomed over his desk in a high-backed executive chair, while across from him I listened from an odd, leggy stool designed to make its occupant struggle to stay upright.

The minister's path had first crossed mine fifteen years earlier, when he'd sought my advice regarding a recently painted portrait of him and his sons, and I'd sought his regarding a dacha near my home village. He had two sons then. The first emigrated before the most recent war to attend an American pharmacology school and now works at a very important drugstore in Muskegon, Michigan. I don't know what happened to the second, but the lack of ministerial boasting serves as a death knell. The portrait, which still hung on the far wall, depicted the three of them in tall leather boots, baggy trousers, long woolen *chokhas*, and sheepskin *papakhas*, heroically bestriding the carcass of a slain brown bear that bore a striking resemblance to Yeltsin.

"Foreign investment," the minister continued. "Most others don't agree with me, but I believe we must attract capital unconnected to the Kremlin if we're to achieve a degree of economic autonomy, and holding the record for the world's largest ruin isn't helping. Rosneft wants to sink its fangs into our oil reserves, but the Chinese will cut a better deal. Have you heard of Oleg Voronov? He's on the Rosneft board, the fourteenth-richest man in Russia, and one of the hawks who pushed for the 1994 invasion. The acquisition of Chechen oil is among his top priorities."

The minister set down his silverware and began sorting through the little bones on his plate, reconstructing the skeleton of the fish he'd consumed. "If we're to entice foreign investment, we need to rebrand Chechnya as the Dubai of the Caucasus. That's where you come in. You're what — the director of the Museum of Regional Art?"

"Deputy director, sir."

"That's right, deputy director. You did fine work sending those paintings to Moscow. A real PR coup. Even British newspapers wrote about the Tretyakov exhibit."

With a small nod, I accepted the compliment for what was the lowest point of my rut-ridden career. In 1999, Russian rockets demolished the museum, and with my staff I saved what I could from the ensuing fires. Soon after, I was ordered to surrender the salvaged works to the Russians. When I saw that I'd been listed as cocurator of an exhibit of Chechen paintings at Moscow's Tretyakov Gallery, I closed my lids and wondered what had happened to all the things my eyes had loved.

The minister tilted his plate over the rubbish bin, and the ribs of the fish slid from the spine. "Nothing suggests stability and peace like a thriving tourism sector," he said. "I think you'd be the perfect candidate to head the project."

"With respect, sir," I said. "The subject of my dissertation was nineteenth-century pastoral landscapes. I'm a scholar. This is all a bit beyond me."

"I'll be honest, Ruslan. For this position we need someone with three qualifications: First, he must speak English. Second, he must know enough about the culture and history of the region to convey that Chechnya is much more than a recovering war zone, that we possess a rich heritage unsullied by violence. Third, and most important, he must be that rare government man without links to human rights abuses on either side of the conflict. Do you meet these qualifications?"

"I do, sir," I said. "But still, I'm entirely unqualified to lead a tourism initiative."

The minister frowned. He scanned the desk for a napkin before reaching over to wipe his oily fingers on my necktie. "According to your dossier, you've worked in hotels."

"When I was sixteen. I was a bellhop."

"Well," the minister beamed, "then you clearly have experience in the hospitality industry."

"In the suitcase-carrying industry."

"So you accept?"

I said nothing, and as is often the case with men who possess more power than wisdom, he took my silence for affirmation.

"Congratulations, Ruslan. You're head of the Grozny Tourist Bureau." And so my future was decided entirely without my consent.

Given how few buildings were still standing, office space was a valuable commodity, so I worked from my flat. I spent the first morning writing *Tourist Bureau* on a piece of cardboard. My penmanship had been honed by years of attempting to appear productive, and I taped the sign to the front door. Within five minutes, it had disappeared. I made a new sign, then another, but the street children who lived on the landing kept stealing them. After the fifth sign, I went to the kitchen and drank the bottle of vodka the minister had sent over in celebration and passed out in tears on the floor. So ended my first day as bureau chief.

Over the following weeks, I designed a brochure. The central question was how to trick tourists into coming to Grozny voluntarily.

For inspiration, I studied pamphlets from the bureaus of other urban hellscapes: Baghdad, Pyongyang, Houston. From them I learned to be lavishly adjectival, to treat prospective visitors as semiliterate gluttons, to impute reports of kidnapping, slavery, and terrorism to the slander of foreign provocateurs. Thrilled by my discoveries, I tucked a notebook into my shirt pocket and raced into the street. Upon discerning the empty space where an apartment block once stood, I wrote, *Wide and unobstructed skies!* I watched jubilantly as a pack of feral dogs chased a man, and noted, *Unexpected encounters with wildlife!* The city bazaar hummed with the sales of looted industrial equipment, humanitarian aid rations, and munitions suited for every occasion: *Unparalleled shopping opportunities!* Even before reaching the first checkpoint, I'd scribbled, *First-rate security!* The copy was easy; the real challenge was in finding images to substantiate it. After all, the siege had transfigured the city. Debris rerouted roads through abandoned warehouses — once I found a traffic jam on a factory floor — and what was not rerouted was razed. A photograph of my present surroundings would have sent a cannonball through my verbiage-fortified illusion of a romantic paradise for heterosexual couples, and I couldn't find suitable alternatives of prewar Grozny within the destroyed archives. In the end, I forwent photographs altogether and instead used the visuals from January, April, and August of the 1984 Grozny Museum of Regional Art calendar. The three nineteenth-century landscapes — in which swallows frolicked over ripening grapevines, and a shepherd minded his flock backlit by a sunset — portrayed a land untouched by war or Communism, and beside them my descriptions of a picturesque Chechnya did not seem entirely dishonest.

I return home after depositing the troika of Chinese oilmen at the Interior Ministry. As I approach the staircase landing, the street children vanish, leaving behind the instruments of their survival: a metal skewer to roast pigeons, a chisel to chip cement from the loose bricks they sell to construction crews for a ruble each.

I knock on the door of the flat adjacent to mine and announce my name. Nadya appears in a headscarf and sunglasses. Turning her unscarred side toward me, she invites me in. "How was the maiden voyage?"

"An excellent success," I say. "They dozed off before we reached the worst of the wreckage."

Nadya smiles and takes measured steps to the Primus stove. She doesn't need her white cane to reach the counter. I scan the room for impediments, yet everything is in order—the floorboards clear but for the kopek coins I'd glued down in paths to the bathroom, the kitchen, the front door so her bare feet could find their way during her early months of blindness. At the end of one such path is a desk neatly stacked with black-and-white photographs, once the subject of her dissertation on altered images from the Stalinist era. I sift through a few while she puts the kettle on. Nadya has circled a single face in each—the same person painted into the background of every photo, aging from childhood to his elderly years, the signature of the anonymous censor.

The kettle whistles in the kitchen. We sip tea from mismatched mugs that lift rings of dust from the tabletop. She sits to hide the left half of her face.

"The tourist brochures will be ready next week," I say. "I'll have to send one along to our Beijing comrades, if the paintings come out clearly. I'm skeptical of Ossetian printers."

"You used three from the Zakharov room?"

"Yes, three Zakharovs."

Her shadow nods on the wall. That gallery, the museum's largest, had been her favorite, too. The first time I ever saw her was there, in 1987, on her initial day as the museum's restoration artist.

"You'll have to save me one," she says. "For when I can see it."

Her last sentence hangs in the air for a long moment before I respond. "I have an envelope with five thousand rubles. For your trip. I'll leave it on your nightstand."

"Ruslan, please."

"St. Petersburg is a city engineered to steal money from visitors. I know—I'm in the industry."

"You don't need to take care of me," she says with a firm but appreciative squeeze of my fingers. "I keep telling you—I've been saving my disability allowance. I have enough for the bus ticket, and I'm staying with the cousin of a university classmate."

"It's not for you. It's for movies, for videocassettes," I say, a beat too quickly. Slapstick and romantic comedies have been my favorite genres in recent years. "Find some that are foreign."

She's looking straight at me, or at my voice, momentarily forgetting the thing her face has become. We were together when rockets turned three floors of our city's preeminent works of art into an inferno she barely escaped. The third-degree burns hardened into a chapped canvas of scar tissue wrapping the left side of her skull. That eye is gone, yet the other was partly spared; in the heat her right lids fused together, sealing the eye from the worst of the flames, and at times it can sense the flicker of light, the faintest movements. There is the possibility, an ophthalmologist has told her, that sight could be restored. However, any optical surgeon clever enough to perform such a delicate operation was also clever enough to have fled Grozny long ago. Nadya hasn't any appointments, but if she can find a surgeon in Petersburg next week, and if she can come up with the money for the procedure, she says she will move to Sweden afterward. I fear for her future in a country whose citizenry is forced to assemble its own furniture.

"If it happens, the surgery, if it's successful," I say, "you don't need to leave."

"What I need is sleep."

When I return to my flat, I scoop the concrete residue of the morning's kasha onto a slice of round bread. The granules wedge into my molar divots, rough and bitter, suggesting the kind of rich, fibrous nutrients that uncoil one's intestines into a vertical chute. I rinse my hands in the sink and let the water run even after they're clean. Indoor plumbing was restored six months ago. Above the doorway hangs a bumper sticker of a fish with *WWJCD?* inscribed across its body, sent by an American church along with a crate of bibles in response to our plea for life-saving aid.

I take a dozen scorched canvases from the closet and lay them on the floor in two rows of six. They were too damaged for the Tretyakov exhibit. Not one was painted after 1879, and yet they look like the surreal visions of a psychedelic-addled mind. Most are charred through, some simply mounted ash, more reminiscent of Alberto Burri's slash-and-burn Tachisme than the Imperial Academy of Arts's classicism. In others the heat-melted oils have turned photo-realistic portraits into dissolved dreamscapes.

My closet holds one last canvas. I set it on the coffee table to examine by the light of an unshaded lamp. The seamless gradation of color, the nearly invisible brushstrokes—not even the three years I spent writing my dissertation on Pyotr Zakharov-Chechenets could diminish my fascination with his work. Born in 1816, on the eve of the Caucasian War that Lermontov, Tolstoy, and Pushkin would later memorialize in their story cycle, he was an orphan before his fourth birthday. Yet his brilliance so exceeded his circumstances that he went on to attend the Imperial Academy in St. Petersburg; and despite exclusion from scholarship, employment, and patronage due to his ethnicity, he eventually became a court painter and a member of the Academy. He was a Chechen who learned to succeed by the rules of his conquerors, a man not unlike the interior minister, to be admired and pitied.

A meadow, an apricot tree, a stone wall in a diagonal meander through the grasses, the pasture cresting into a hill, a boarded well, a house. In 1937, the censor who would become the subject of Nadya's dissertation painted the figure of the Grozny party boss beside the dacha, like a mislaid statue of Socialist Realism. Soviet dogma pervaded the whole of the present, and here was a reminder that the past was no less revisable.

In 1989, when the Berlin Wall fell and Soviet satellite states began breaking away, when the politicians and security apparatus had more pressing concerns than nineteenth-century landscapes, I asked Nadya to restore the Zakharov, and over the course of several weeks she did. We didn't take to the streets; we didn't overthrow governments or oust leaders; our insurrection was ten centimeters of canvas.

It's among the least ambitious of all Zakharov's work. Here is an artist who painted the portraits of Tsar Nicholas I, General Alexei Yermolov, and Grand Duchess Maria Nikolaevna, along with the famed depiction of Imam Shamil's surrender; and this, in my hands, portrays all the drama its title suggests: *Empty Pasture in Afternoon*.

I grew up in the southern highlands, just a few kilometers from the pasture. Though the land was technically part of a state farm, nothing was ever planted, and flocks were banned from grazing because no one liked the idea of sheep relieving themselves on Zakharov's soil. During secondary school, on a class trip to the Grozny Museum of Regional Art, I finally beheld the canvas that existed with greater vibrancy in village lore than it ever could on a gallery wall.

More than anything, it was that painting that led me to study art at university, and there I met and married Liana. We lived with my parents in cramped quarters well into our twenties, and found the privacy to speak openly only in deserted public areas: on the roof of the village schoolhouse, in the waiting room of the shuttered clinic, in Zakharov's pasture. After I received my doctorate and a position at the museum, we relocated to a Grozny flat, where we learned to talk in bed.

The USSR fell. We had a son. With the assistance of the interior minister, I purchased the dacha in Zakharov's pasture amid the frenzied privatization of the post-Soviet, prewar years. When the First War began, I stayed in Grozny to protect the museum from the alternating advances of foreign soldiers and local insurgents. My wife and son fled to the dacha, far from the conflict.

In my research for the tourist bureau, I've learned that the First and Second Chechen Wars have rendered the republic among the most densely mined regions in human history. The United Nations estimates that five hundred thousand were planted, roughly one for every two citizens. I was unaware of this statistic when I visited the dacha during the First War, taking what provisions I could from the ruined capital, a few treats for which I paid dearly—tea leaves for my wife, sheets of fresh drawing paper for my son—but I knew enough to warn my family never to venture into the pasture. Initially, they heeded my words.

I don't know how it happened, on that May day in 1996, if they were pursued by depraved men, if the perilous field were a relative sanctuary, if they were afraid, if they called for help, if they called for me. I'd like to believe that it was a day so beautiful they couldn't resist the crest of the hill, the open sky, that radiance. I'd like to believe that my wife suggested a picnic, that their penultimate moment was one of whimsy, charm. I'd like to believe anything to counter the more probable realities at the edge of my imagination. With terror or joy, with abasement or delight, they remained my wife and child to the end—I must remind myself of this, because in the mystery that subsumes those final moments they are strangers to me. I was in Grozny, at the museum, and never heard the explosion.

* * *

For the two weeks Nadya is in Petersburg, my evenings stagnate. Russian dignitaries, potential investors, state-approved journalists, the omnipresent oilmen fill my mornings and afternoons, but when I return to my flat I'm reminded that I am, at the end of the day, alone. Twice I go to Nadya's flat to clean her bedroom closet, the back corners of shelves, behind the toilet, the little places that even in her fastidiousness she misses. I'm uncomfortable with the neediness that underlies my interventions in her life under the pretext of concern. I am concerned, of course. Some nights I wake from nightmares that she's tripped over a chair, a shoe, a broomstick I could have moved. Yet in rare spells—like now, as I scour the mildew from her bathroom tiles—clarity surfaces through the murky soup of daily life, and I know that I've purposefully made myself into a crutch she cannot risk discarding. What I don't know is whether I've done so out of love or loneliness, or if in this upside-down world where roofs lie on streets, intentions have lost their moral weight altogether.

One Wednesday night, feeling unusually alert given the hour, I contemplate Zakharov's pasture. It's the least ruined of the canvases, the principal damage—aside from the stains of ash and soot—being the burn hole at its center, upon the hill, which I see as the aftermath not of the museum fire but of the mine blast, the crater into which everything disappeared. A few years ago, Nadya could have restored it in days.

An idea. I let myself back into her flat to retrieve her restoration kit. It's at the desk, amid the photographs. I pause on one in which the party boss is just a boy, chubby face and gray eyes below the accent mark of a cowlick, hardly noticeable in the crowd. I feel him staring up at me with an intensity approaching sentience, and for a moment I'm immobilized. How did he die? I've never before asked such a question about a child who was not my son.

Back home I set the contents of the kit beside the Zakharov. Plastic bottles of emulsion cleaner, neutralizer, gloss varnish, conditioner, varnish remover. A tin of putty. Eight meters of canvas lining. A depleted packet of cotton-tipped swabs. A dozen disposable chloroprene gloves. I'd taken a yearlong course in conservation at university, but my real education came from Nadya, when in the months after my family died, I neglected my duties as deputy director and spent most afternoons in her office, watching her work.

Every evening for the next week I snap on the chloroprene gloves and wash away the surface dirt with cotton balls dampened in neutralizer. The emulsion cleaner smells of fermented watermelon, and I apply it with the swabs in tight circles until the tips gray and the unadulterated color of Zakharov's palette is revealed. Employing the repair putty as sealant, I patch the burn hole with a square of fresh canvas. Then I paint.

The totality of my attention is focused on an area the size of a halved playing card. The grass, turned emerald by sunlight, must be flawless, and I spend several hours testing different blends of oils. As I apply them with delicate brushstrokes, I realize that even in his rendering of a distant field, Zakharov is beyond imitation, and that were Nadya here to witness my final infidelity, she would never forgive me.

With precise, strong lines, I draw them as silhouettes. The boy's arms are raised, his body elongated as he makes for the crest, his head thrown back in rapture. The woman hurries a step behind, animated by his anticipation. Their backs are to me. The sun rakes the grass, and ripe apricots bend the branches. No one chases them. They run from nothing.

Nadya has returned, and the white tea has cooled in our cups, and still she hasn't mentioned the Petersburg eye surgeons.

"Good news," she says, and feels across the floor for her suitcase, then hands me two VHS tapes. "These are the ones you wanted, right?"

I examine the cases. Soviet comedies, regrettably. "Yes, these are exactly the ones."

"I was afraid the street vendor had swindled me."

"What did the doctors say, Nadya?"

The pause is long enough to peel a plum.

She delivers her reply with a downcast frown. "Reconstructive surgery is possible."

I force as much gusto as I can muster into my congratulations, slapping a palm on the table while my spine wilts. What will I be if Nadya no longer needs me? This is truly good news, though, certainly it is, but her face is joyless. "What's wrong? Is there a long wait for the operation?"

"There won't be one."

"What? Why not?"

"Too expensive." She's facing the empty chair across the table, thinking that I'm still sitting there. "One hundred and fifteen thousand."

One hundred and fifteen thousand rubles. A huge yet not impossible sum. Years to save for, but within the realm of possibility, like a vacation to Belarus. I'm already scheming ways to defraud the Interior Ministry when she says, "Dollars."

My heart spirals and crash-lands somewhere deep in my gut. At thirty-three rubles to a dollar, the figure is insurmountable. Nadya reaches for her purse and pulls out an envelope.

"What I owe you for the trip. Help me count it out," she says. For a moment her instinct to trust anyone, even me, is infuriating. Isn't suspicion the natural condition of the blind? Haven't I warned her, told her to be careful, cautioned that she can't rely on anyone? But by some perversion she's become more credulous, more willing to believe that people aren't by nature hucksters and scoundrels, which is why, I suppose, my VHS collection is rounded out with *Gentlemen of Fortune*.

"It's nothing," I say.

"I'm paying you back."

"If you want to be a martyr, go join them in the woods."

"Help me count it out," she insists, her voice stern, cool, serious. "I still have money left from the disability fund. I'm not a charity."

Of course there's no disability fund. Of course the government isn't providing her a stipend or subsidizing the flat adjacent to mine. The cash delivered in the Interior Ministry envelope on the first of the month comes from me, as does her rent.

"I'm waiting," she says. We both know this is a farce. But I sit beside her. I play my part in the lie that preserves the illusion that our friendship, our romance, whatever this is, is based in affection rather than dependence. I count the bills that I will return to her, and we shake hands as if our business were concluded, as if there were nothing left that we owe one another.

In bed I run my fingers through what remains of her hair, press my fingertips to her cheeks, slowly scrolling to decipher the dense braille scrawled across her face. I slide my hand down her torso, over the bulge of her left breast, the hook of her hip bone, to thighs so smooth and unmarked they're hers only in darkness. She turns away.

Lying here, I nearly forget the falling rockets, the collapsing museum, the cinder blocks shifting like ice cubes in a glass, the air of a clean sky impossibly distant. The Zakharov was in my hands when I found her, her face halved, her teeth chattering. I nearly forget how I lifted her cheek to cool it with my breath, how her broken eyes searched for me as I held her. So many times I've warned her of monsters, ready to prey on the vulnerable, and as she turns, I nearly forget to ask myself, *What monster have I become today?*

In the morning I return to my flat and find the paintings on the floor where I left them. Daylight grants the scorch and char an odd beauty, as if the fires haven't destroyed the works but revised them into expressions of a brutal present. I pick up the nearest one, a family portrait commissioned by a nobleman as a wedding present for his second son. The top third of the canvas has been incinerated, taking with it the heads of the nobleman, his wife, the first son, and the newly betrothed, but their bodies remain, dressed in soot-stained breeches and petticoats, and by their feet sits a dachshund so fat its little legs barely touch the ground, the only figure—in a painting intended to convey the family's immortal honor—to survive intact.

I hang the canvas on the wall from a bent nail and step back, marveling that here, for the first time in my career, I've displayed a work of modern art. After pulling the furniture into the kitchen, I mount the remaining canvases throughout the living room, finally coming to the restored Zakharov, which I consider returning to the closet, where it would exist in darkness for me alone. Yet my curatorial instincts win out, and I place it beside the others, where it is meant to be. I scrawl one more sign on a cardboard shingle and nail it to the door: *Grozny Museum of Regional Art.*

Now, for guards. I toss a crumpled hundred-ruble note down the stairs, thinking that the young landing-dwellers, like the Sunzha trout, are too hungry to pass up a baited hook. A small hand reaches around the corner, and I spring out and grab it, yanking on the slender arm to reel in the rest of the child. He squirms wildly, biting at my wrists, until I shake him into submission and offer him a job in museum security.

His body quiets, perhaps out of shock, and I close his hand around the bill. His fingernails look rusted on. His shirt is no thicker than stitched dust.

"Bandits are stealing the signs from my door," I tell him. "I'll pay you and your friends three hundred rubles a week to keep watch."

Over the following month, I bring all my tours through the museum. A delegation from the Red Cross. More Chinese oilmen. A heavyweight boxing champion. A British journalist. *This is what remains*, the canvases cry. *You cannot burn ash! You cannot raze rubble!* As the only museum employee besides the street children, I give myself a long overdue promotion. Henceforth, I am director.

The newly installed telephone rings one morning, and the gloomy interior minister greets me. "We're properly fucked."

"Nice to hear from you, sir," I reply. I'm still in my sleeping clothes, and even for a phone conversation I feel unsuitably dressed.

"The Chinese are out. They traded their drilling rights to Rosneft for a few dozen Russian fighter jets."

I nod, grasping why Beijing didn't sent its shrewdest or most sober representatives. "So this means Rosneft will drill?"

"Yes, and it gets even worse," he heaves. "I may well be demoted to deputy minister."

"I was a deputy for many years. It's not as bad as you think."

"When the world takes a dump, it lands on a deputy's forehead."

I couldn't deny that. "What does this mean for the Tourist Bureau?"

"You should find new employment. But first, you have one final tour. Oleg Voronov. From Rosneft."

It takes a beat for the name to register. "The fourteenth-richest man in Russia?"

"Thirteenth now."

"With respect, sir, I give tours to human rights activists, print journalists, state and corporate underlings—people of no power or importance. What does a man of his stature want with me?"

"My question precisely! Yet apparently his wife, Galina Something-or-other-ova, the actress, has heard of this art museum you've cobbled together. What've you been up to?"

"It's a long story, sir."

"You know I hate stories, but do show him our famed Chechen hospitality — perhaps with a glass of unboiled tap water. Let's give the thirteenth-richest man in Russia an intestinal parasite!"

"I understand, sir. I'm a limo driver."

Three weeks pass and here he is, Oleg Voronov, in the backseat of the Mercedes, with his wife, the actress Galina Ivanova. Sitting up front is his assistant, a bleached-blonde parcel of productivity who takes notes even when no one is speaking. Still, try as I might, I'm unable to properly hate Voronov. So far he's been nontalkative, inattentive, and uncurious — in short, a perfect tourist. Galina, on the other hand, has read Khassan Geshilov's *Origins of Chechen Civilization* and recites historical trivia unfamiliar to me. As the office doors of dead administrators clatter beneath us, she asks thoughtful questions, treating me not as a servant, or even as a tour guide, but as a scholar. I casually mention the land mines, the street children, the rape and torture and indiscriminate suffering, and Voronov and his wife shake their heads with sympathy. Nothing I say will turn them into the masks of evil I want them to be; and when the oligarch checks his watch, a cheap plastic piece of crap, I feel an affinity for a man who deserves its opposite.

The tour concludes at my flat. As I open the door, I say, "This is what remains of the Grozny Museum of Regional Art."

Voronov and Galina pass the burned-out frames to the pasture. "Is this the one?" he asks her. She nods.

"A Zakharov, no?" he inquires, fingering his lapel as he turns to me. "There was an exhibit of his at the Tretyakov, if memory serves."

Only now do I recognize clearly the animals I have invited into my home. "When the museum was bombed, the fires destroyed most of the original collection. We sent what was saved to the Tretyakov."

"But not this?"

"Not this."

"Rather reckless, don't you think, to leave such a treasure on an apartment wall guarded only by street urchins?"

"It's a minor work."

"Believe it or not, my wife has been looking for this painting. She collects art from every region where I drill oil."

"Could I offer you a glass of water?"

"You could offer me the painting."

I force a laugh. He laughs, too. We are laughing. Ha-ha!

"The painting is not for sale," I say.

His mirth disappears. "It is if I want to buy it."

"This is a museum. You can't have a painting just because you want it. The director of the Tretyakov wouldn't sell you the art from his walls just because you can afford it."

"You are only a deputy director, and this isn't the Tretyakov." There's real pity in his voice as he surveys the ash flaking from the canvases, the dirty dishes stacked in the sink; and yes, now, at last, I hate him. "I have a penthouse gallery in Moscow. Temperature- and moisture-controlled. The utmost security. No one but Galina and I and a few guests will ever see it. You must realize that I'm being more than reasonable." In a less-than-subtle threat, he nods out the window to the street below, where his three armed Goliaths skulk beside their Land Rover. "What is the painting worth?"

"It's worth," I begin, but how can I finish? What price can I assign to the last Zakharov in Chechnya, to the last image of my home? One sum comes to mind, but it terrifies me. Wouldn't that be the worst of all outcomes, to lose both the Zakharov and Nadya in the same transaction? "Just take it," I say. "You took everything else. Take this, too."

Voronov bristles. "I'm not a thief. Tell me what it's worth."

My gaze floats and lands upon the bumper sticker: *WWJCD?* What would he do? Jim Carrey would be brave. No matter how difficult, Jim Carrey would do the right thing. I close my eyes. "One hundred and fifteen thousand dollars. U.S."

"One fifteen?"

I nod.

"That's what—3.7, 3.8 million rubles?" Voronov fixes me with a venomous stare, then turns to his wife, who still hasn't glanced away from the painting. I look into it, too, to its retreating figures, wondering if we might be reunited soon.

A single, fleshy clap startles me like a gunshot, and I spin to find

Voronov smiling once more. "Let's make it an even four," he says expansively.

The assistant unyokes herself from a mammoth purse and spills eight stacks of banded five-thousand-ruble bills onto the floor.

"Never trust banks," Voronov says. "You can have that advice for free. It's been a pleasure." He slaps my back, tells the assistant to bring the canvas, and heads for the door. Then he's gone.

Galina remains at the Zakharov. Even as I'm losing it, I'm proud that my painting can elicit such sustained attention. She dabs her eyes, touches my shoulder, and follows her husband out.

I'm left with the assistant, whose saccharine perfume reeks of vaporized cherubs.

"And you'll have to give us a curatorial description," she says. "Something we can mount on a placard." She passes me the notepad, and I stand at my painting for a long while before I begin.

Notice how the shadows in the meadow mirror the clouds in the sky, how the leaves of the apricot tree blow with the grass. No verisimilitude escapes such a master. The wall of white stones cuts an angle across the composition, both establishing depth and offsetting the horizon line. Channels of turned soil run along the left flank of the hill, as if freshly dug graves, or recently buried land mines, but closer inspection reveals the furrows of a newly planted herb garden. The first shoots of rosemary already peek out. Zakharov portrays all the peace and tranquility of a spring day. The sun shines comfortingly, and hours remain before nightfall. Toward the crest of the hill, nearing the horizon, you may notice what look to be the ascending figures of a woman and a boy. Pay them no mind, for they are merely the failures of a novice restoration artist, no more than his shadows. They are not there.

MATEO HOKE AND CATE MALEK

■

An Oral History of Abdelrahman Al-Ahmar

FROM *Palestine Speaks*

VOICE OF WITNESS *is a nonprofit organization that publishes oral histories of human rights crises. The following is an excerpt drawn from their book* Palestine Speaks, *which explores the experiences of Palestinians living in the West Bank and Gaza.*

AGE: 46
OCCUPATION: Lawyer
PLACE OF BIRTH: Deheisheh refugee camp, West Bank
INTERVIEWED IN: Bethlehem, West Bank

Abdelrahman Al-Ahmar lives with his wife and four children in a small apartment complex on the edge of the refugee camp where he grew up. The complex is surrounded by trees and garden greenery and is also home to four of his brothers and their families, as well as rabbits, birds, puppies, and even a horse. During the course of several interviews, the house is full of the sounds of his children playing. Sometimes they come to sit and listen to their father's story, interjecting parts of the narrative they know by heart.

Abdelrahman's comfortable house is a retreat from the harsh conditions he has faced his entire life. He was born in the Deheisheh refugee camp, where his family struggled against extreme poverty and regular attacks from soldiers and settlers. He later spent nearly twenty years in prison, most of it in administrative detention, where he was interrogated *using torture techniques that have now been outlawed by the Israeli High Court.* In 1999, the court ruled that the Israeli Security Agency (Shin Bet) does not have legal authority to use physical means of interrogation. It found tactics must be "fair and reasonable" and not cause the detainee to suffer. According to the Supreme Court case, a common practice during questioning was shaking prisoners violently enough to lead to unconsciousness, brain damage, or even death (in at least one reported case). However, in a society where 40 percent of men have spent time in prison, thousands of people still bear the physical and psychological marks of these methods.*

Abdelrahman seems reserved at first during our initial meeting—he speaks little and watches us carefully as we ask questions. But as he relaxes, his dark humor and natural gift for storytelling begin to emerge. He switches between English, Arabic, and Hebrew as he speaks, and the only time he becomes quiet again is when talking about the most extreme forms of torture he endured. However, he also tells us about how the most difficult moments in his life have inspired him to become a leader in his community.

We Didn't Even Have Coca-Cola

I'm the same age as the occupation. The war of '67 started in June, and my mother was pregnant with me at the time.† She and my father were living in the Deheisheh refugee camp in Bethlehem.‡ They'd been pushed out of their homes in Ramla during the war in '48, and that's when they'd moved to the camp.§ They lived in tents in camp for over ten years, and then my father was able to build a small house in camp in the fifties. Then during the war in '67, a lot of peo-

---

* Administrative detention is a system of incarceration without official charges used by occupying military forces.

† The war in 1967 is known as the Six-Day War.

‡ The Deheisheh refugee camp was established for 3,000 refugees in 1949 and is one of three refugee camps in the Bethlehem metropolitan area. Deheisheh is located just south of the city. Current estimates of the camp's population range up to 16,000 persons living in an area that is roughly one square mile.

§ Ramla is a city of 65,000 people in central Israel. Today the city is approximately 20 percent Muslim—most Arabs fled the city during the 1948 war.

ple fled the camp and ended up living in Jordan, especially in Amman.* But my father said, "We're not leaving again." He didn't want to lose his home again. So during the war in '67, my father stayed to protect the house while my mother went up in the woods and hid for a few days. She gave birth to me a few months later in the camp, with the help of a midwife.†

I remember the camp of my childhood was a neighborhood of shacks made of cinder blocks and aluminum roofs. Most people in the camp built their own houses, like my father had. We all had leaky ceilings, no plumbing, no bathrooms. There were just a few public restrooms we would all share, and the toilets would flush into the gutters in the streets. We didn't have showers. We'd heat up water in a basin and wash with that. We depended on UNRWA for clothes.‡ I remember getting clothes twice a year, and they were often the wrong size, and sometimes all that was available were girl clothes. We were so cold in the winter. For heat, we had fires in old oil barrels outside our homes, and families would gather around them to warm up. I remember the fires would get so high, we couldn't see the faces of the people on the other side of the barrel. And there was so much disease — cholera, infections of all sorts.

Growing up, we could hear our next-door neighbors every day. We knew their fights, conversations, everything. And there were so many places that you couldn't get to by car because the spaces between buildings were too narrow. You had to walk between the houses.

As children from the camp, we'd feel different from other kids when we went out into Bethlehem, the city. We would see kids who had bicycles, but we didn't have any. They had good clothes, but we didn't have them. They even had Coca-Cola! My parents weren't accustomed to the kind of poverty we were living in. They were born in villages with homes on large pieces of land. When I was a kid, my fa-

---

* Amman, the capital of neighboring Jordan, is a city of around 2 million residents. Amman grew rapidly with the influx of Palestinian refugees after 1967

† In 1967, the Israelis seized the West Bank from Jordan, which had administered the region since 1948.

‡ The United Nations Relief and Works Agency (UNRWA) has provided services such as education and medical care to Palestinian refugees since 1949.

ther used to work in Israel. He was a stonecutter. But he wasn't making enough money for the family—he had four boys and two girls to support. There was no one in Deheisheh with money. So everybody was struggling financially, but at least it gave us this feeling of being equal.

Our Windows Were Always Open, So We Got Used to the Smell of Tear Gas

I felt pressure from the Israeli army and Israeli settlers at an early age. The most difficult issue that we had to deal with was the settlers. I was only six years old when the settlers started coming through the camp in the early seventies, so I grew up seeing them. The main road from the settlements in the south runs through Bethlehem to Jerusalem, and it goes right through the camp. I think the settlers who passed through saw Deheisheh as something they needed to control.

The settlers were led by a man named Rabbi Moshe Levinger, who saw all of the West Bank as part of Israel.* They wanted Israel to claim the land around the camp, and they found ways to make life miserable for us. They would come in buses maybe once a week. They'd get off and start shooting randomly in the refugee camp with live bullets. They'd shout, throw stones, provoke fights. Whenever anyone tried to fight back, the settlers would alert Israeli soldiers, who would chase us through the streets and fire tear-gas canisters. Our windows were always open, so we got used to the smell of tear gas.

I remember settlers entering my UNRWA school and smashing desks, doors, windows. The teachers couldn't protect us. There was always a sense of fear and insecurity. When I was younger, these things affected me tremendously. They affected my relationship with my teachers and the way I looked at them. I kind of lost respect for them because I'd seen them degraded. And after some time, other students and I stopped listening to them because we knew they were powerless.

---

* Rabbi Moshe Levinger was born in Jerusalem in 1935 and helped lead the movement to settle the West Bank after the Six-Day War. He was especially active in asserting settler presence around Hebron, a large West Bank city fifteen miles south of the Deheisheh camp.

Then in the early eighties, the military built a fence around the camp. It was twenty feet high, and the only way in and out was a gate leading to the Hebron–Jerusalem Road, the one that the settlers passed through. I once heard that some tourists who came to Bethlehem saw the fence and wondered if it was the wall of a city zoo! In the camp, we had a curfew—we had to be in by seven p.m., or the soldiers guarding the entryway wouldn't let us back in through the gate. And we couldn't leave after curfew under any circumstances. Some people died because they couldn't go to the hospital after the gate closed at seven.

Around the same time, settlers brought trailers across from the camp and tried to establish an outpost there. I remember being stuck in the camp after curfew and hearing the patriotic music of the settlers blaring through the night.

The soldiers worked closely with the settlers most of the time. When I was fourteen, I got a backpack—the first I ever owned. Before that, I would carry my books in plastic bags, like most kids in the camp. I was so happy I finally had a backpack. It was green. My dad bought it for me. I was going to school one morning, and a group of six soldiers and an armed man in civilian clothes—a settler—called me over. The settler kicked me and slapped me and then took my backpack and threw it into the gutter. I tried to get it out of the gutter, but the soldiers hit me and threw the backpack back in. My books were wet and ruined, and they still didn't allow me to get the pack. I watched them do the same thing to some of my friends—they threw their books in the gutter, too.

At the UNRWA school, they would give us the books for free. I told them what the soldiers had done, and they gave me new books. But I had to put them back in plastic bags again. Of course, the soldiers knew the backpack was important to me because they could see how impoverished we all were and that we were deprived of everything.

Refugees in the camp would retaliate against the settlers by throwing stones. I started throwing stones at age ten. Kids a little older might be a little more organized. Different groups of kids would decide to do something—a group of five over here, a group of six over there. By the time I was thirteen, I was among them. We started to incite other children to put flags up. At that time, it was illegal to hang the Palestinian flag.* So, we would tell the kids to hang the flag and to write slogans on the walls. That was also illegal then. You could be arrested by the Israeli army and go to prison.

When they saw us throwing stones, the soldiers or settlers might shoot. When they shot at us, yes, we were afraid. But with time, with all the injustice and the frustration, we were just stuck, and we didn't care if we died. But we thought throwing stones made a difference. We saw the settlers as the occupiers, and they were the source of injustice and deprivation, so we had to fight back. This was before the First Intifada, but for us in the camp it was already Intifada—it was always Intifada.†

"What did you do? What did you do? What did you do?"

Eventually, my friends and I graduated from throwing stones to thinking about throwing Molotov cocktails. It wasn't hard to make a weapon out of a bottle of kerosene and a wick. We wanted to throw them at the outpost set up by Moshe Levinger and at the soldiers who were helping the settlers to come and wreck our neighborhood. By this point I was fifteen, almost sixteen. Some in our group were younger—one was fourteen. We made a couple of Molotov cocktails and tested them out by smashing them against walls in the camp when we thought nobody was looking.

December 11, 1984, was a cold, snowy night. I was home asleep, and suddenly soldiers swarmed in. I was cuffed and put in a vehicle with some other boys from my group that had already been arrested. That night they picked up me and four of my friends, and we were driven to Al-Muskubiya.‡

---

* After the Oslo Accords were put into full effect in 1995, Bethlehem was administered by the Palestinian Authority. Between 1967 and 1995, however, Israel maintained full control of the region and outlawed symbols of Palestinian nationalism such as flags.

† The First Intifada was an uprising throughout the West Bank and Gaza against Israeli military occupation. It began in December 1987 and lasted until 1993. Intifada in Arabic means "to shake off."

‡ Al-Muskubiya ("the Russian Compound") is a large compound in Jerusalem that was built in the nineteenth century to house an influx of Russian Orthodox pilgrims

When we got to the interrogation center, it was very chaotic. There were maybe forty guys in all who had been arrested and brought to Al-Muskubiya that night. For the five of us, they took off all of our clothes, stripped us naked. Then they tightened our handcuffs, took us outside in an open area, and put bags on our heads. The snow was coming down, and we were naked out there. I couldn't see the others, but I could hear their teeth chattering, and the sound of the handcuffs shaking was so loud. The cold weather still bothers me now—it makes me remember that night. This is where we stayed for forty-five days between interrogations. Our bodies turned blue, we were out in the cold so long.

My interrogation lasted two months. During the interrogations, they beat me, and there was loud music playing the whole time. We were allowed to go to the bathroom just once a day. They would tie our hands to the pipes. It was really painful for me. After some time, I stopped feeling my arms—sometimes I didn't know if I still had them or if they had been amputated. There was constant beating, all over my body, to the point where my skin would be as black as my jacket. If I lost consciousness, they would throw water on me or slap me so I'd wake up.

This mark on my wrist is actually from the handcuffs during that time in prison. The handcuffs were so tight, they cut to the bone. I still have marks on my legs from the beatings. They wouldn't give us any medical treatment. And the interrogators wouldn't ask you direct, obvious questions. They would just keep saying, "What did you do? What did you do? What did you do?" And that was it. With all the beating, I couldn't focus anymore, even if I was conscious. I couldn't remember anything that I did from the time before prison, even if I had anything to confess. Most of the other kids told the police what they'd done—they made some Molotov cocktails and tested them out. I didn't tell them anything. Not because I was being secretive, but because I was too confused and disoriented from the beatings. It was a very hostile environment.

Sometimes they would keep me awake for many days straight be-

---

into the city during the time of Ottoman rule. Today, the compound houses Israeli police headquarters, criminal courts, and a prison and interrogation center.

fore they gave me four hours of sleep. And with the pressure of sleep deprivation, I started hallucinating, and I didn't actually know what was happening around me. I would imagine I was in a kindergarten and there were a lot of crying kids causing all this chaos, but I couldn't do anything to calm them down. I stopped knowing if what was happening was real or just a product of my imagination.

Eventually, a lawyer came to visit me. Her name was Lea Tsemel. She was an Israeli lawyer.* She came to meet me in the visiting room one day and she gave me cigarettes. She told me she was taking on my case. I was so confused. I just asked her if what was happening to me was real, or was I just trapped in my imagination. So many times I was convinced that the prison was full of snakes. I asked her about that, and she told me I was just hallucinating. She told me about my charges and let me know we'd be in court soon.

There was one police officer who was nice. One morning, I asked to go to the bathroom, and the interrogators wouldn't let me go until midnight. When this one police officer saw me in pain because I had to go so badly, he said, "Godammit! What happened to these people? Why do they torture people? Godammit!" He was angry, and he let me go to the bathroom. Then he brought me tea and cigarettes and said, "Rest, rest." This was very risky for him, and I really appreciated it.

The whole interrogation was two months. I was afraid that they were going to kill me and my friends, because we had heard all these terrible stories of torture. I had an uncle who had been arrested a while before, and I knew that he'd died in prison. He participated in a hunger strike, and when the prison guards force-fed him, he choked to death.

The main thing that consumed my thinking was that these people were crazy, and they wanted to torture me and mentally destroy me. And they would actually say it right to our faces. They would tell us, "We want to ruin you psychologically." In fact, many prisoners do become mentally ill. Some of them die. I didn't go crazy. I focused on all the other people suffering besides me. And also, I think people who are really religious have a hard time with this kind of abuse some-

---

* Lea Tsemel is a prominent human rights lawyer in Israel.

times. They pray to God for help, and when none comes, it breaks them mentally. But that wasn't me, and I was able to focus on the future and what I needed to do to get myself out of that situation.

After two months of interrogation, my friends and I were taken to trial and charged with terrorist activities. The judge sentenced us to four to six years each. My mother was in the courtroom, and she fainted when she heard the sentence.

We Were All Still Dreaming of Growing a Moustache

After my sentence, I was sent to Damun Prison.* I learned more in prison than I would have at a university. I met some leaders of the resistance. I was so proud of myself. They were the big fighters. And the other boys I was arrested with, they were all so happy. We thought we were so grown up, even though we were all still dreaming of growing a mustache. We'd actually shave four times a day to try to get our beards to grow in stronger so we could look older. I acted angry about my sentence—not because I thought it was too long, but because I thought it was too short! They gave me four years, I wanted twelve years. I thought it was sort of an honor.

In Damun, I was in with a bunch of Israeli mafia guys, drug dealers—all sorts of criminals. I think the soldiers wanted to put young guys in the resistance in with real degenerates, sort of to corrupt us. But we all got along, and before long I was one of the leaders in prison. I became the representative of a group of young prisoners in dealing with the guards. I'd voice our demands and objections to the ways we were being treated.

In 1986, I led a hunger strike. We were actually protesting about not getting enough food. Besides that, it was winter, and there was no heat, and we only had one thin blanket each. And we weren't getting enough exercise time outside. So there were dozens of us not eating as a protest. I remember we used to dream of food at night. The Israeli soldiers, they would tease us. They'd have barbecues out-

---

* Damun Prison is in northern Israel, near Haifa. The facilities were once used as a tobacco warehouse during the British Mandate, but they were converted to a prison by Israel in 1953. It houses up to 500 prisoners.

side the walls of our cells, and the smell would come into our cells through the windows.

We stuck at it for eighteen days, and on the eighteenth day I announced we were going on a water strike as well. The guards quickly brought in doctors from the Red Cross, and they told us that we'd be dead in two days if we tried that. So I said, "Okay, we won't do that." But it was enough to make the guards think we were crazy enough to try. The next day, the prison administrators came and agreed to our demands—more food, two more blankets at night, and fifteen more minutes of exercise time a day. It felt like a big victory. For two weeks afterward, we had to relearn to eat, like we were babies all over again. All our stomachs could handle was milk, a little soft potato, that sort of thing.

So I had a reputation as a dangerous prisoner. Not because I was violent, but because I could lead the prisoners to rebel against our conditions. The authorities decided to transfer me to Ashkelon, which was where they put the prisoners they considered the most dangerous.* Inside Ashkelon, there were a lot of leaders of Palestine's resistance movement. To Israel, this was where the worst of the worst went. But as a Palestinian, I felt much safer in Ashkelon than I had at Damun.

Those of us who were young and in prison for the first time started to study. We wanted to know everything. We would sit with the older men in Ashkelon, and they told us about their experience. The older prisoners would even organize more formal education—lectures and lessons every day. These were guys who had been in prison forever. Some of them had been in since 1967. I think a few of those guys had been around to hear Jesus lecture! So they had a lot of wisdom to pass on.

We learned about history, economics, philosophy. We had to wake up at six in the morning and start reading and studying. At ten there was a lecture until noon, and then there was a ninety-minute break.

---

* Now called Shikma Prison, the facility is a maximum-security prison just outside Ashkelon, a city of 115,000 people just north of the Gaza Strip. Shikma was built following the Six-Day War in 1967 as a lockup for security prisoners in the newly occupied Palestinian territories.

After the break, we had to write an article — it could be political, educational, whatever. But we had to write something. Every day one of the inmates had to lecture the others about what he had written and read earlier. And then we would go back to reading. They served us dinner at seven, and then between seven and ten we could read, and then we would go back to sleep. If we didn't finish our writing, we could stay up late and write. We didn't have enough time for all our activities. It became an addiction, and I was consumed with *What am I going to read next? What am I going to write?*

Every inmate had his own specialty. Some of them were political, some of them philosophical. One specialized in economics, another in Marx. Some people taught chemistry and explosives inside the prison. We also learned languages. Some of the prisoners knew Greek, Russian, Turkish, so they would pass on their languages. Getting into Ashkelon for me was like getting accepted to Harvard or Oxford, or even better!

But the treatment in the prison was still very harsh. Solitary confinement at Ashkelon was the worst in all the prisons in Israel. Prisoners could be isolated from others for years.* One inmate I knew lost his mind because of all the pressure from solitary. He needed psychiatric help.

To protest this, we set all the cells on fire. Every prisoner was part of it. We all piled up clothes in the middle of our cells and lit them with smuggled matches. The smoke was terrible, and many of us suffocated. Forty-eight prisoners had to be hospitalized, but our protest got attention. They still used solitary confinement to torture people afterward, though.

The relationships you form inside the prison are very strong. There are a lot of people from different cities — Ramallah, Nablus, Hebron, so many places. So there's a lot to learn, and you become more knowledgeable about the situations in other cities. When you

---

* In 1986, the same year Abdelrahman was transferred to Shikma Prison, Israeli nuclear technician Mordechai Vanunu was captured by Israeli intelligence officers in Rome and sentenced by military tribunal to Shikma for leaking details of Israel's secret nuclear weapons program. He spent eleven of his eighteen years in prison in solitary confinement.

get out of prison, you're going to stay friends with them. And they're really influential in their own societies. So many of the leaders of the First Intifada met in prison.

I got out of prison in 1989, during the First Intifada. I was still only twenty, but I was more influential in our society because people respect someone who's been in jail—we weren't seen as criminals, but leaders.

I Was Just Like the Pope

I didn't stay out long after my release in 1989. I was only out for six months. I hadn't done anything this time, but because of my record and people I knew, and because it was the Intifada, I was rounded up.*

This time after my trial I was sent to Ktzi'ot Prison.† In Ktzi'ot, I improved my Hebrew. Ktzi'ot was like a big open-air prison with lots of tents, and one of the tents was the "Hebrew tent," where only Hebrew was spoken. I taught Hebrew lessons there and trans-lated Hebrew-language newspapers for the other inmates.

I had a lot of experience and I knew a lot, so the new inmates would ask me how to do things. I was just like the Pope. They would respect me and ask me for things. In prison culture, if you're an alumnus of prison, you get special treatment from both the inmates and the wardens and guards. I would get the best bed in the tent, you know, the one in the corner. The guards also gave me special treat-ment because I was an asset to the prison. They knew that I could in-fluence everyone else, and if I said something, everyone was going to listen to me. It was a give and take.

I was out of prison in 1994, but of course, the Israeli authorities

---

* Abdelrahman was arrested under suspicion of being a member of the Popular Front for the Liberation of Palestine (PFLP).

† The Ktzi'ot Prison is a large, open-air prison camp in the vast Negev desert, located forty-five miles southwest of Be'er Sheva. Ktzi'ot was opened in 1988 and closed in 1995 after the end of the First Intifada, and then reopened in 2002 during the Second Intifada. According to Human Rights Watch, one out of every fifty West Bank and Ga-zan males over the age of sixteen was held at Ktzi'ot in 1990 during the middle of the First Intifada.

kept an eye on me. The authorities have this obsession, that once someone like me has been to prison, then we're a terrorist for life. I got picked up a few times, and sometimes I'd be held for a day, sometimes for two weeks. Then, in 1995, I was arrested, and this time they took me to Al-Muskubiya. They didn't have charges, they just wanted to interrogate me about people I knew. During the interrogation, I was tortured.

After twelve days of not being allowed to sleep, not getting enough to eat, that's when the interrogators started shaking me. There are two kinds of shaking they'd do—one of the head and neck only, and one for the whole body. Of course when they start after nearly two weeks of no food or no sleep, you can't really physically resist at all. You're too weak, and your neck starts to flop around, you don't get oxygen, and you pass out. They'd bring us prisoners close to death.

I remember waking up in the hospital. I'd been taken to Hadassah.* After I was better, I was taken back to Al-Muskubiya and interrogated some more. They'd use other methods, too. One thing the interrogators liked to do was to make the handcuffs really tight and bind me to a chair that slanted downward. They would leave me like that for twelve days at a time, with the handcuffs slowly cutting into my wrists. They would also put a dirty bag over my head that was soaked in vomit or that had been dunked in the toilet. After twelve days, they'd give me four hours of rest. This went on for months. Sometimes they'd only ask me a few questions, for just fifteen minutes a day. And then I'd be bound up in the chair for the rest of the day. Sometimes they'd say they were going to give me "stomach exercises," and then two interrogators would twist my body in opposite directions while my hands were cuffed. They would put me in these stress positions until I threw up or fainted.

They didn't have anything to accuse me of in Al-Muskubiya, but they didn't want me out on the streets. Also, they wouldn't let my lawyer see me for many weeks. Finally, a lawyer came. She was a new lawyer I'd never heard of named Allegra Pacheco. I think as a prisoner, I had developed a keen sense of who was dangerous, who was

---

* Hadassah Medical Center is a health care complex in Jerusalem.

safe, and who I could trust. I knew I could trust Allegra right away.

After six months, they sent me to Megiddo Prison in northern Israel. They never charged me with anything. They just gave me a one-year sentence of administrative detention that they renewed for a second year. By this time, I was a real expert at life in prison. I was able to convince some of the guards that I was a Jew because of my good Hebrew. They used to ask me, "You're among Arabs. How can we help you?" I asked them for a mobile phone, because we couldn't have one inside prison. They gave me the phone.

I got away with other tricks because of my good Hebrew. We had newspapers inside, and there were ads in the back. One ad was for a pizza place. I used one of our smuggled phones and called the pizza place, and I pretended as if I was the prison director. I ordered seventy-five slices, enough for all the inmates. And the pizza guy told me they'd deliver in two hours. In three hours, the prison director came to my tent and gave me a long look. He asked, "Do you still want pizza?" So I answered him, "If you're going to give it to us, why not?" He was pretty mad. He said, "I know that you're the one who asked for the pizza, because you have really good Hebrew. Now you're going to solitary." So I had to spend two weeks in solitary. There was another ad in the newspaper for belly dancers. I wanted to call and ask for dancers as well, but because I got busted for the pizzas I didn't have the nerve to do it.

The Judges Had No Mercy

During the time I was in prison, I kept seeing my lawyer, Allegra. She helped me appeal every six months during my administrative detention hearings, and she kept me thinking about the future. I must have proposed to her twenty times while I was at Megiddo. She told me I was crazy.

Finally, I got out of administrative detention in 1998, and I started working for human rights groups, like the Palestinian Human Rights Monitoring Group and B'Tselem.* We'd investigate cases of human

---

* The Palestinian Human Rights Monitoring Group was founded in 1996 partly by members of the Palestinian Authority to record instances of human rights abuses in

rights abuses against Palestinians. And I stayed in touch with Lea and Allegra and other lawyers who were fighting in courts to end the torture of prisoners. In 1999, they took some cases to the high court in Israel, and they won a huge victory that made certain kinds of torture illegal.

It was also around this time that I got Allegra to agree to marry me. I think I just had to ask her enough times. As a prisoner, I'd learned to be persistent in speaking out for what I wanted, and I used the same tactics to win over Allegra. We just sort of agreed we might get married someday soon, and then she went to the U.S. on a fellowship. She was working on a book about how a Second Intifada might be right around the corner. But she didn't finish it, because the Second Intifada started in 2000 while she was still writing and that spoiled the concept of her whole book!

During the Second Intifada, I was still working for B'Tselem, and sometimes I'd sneak into Jerusalem to talk to Palestinians for reports on human rights abuses. I also worked with Gideon Levy, a reporter for *Ha'aretz*, which is Israel's major newspaper. I'd show him around the refugee camps and help with stories. When I went to Jerusalem, I'd always bring a really nice leather briefcase, so I'd look like a businessman. But in May 2001, I was stopped by a police officer in Jerusalem and arrested for not having a proper permit to travel into the city. So once again I was headed to prison.

I was taken back to Al-Muskubiya. Already, interrogation had changed, but not much. They still put me on a chair that was angled downward with tight cuffs. But now, instead of hitting, shaking, that sort of thing, they tried to mess with my mind more. They would do things like show me a photo of my house in ruins and tell me it had been demolished. But it was all Photoshop work.

At the time, Allegra was in the United States. She was supposed to be done with her fellowship and come back to Israel in June. She was in Boston trying on a wedding dress when she heard I'd been picked up. She got back just in time to represent me during my administrative detention hearing. She showed up along with Lea, her men-

---

the West Bank and Gaza. B'Tselem was founded by Israeli citizens in 1989 to document human rights abuses in the occupied territories.

tor and my first lawyer. They had a photographer from *Ha'aretz* with them who was going to testify on my behalf, and they brought a lot of snacks—*burek*, cola, and cigarettes.* Allegra also brought wedding bands with her. We got to have a reunion in the lawyer's meeting room, and that's where we announced that we were engaged. We had a little party with the burek and cola, and then Lea took some pastry to the judges to tell them we were getting engaged, and she asked if we could have a little more time in the meeting room. Meanwhile, the *Ha'aretz* photographer took pictures of us exchanging rings. It was beautiful!

But the judges had no mercy. The prosecutors kept bringing up how I was mean to my interrogators, cursed at them, called them sons of bitches, and how I wouldn't cooperate. That was their big case for me being a security risk to Israel, just that I wasn't nice enough in the interrogation room. Allegra was wonderful—she demanded that the judges look at the deep grooves in my wrists from my recent interrogation. But they refused. And so I ended up spending another year in administrative detention.

When I got out in May 2002, Allegra and I were married, and she was five months pregnant when I was arrested again in November. This was right in the middle of the Second Intifada still, and a lot of former prisoners were being arrested. The night they picked me up, they were looking for my brother. But because I had a record, they decided they'd pick me up as well. I was sentenced to six months administrative detention and sent to Ofer Prison.† I was in prison when our son Quds was born in April 2003. Allegra was all by herself during the birth. When June 2003 came around, I was up for another renewal of detention. This would have been the seventeenth six-month detention I'd been given during my lifetime. My lawyer Lea tried to bring photos of Quds into court near Ofer to show me. It would have been the first time I'd seen my son, but the judge refused to let me see the photos. He gave me another sentence of six months. During

---

* Burek is a traditional Turkish pastry stuffed with cheese, potatoes, or other fillings.

† Ofer Prison is a large open-air prison near Ramallah. At the time of Abdelrahman's arrest in 2003, there were approximately 1,000 Palestinian men and women serving administrative detention sentences.

the hearing, I was able to slip the photos of my son into my prison uniform when nobody was looking, so I at least had the photos of my son in prison with me. My detention was renewed twice more for a year and a half total, so I didn't get to go home and meet Quds until he was almost two. By that time I had spent almost seventeen years in prison altogether, with at least thirteen of those years being in administrative detention without charges.

This Is Life for Thousands of People

I've been out of prison since 2004. When I got out the last time, I started studying law, and now I'm a lawyer, like Allegra. Last January, I was in military court to help my friend. I argued his case in front of a judge who has sentenced me to administrative detention many times before. I was going to rub it into his face that I was a lawyer now. But they didn't let me enter the courtroom.

I also defend prisoners who have been arrested by the Palestinian Authority.* The conflict with the Palestinian Authority is even more complicated than the occupation. I make visits to the prisoners in the PA prisons, and in some cases they get tortured and humiliated there even more than with the Israelis. I visit my clients in prison every day. And I sit down and talk to them and listen to them. The conditions are extremely harsh. In the important cases, the information from the interrogation is shared among the intelligence agencies of the Americans, Israelis, and the Palestinians, together.

I still see many of the people from my time in prison, including other prisoners and my first lawyer, Lea Tsemel. She's like a mother to my wife and me. She still visits me now. She's a good person.

Now we have two girls and two boys. It's even. The boys are ten and seven, and then the girls, five and two. To raise a baby girl is much easier than raising a boy. They're much calmer, and they're nicer, easier to deal with. Boys just want to rebel all the time. But my

---

* The Palestinian Authority was chartered to administer parts of the West Bank and Gaza following the Oslo Accords in 1993. As part of the Oslo agreement, the Palestinian Authority is responsible for security control in parts of the West Bank such as Bethlehem.

boys are not aggressive. The kids just want to play. They're very sweet.

Of course, I worry about my kids and the situation they're growing up in. I want my kids to grow up in a good atmosphere, with justice and liberty and freedom, and a life with no problems. We've been deprived of so many things, and that, of course, always takes its toll on you. So whatever my kids ask from me I get for them. I buy them expensive bicycles and that sort of thing. Allegra says no, but I spoil them because I was deprived of so many things when I was a child. I want my children to have what I never had. I admit, I have a psychological problem with shoes! I buy them for my kids all the time. Every one of my four children has dozens of pairs of shoes. Every time Allegra asks me, "Why did you buy that?" I say, "You can't possibly understand." One of my daughters also has five little backpacks.

I would like to go to the U.S. to visit my wife's parents. My wife is an American, but the U.S. government rejected our visa application on security grounds.* What's the security problem? I haven't been convicted of any crime by an Israeli court since I was a child. I've been trying to get a visa for a long time. The lawyer for the visa asked for $120,000. We've stopped trying.

From a physical aspect, I do still have effects from the torture. I still can't feel my left hand completely due to the nerve damage I got from being handcuffed. And it's not easy to live with the fact that I went through such a horrible experience. It has impacted me.

I probably would be different today if I hadn't gone to prison. Probably I would've gone to med school instead of law school. But I've never really thought much about how my life would be different if I hadn't gone to prison, because this is life for thousands—millions even—of people in refugee camps in Palestine, in Lebanon, or in Syria. It's not a personal problem, it's a broader thing. I want to solve it because it affects everybody else, not just me. If the situation doesn't change, my son Quds may soon have the same experience. This is a problem for generation after generation—we've been fighting for sixty-five years. It's going to be the same thing until we break the cycle.

---

* It is very difficult for any Palestinians who have spent time in prison to travel, and especially to get visas to the United States, even if they were held under administrative detention and never charged with a crime.

DANA SPIOTTA

■

Jelly and Jack

FROM *The New Yorker*

IN THE DAMP LATE spring of 1985, Jelly picked up the handset of
her pink plastic Trimline phone and the dial tone hummed into her
ear. She tilted the earpiece slightly away from her and heard the sad
buzz of a distant sound seeking a listener. How many times had she
fallen asleep after saying goodbye and not managed to get the thing
on the cradle? The little lag when he had hung up but she was still
on the line, semiconnected, in a weird half-life of the call, followed
by the final disconnection click, then silence, and then, if she didn't
hang up, sharp insistent beeps. These were the odd ways in which
the phone communicated: urgent beeps to say, "Hang up"; long-
belled rings to say, "Answer"; rude blasts of the busy signal to say,
"No." The phone was always telling her things.

She pushed the eleven buttons — the 1, the area code, the number,
zeroing in, the nearly infinite combinations ousted — her fingertips
not needing to feel the groove of the numbers but feeling it nevertheless. So many distractions, unneeded and unwanted. She had to
concentrate to keep the information away. There was a bird outside,
trilling at her. It was at least fifteen feet from the closed window, but
it still bothered her. It was probably in the Chinese oak in the court-
yard. The ring of another person's phone sounded so hopeful at first,
and then it grew lonelier. It lost possibility, until you could almost see
the sound in an empty house.

He didn't have an answering machine. Make a note of that. A dis-
tinction. She could let it ring all day. Was that true? Had anyone ever

tried it? The plastic handset rubbed against her jaw and her ear. She tilted it away again. If she lay on her side and let it rest on her head, using a hand only for balance, she could talk for hours.

"Hello?" said a male voice, clearing itself as it spoke, so that the end of the word had a cough pushing through it. Then came another cough. Was this the first time he had spoken today? Or had she woken him up? Talking to someone just roused from sleep offered a special, intimate opportunity. But it carried high risk, also. The woken person could feel startled or vulnerable, and then grow angry as the reality of the call's interruption reached his conscious mind. It had happened to Jelly once: "Why the fuck are you disturbing my sleep? You have no idea how hard it is for me to fall asleep. And now. Well, now I'm awake for the goddamn duration, you bitch." Even Jelly couldn't break through a feeling like that. But this man just finished coughing and waited. She closed her eyes and focused on the white of ease, of calm, of joy. The pure and loving human event of calling a stranger, reaching across the land and into a life.

"Hello," she said. Her voice sliding easily through the "l"s, to the waiting, hopeful "o." She always took her time. Nothing made people more impatient than rushing.

"Who is this?"

"It's Nicole."

"Nicole? Nicole who? I think you have the wrong number."

This was a crucial moment.

"Is this Mark Washborn?"

"Uh, no. I mean, Mark. It isn't. Who is this again?"

"Nicole. I'm a friend of Mark's. I thought this was his new number."

"No. That's weird. I know Mark. I mean, he's a good friend of mine."

"Oh my. How awkward. I am so sorry I disturbed you, uh . . ." She rarely used "uh," but it was an important wordish sound that introduced a powerful unconscious transaction. Used correctly, not as a habit or a rhythmic tic, it invited the other person to finish the sentence. It was an opening without content, just the pull of syntax and the human need to complete.

"Jack. Jack Cusano."

"Jack Cusano? Not Jack Cusano the record producer?"

"Uh, yeah."

"Jack Cusano who also composes film scores? You did that gorgeous work on those Robert DeMarco films."

"That's right." He laughed. His laugh cleared out his throat a bit more. She lay back on the pillow, held the phone so that it barely touched her cheek. She imagined her voice going into the transmitter, sound waves being turned into electrical pulses, sent up the wires to the phone lines to a Syracuse switching station, then turned into microwaves speeding across the country with the memory—the imprint—of her exact tone, her high and low frequencies, her elegant modulations, to the switching station in Santa Monica, which sent electric current up the P.C.H. to a Malibu beach house and into Jack's receiver—undoubtedly a sleek black cordless phone. So fast, too: instantly turned back into a sound wave by the tiny amplifier near his ear. All that way, all those transformations, but no distortions. A miracle of technology. The sound was as clear as speech in a room. She could—amazing—hear the ocean in the background. A gull, the sound of water pulling back from beach. She could almost hear the sun shining through his west-facing windows.

This was another crucial moment. She knew that she could not initiate anything more. She had to wait for him to open it further. She could not get anxious. She crossed her legs at the ankles, pulled her kimono robe over her knees. She was a little cold. She wanted to be in that room with the beach smell and the sun on the windows. She waited, closed her eyes. She heard him cough.

"So how do you know Mark?" he said. He sounded friendly and a bit amused now.

Jelly made an "em" sound in her throat, with a little push through her nose. It sounded thoughtful, vaguely affirmative. She knew that, even if she had to say no at some point, she would say it low and round and long, so that it sounded as if it had a yes in it somehow. Or an up-pitched-down-pitched mmm-mmm, like a hill. The hum took you for a ride, just under the nose with the mouth closed.

"We talk a lot. Early-morning talks, middle-of-the-night talks. Sometimes we talk for hours."

"Yeah? What about? Are you a girlfriend?"

Jelly laughed. These men all had "a" girlfriend, meaning several at any time. She never wanted to be one of a number. What Jelly wanted was to be singular. Not even "a friend." She wanted a category of her own construction. Something they never knew existed.

"No," she said. "Actually, he talks to me about his writing. He reads me what he's written that day. I listen and tell him what I think. He says it gives him motivation, knowing that I'll call, and he has to have something good to read to me."

"Really?"

"He never told you about me?" she said.

"No, but I don't listen to everything Mark says. He tends to fill the air with static. At a certain point, it's just ambient noise."

She laughed. He laughed. Jelly sat up, stretching her back straight, feeling her spine arrange itself in a line above her hips. She switched the phone to the other ear and relaxed the tension in her neck. She took a breath. So much of this involved waiting, silence, timing.

"So I have to go, Jack. I am so sorry I disturbed you."

"No. I mean, no problem. I had to get up. I usually don't sleep this late. But I was working all night on this piece."

"You probably want to make some coffee and get back to work."

"Yeah, but not really."

"Is it for a film score?"

"You know, it isn't. It is just a thing I had in my head, and I was playing with it. Using the keyboard. It'll end up in a film score at some point, I'm guessing."

"Really? You don't watch the film and then compose to it?" she said.

"Yeah, I do. But I also import melodies and musical ideas I have. On file, so to speak."

"Fascinating."

"So, would you like to hear some of it?"

"Really?"

"Sure."

"Oh, wow, I would really love that. Yes, please."

"OK, good," he said. "Hold on."

Jelly closed her eyes and leaned back again. She called this body listening. It was when you surrendered to a piece of music or a story. By reclining and closing your eyes, you could respond without tracking your response. Some people started to speak the second the other person stopped talking or playing or singing. They were so excited to render their thoughts into speech that they practically overlapped the person. They spent the whole experience formulating their response, because their response was the only thing they valued. Jelly had a different purpose in listening to anything or anyone. It had something to do with submission, and it had something to do with sympathy. She would lie back and cut off all distraction. The phone was built for this. It had no visual component, no tactile component, no scent wafting, no acid collection in the mouth, no person with a hopeful or embarrassed face to read. Just vibrations, long and short waves, and to clutch at them with your own thoughts was just wrong. A distinct resistance to potential. A lack of love, really. Because what is love, if not listening, as uninflected—as uncontained—as possible.

She took a deep breath, relaxed, and let the music find her.

"So that's it," he said, and let out a tight, nervous laugh.

Jelly opened her eyes, expelled a small sigh into the receiver. "It's wonderful," she said.

"Yeah?" he said.

"Yes," she said. "Thank you."

"Good," he said.

"There were these little leaps with each reprise."

"That's right," he said.

Only after she was done listening did she form her response. And it worked like this: you found the words—out of a million possible words—that truly described the experience. That part, the search for the right language, was fun, almost like solving a puzzle. You thought of the word, and then you felt it in your mouth, pushed breath into it, and said it out loud. The sound of it contained the meaning—she had to hear the words to know if she had it right. Then, as it hung there, she revised it, re-attacked it, applied more words to it.

"It gave me a remarkable feeling of lifting. Not being picked up or climbing. Not even like rising in an elevator," she said. "Or an escalator. Not quite. More float in it. Maybe like . . . levitating."

"You levitated while listening to my little piece? Right on."

It did feel like levitation. Waves of sound. Waves on the ocean.

Floating on the water. Floating on sound waves. Levitation. What Jack didn't know was how easily this came to her.

"I have to go, Jack. I'm afraid I'm late."

"Oh, no, really?" he said. She heard the hard fizzle of a match strike, and then a sharp intake of breath followed by a blowing sound: lighting a cigarette. She knew the sounds that people made on the phone: the bottle unscrewed or uncorked, the pour of liquid over ice and the cracking of the ice. The sip — so slow it was painful, the delicate, discreet sound of a swallow. And this sound, lighting a cigarette. But with a match, not a lighter. He was a smoker who used matches instead of a lighter, which made him a certain kind of person. Because a match had drama. A match left you with a flame to shake or blow out. And a match left a pleasant phosphorus smell lingering in the air.

"So nice to talk with you this morning. Nice to meet you, Jack," she said.

"The pleasure, Nicole, is mine. So when can we talk again? Can I call you sometime?"

Jelly sat up. Held the phone back for a minute. She moved slowly in these moments. The giveaway was not his request. The giveaway was that he'd used her name. She had him.

"I do have to run. I promise I'll call you soon," she said.

"I look forward to it. Anytime," Jack said.

"Goodbye," she said.

"Bye."

She would not call anytime. She would call on Sunday, at the same time. Only Sunday, and it would only be her calling him. Parameters. Predictability. That was the way it would work best for both of them, for this thing they were building between them. He wouldn't understand. He would want to call her, have her number. He would want to talk at other times, more often. But she knew what was best, how to do this. Pace was important. She would make him her Sunday call, and, as the weeks of talks went by, he would accept her terms. He would begin to get great pleasure out of counting the days until Sunday.

"Hey, babe," Jack said when he answered the phone.

"Hi, Jack," Jelly said. She was sitting on her couch. She had the trade papers—*Variety* and *The Hollywood Reporter*—on the coffee table in front of her. Next to the papers were a large magnifying glass and a highlighter. The rain was coming down hard. Later it would turn into wet, sticky snow. The news called it a "wintry mix." It would freeze up and make the sidewalks ice sheets by morning. The weather made it difficult for her: if the sun wasn't out, it was low-lit, low-contrast gray with hidden ice. If she was lucky, she would hear and feel the ice cracking under her feet as she stepped, but mostly it was silent slick surfaces, which made walking frightening. And if the sun came out it was high-glare, every surface a beautiful but painful shimmer of reflected light. The winter was different every day, and you had to plan and react and accommodate it. There were easier places for a low-vision person like her. For anyone, really.

"Congratulations on the Grammy nomination," she said.

"Thank you. To tell you the truth, it doesn't mean that much. They can barely find five people who qualify in that category. Some of these things, if you submit and your name is known, you're automatically nominated," he said.

"But you've won before, and surely there's nothing automatic in that?" Jelly pulled her thick chenille robe around her. She had a cold, and she'd spent the morning sipping tea with lemon and honey. Her throat felt swollen, and even swallowing her saliva caused a sharp pain, but it hadn't affected her voice yet. She held an ice pack wrapped in a dishtowel. As she listened to Jack, she pressed the cold compress to her throat.

"True," he said.

"And it's such a perfectly realized recording. The production is outstanding—anyone would recognize that," she said. She heard him light a cigarette.

"I watched 'A Woman Under the Influence' yesterday," Jelly said. Jack loved John Cassavetes movies, and he had sent her a private video copy, impossible to find.

"Yeah? What did you think?"

"I think it's my favorite one. Gena Rowlands is mesmerizing, the way her vulnerability just crushes everyone around her."

"I never thought of it that way," he said. "I love that scene where she's waiting for her kids to get off the bus."

"Yes, she's so excited she's jumping from foot to foot, looking down the street, asking people for the time."

"Right! I love that. That's what I'm really like, way too much. When I was working at home and my daughter was little, I used to get so excited when it was three o'clock and she was coming home."

"You?"

Jack laughed. "Nicole, inside I am Gena Rowlands."

"I believe it. I'm glad," she said. She made herself swallow a sip of tea. She felt the movement in her ears. "So how did it go last night?"

"Shitty. I'm not feeling it these days."

Jack frequently stayed up all night working. Jelly called at 2 p.m., about an hour after he got up, by which time he had eaten his eggs and drunk his coffee. Read the Sunday *New York Times*.

"You always say that, and then you have an amazing breakthrough," she said. "A few weeks ago you said you felt spent and uninspired, and then you wrote that perfect, haunting melody for the new DeMarco film."

"That's true. I mean, I do usually feel shitty about what I'm working on, but that's no guarantee that the piece will ever get better. And then I complain about it, which must be boring."

"You feel bad because you care deeply and you're hard on yourself. Maybe it's all just part of your process."

"What?"

"Feeling hopeless makes room for something, maybe," she said. She heard him exhale.

"You think I need to despair and give up in order to get to something?"

Jelly cooed a sound that concurred with but did not interrupt his thoughts. "Mmm."

"Maybe." A long drag on his cigarette. "Maybe I have to push the obvious cliché crap out of my head. I have to exorcise it, throw it all out, and then, when all the bullshit has been heard and rejected, there's only something new—or, at least, interesting—left." Jelly heard the *ting* of a spoon stirring coffee, a sip, and then an exhale. "Maybe that's true. But it's a hell of a way to do it."

"What you are doing works. You always get what you need in the end. Inspiration comes."

"I really do that, don't I?" he said. "Never thought of it like that before. But I wonder if I could be more deliberate about it? Know that
I'm clearing out the cobwebs, so to speak. Going through the litany
of the obvious. The first wave of crap. Maybe I could be more efficient about the process."

"You could feel confident that, after you've rid yourself of it, the
real work will start," she said.

"I'd avoid the feeling of utter despair," he said. "Just by telling myself a different story about what I was doing."

"If you can reassure yourself in the midst of it, it won't cost you
so much," she said. "Because you need—you deserve—the feeling
of competence. You know what you're doing, and your bad moments
are just part of a process."

"Now I feel a little better about working again tonight," he said.

"Wonderful," she said.

"You always make me feel better," he said.

"I hope so," Jelly said. She pressed the ice to her throat. "Shall I go
and let you get back to work? I don't mind."

"No!" he said. "Don't you dare hang up yet."

"All right," she said, though she usually didn't let herself get talked
out of her instinct for exit timing. Most Sundays, they talked for an
hour, sometimes only half an hour. The times when she was on the
line for two or even three hours were unusual but had been more
frequent lately. Jack would play music—his or someone else's—or
they would watch a movie together, talking during the breaks in the
action. He now regularly sent her VHS cassettes in the mail, along
with letters and other little gifts. She had given him her Syracuse address, and if he got the impression that she was a graduate student at
Syracuse University it wasn't from anything she said directly. She left
gaps, and Jack filled them in. The contours were a collaboration, built
of his desires and her omissions. She didn't think of these as lies.
And she did feel like a graduate student. She was a kind of graduate
student in sociology. She had been helped by social workers when
she'd really needed help, after a meningitis infection nearly killed
her and blinded her overnight. Then, slowly, she had recovered some
sight. And now she volunteered to work with blind kids at the Center. Helped their parents. She felt like a grad student in the same way

that she felt blond and supple and young when she talked to Jack. She felt elegance in her hands and wrists.

Here is what she did not feel: She did not feel dowdy and heavy. She did not feel the doughy curve of her large belly. She did not feel the flesh of her thighs growing into her knees, making them dimpled and lumpy. She did not feel knots of spider veins or calluses or stretch marks. Was it fair that she hadn't even had a baby, that mere quick adolescent growth had given her red stripes that faded to permanent white ridges in the skin of her breasts, her upper arms, and thighs? Did it make sense that, before she had even shown anyone her body, her body had felt old and damaged? She did not feel like a forty-one-year-old woman, did not feel like being this heavy, invisible, unremarkable creature. She felt young and taut, a person who could beguile, a person who loved and understood men. That was the truth, and the rest was not of import to either of them.

"But I have to go soon," she said.

"No, Nico," Jack said.

Jelly wanted to hang up while he was still wanting her, long before he'd had his fill. But Jack was hard to resist. She liked the way he called her Nico. The way he asked things of her so openly.

"No? Why not?" she said, her sore throat making her voice crack slightly.

"Because your voice sounds so sultry today, and I need to listen to it," he said. His naked want worked on her. It skirted toward the sexual, but she never let it go there. She was reserved about overt sexuality, and the men she talked to got that somehow. They knew that some women were butterflies in your hands. You didn't say crude things to them. You breathed gently and you didn't make any sudden moves.

However, it was also true that a few men she had called in the past hadn't got her at all. They didn't understand her, despite her guidance, her clear vision for them, her parameters. They weren't interested in her, not truly.

"You are making me so hard," one unworthy contact had said, apropos of nothing she had told him. This despite her subtle, demure approach, and the fact that she knew someone in his circle. She'd hung up immediately and never called him again.

Jack was polite. He cursed and he hacked his cigarette cough, but he was gentle. A gentleman.

"I don't have to go yet," she said. "Are you feeling sad? You sound a little sad."

"Maybe a little."

"It isn't just about your work?"

"I don't know. It's a nice Sunday sad, some old-fashioned melancholy. Sometimes I sit around and just feel sad about things. Is that odd? I am odd—you know I am. It isn't just loneliness. I miss certain people, or feel sad about certain people, which is different, I think."

"Who?"

"I miss my Uncle Joe. He died a few years back, but I thought of him today. He was a funny guy. He didn't really understand me or what I do, but that didn't matter. We were family, and he always liked me and made me feel that. Up until he died, he gave me money every time I saw him. Even though he was a retired insurance salesman and I was making a lot of money, a successful guy, an adult with a kid, when he'd see me at a family dinner or whatever, when he was leaving he'd press a hundred dollars into my hand and say, 'A little gas money,' and wink. I'd try to refuse, but it was his way of showing he was looking out for me. An Italian thing, I guess. I miss that little jolt of family." Jack coughed. "I should have, I don't know, asked his advice or something, instead of just talking to my cousins. And I miss my dog Mizzie. She was a mutt with these droopy hound eyes and long velvet ears. I got her when I was in my twenties and had her through my first divorce and second marriage. I never walked her as much as she wanted me to. I rushed her or let the housekeeper do it. Now I wish she were here so I could take her for a long walk."

"Oh, you are being very hard on yourself," she said.

"Not just that." She heard him light another cigarette and exhale. "Not just that. I miss my daughter and my mother. I mean, my daughter is still around, but—" He laughed.

"What's funny?" she asked.

"I don't know. My spiel of regrets."

Jelly fingered her tender throat and listened to Jack smoke.

"It's difficult," she said. "So difficult."

"Do you miss anyone, Nico?" he said. "Maybe you're too young—"

"No, I do," Jelly said, starting to talk before Jack finished, which was something she tried never to do.

"Yeah? Who?"

"My father died when I was sixteen," Jelly said. "He never lived with us, so I didn't see him too often. Once a week he'd take me out. Usually we saw a movie and then went to a diner and had hamburgers. It was hard, because he died suddenly, of a heart attack, and I kept thinking about the last time I saw him. I was in a bad mood, and I didn't want to go out to dinner with him. I wanted to be with my friends. So I went, but I sulked. I didn't want to see a movie, and I barely ate my dinner. I remember peeling the label off the Coke bottle and how he kept asking awkward questions about my life. I found everything he said irritating and boring. And then after he died, I felt bad about that dinner. I remember sitting on my bed and realizing that I could actually count the number of times I had seen my father. One night a week, plus a full week every summer. Multiplied by my age, or at least the years I could remember, so let's say twelve. That was all we had, and yet I couldn't be bothered to even look at him the last time I saw him." This was a true story that she had never told anyone before. Part of her thought, Stop. What are you doing? But she pushed that thought away. Jack would love her; she knew it.

"Oh no," Jack said. "I'm sorry. But you were a kid. He knew you loved him under the sulk. My daughter did the same thing—all kids do it. I promise you he understood that."

"Yes," Jelly said. The word squeezed through her tight throat. She could feel patches of heat on her cheeks and her eyes started to sting.

"I mean, my daughter—I haven't seen her in months," he said. He made a loud exhale, half sigh, half noise. "We had a stupid thing a few months ago. We—I mean, I—I should be able to do better, but every day I don't." Jelly said nothing, just waited for what he would say or sound next. A sniff. "It's OK," he said. "It's good sometimes to feel this way, even if it fucks me up a little." Jelly could hear that his voice had a catch in it—a failure of breath mid-word—and it undid her. Her own throat caught.

"I know," she said, and she heard the unmistakable sounds of a man weeping, a man unused to it, and she let him get it all out. She could hear his hard breaths, his sniffs, the little human sounds of feeling. "I know." She did know.

"Yes," he said. "I'm sorry."

"Don't be sorry, Jack. You're OK with me."

"Yeah, yeah. I am OK with you. I am."

She felt so close to Jack that she did something she had never done before. She stopped calling other men, her other phone dates. She gave Jack her number and let him call her whenever he felt like it. They began to talk every day. This thing between them was quickly escalating, and she tried not to worry or think about where it would lead. She tried, in her own soft, quiet way, to maintain a little reserve and slow things down. But it was hard because, well, she was in love with Jack. She felt connected to him in ways that made her feel happy all the hours of her day.

He trusted her and she trusted him, and when she hung up the phone she felt so loved. But then all at once her life—her real life, her harsh, real life—was all around her. She looked down at her hand holding the phone, at her legs in her robe, at her notebook full of notes about her phone conversations. She squinted up at her apartment, and imagined how she'd look to anyone else. She tried to tell herself that things might work out, but the gap was so big. It made her gasp.

The phone rang very early one morning. Jelly woke in her bed, the room dark. She had fallen asleep talking to Jack but must at some point have returned the phone to its cradle on the nightstand. She reached out from under the covers and picked up the phone. She held it to her ear and, half-asleep, whispered, "Hello?"

"Nico," Jack said in a low voice.

"Are you OK?" she asked, and her voice sounded drowsy and girl-ish.

"Yes," he said. "Are you asleep?" Jelly pulled the covers over her head and held the phone to her ear as she closed her eyes.

"A little," she said, and she sighed into the mattress by the receiver.

Years earlier, when Jelly was in college, she had rented her first apartment, just off campus. She'd been excited to have her own space and her own phone. One night the phone woke her. She was still partially asleep when a man's voice said, "Hi," as if he knew her.

"Hi," she said.

"It's me," he said. "Did I wake you?"

"No," she said.

"You sound sleepy."

"I am a little sleepy," she said.

"Good," he said. And then she heard something in his voice. "So good," he whispered. "And you like it, don't you?"

"Who is this?" she said, now awake and angry, and he moaned a little into the phone. She heard it, paused for just a moment, and slammed the phone onto the cradle. It wasn't anyone she knew. He'd just randomly called her, a crank call. He called women in the phone book, probably, and got them to talk to him by acting intimate, by whispering to them while they were disoriented after being woken in the middle of the night. What upset Jelly the most was how he'd sounded—gentle and easy. She'd replayed the voice in her head, and it wasn't a deviant voice. It was sexy. He never called again, although she almost wished he had. It was the first time she'd understood what the phone could be—a weapon of intimacy.

Jelly closed her eyes and said his name into the receiver, "Jack." She lay on her stomach with the phone next to her. "I'm in bed." And she listened to him breathe.

"Good morning," he said.

"Good morning! How are you?"

There was a long pause. Jelly pulled a velvet pillow onto her lap. She rested her elbows on it, the phone cradle on the pillow between her arms, the receiver held lightly by her ear. The room was bright. It was midmorning. She was still in her silk pajamas. Her kimono robe opened to the morning air. The sun was strong and warmed her face as she spoke. She heard Jack light a cigarette. She resisted the urge to fill in, talk. She waited for him to speak.

"What if I said something crazy?"

Jelly waited some more. But she knew what was coming. It always came.

"What if I bought you a ticket and you got on a plane to come see me?"

She laughed. Not a mocking laugh but a fluttery, delighted laugh. It was a delicate situation. She could feel his want. All down the wires the want travelled. In his scratchy morning voice, his cigarette voice, his sentence didn't sound like a question until it went up a half-register on the word "me." It was touching.

Still she didn't speak. This was the moment she'd been longing for but also dreading. Things always fell apart after this.

"I mean it. I've been thinking. I think — well, not thinking. That's the wrong word. Feeling. I have these feelings for you. I want to be with you."

"I have feelings for you, too," she said.

"I'm in love with you," he said.

"Yes," she said.

"Is that crazy? Never meeting in person, and feeling this way."

After she got off the phone, Jelly began to cry. She let herself feel loved, in love, immersed in their particular devotion, however fleeting. But there was no chance for them, not after what she had done. She had no choice.

The first time Jelly had come to such a pass was with another man she called, Mark Jenks. He was a mildly successful film director. Things had gone on for months; things had gone as far as they could (nothing stays in one place, people always want more), and one day he had asked her what she looked like. She had described herself accurately but not specifically: long blond hair, fair skin, large brown eyes. Those true facts would fit into a fantasy version of her. She knew, because she had the same fantasy of how she looked. But, after a few weeks of that, there came the request for a photograph.

She had taken some photos of her friend Lynn. She'd met Lynn through the Center. She was the mother of one of the low-vision kids Jelly worked with. Lynn was lovely to look at: a slender girl with delicate but significant curves. She was not that bright and had a flat, central-New York trailer accent, but she also had a most appealing combination of almost too pouty lips, heavy-lidded eyes, and an innocent spray of freckles across her tiny nose. Lynn had invited her to the beach with her son, Ty, who was six. Jelly met with Ty once a week to help him adjust to his fading eyes. Although she had regained nearly all of her own sight, she still had to use extremely thick glasses; she was tunnel-visioned and had difficulty in low-contrast situations. Like Ty, she didn't fully belong in either world, sighted or blind. She was like a character in a myth, doomed to wander between two places, belonging nowhere. That was the word, "belong." How much she would like to be with someone, and *be long*—not finite, not ending—with someone.

At the beach that day, Lynn had looked even more beautiful than usual. She wore very little makeup. She had a tan and a white macramé bikini. She looked happy, relaxed. Jelly took three shots of her. Just held up her cheap camera and clicked. One showed Lynn looking away, thoughtful. One was blurred. The third showed her smiling into the camera. Lynn looked sexy but not mean. A happy, open, sweet-looking girl. Jelly knew as she took the photos what she would do with them. She dropped the film at the Fotomat to be developed. She made sure she kept the negatives in a safe place.

The photos bought her some time with Mark, but they also escalated things. She knew there was no coming back from the lie. She tried to enjoy the moment, the delicious male desire directed at her. In her fantasies, she often imagined herself looking like Lynn and being worshipped by Mark. She was always Jelly but not Jelly, even as she lay in her bed with the lights out, after Mark had whispered his love for her and she had replaced the phone on the cradle. She closed her eyes and leaned back into her pillow. Her hand found the elastic top of her panties, the curly hair, and then the tiny wet bump. With all the possibilities of the world at her beckon, she never imagined Mark loving Jelly, squishy middle-aged Jelly. She was herself but in Lynn's body. She imagined Mark undressing her and touching her perfect, pink-tipped breasts as they spilled out of her bra, her smooth thighs under her skirt, her supple but taut midsection, her round high ass. She watched her fantasy as if it were a movie. After she came, she didn't think too much about it. Was it unusual to exclude your own body from your fantasy? Why not, if anything is possible, imagine him loving you as you are? Because (and she knew this absolutely without ever saying it to herself) her desire depended on her perfection in the eyes of the man. The fantasy—and her arousal—was about her perfect body. And how a man like Mark—a man who already loved her in theory—would worship her in that body. Her fantasy was impossible to fulfill, and she was never dumb enough to believe that Mark could love her as she actually was.

After Mark, she had used the photos with two other men. Things always proceeded in the same direction, and when a meeting became unavoidable she ended them.

But what about Jack? Some part of her thought that maybe Jack would love her no matter what. She thought about sending a neck-up flattering photo of herself, just to see what happened. Before he asked for a photo, before he invited her to visit him, he'd asked her the question they'd all asked at some point. Though Jack's version was artful, gentle: "You sound so young when you laugh. How old are you?"

Jelly laughed again. She knew how to avoid answering questions. But you couldn't laugh off questions forever. And all of his circling around eventually came to the point. *What do you look like?* It wasn't that she didn't expect it or that she didn't understand it; it was just so hopeless to always wind up against it. And how could she answer it? After she hung up the phone, she sat on the couch for a long time, staring into the faint dusk light.

What do I look like? If you look, or if I look? It is different, right? There is no precision in my looking. It is all heat and blurred edges. Abstractions shaped by emotion—that is looking. But he wants an answer.

What do I look like? I look like a jelly doughnut.

Jelly got up and went to the mirror. What to do if what you look like is not who you are? If it doesn't match?

I am not this, this woman. And I am not Lynn-in-the-photograph. Jack must know. Jack knows who I am. I am a window. I am a wish. I am a whisper. I am a jelly doughnut. Sometimes, when my hair falls against my neck and my voice vibrates in my throat, I feel beautiful. When I am on the telephone, I am beautiful.

How would it go? Jelly knew, just as she knew so many things without having experienced them. She knew that if she met Jack he would be disappointed, even if she were beautiful in the common sense of "beautiful." "Common" was an interesting word. It could be comforting if you meant what we all have in common. But it also meant ordinary—something we have all seen many times or can find easily. So a common beauty was agreed upon by all and also dull, in a way.

Still, his disappointment would come out of something human and inescapable: the failure of the actual to meet the contours of the imaginary. As he listened to her words come across the line and into his ear, he imagined a mouth saying them. As he spoke into the receiver, he imagined a face listening, and an expression on that face. Maybe he imagined a woman made up of an actress he'd seen on TV the night before, plus a barely remembered photograph of his mother when she was very young, and a girl with long hair he'd once glimpsed at the beach. But there was no talking without imagining. And, when imagining preceded the actual, there was no escaping disappointment, was there?

What about Jelly? Would Jelly feel disappointment with Jack if he showed up sweaty, old, smelling of breath mints and cigarettes? It never occurred to her to think this way. She would be so focused on him that her own feelings wouldn't matter. She would feel disappointed if he felt disappointed. She would hear it in his voice, and she would know that she was losing everything, all the perfect, exquisite moments that she had made with him.

"I want to see you," Jack had said. "I need to see you."

"I know. I know. OK," Jelly had said. "I will send you some pictures."

Of course she was right to send the photographs of Lynn; she needed to make things last just a little longer. But she cried as she sealed the envelope, because for a moment she thought it might have gone a different way.

SHARON LERNER

■

The Teflon Toxin

FROM *The Intercept*

This story is the first part of a three-part investigative series regarding C8, a toxic chemical used in Teflon and other products. Today, C8 is present in the blood of 99.7 percent of Americans. You can find parts two and three of this series online at theintercept.com. The Intercept was founded in 2014 by journalists Glenn Greenwald, Laura Poitras, and Jeremy Scahill. It seeks to bring transparency and accountability to powerful governmental and corporate institutions.

KEN WAMSLEY sometimes dreams that he's playing softball again. He'll be at center field, just like when he played slow-pitch back in his teens, or pounding the ball over the fence as the crowd goes wild. Other times, he's somehow inexplicably back at work in the lab. Wamsley calls them nightmares, these stories that play out in his sleep, but really the only scary part is the end, when "I wake up and I have no rectum anymore."

Wamsley is 73. After developing rectal cancer and having surgery to treat it in 2002, he walks slowly and gets up gingerly from the bench in his small backyard. His voice, which has a gentle Appalachian lilt, is still animated, though, especially when he talks his happier days. There were many. While Wamsley knew plenty of people in Parkersburg, West Virginia, who struggled to stay employed, he made an enviable wage for almost four decades at the DuPont plant here. The company was generous, helping him pay for college courses and training him to become a lab analyst in the Teflon division.

He enjoyed the work, particularly the precision and care it required. For years, he measured levels of a chemical called C8 in various products. The chemical "was everywhere," as Wamsley remembers it, bubbling out of the glass flasks he used to transport it, wafting into a smelly vapor that formed when he heated it. A fine powder, possibly C8, dusted the laboratory drawers and floated in the hazy lab air.

At the time, Wamsley and his coworkers weren't particularly concerned about the strange stuff. "We never thought about it, never worried about it," he said recently. He believed it was harmless, "like a soap. Wash your hands [with it], your face, take a bath."

Today Wamsley suffers from ulcerative colitis, a bowel condition that causes him sudden bouts of diarrhea. The disease also can—and his case, did—lead to rectal cancer. Between the surgery, which left him reliant on plastic pouches that collect his waste outside his body and have to be changed regularly, and his ongoing digestive problems, Wamsley finds it difficult to be away from his home for long.

Sometimes, between napping or watching baseball on TV, Wamsley's mind drifts back to his DuPont days and he wonders not just about the dust that coated his old workplace but also about his bosses who offered their casual assurances about the chemical years ago.

"Who knew?" he asked. "When did they know? Did they lie?"

Until recently, few people had heard much about chemicals like C8. One of tens of thousands of unregulated industrial chemicals, perfluorooctanoic acid, or PFOA—also called C8 because of the eight-carbon chain that makes up its chemical backbone—had gone unnoticed for most of its eight or so decades on earth, even as it helped cement the success of one of the world's largest corporations.

Several blockbuster discoveries, including nylon, Lycra, and Tyvek, helped transform the E. I. du Pont de Nemours company from a 19th-century gunpowder mill into "one of the most successful and sustained industrial enterprises in the world," as its corporate website puts it. Indeed, in 2014, the company reaped more than $95 million in sales each day. Perhaps no product is as responsible for its dominance as Teflon, which was introduced in 1946, and for more than 60 years C8 was an essential ingredient of Teflon.

Called a "surfactant" because it reduces the surface tension of water, the slippery, stable compound was eventually used in hundreds of products, including Gore-Tex and other waterproof clothing; coatings for eye glasses and tennis rackets; stain-proof coatings for carpets and furniture; fire-fighting foam; fast food wrappers; microwave popcorn bags; bicycle lubricants; satellite components; ski wax; communications cables; and pizza boxes.

Concerns about the safety of Teflon, C8, and other long-chain perfluorinated chemicals first came to wide public attention more than a decade ago, but the story of DuPont's long involvement with C8 has never been fully told. Over the past 15 years, as lawyers have been waging an epic legal battle—culminating as the first of approximately 3,500 personal injury claims comes to trial in September—a long trail of documents has emerged that casts new light on C8, DuPont, and the fitful attempts of the Environmental Protection Agency to deal with a threat to public health.

This story is based on many of those documents, which until they were entered into evidence for these trials had been hidden away in DuPont's files. Among them are write-ups of experiments on rats, dogs, and rabbits showing that C8 was associated with a wide range of health problems that sometimes killed the lab animals. Many thousands of pages of expert testimony and depositions have been prepared by attorneys for the plaintiffs. And through the process of legal discovery they have uncovered hundreds of internal communications revealing that DuPont employees for many years suspected that C8 was harmful and yet continued to use it, putting the company's workers and the people who lived near its plants at risk.

The best evidence of how C8 affects humans has also come out through the legal battle over the chemical, though in a more public form. As part of a 2005 settlement over contamination around the West Virginia plant where Wamsley worked, lawyers for both DuPont and the plaintiffs approved a team of three scientists, who were charged with determining if and how the chemical affects people.

In 2011 and 2012, after seven years of research, the science panel found that C8 was "more likely than not" linked to ulcerative colitis—Wamsley's condition—as well as to high cholesterol; pregnancy-induced hypertension; thyroid disease; testicular cancer; and kidney cancer. The scientists' findings, published in more than three dozen peer-reviewed articles, were striking, because the chemical's effects were so widespread throughout the body and because even very low exposure levels were associated with health effects.

We know, too, from internal DuPont documents that emerged through the lawsuit, that Wamsley's fears of being lied to are well-founded. DuPont scientists had closely studied the chemical for decades and through their own research knew about some of the dangers it posed. Yet rather than inform workers, people living near the plant, the general public, or government agencies responsible for regulating chemicals, DuPont repeatedly kept its knowledge secret.

Another revelation about C8 makes all of this more disturbing and gives the upcoming trials, the first of which will be held this fall in Columbus, Ohio, global significance: This deadly chemical that DuPont continued to use well after it knew it was linked to health problems is now practically everywhere.

A man-made compound that didn't exist a century ago, C8 is in the blood of 99.7 percent of Americans, according to a 2007 analysis of data from the Centers for Disease Control, as well as in newborn human babies, breast milk, and umbilical cord blood. A growing group of scientists have been tracking the chemical's spread through the environment, documenting its presence in a wide range of wildlife, including loggerhead sea turtles, bottlenose dolphins, harbor seals, polar bears, caribou, walruses, bald eagles, lions, tigers, and arctic birds. Although DuPont no longer uses C8, fully removing the chemical from all the bodies of water and bloodstreams it pollutes is now impossible. And, because it is so chemically stable—in fact, as far as scientists can determine, it never breaks down—C8 is expected to remain on the planet well after humans are gone from it.

Eight companies are responsible for C8 contamination in the U.S. (In addition to DuPont, the leader by far in terms of both use and emissions, seven others had a role, including 3M, which produced C8 and sold it to DuPont for years.) If these polluters were ever forced to clean up the chemical, which has been detected by the EPA 716 times across water systems in 29 states, and in some areas may be present at dangerous levels, the costs could be astronomical—and C8 cases could enter the storied realm of tobacco litigation, forever changing how the public thinks about these products and how a powerful industry does business.

In some ways, C8 already is the tobacco of the chemical industry—a substance whose health effects were the subject of a decades-long corporate cover-up. As with tobacco, public health organizations have taken up the cause—and numerous reporters have dived into the mammoth story. Like the tobacco litigation, the lawsuits around C8 also involve huge amounts of money. And, like tobacco, C8 is a symbol of how difficult it is to hold companies responsible, even when mounting scientific evidence links their products to cancer and other diseases.

There is at least one sense in which the tobacco analogy fails. Exposure to tobacco usually contains an element of volition, and most people who smoked it in the past half century knew about some of the risks involved. But the vast majority of Americans—along with most people on the planet—now have C8 in their bodies. And we've had no choice in the matter.

For its first hundred years, DuPont mostly made explosives, which, while hazardous, were at least well understood. But by the 1930s, the company had expanded into new products that brought new mysterious health problems. Leaded gasoline, which DuPont made in its New Jersey plant, for instance, wound up causing madness and violent deaths and lifelong institutionalization of workers. And certain rubber and industrial chemicals inexplicably turned the skin of exposed workers blue.

Perhaps most troubling, at least to a DuPont doctor named George Gehrmann, was a number of bladder cancers that had recently begun to crop up among many dye workers. Worried over "the tendency to believe [chemicals] are harmless until proven otherwise," Gehrmann pushed DuPont to create Haskell Laboratories in 1935. Haskell was one of the first in-house toxicology facilities and its first project was to address the bladder cancers. But the inherent problems of assigning staff scientists to study a company's own employees and products became clear from the outset.

One of Haskell's first employees, a pathologist named Wilhelm Hueper, helped crack the bladder cancer case by developing a model of how the dye chemicals led to disease. But the company forbade him from publishing some of his research and, according to epidemiologist and public health scholar David Michaels, fired him in 1937 before going on to use the chemicals in question for decades.

C8 would prove to be arguably even more ethically and scientifically challenging for Haskell. From the beginning, DuPont scientists approached the chemical's potential dangers with rigor. In 1954, the very year a French engineer first applied the slick coating to a frying pan, a DuPont employee named R. A. Dickison noted that he had received an inquiry regarding C8's "possible toxicity." In 1961, just seven years later, in-house researchers already had the short answer to Dickison's question: C8 was indeed toxic and should be "handled with extreme care," according to a report filed by plaintiffs. By the next year experiments had honed these broad concerns into clear, bright red flags that pointed to specific organs: C8 exposure was linked to the enlargement of rats' testes, adrenal glands, and kidneys. In 1965, 14 employees, including Haskell's then-director, John Zapp, received a memo describing preliminary studies that showed that even low doses of a related surfactant could increase the size of rats' livers, a classic response to exposure to a poison.

The company even conducted a human C8 experiment, a deposition revealed. In 1962, DuPont scientists asked volunteers to smoke cigarettes laced with the chemical and observed that "Nine out of ten people in the highest-dosed group were noticeably ill for an average of nine hours with flu-like symptoms that included chills, backache, fever, and coughing."

Because of its toxicity, C8 disposal presented a problem. In the early 1960s, the company buried about 200 drums of the chemical on the banks of the Ohio River near the plant. An internal DuPont document from 1975 about "Teflon Waste Disposal" detailed how the company began packing the waste in drums, shipping the drums on barges out to sea, and dumping them into the ocean, adding stones to make the drums sink. Though the practice resulted in a moment of unfavorable publicity when a fisherman caught one of the drums in his net, no one outside the company realized the danger the chemical presented. At some point before 1965, ocean dumping ceased, and DuPont began disposing of its Teflon waste in landfills instead.

In 1978, Bruce Karrh, DuPont's corporate medical director, was outspoken about the company's duty "to discover and reveal the unvarnished facts about health hazards," as he wrote in the *Bulletin of the New York Academy of Medicine* at the time. When deposed in 2004, Karrh emphasized that DuPont's internal health and safety rules often went further than the government's and that the company's policy was to comply with either laws or the company's internal health and safety standards, "whichever was the more strict." In his 1978 article, Karrh also insisted that a company "should be candid, and lay all the facts on the table. This is the only responsible and ethical way to go."

Yet DuPont only laid out some of its facts. In 1978, for instance, DuPont alerted workers to the results of a study done by 3M showing that its employees were accumulating C8 in their blood. Later that year, Karrh and his colleagues began reviewing employee medical records and measuring the level of C8 in the blood of the company's own workers in Parkersburg, as well as at another DuPont plant in Deepwater, New Jersey, where the company had been using C8 and related chemicals since the 1950s. They found that exposed workers at the New Jersey plant had increased rates of endocrine disorders. Another notable pattern was that, like dogs and rats, people employed at the DuPont plants more frequently had abnormal liver function tests after C8 exposure.

DuPont elected not to disclose its findings to regulators. The reasoning, according to Karrh, was that the abnormal test results weren't proven to be adverse health effects related to C8. When asked about the decision in deposition, Karrh said that "at that point in time, we saw no substantial risk, so therefore we saw no obligation to report."

Not long after the decision was made not to alert the EPA, in 1981, another study of DuPont workers by a staff epidemiologist declared that liver test data collected in Parkersburg lacked "conclusive evidence of an occupationally related health problem among workers exposed to C-8." Yet the research might have reasonably led to more testing. An assistant medical director named Vann Brewster suggested that an early draft of the study be edited to state that DuPont should conduct further liver test monitoring. Years later, a proposal for a follow-up study was rejected.

If the health effects on humans could still be debated in 1979, C8's effects on animals continued to be apparent. A report prepared for plaintiffs stated that by then, DuPont was aware of studies showing that exposed beagles had abnormal enzyme levels "indicative of cellular damage." Given enough of the stuff, the dogs died.

DuPont employees knew in 1979 about a recent 3M study showing that some rhesus monkeys also died when exposed to C8, according to documents submitted by plaintiffs. Scientists divided the primates into five groups and exposed them to different amounts of C8 over 90 days. Those given the highest dose all died within five weeks. More notable was that three of the monkeys who received less than half that amount also died, their faces and gums growing pale and their eyes swelling before they wasted away. Some of the monkeys given the lower dose began losing weight in the first week it was administered. C8 also appeared to affect some monkeys' kidneys.

Of course, enough of anything can be deadly. Even a certain amount of table salt would kill a lab animal, a DuPont employee named C. E. Steiner noted in a confidential 1980 communications meeting. For C8, the lethal oral dose was listed as one ounce per 150 pounds, although the document stated that the chemical was most toxic when inhaled. The harder question was to determine a maximum *safe* dosage. How much could an animal—or a person—be exposed to without having any effects at all? The 1965 DuPont study of rats suggested that even a single dose of a similar surfactant could have a prolonged effect. Nearly two months after being exposed, the rats' livers were still three times larger than normal.

Steiner declared that there was no "conclusive evidence" that C8 harmed workers, yet he also stated that "continued exposure is not tolerable." Because C8 accumulated in bodies, the potential for harm was there, and Steiner predicted the company would continue medical and toxicological monitoring and described plans to supply workers who were directly exposed to the chemical with protective clothing.

Two years after DuPont learned of the monkey study, in 1981, 3M shared the results of another study it had done, this one on pregnant rats, whose unborn pups were more likely to have eye defects after they were exposed to C8. The EPA was also informed of the results. After 3M's rat study came out, DuPont transferred all women out of work assignments with potential for exposure to C8. DuPont doctors then began tracking a small group of women who had been exposed to C8 and had recently been pregnant. If even one in five women gave birth to children who had craniofacial deformities, a DuPont epidemiologist named Fayerweather warned, the results should be considered significant enough to suggest that C8 exposure caused the problems.

As it turned out, at least one of eight babies born to women who worked in the Teflon division did have birth defects. A little boy named Bucky Bailey, whose mother, Sue, had worked in Teflon early in her pregnancy, was born with tear duct deformities, only one nostril, an eyelid that started down by his nose, and a condition known as "keyhole pupil," which looked like a tear in his iris. Another child, who was two years old when the rat study was published in 1981, had an "unconfirmed eye and tear duct defect," according to a DuPont document that was marked confidential.

Like Wamsley, Sue Bailey, one of the plaintiffs whose personal injury suits are scheduled to come to trial in the fall, remembers having plenty of contact with C8. When she started at DuPont in 1978, she worked first in the Nylon division and then in Lucite, she told me in an interview. But in 1980, when she was in the first trimester of her pregnancy with Bucky, she moved to Teflon, where she often sat watch over a large pipe that periodically filled up with liquid, which she had to pump to a pond in back of the plant. Occasionally some of the bubbly stuff would overflow from a nearby holding tank, and her supervisor taught her how to squeegee the excess into a drain.

Soon after Bucky was born, Bailey received a call from a DuPont doctor. "I thought it was just a compassion call, you know: can we do anything or do you need anything?" Bailey recalled. "Shoot. I should have known better." In fact, the doctor didn't express his sympathies, Bailey said, and instead asked her whether her child had any birth defects, explaining that it was standard to record such problems in employees' newborns.

While Bailey was still on maternity leave, she learned that the company was removing its female workers from the Teflon division. She remembers the moment—and that it made her feel deceived. "It sure was a big eye-opener," said Bailey, who still lives in West Virginia but left DuPont a few years after Bucky's birth.

The Federal Toxic Substances Control Act requires companies that work with chemicals to report to the Environmental Protection Agency any evidence they find that shows or even suggests that they are harmful. In keeping with this requirement, 3M submitted its rat study to the EPA, and later DuPont scientists wound up discussing the study with the federal agency, saying they believed it was flawed. DuPont scientists neglected to inform the EPA about what they had found in tracking their own workers.

When DuPont began transferring women workers out of Teflon, the company did send out a flier alerting them to the results of the 3M study. When Sue Bailey saw the notice on the bench of the locker room and read about the rat study, she immediately thought of Bucky.

Yet when she went in to request a blood test, the results of which the doctor carefully noted to the thousandth decimal point, and asked if there might be a connection between Bucky's birth defects and the rat study she had read about, Bailey recalls that Dr. Younger Lovelace Power, the plant doctor, said no. According to Karrh's deposition, he told Karrh the same. "We went back to him and asked him to follow up on it, and he did, and came back saying that he did not think it was related."

"I said, 'I was in Teflon. Is this what happened to my baby?'" Bailey remembered. "And he said, 'No, no.'" Power also told Bailey that the company had no record of her having worked in Teflon. Shortly afterward, she considered suing DuPont and even contacted a lawyer in Parkersburg, who she says wasn't interested in taking her case against the town's biggest employer. When contacted for his response to Bailey's recollections, Power declined to comment.

By testing the blood of female Teflon workers who had given birth, DuPont researchers, who then reported their findings to Karrh, documented for the first time that C8 had moved across the human placenta.

In 2005, when the EPA fined the company for withholding this information, attorneys for DuPont argued that because the agency already had evidence of the connection between C8 and birth defects in rats, the evidence it had withheld was "merely confirmatory" and not of great significance, according to the agency's consent agreement on the matter.

Ken Wamsley also remembers when his supervisor told him they had taken female workers out of Teflon. "I said, 'Why'd you send all the women home?' He said, 'Well, we're afraid, we think maybe it hurts the pregnancies in some of the women,'" recalled Wamsley. "They said, 'Ken, it won't hurt the men.'"

While some Dupont scientists were carefully studying the chemical's effect on the body, others were quietly tracking its steady spread into the water surrounding the Parkersburg plant. After it ceased dumping C8 in the ocean, DuPont apparently relied on disposal in unlined landfills and ponds, as well as putting C8 into the air through smokestacks and pouring waste water containing it directly into the Ohio River, as detailed in a 2007 study by Dennis Paustenbach published in the *Journal of Toxicology and Environmental Health*.

By 1982, Karrh had become worried about the possibility of "current or future exposure of members of the local community from emissions leaving the plant's perimeter," as he explained in a letter to a colleague in the plastics department. After noting that C8 stays in the blood for a long time — and might be passed to others through blood donations — and that the company had only limited knowledge of its long-term effects, Karrh recommended that "available practical steps be taken to reduce that exposure."

To get a sense of exactly how extensive that exposure was, in March 1984 an employee was sent out to collect samples, according to a memo by a DuPont staffer named Doughty. The employee went into general stores, markets, and gas stations, in local communities as far as 79 miles downriver from the Parkersburg plant, asking to fill plastic jugs with water, which he then took back for testing. The results of those tests confirmed C8's presence at elevated levels.

Faced with the evidence that C8 had now spread far beyond the Parkersburg plant, internal documents show, DuPont was at a crossroads. Could the company find a way to reduce emissions? Should it switch to a new surfactant? Or stop using the chemical altogether? In May 1984, DuPont convened a meeting of 10 of its corporate business managers at the company's headquarters in Wilmington, Delaware, to tackle some of these questions. Results from an engineering study the group reviewed that day described two methods for reducing C8 emissions, including thermal destruction and a scrubbing system.

"None of the options developed are . . . economically attractive and would essentially put the long term viability of this business segment on the line," someone named J. A. Schmid summarized in notes from the meeting, which are marked "personal and confidential."

The executives considered C8 from the perspective of various divisions of the company, including the medical and legal departments, which, they predicted, "will likely take a position of total elimination," according to Schmid's summary. Yet the group nevertheless decided that "corporate image and corporate liability"—rather than health concerns or fears about suits—would drive their decisions about the chemical. Also, as Schmid noted, "There was a consensus that C-8, based on all the information available from within the company and 3M, does not pose a health hazard at low level chronic exposure."

Though they already knew that it had been detected in two local drinking water systems and that moving ahead would only increase emissions, DuPont decided to keep using C8.

In fact, from that point on, DuPont increased its use and emissions of the chemical, according to Paustenbach's 2007 study, which was based on the company's purchasing records, interviews with employees, and historical emissions from the Parkersburg plant. According to the study, the plant put an estimated 19,000 pounds of C8 into the air in 1984, the year of the meeting. By 1999, the peak of its air emissions, the West Virginia plant put some 87,000 pounds of C8 into local air and water. That same year, the company emitted more than 25,000 pounds of the chemical into the air and water around its New Jersey plant, as noted in a confidential presentation DuPont made to the New Jersey Department of Environmental Protection in 2006. All told, according to Paustenbach's estimate, between 1951 and 2003 the West Virginia plant eventually spread nearly 2.5 million pounds of the chemical into the area around Parkersburg.

Essentially, DuPont decided to double-down on C8, betting that somewhere down the line the company would somehow be able to "eliminate all C8 emissions in a way yet to be developed that would not economically penalize the bussiness [sic]," as Schmid wrote in his 1984 meeting notes. The executives, while conscious of probable future liability, did not act with great urgency about the potential legal predicament they faced. If they did decide to reduce emissions or stop using the chemical altogether, they still couldn't undo the years of damage already done. As the meeting summary noted, "We are already liable for the past 32 years of operation."

When contacted by *The Intercept* for comment, 3M provided the following statement. "In more than 30 years of medical surveillance we have observed no adverse health effects in our employees resulting from their exposure to PFOS or PFOA. This is very important since the level of exposure in the general population is much lower than that of production employees who worked directly with these materials," said Dr. Carol Ley, 3M vice president and corporate medical director. "3M believes the chemical compounds in question present no harm to human health at levels they are typically found in the environment or in human blood." In May 2000, 3M announced that it would phase out its use of C8.

Dupont confronted its potential liability in part by rehearsing the media strategy it would take if word of the contamination somehow got out. In the weeks after the 1984 meeting, an internal public relations team drafted the first of several "standby press releases." The guide for dealing with the imagined press offered assurances that only "small quantities of [C8] are discharged to the Ohio River" and that "these extremely low levels would have no adverse affects." When a hypothetical reporter, who presumably learned that DuPont was choosing not to invest in a system to reduce emissions, asks whether the company's decision was based on money, the document advises answering "No."

The company went on to draft these just-in-case press releases at several difficult junctures, and even the hypothetical scenarios they play out can be uncomfortable. In one, drafted in 1989, after DuPont had bought local fields that contained wells it knew to be contaminated, the company spokesperson in the script winds up in an outright lie. Although internal documents list "the interests of protecting our plant site from public liability" as one of the reasons for the purchase, when the hypothetical reporter asks whether DuPont purchased the land because of the water contamination, the suggested answer listed in the 1989 standby release was to deny this and to state instead that "it made good business sense to do so."

DuPont drafted another contingency press release in 1991, after it discovered that C8 was present in a landfill near the plant, which it estimated could produce an exit stream containing 100 times its internal maximum safety level. Fears about the possible health consequences were enough to spur the company to once again rehearse its media strategy. ("What would be the effect of cows drinking water from the . . . stream?" the agenda from a C8 review meeting that year asked.) Yet other recent and disturbing discoveries had also provoked corporate anxieties.

In 1989, DuPont employees found an elevated number of leukemia deaths at the West Virginia plant. Several months later, they measured an unexpectedly high number of kidney cancers among male workers. Both elevations were plant-wide and not specific to workers who handled C8. But, the following year, the scientists clarified how C8 might cause at least one form of cancer in humans. In 1991, it became clear not just that C8-exposed rats had elevated chances of developing testicular tumors—something 3M had also recently observed—but, worse still, that the mechanism by which they developed the tumors could apply to humans.

Nevertheless, the 1991 draft press release said that "DuPont and 3M studies show that C-8 has no known toxic or ill health effects in humans at the concentrations detected" and included this reassuring note: "As for most chemicals, exposure limits for C-8 have been established with sufficient safety factors to ensure there is no health concern."

Yet even this prettified version of reality in Parkersburg never saw the light of day. The standby releases were only to be used to guide the company's media response if its bad news somehow leaked to the public. It would be almost 20 years after the first standby release was drafted before anyone outside the company understood the dangers of the chemical and how far it had spread beyond the plant.

In the meantime, fears about liability mounted along with the bad news. In 1991, DuPont researchers recommended another study of workers' liver enzymes to follow up on the one that showed elevated levels more than a decade before. But Karrh and others decided against the project, which was predicted to cost $45,000. When asked about it in a deposition, Karrh characterized the decision as the choice to focus resources on other worthy scientific projects. But notes taken on a discussion of whether or not to carry out the proposed study included the bullet point "liability" and the hand-written suggestion: "Do the study after we are sued."

In a 2004 deposition, Karrh denied that the notes were his and said that the company would never have endorsed such a comment. Although notes from the 1991 meeting describe the presence of someone named "Kahrr," Karrh said that he had no idea who that person was and didn't recall being present for the meeting. When contacted by *The Intercept*, Karrh declined to comment.

As the secrets mounted so too did anxiety about C8, which DuPont was by now using and emitting not just in West Virginia and New Jersey, but also in its facilities in Japan and the Netherlands. By the time a small committee drafted a "white paper" about C8 strategies and plans in 1994, the subject was considered so sensitive that each copy was numbered and tracked. The top-secret document, which was distributed to high-level DuPont employees around the world, discussed the need to "evaluate replacement of C-8 with other more environmentally safe materials" and presented evidence of toxicity, including a paper published in the *Journal of Occupational Medicine* that found elevated levels of prostate cancer death rates for employees who worked in jobs where they were exposed to C8. After they reviewed drafts, recipients were asked to return them for destruction.

In 1999, when a farmer suspected that DuPont had poisoned his cows (after they drank from the very C8-polluted stream DuPont employees had worried over in their draft press release eight years earlier) and filed a lawsuit seeking damages, the truth finally began to seep out. The next year, an in-house DuPont attorney named Bernard Reilly helped open an internal workshop on C8 by giving "a short summary of the right things to document and not to document." But Reilly—whose own emails about C8 would later fuel the legal battle that eventually included thousands of people, including Ken Wamsley and Sue Bailey—didn't heed his own advice.

Reilly clearly made the wrong choice when he used the company's computers to write about C8, which he revealingly called "the material 3M sells us that we poop to the river and into drinking water along the Ohio River." But the DuPont attorney was right about two things: If C8 was proven to be harmful, Reilly predicted in 2000, "we are really in the soup because essentially everyone is exposed one way or another." Also, as he noted in another prescient email sent 15 years ago: "This will be an interesting saga before it's thru."

EDITOR'S NOTE: DuPont, asked to respond to the allegations contained in this article, declined to comment due to pending litigation.

In previous statements and court filings, however, DuPont has consistently denied that it did anything wrong or broke any laws. In settlements reached with regulatory authorities and in a class-action suit, DuPont has made clear that those agreements were compromise settlements regarding disputed claims and that the settlements did not constitute an admission of guilt or wrongdoing. Likewise, in response to the personal injury claims of Ken Wamsley, Sue Bailey, and others, DuPont has rejected all charges of wrongdoing and maintained that their injuries were "proximately caused by acts of God and/or by intervening and/or superseding actions by others, over which DuPont had no control." DuPont also claimed that it "neither knew, nor should have known, that any of the substances to which Plaintiff was allegedly exposed were hazardous or constituted a reasonable or foreseeable risk of physical harm by virtue of the prevailing state of the medical, scientific and/or industrial knowledge available to DuPont at all times relevant to the claims or causes of action asserted by Plaintiff."

MICHELE SCOTT

■

How I Became a Prison Gardener

FROM *The Marshall Project*

AS A GARDENER in a prison I know a considerable amount about a few plants, the plants that have been in captivity along with me. We have been sharing the same confined space for decades. When you have been around someone for 24 years, you pick up a few things about what they like, what their needs are, what it takes to make them happy or what to do when they are sick.

This is not a one-way relationship. By observing, studying, and tending to the plants, I have reconnected with myself. Seeing them thrive and grow and live has opened a window for my guilt, my self-hatred from the ever-present fact that I took two lives.

And with all the hard work of establishing a garden, it is as if I created new time. All the drudgery of gardening has created time for thinking—about how I ever had gotten to where I'd gotten to begin with. As the years have unfurled in the garden, I have become a nurturer, at least in my own heart, and my remorse has begun to serve a purpose.

But it did not start out that way. At first, kneeling in the dirt outside my housing unit and preparing a place for that first marigold was a means of carving out personal space—an effort to be left alone, to get free, if only for a moment. It came from my inability to handle my new environment.

There were few birds; I did not see my first seagull until a few years into my time. A rabbit came and went.

A Beginning

In October of 1991, after they mowed the Reception Yard lawn for the first time in almost a year, I was part of the volunteer inmate crew that swept up the blades of grass. They did not give us rakes to use—just brooms, bare hands, and plastic bags.

I can remember the tang of the lawn's scent in the air. It was familiar, reminding me of home, Saturday mornings, picnics. Yet it was contained within the 40-yard circumference of a prison I would call "home" until I died.

By that time, I had found that prison had a culture unto itself, with customs and unwritten codes of expected behavior everywhere I turned. When you saw something going down (drugs snorted off the counter in the Laundry Room; or a quarter gram of dope getting sold at 300 percent profit; or a fight jumping off in the Port-a-Potty), you "saw nothing." No staring; no slowing down. Getting noticed might mean your room would get searched, and they would confiscate the "pruno" (inmate-manufactured alcohol) that your bunkie was brewing under her bed. And your bunkie would get pissed at you, not the officer.

No staring, no slowing down. Responding was what drew the officers' attention.

So what could I put my attention on? I had been a gardener before I was inside, so after that day collecting the grass, I applied myself to the front yard of my housing unit.

I remember how solitary it was outside, how quiet. There were never any birds. The bare dirt was not adorned. It was muddy, uneven. It contained remnants from the prison's construction—bits and pieces of concrete, rebar, wood, and nails, familiar things in an unfamiliar setting.

Clearing the dirt was a beginning, an unconscious permission for me to clear the insides of myself. I was desperate, frantic, for anything to be present inside of me but self-hatred and ceaseless guilt—the sweeping and unmanageable awareness that I had taken life.

The Life of Physical Things in Prison

But the building blocks I needed were now deemed both contraband and weapon material.

This was another frequent lesson in my prison education, when the secret life of everyday objects was revealed. Every solid thing in this place was warped and twisted, viewed by the officers as having ulterior possibilities that I, in my new role as prisoner, was expected to "be up on." It was a given that I was "up on" the fact that the brown plastic cup I was issued to take with me to my meals was actually a favored utensil for cutting cheeks, noses, and foreheads when in a fight with another woman.

To this day, I keep an eye on the inmates I pass on a walkway—perhaps that one over there who is gesturing too energetically. I veer away from her, just in case.

I never said the officers were wrong.

The Opportunity

A year after I arrived in prison, I was scheduled to have my annual program review. I knew my available job assignments were Auto Body Repair, Welding, Upholstery, Cosmetology—and Vocational Landscaping.

I knew which job I wanted. My patch outside my housing unit was waiting.

When I walked into the conference room, I saw the five committee members facing me. I took a deep breath. Then I said it as simply as I could: I enjoyed gardening and I really liked plants.

I saw a slight smile on the Inmate Assignment Lieutenant's face. Perhaps he was paying attention.

The next day, I received a job ducat—assigning me to Vocational Landscaping. From then on, the Landscaping Building and adjacent greenhouse were my sanctuaries.

How to Start a Garden in Prison

It is all about your interactions with staff. Whether it's asking for a "one-way" to get back into your room after the designated time has passed, or trying to get back out the door again in the morning—at 7:00 a.m.—to go play in the dirt, your housing officer holds all the keys.

After all, I was a Close B Custody inmate, which meant that I was at a higher "level of staff supervision required to ensure institutional security and public safety" and that my "activities shall be within the confines of the approved program housing unit."

What that really meant was I was not supposed to be let outdoors by myself, and certainly not unsupervised. But my staff observed that they had a stressed-out newbie LWOP inmate on their hands, and that being outside seemed to keep me sane.

Welcome to Hardpan

Do you know what hardpan is? It's a layer of hard soil cemented by almost insoluble construction materials that restrict the downward movement of water and roots.

To dig into that hard ground, I used plastic spoons, can lids, the metal plate that screwed the mop head into the mop stick. Anything I could get my hands on.

But I didn't care. It was a distraction, a kind of half-freedom from the constant loop always sounding in my thoughts: I'm here forever, and will never be free, I'm here forever and will never be free. That loop began each morning the moment the cinder blocks greeted me.

So I welcomed the hardpan, the exhausting labor. I pored over the textbooks at Landscaping, teaching myself about soil composition, the importance of soil aeration, and what substances it takes to make "good" soil.

I realized I needed to introduce some sand into the hardpan. Where to get sand? There were no garden store outlets in prison.

But while waiting in line behind the Work Change processing building, I noticed that a construction project was going on in the kitchen. There were sandbags on the ground to keep the water away from the inmate dining area. There was the sand I needed!

But I looked at the size of the burlap sacks, then looked down at my pants pockets. Not gonna happen, I thought. I would have to get this sand on the up-and-up. But who to ask?

Unwritten Rules

Another unwritten rule I was learning was that the apathetic staff are the best to deal with. As long as they don't have to work harder, and they are not "fronted off" (meaning that no unwanted attention is drawn to them), then these staff will let you handle what you need to handle.

(As for us, we inmates become known for how we do our time. The staff categorize us—some of us are "management concerns"; some are "dope fiends"; some are "ass kissers"; and some are "Polly Programmers," the good girls who are doing programs all the time. Early on, I was known for my mouth and my attitude. But now I was becoming the "Plant Lady.")

After explaining to a guard why I was so interested in the sand and what I was going to use it for (and with a promise to return the burlap bags), I was allowed to empty out the bags, with the help of a friend, and collect the sand.

I Get a Tractor

The landscaping program had a full set of tools, materials, and equipment. There was even a mini-tractor with an attachable loading cart.

Work crews were often assigned to go prune rosebushes, privet hedges, or install plants in front of the housing units. Part of my job was to load whatever we needed for those projects onto the loading cart and drive it to wherever it needed to go. Many times the staff saw me drive by with potted plants loaded into the back of my cart.

What they didn't know was that I often hid hormone powder, seed packets, a hose spray nozzle, plant fertilizer, and even worms (which would also improve the quality of the hardpan) in the bottom of those pots, hidden in the soil. I dropped my hidden supplies off at my unit and then continued on my way. The staff didn't have a clue.

It was the art of procurement, the act of liberating something from its captivity in one place to bring it someplace else, usually nearer to me.

When I read in one of my gardening books that vermiculite and perlite were soil amendments, I knew I would have to procure them. But how? The bags of this stuff were five feet long, three feet wide, and very bulky. There was no way to sneak them through Work Change, as I had with the worms. It had to look legitimate, at least at first glance. And that was what I was counting on—that staff would look only once at me, and then move on.

Timing my drop-offs was most important of all—when were certain staff taking lunch? Who had called in sick? I had to be watchful for opportunity.

So I was—and not only did I get the big sacks, I also got loads and loads of cinder blocks, which I needed to make a barrier around my plants. The material of the walls imprisoning me were becoming useful in my garden.

The Payoff

Here is why I push so hard to create my garden.

It is those moments when I shed the skin of an inmate, and feel the sunshine directly on me and listen to the droning bees as they tumble through the circuit of flowers planted months before.

Rabbits now lay supine in my garden and even near the walkways. And the birds that were once uncommon have come to join me too. It is common now to have to duck and take cover under a jacket or folder when an immense flock of gulls leaves its perch atop the dining hall, and swoops toward me. They have become my companions, encouraging me to come outside on a warm day and leave behind whoever I was before.

After two decades, I have learned the difference in birdsong—from the agitated pitch of white-crested house sparrows, fussing as they chase each other through the small bushes, to the excited chirping of the gulls when they realize water is available. A simple delight for me is to observe the splashing of these tiny feathered animals when a small pool of water collects in a shallow in the ground.

I glimpse a bird just being a bird.

And within these moments of observation, I am not thinking about this place. I do not see the concrete buildings encircling me, or notice the fencing topped with razor wire. My ears are closed to the arguments—about dope, or "prison love"—that drift along the walkway.

The innocence of creatures being their true selves offers me a diversion, though temporary, from the truth that another year has passed here in this place of sorrow. I am in that shared moment with the birds. Water cascades upon my feathers, my beak dipping into rivulets of water. For an instant I am free like the creatures I watch so closely.

JESSE BALL

■

The Gentlest Village

FROM *Granta*

I.

—This is a chair, said the examiner. A person is made in such a way that he can sit where he likes. He can sit on the ground,

she knelt and patted the floor.

—Or even on the table itself,

she patted the table.

—However, if you are in company, it is best to sit in a chair unless there is a good reason to sit elsewhere. In a chair, one can sit with good posture, that is, with the skeleton set into good order.

He looked at her with puzzlement.

—The skeleton, she said, is a hard substance, hard like wood, like the wood of this chair. It is all through the inside of your body, and mine. It keeps us stiff, and allows our muscles something to pull and push on. That is how we move. Muscles are the way the body obeys the mind.

—Here, she said. Come sit in the chair.

She gestured.

The claimant came across the room slowly. He moved to sit in the chair, and then sat in it. He felt very good sitting in the chair. Immediately he understood why the house was full of chairs.

—They put chairs wherever someone might sit.

—They do, she said. And if your needs change, you can move chairs from place to place. Come, let us eat. We shall walk to the kitchen, and there we will get the things we shall eat; also, we will get the things on which we shall eat, and the things with which we shall eat. We will not eat our food there; we'll go to the dining room, or to the enclosed porch. This will be a nice thing for us. Having gotten the food and the implements, we will decide whether we want to eat on the porch or in the dining room. Do you know how we will decide that?

The claimant shook his head.

—You do. Think carefully. Say what comes to mind.

—If it is a nice day, outside . . .

—That is one reason, one of many reasons, why a person would choose to sit outside. It is a good reason. It is always best to have a good reason for doing things, a reason that can be explained to others if you must. One should not live in fear of explaining oneself—but a rational person is capable of explaining, and even sometimes likes to do so.

—Rational?

—A person whose life is lived on the basis of understanding rather than ignorance.

—Am I ignorant?

—Ignorance is not about the amount of knowledge. It is about the mechanism of choosing actions. If one chooses actions based upon that which is known to be true—and tries hard to make that domain grow, the domain of knowledge—then he will be rational. Meanwhile, someone else who has much more knowledge might make decisions without paying any attention to truth. That person is ignorant.

—A mechanism, she continued, is the way a thing is gone about.

They went into the kitchen. On the wall was a painting of a woman feeding chickens with millet. The millet poured from her hand in a gentle arc. Around about her feet the chickens waited in a ring, looking up at her. When the arc made its way to the ground, they would eat.

Beside it was a photograph of a hill. There was a hole somewhere in it.

The claimant paused at these wall hangings, and stood looking. The examiner came and stood by him.

—What is different about these? she asked him.

He thought for a while.

—About them?

—What's the difference between them? I should say. When I say, what is different about these, I am making two groups—them and the rest of the world. When I say between them, I am setting them against each other. Do you see?

—This one happens less often.

He pointed to the woman with the chickens.

—Less often?

—If you go looking for them, outside the house, he said, you could probably find the other one, no matter when you looked. But, you can't find this one.

—Why not? Because it is a painting?

—A painting?

—Because it is made by hand—with strokes of a brush? Or for another reason?

—I didn't mean that, he said. I am tired. Can I sit down?

—Yes, let's go to our lunch. We can return to this later.

2.

The claimant sat watching her. He was in something she called a window seat. She had her hands folded and was sitting in a chair. They were in a room with what she called a piano. It made loud noise and also soft noise.

The examiner was a girl. The claimant didn't know that word, but it is how he saw her. He had known others, he was sure of it. Her soft yellow hair fell about her shoulders, and her bones were thin and delicate. He felt that he could see where the bones were through the skin. His own bones were larger.

She was helping him. He didn't know why. It occurred to him that he hadn't asked.

—Why am I here? he said suddenly.

The examiner looked up from her book. She smiled.

—I was waiting for you to ask that. Actually, she looked at a little clock that lay across her leg, it is just about the right time for you to be asking that. Nearly to the minute.

She laughed—a small, distinct laugh.

—You are here because you have been very sick. You almost died. But, you realized that you were sick, and you went to get help. You asked for help, and you were brought here. It is my job to make you better. You and I shall become good friends as you grow stronger, and as you learn. There is much for you to learn.

—But, he asked, where was I before?

—In a place like this, she said. Or in some place so different as to be unknowable to us when we are here. I can't say.

—Why do I keep falling asleep?

—You are learning—learning a great deal. It is too much for you, so your body bows out. Then you wake up and you can continue. It will be like this for a time. I have seen it before.

—Are you the only one like me? he asked.

—No, no, no.

She laughed to herself.

—There is a whole world full of people like us. Soon, you will meet others, when you are ready.

—How will we know?

—I will know, she said.

3.

On the third day, she pointed out to him a gardener. The man was in the distance, trimming a bush.

—There, she said. There is one.

He stood and watched the man for at least an hour. The man had gone away, and the claimant stood looking at the bush that had been clipped, and at the place where the man had been. He asked the examiner if the gardener was likely to be in that spot again. Not that exact spot, she said, but another near to it. This was the gardener window, then, he said. I can watch the gardener from here. They are all gardener windows, she said. There are others, and others. It's a matter of how far you can look, and if things are in the way. She took him to another window. Out of that one, he could see three people in a field, in the extreme distance. They were scarcely more than dots, but they were moving. At this distance, she said, you can't tell if they are men or women. They could even be children, he said. It might be hard to see a child that far off, she said. They could be, he insisted. The examiner did not tell him: there are no children in the gentlest village.

On the fifth day, she told him about fire, and explained what cooking was. He found fire to be very exciting. He could hardly bear the excitement of it. She wrote this down.

On the sixth day, he closed a cupboard door on his hand, and cried. She explained crying to him. He said that it felt very good. In his opinion, it was almost the same as laughing. She said that many people believe it is the same. She said there was perhaps something to that view, although of course it appeared to be a bit reductive.

4.

She wrote things in her notes, things like: Claimant is perhaps twenty-nine years of age, in good health. Straight black hair, grayish-brown eyes, average height, scars on left side from (childhood?) accident, scar under left eye, appears to be a quick learner, inquisitive. Memory is returning relatively quickly. Claimant is matching given data with remembered data—a troubling development.

5.

On the morning of the seventh day, he refused to get up. She told him to get up. He refused.

—What's wrong?

—The other day, you said that I almost died. That I was sick and that I almost died.

—You were sick. Now you are convalescing. You are regaining your strength. You are young and have a long life ahead of you in a world full of bright amusements and deep satisfactions, but you have been sick, and you must regain your ability to walk far and parse difficult things.

—What did you mean when you said I almost died?

—It isn't very much. It is a small thing. The world is full of organisms. You are an organism. A tree is an organism. These organisms, they have life, and they are living. They consume things, and grow, or they have no life, and they become the world in which other organisms live and grow. You almost became part of the world in which organisms live, rather than that which lives. It is nothing to be afraid of—just . . .

—But it would be the end? he said. There wouldn't be anymore?

—It would be an end, she said. Do you remember the conversation we had, the second night? About going to sleep?

He nodded.

—What happened?

—I went to sleep, and then in the morning everything was still here.

—Death is like that. Only, you work in the world with a different purpose. The world works upon you.

—How did I die?

—You didn't die. You nearly did.

—How?

—We will talk about this later, when you have more to compare it with. Here, get out of bed. Perhaps it is time for us to go for a walk. Perhaps we should leave the house.

He got up and she helped him dress. They had clothes for him, just his size, in a wardrobe that stood against the wall. They were simple, sturdy clothes: trousers, shirt, jacket, hat. She wore a light jacket also, and a scarf to cover her head. He had never seen her do this. I often cover my head, she said, when I go outside. One doesn't need to, but I like to.

They went into the front hallway, an area that he had not understood very well. It appeared to have no real use. But now when the door was opened he could see very well why there should be this thing: front hallway. He went out the door and down the stairs and stood by her in the street. He could feel the length of his arms and legs, the rise of his neck.

Going outside, he thought—it is so nice! The things that he had seen through the window were much closer. He could see houses opposite and, suddenly, there were people inside of them, and lights on. There was no one in the street, though. He walked with the examiner, arm in arm, and they went up the street a ways.

The houses looked very much the same. He said so.

—Do you know, she asked—do you know which one is ours?

He looked back in fright. The houses were all the same. They were exactly the same. He had no idea which one was theirs. She saw his fright and squeezed his arm. I will take you back to it, don't worry. I know which one is ours.

The street wound past more houses, and they gave way to buildings that she called shops. No one was in these shops, but the windows were full of things that she said might be bought. He did not understand, and did not ask.

On down they went to a little lake. Fine buildings were in a circle around the lake. There was a bridge in the lake to a little island (as she called it), and on the island there was a small house with no walls. They sat in it, and she poured him a glass of water from a pitcher that sat on a tray on a bench at the very center.

6.

When he woke up, he was back at the house again, in bed. It was the afternoon, he guessed—as light was all in the sky.

—Did I fall asleep again?

But she was not in the room. He went out to the landing. There was a carpet, but the old wooden boards of the house creaked beneath his feet. He winced, trying to step as quietly as possible. The railing ran along the top of the landing. The balusters were worked with lions and other beasts. He knelt by the edge and listened.

She was speaking to someone else. He couldn't hear what she was saying. The door shut, and she came up the stairs. When she saw him kneeling there, she smiled.

—Did you wake already?

—Who was that?

—Friends. They helped to bring you here. You didn't think I could carry you all by myself?

—Can I see them?

—Not yet, she said.

—What about the other people—the people in the other houses?

—Not yet, she said.

—How will you know?

—I will know.

7.

She wrote in her report:

> As I stated before, in the case of this claimant, the dream burden of his treatment was severe. His every sleep period is marred with nightmares. He is still in the first period, prior to Mark 1, so he remembers little to nothing of this, but it is a cause for concern. If it continues this way, I may need to directly address it. He talks in his sleep, muttering about a person who has died, and speaking with a vocabulary that he does not possess during the day. It is my hope that reprocessing is not necessary. He is mid to high functioning and could do very well as things stand but would lose much after a second injection.

She leaned back in her chair and her gaze ran along the wall. There was a stopped clock, an embroidered handkerchief in a glass case and an antique map. The map showed the known world as of a time when nothing was known. How apt for the Process of Villages.

She wrote:

> The previous case that I worked on involved a woman prone to violence
> and anger. None of that struggle is evident with this current claimant. It
> appears that his difficulty may have been entirely situational. If that is so,
> there is a good chance that our process will bring him to balance, as there
> may be no flaw whatsoever in his psyche.

8.

—Gardener is there! He's there!

She came to the window where the claimant was sitting.

—Is it the same one—or a different one?

—This one is wearing . . .

—Glasses.

—The other didn't have them.

—Is that a good way to tell them apart? she asked.

—It is one way.

—What if I were to wear glasses?

She took a pair out of a drawer and put them on.

—Would I be a different person?

She did look like a different person with glasses on, but he didn't
want to say that, so he said nothing.

—It is usually safe to assume that a person is different if their physical characteristics are different, said the examiner. But even then

sometimes people change—by accident or on purpose—and the same person can look different. Likewise, two people can look very alike.

—Or be exactly the same, he said.

—What do you mean?

—Twins are alike. They are the same.

—But even if the bodies are the same, the minds inside are different—their experiences are different. They are different people.

—Even if they can't be told apart?

—Even then.

—I knew someone, I think, who was a twin.

She looked at him very seriously and said nothing.

—She had a twin, but the twin died.

—How do you know this? asked the examiner.

—I remember it.

—But not from life, she said. You remember it from a dream. When you sleep at night, your mind wreathes images and scenes, sounds, speech, tactile constellations—anything that is sensory—into dreams. One feels that one has lived these things, of course one does. But dreams are imagined. They are a work of the imagination.

—What is the imagination for?

—It is a tool for navigating life's random presentation of phenomena. It enables us to guess.

—But I am sure that I knew her.

—Know her you did, but it was in a dream. You may dream of her again. That is the world where you can meet such a person. The actual world is different. For you, it is this house, and the street beyond. It is the lake at the center of the village, and the gazebo in the lake. It is the meal we take together at midday, and again at nightfall.

She sat for a moment quietly.

—Do you remember the book that I was reading to you from?

—About the poacher and his dog?

—Yes. You remember how real it seemed? Well, it is not real. It just seems to be real. And that is just a toy of words on a page—not anything close to the vibrant power of the mind's complete summoning that you find in the night. Is it any wonder that you believe it to be real? That you confuse memory and sleep's figment?

He shook his head.

She took off the glasses, and put them in the drawer.

—I still feel that you are different with glasses, he said.

She laughed.

—People do look quite different with glasses, I suppose. I suppose that must be true.

—Will you play for me on the piano? he asked.

She went to the piano and opened it.

—I can know that it is you because you play for me on the piano, he said. Someone else wouldn't do that.

—So, she said—you believe an individual's function and service are identical to their person?

She began to play.

He looked out the window again. It was open, and the air was moving now and then, sometimes in, sometimes out. Or, it must move out whenever it moves in. It couldn't just move in, or it would all end up inside. But, he supposed, that wasn't entirely impossible. After all, he was completely inside.

He put his arm out the window and felt the air on it.

Below, the neatly trimmed yard lay flat on its side. The street unrolled from left to right, and beyond the houses, other streets could be seen by the white chalk of their surface. The tops of houses could be seen downhill, the glint of light off the lake in the distance. In the long fields of the distance, and in the canopies of the trees, in waves at their edges, he felt a coy energy. It was as though the edges of things were where the greater part might be hidden—where he could find more.

9.

—There is a thing I want to tell you about, she said. It is called naming. Many things have names. You know that. The bottom post on the staircase is called the newel post. The staircase is called a staircase. The post is called a post. The bottom of the staircase is called the bottom. These are all names. People can have names too, and naming is a privilege. In human history, names have been used as a form of power. Poor families, for instance, would sometimes have three or four sons, and those sons would simply be given numbers for names. First son, second son, third son. Some people would be named just for their position. Blacksmith, or Miller. In fact, that naming system was so strong that there remain people today who have as part of their names those old positions.

She paused.

—Can you think of someone you speak about in that way?

—The men who work outdoors.

—You call them gardener. And if you spoke to them that way, they would understand. This is why it is useful—because it is effective communication. You speak to them, and they understand. Now, let us imagine that such a person had a different name—a name that had nothing to do with what he or she did. What would you say to that?

—It wouldn't make sense, he said. How would you get such a name? There would be no reason for you to have it instead of a different name.

—That's true. What would you call me?

—I would call you examiner.

—That's right, and why am I an examiner?

—Because your work is to examine people and things and help to achieve balance.

—That's what I told you, and I have shown it to be true through my actions. So, to you, a sound name for me is examiner. However, that is not my name. That is the name of my position. In the world, there are many examiners, but there is only one person with my particular allotment of cells who stands in my geographical and temporal position. That person is myself, and so I have a name to help differentiate me from other people who are similar to me.

—But, if you are the only one in your circumstance, why do you need a different name? Shouldn't your circumstance alone be the name itself? If it is specific to you?

The examiner laughed.

—Very good, very good. But it isn't necessarily so, because not everyone has perfect information. So, if they saw me on one day at the lake, and then a week later by that distant field, they might not know that I was the same person, unless I had told them my name. If I had, they could speak to me and use my name, and thereby confirm that it was me.

—But what if there were two of you with the same name?

—That is a problem. It is—and it comes up. In any case, I have a name. That gardener has a name. Everyone has a name. Everyone but you.

—Why don't I have a name?

—You don't have a name because you are starting over. You are beginning from the beginning. You are allowed to make mistakes and to fail. You don't need to do that under a real name, a name that will stay with you. We give you the freedom to make every conceivable mistake and have them all be forgotten. So, for now you will have a conditional name. You will have a name while you are here in this first village. Here your name is Anders.

—Anders. Anders.

He said it quietly to himself.

—Can you say it again? Say it again, she said.

—Anders. Anders, he said. But what shall I call you?

—You can call me Teresa. That is not my real name either. It is the name for the examiner that orbits you. Teresa and Anders. Names always function this way, though people don't think about it. They only exist in reference to each other.

—I'm not any more Anders to that gardener than I was a moment ago.

—You aren't. And his name is hidden from you. Perhaps forever.

—Where did my name come from? What does Anders mean?

She thought for a minute.

—I believe it is a Scandinavian name, or perhaps it is German. Let me say completely how it was for me in the moment I named you Anders. That is as close to the meaning of this use of Anders as we can get.

She stood up and went to the window.

—When I was young, there was a girl who lived on the same street as me. Her name was Matilda Colone. She was very pretty and she wore beautiful clothes. She was the envy of everyone at my school, and she was blind. How can that be? Of course, it isn't silly for grown people with circumspection and wisdom to envy a blind person who happens to be extraordinary. However, for children to do so—when the world is so bright and good to look at . . . you may imagine that it is surprising.

He nodded.

—She was elegant and calm. She learned her lessons perfectly. She had a seat in the classroom by a window, and the breeze would ruffle her hair or the scarf she wore, and we would all look at her and look at her and look at her. Matilda Colone, we would say under our breath. The teachers adored her, and everyone wanted to be her friend. But, she needed no friends, and would have none. Of all the things she had, and she had many, the best thing was that she had a brother, named Anders, and he sat beside her in class. He walked beside her to school. He brought her her lunch. He held her coat; he held it up, and then she would put it on. He was very smart, smarter than anyone in the class, except perhaps Matilda, but it was hard to say, because they would never cross each other. It was a school for the smartest children in the region. We all loved her so much that we could almost weep.

—What happened to her?

—This was in the old days. Her father shot himself, and she and Anders were separated and put into homes. Some years after that she died of pneumonia.

—Anders, he said to himself.

10.

Each night, the examiner would say to the claimant something like this (not this, but something like it):

Tomorrow we are going to wake up early. I am going to wake early and you are going to wake early. This will happen because I am sure to do so, and I will come and see to it that you are woken up. Then, I shall dress and you shall dress, and we will go downstairs to the kitchen. In the kitchen, we shall have our breakfast and we will enjoy the morning light. We will talk about the furnishings in the room. We will talk about the paintings and the photographs that we talk about each morning. You will have things to say about them and I will listen. I will have things to say to you about the things you have said. In this way, we shall speak. After breakfast, we will wash the dishes we have used and we will put them away. We will stand for a moment in the kitchen, which we will have cleaned, and we will feel a small rise of pleasure at having set things right. It is an enduring satisfaction for our species to make little systems and tend to them.

Yes, she would continue, we shall go on a walk to the lake, and perhaps this time we will walk around it to the small wood at the back. There we will find the trees that we like. Do you remember them? Do you remember that I like the thin birch that stands by the stream, and that you prefer the huge maple with the roots that block the path? Do you remember when you first saw it, and you ran to it? We shall go there tomorrow, and spend as much time as we want to sitting with those trees, in that quiet place. And when we have done that, we shall come home, walking fast or slow, and we shall . . .

And in this way she would go through the day and give him a sense that there was something to look forward to, and nothing to fear.

■

An Interview with President Obama

FROM *The New York Review of Books*

The following conversation between President Obama and Marilynne Robinson was conducted in Des Moines, Iowa, on September 14, 2015. Robinson is the author of the novels Lila, Home, Housekeeping, *and* Gilead, *which was awarded a Pulitzer Prize. President Obama is the president.*

THE PRESIDENT: Marilynne, it's wonderful to see you. And as I said as we were driving over here, this is an experiment, because typically when I come to a place like Des Moines, I immediately am rushed over to some political event and I make a speech, or I have a town hall, or I go see some factory and have wonderful conversations with people. But it's very planned out and scripted. And typically, we're trying to drive a very particular message that day about education or about manufacturing.

But one of the things that I don't get a chance to do as often as I'd like is just to have a conversation with somebody who I enjoy and I'm interested in; to hear from them and have a conversation with them about some of the broader cultural forces that shape our democracy and shape our ideas, and shape how we feel about citizenship and the direction that the country should be going in.

And so we had this idea that why don't I just have a conversation with somebody I really like and see how it turns out. And you were first in the queue, because—

MARILYNNE ROBINSON: Thank you very much.

THE PRESIDENT: Well, as you know—I've told you this—I love your books. Some listeners may not have read your work before, which is good, because hopefully they'll go out and buy your books after this conversation.

I first picked up *Gilead*, one of your most wonderful books, here in Iowa. Because I was campaigning at the time, and there's a lot of downtime when you're driving between towns and when you get home late from campaigning. And you and I, therefore, have an Iowa connection, because *Gilead* is actually set here in Iowa.

And I've told you this—one of my favorite characters in fiction is a pastor in Gilead, Iowa, named John Ames, who is gracious and courtly and a little bit confused about how to reconcile his faith with all the various travails that his family goes through. And I was just—I just fell in love with the character, fell in love with the book, and then you and I had a chance to meet when you got a fancy award at the White House. And then we had dinner and our conversations continued ever since.

So anyway, that's enough context. You just have completed a series of essays that are not fiction, and I had a chance to read one of them about fear and the role that fear may be playing in our politics and our democracy and our culture. And you looked at it through the prism of Christianity and sort of the Protestant traditions that helped shape us, so I thought maybe that would be a good place to start.

Why did you decide to write this book of essays? And why was fear an important topic, and how does it connect to some of the other work that you've been doing?

ROBINSON: Well, the essays are actually lectures. I give lectures at a fair rate, and then when I've given enough of them to make a book, I make a book.

THE PRESIDENT: So you just kind of mash them all together?

ROBINSON: I do. That's what I do. But it rationalizes my lecturing, too. But fear was very much—is on my mind, because I think that the basis of democracy is the willingness to assume well about other people.

You have to assume that basically people want to do the right thing. I think that you can look around society and see that basically people do the right thing. But when people begin to make these conspiracy theories and so on, that make it seem as if what is apparently good is in fact sinister, they never accept the argument that is made for a position that they don't agree with—you know?

THE PRESIDENT: Yes.

ROBINSON: Because [of] the idea of the "sinister other." And I mean, that's bad under all circumstances. But when it's brought home, when it becomes part of our own political conversation about ourselves, I think that that really is about as dangerous a development as there could be in terms of whether we continue to be a democracy.

THE PRESIDENT: Well, now there's been that strain in our democracy and in American politics for a long time. And it pops up every so often. I think the argument right now would be that because people are feeling the stresses of globalization and rapid change, and we went through one of the worst financial crises since the Great Depression, and the political system seems gridlocked, that people may be particularly receptive to that brand of politics.

ROBINSON: But having looked at one another with optimism and tried to facilitate education and all these other things—which we've done more than most countries have done, given all our faults—that's what made it a viable democracy. And I think that we have created this incredibly inappropriate sort of in-group mentality when we really are from every end of the earth, just dealing with each other in good faith. And that's just a terrible darkening of the national outlook, I think.

THE PRESIDENT: We've talked about this, though. I'm always trying to push a little more optimism. Sometimes you get—I think you get discouraged by it, and I tell you, well, we go through these moments.

ROBINSON: But when you say that to me, I say to you, you're a better person than I am.

THE PRESIDENT: Well, but I want to pick up on the point you made about us coming from everywhere. You're a novelist but you're also—can I call you a theologian? Does that sound, like, too stuffy? You care a lot about Christian thought.

ROBINSON: I do, indeed.

THE PRESIDENT: And that's part of the foundation of your writings, fiction and nonfiction. And one of the points that you've made in one of your most recent essays is that there was a time in which at least reformed Christianity in Europe was very much "the other." And part of our system of government was based on us rejecting an exclusive, inclusive—or an exclusive and tightly controlled sense of who is part of the community and who is not, in favor of a more expansive one.

Tell me a little bit about how your interest in Christianity converges with your concerns about democracy.

ROBINSON: Well, I believe that people are images of God. There's no alternative that is theologically respectable to treating people in terms of that understanding. What can I say? It seems to me as if democracy is the logical, the inevitable consequence of this kind of religious humanism at its highest level. And it [applies] to everyone. It's the human image. It's not any loyalty or tradition or anything else; it's being human that enlists the respect, the love of God being implied in it.

THE PRESIDENT: But you've struggled with the fact that here in the United States, sometimes Christian interpretation seems to posit an "us versus them," and those are sometimes the loudest voices. But sometimes I think you also get frustrated with kind of the wishy-washy, more liberal versions where anything goes.

ROBINSON: Yes.

THE PRESIDENT: How do you reconcile the idea of faith being really important to you and you caring a lot about taking faith seriously with the fact that, at least in our democracy and our civic discourse, it seems as if folks who take religion the most seriously sometimes are also those who are suspicious of those not like them?

ROBINSON: Well, I don't know how seriously they do take their Christianity, because if you take something seriously, you're ready to encounter difficulty, run the risk, whatever. I mean, when people are turning in on themselves—and God knows, arming themselves and so on—against the imagined other, they're not taking their Christianity seriously. I don't know—I mean, this has happened over and over again in the history of Christianity, there's no question about that, or other religions, as we know.

But Christianity is profoundly counterintuitive—"Love thy neighbor as thyself"—which I think properly understood means your neighbor is as worthy of love as you are, not that you're actually going to be capable of this sort of superhuman feat. But you're supposed to run against the grain. It's supposed to be difficult. It's supposed to be a challenge.

THE PRESIDENT: Well, that's one of the things I love about your characters in your novels, it's not as if it's easy for them to be good Christians, right?

ROBINSON: Right.

THE PRESIDENT: It's hard. And it's supposed to be hard. Now, you grew up in Idaho, in a pretty—it wasn't a big, cosmopolitan place.

ROBINSON: The word "cosmopolitan" was never applied.

THE PRESIDENT: Which town in Idaho did you grow up in?

ROBINSON: [Coeur d'Alene] is where I really grew up.

THE PRESIDENT: How big was the town when you were growing up?

ROBINSON: 13,500 people.

THE PRESIDENT: All right. So that's a town.

ROBINSON: Yes, the second-largest city in the state at the time.

THE PRESIDENT: And how do you think you ended up thinking about democracy, writing, faith the way you do? How did that experience of growing up in a pretty small place in Idaho, which might have led you in an entirely different direction—how did you end up here, Marilynne? What happened? Was it libraries?

ROBINSON: It was libraries, it was—people are so complicated. It's like every new person is a completely new roll of the dice, right?

THE PRESIDENT: Right.

ROBINSON: I followed what was for me the path of least resistance, which meant reading a lot of books and writing, because it came naturally to me. My brother is excellent in many of these things, you know? And I think we reinforced each other, he and I, but it was perfectly accidental.

With all respect to that environment, many very smart people do not follow the path in life that people like my brother and I did. You learn from them even if you don't learn from them in a formal sense. But I always knew what I wanted to do in a sense — I mean, not be, but do. I didn't really have the concept of author until I was in high school. But I was writing.

THE PRESIDENT: But you knew you wanted to read and write.

ROBINSON: Yes, that's what I wanted to do.

THE PRESIDENT: Were your parents into books, or did they just kind of encourage you or tolerate your quirkiness?

ROBINSON: There was great tolerance in the house for quirkiness. No, it's a funny thing because on the one hand, I'm absolutely indebted to my origins, whatever they are, whatever that means. On the other hand, with all love and respect, my parents were not particularly bookish people.

THE PRESIDENT: Well, that's why you have good sense along with sort of an overlay of books on top of good sense. What did your mom and dad do?

ROBINSON: My mother was a stay-at-home mother. My father was a sort of middle-management lumber company guy.

THE PRESIDENT: But they encouraged it.

ROBINSON: You know what, they were the adults and we were the kids, you know what I mean? Sort of like two species. But if they noticed we were doing something — drawing or painting or whatever we were doing — then they would get us what we needed to do that, and silently go on with it. One of the things that I think is very liberating is that if I had lived any honest life, my parents would have been equally happy. I was under no pressure.

THE PRESIDENT: Well, you told me about a certain attitude that your parents had that was—there was a certain set of homespun values of hard work and honesty and humility. And that sounded really familiar to me when I think about my grandparents who grew up in Kansas.

And that's part of what I see in your writing. And part of my connection to your books, I think, is an appreciation for—without romanticizing Middle America or small-town America—that sense of homespun virtues. And that comes out in your writing. And it sometimes seems really foreign to popular culture today, which is all about celebrity and being loud and bragging and—

ROBINSON: I mean, I really think that you have to go very far up in American culture to get beyond the point where people have good values. I mean, you really have that feeling sometimes that honesty is more intrinsic in some person that's doing very low-level work than it is in perhaps somebody that's trying to find his way into some sensation—

THE PRESIDENT: These big systems where everything is all about flash. But that's not how your parents saw the world, right? When you said that all they cared about was just you being honest and—

ROBINSON: Yes, exactly.

THE PRESIDENT: —doing your best in some enterprise.

ROBINSON: In whatever. Exactly.

THE PRESIDENT: It's interesting, because we're talking in Iowa; people always, I think, were surprised about me connecting with folks in small-town Iowa. And the reason I did was, first of all, I had the benefit that at the time nobody expected me to win. And so I wasn't viewed through this prism of Fox News and conservative media, and making me scary. At the time, I didn't seem scary, other than just having a funny name. I seemed young. Sometimes I look at my pictures from then and I say, I can't believe anybody voted for me because I look like I'm twenty-five.

But I'd go into these towns and everybody felt really familiar to me, because they reminded me of my grandparents and my mom and that attitude that you talk about. You saw all through the state—and I saw this when I was traveling through southern Illinois when I was first campaigning for the United States Senate—and I actually see it everywhere across the country.

The issue to me, Marilynne, is not so much that those virtues that you prize and that you care about and that are vital to our democracy aren't there. They are there in Little League games, and—

ROBINSON: Emergency rooms.

THE PRESIDENT: —emergency rooms, and in school buildings. And people are treating each other the way you would want our democracy to cultivate. But there's this huge gap between how folks go about their daily lives and how we talk about our common life and our political life. And people describe it as the distance between Washington and Main Street. But it's not just Washington; it's the way we talk about our politics, our foreign policy, our common endeavors. There's this gap.

And the thing I've been struggling with throughout my political career is how do you close the gap. There's all this goodness and decency and common sense on the ground, and somehow it gets translated into rigid, dogmatic, often mean-spirited politics. And some of it has to do with all the filters that stand between ordinary people who are busy and running around trying to look after their kids and do a good job and do all the things that maintain a community, so they don't have the chance to follow the details of complicated policy debates.

They know they want to take care of somebody who's sick, and they have a generous impulse. How that gets translated into the latest Medicare budgets [isn't] always clear. They know they want us to use our power wisely in the world, and that violence often begets violence. But they also know the world is dangerous and it's very hard to sort out, as you talk about in your essay, fear when violence must be met, and when there are other tools at our disposal to try to create a more peaceful world.

So that, I think, is the challenge. I'm very encouraged when I meet people in their environments. Somehow it gets distilled at the national political level in ways that aren't always as encouraging.

ROBINSON: I think one of the things that is true is that many Americans on every side of every issue, they think that the worst thing they can say is the truest thing, you know?

THE PRESIDENT: No. Tell me what you mean.

ROBINSON: Well, for example—I mean, I'm a great admirer of American education. And I've traveled—I mean, a lot of my essays, you know, are lectures given in educational settings—universities everywhere. And they're very impressive. They are very much loved by people who identify with them. You meet faculty and they're very excited about what they're doing; students that are very excited, and so on.

And then you step away and you hear all this stuff about how the system is failing and we have to pull it limb from limb, and the rest of it. And you think, have you walked through the door? Have you listened to what people say? Have you taught in a foreign university?

We have a great educational system that is—it's really a triumph of the civilization. I don't think there's anything comparable in history. And it has no defenders. Most of the things we do have no defenders because people tend to feel the worst thing you can say is the truest thing you can say.

THE PRESIDENT: But that's part of what makes America wonderful is we always had this nagging dissatisfaction that spurs us on. That's how we ended up going west, that's how we—"I'm tired of all these people back east; if I go west, there's going to be my own land and I'm not going to have to put up with this nonsense, and I'm going to start my own thing, and I've got my homestead." . . . It is true, though, that that restlessness and that dissatisfaction which has helped us go to the moon and create the Internet and build the Transcontinental Railroad and build our land-grant colleges, that those things, born of dissatisfaction, we can very rapidly then take for granted and not tend to and not defend, and not understand how precious these things are.

And this is where conceptions of government can get us in trouble. Whenever I hear people saying that our problems would be solved without government, I always want to tell them you need to go to some other countries where there really is no government, where the roads are never repaired, where nobody has facilitated electricity going everywhere even where it's not economical, where—

ROBINSON: The postal system.

THE PRESIDENT: —the postal system doesn't work, or kids don't have access to basic primary education. That's the logical conclusion if, in fact, you think that government is the enemy.

And that, too, is a running strain in our democracy. That's sort of in our DNA. We're suspicious of government as a tool of oppression. And that skepticism is healthy, but it can also be paralyzing when we're trying to do big things together.

ROBINSON: And also, one of the things that doesn't take into account is that local governments can be great systems of oppression. And it's a wonderful thing to have a national government that can intervene in the name of national values.

THE PRESIDENT: Well, that was the lesson of the entire movement to abolish slavery and the civil rights movement. And that's one thing—I mean, I do think that one of the things we haven't talked about that does become the fault line around which the "us" and "them" formula rears its head is the fault line of race. And even on something like schools that you just discussed, part of the challenge is that the school systems we have are wonderful, except for a handful of schools that are predominantly minority that are terrible.

Our systems for maintaining the peace and our criminal justice systems generally work, except for this huge swath of the population that is incarcerated at rates that are unprecedented in world history.

And when you are thinking about American democracy or, for that matter, Christianity in your writings, how much does that issue of "the other" come up and how do you think about that? I know at least in *Gilead* that factors into one major character, trying to figure out how he can love somebody in the Fifties that doesn't look like him.

ROBINSON: Iowa never had laws against interracial marriage. Only Iowa and Maine never had [them]—

THE PRESIDENT: Those were the only two.

ROBINSON: Yes. And [Ulysses S.] Grant really did call [Iowa] the shining star of radicalism, and so on. We never had segregated schools; they were illegal from before, while it was still a territory, and so on. And these laws never changed and they became the basis for the marriage equality ruling that the Supreme Court here [in Iowa] did.

So that whole stream of the culture never changed. And at the same time, the felt experience of the culture was not aligned with the liberal tradition [of the] culture. And so in that book, Jack has every right to think he can come to Iowa, and yet what he finds makes him frightened even to raise the question.

THE PRESIDENT: I'm going to shift gears for a second. You told me that when you started writing it just kind of showed up in some ways. When you started writing your novels, that it was just forced upon you and that you didn't map it out. Tell me about when you were writing *Gilead* and *Home* and some of my favorite books, how did you decide, I'm going to start writing about some old pastor in the middle of cornfields?

Because by that time you had gone to the East Coast, you had traveled in France.

ROBINSON: The Midwest was still a very new thing for me. I got a voice in my head. It was the funniest thing. I mean, [I'd] been reading history and theology and all these things for a long time. And then I was in Massachusetts, actually, just [waiting to spend] Christmas with my son[s]. They were late coming to wherever we were going to meet, and I was in this hotel with a pen and blank paper, and I started writing from this voice. The first sentence in that book is the first sentence that came to my mind. I have no idea how that happens. I was surprised that I was writing from a male point of view. But there he was.

THE PRESIDENT: He just showed up.

ROBINSON: He just showed up. And the first things that I knew about him—that he was old, that he had a young son, and so on—they create the narrative.

THE PRESIDENT: Are you somebody who worries about people not reading novels anymore? And do you think that has an impact on the culture? When I think about how I understand my role as citizen, setting aside being president, and the most important set of understandings that I bring to that position of citizen, the most important stuff I've learned I think I've learned from novels. It has to do with empathy. It has to do with being comfortable with the notion that the world is complicated and full of grays, but there's still truth there to be found, and that you have to strive for that and work for that. And the notion that it's possible to connect with some[one] else even though they're very different from you.

And so I wonder when you're sitting there writing longhand in some—your messy longhand somewhere—so I wonder whether you feel as if that same shared culture is as prevalent and as important in the lives of people as it was, say, when you were that little girl in Idaho, coming up, or whether you feel as if those voices have been overwhelmed by flashier ways to pass the time.

ROBINSON: I'm not really the person—because I'm almost always talking with people who love books.

THE PRESIDENT: Right. You sort of have a self-selecting crew.

ROBINSON: And also teaching writers—I'm quite aware of the publication of new writers. I think—I mean, the literature at present is full to bursting. No book can sell in that way that *Gone with the Wind* sold, or something like that. But the thing that's wonderful about it is that there's an incredible variety of voices in contemporary writing. You know people say, is there an American tradition surviving in literature, and yes, our tradition is the incredible variety of voices . . .

And [now] you don't get the conversation that would support the literary life. I think that's one of the things that has made book clubs so popular.

THE PRESIDENT: That's interesting. Part of the challenge is—and I see this in our politics—is a common conversation. It's not so much, I think, that people don't read at all; it's that everybody is reading [in] their niche, and so often, at least in the media, they're reading stuff that reinforces their existing point of view. And so you don't have that phenomenon of here's a set of great books that everybody is familiar with and everybody is talking about.

Sometimes you get some TV shows that fill that void, but increasingly now, that's splintered, too, so other than the Super Bowl, we don't have a lot of common reference points. And you can argue that that's part of the reason why our politics has gotten so polarized, is that—when I was growing up, if the president spoke to the country, there were three stations and every city had its own newspaper and they were going to cover that story. And that would last for a couple of weeks, people talking about what the president had talked about.

Today, my poor press team, they're tweeting every two minutes because some new thing has happened, which then puts a premium on the sensational and the most outrageous or a conflict as a way of getting attention and breaking through the noise—which then creates, I believe, a pessimism about the country because all those quiet, sturdy voices that we were talking about at the beginning, they're not heard.

It's not interesting to hear a story about some good people in some quiet place that did something sensible and figured out how to get along.

ROBINSON: I think that in our earlier history—the Gettysburg Address or something—there was the conscious sense that democracy was an achievement. It was not simply the most efficient modern system or something. It was something that people collectively made and they understood that they held it together by valuing it. I think that in earlier periods—which is not to say one we will never return to—the president himself was this sort of symbolic achievement of democracy. And there was the human respect that I was talking about before, [that] compounds itself in the respect for the personified achievement of a democratic culture. Which is a hard thing—not many people can pull that together, you know . . . So I do think that one of the things that we have to realize and talk about is that we cannot take it for granted. It's a made thing that we make continuously.

THE PRESIDENT: A source of optimism—I took my girls to see *Hamilton*, this new musical on Broadway, which you should see. Because this wonderful young Latino playwright produced this play, musical, about Alexander Hamilton and the Founding Fathers. And it's all in rap and hip-hop. And it's all played by young African-American and Latino actors.

And it sounds initially like it would not work at all. And it is brilliant, and so much so that I'm pretty sure this is the only thing that Dick Cheney and I have agreed on—during my entire political career—it speaks to this vibrancy of American democracy, but also the fact that it was made by these living, breathing, flawed individuals who were brilliant. We haven't seen a collection of that much smarts and chutzpah and character in any other nation in history, I think.

But what's most important about [*Hamilton*] and why I think it has received so many accolades is it makes it live. It doesn't feel distant. And it doesn't feel set apart from the arguments that we're having today.

And Michelle and I, when we went to see it, the first thing we thought about was what could we do to encourage this kind of creativity in teaching history to our kids. Because, look, America is famously ahistorical. That's one of our strengths—we forget things. You go to other countries, they're still having arguments from four hundred years ago, and with serious consequences, right? They're bloody arguments. In the Middle East right now, you've got arguments dating back to the seventh century that are alive today. And we tend to forget that stuff. We don't sometimes even remember what happened two weeks ago.

But this point you made about us caring enough about the blood, sweat, and tears involved in maintaining a democracy is vital and important. But it also is the reason why I think those who have much more of an "us" versus "them," fearful, conspiratorial brand of politics can thrive sometimes is because they can ignore that history.

If, in fact, you don't know much about the evolution of slavery and the civil rights movement and the Civil War and the postwar amendments, then the arguments that are being had now about how our criminal justice system interacts with African-Americans seem pretty foreign. It's like, what are the issues here? If you're not paying attention to how Jefferson and Madison and Franklin and others were thinking about the separation of church and state, then you're not that worried about keeping those lines separate.

ROBINSON: Exactly. I believe very much in teaching history. I spend an enormous amount of time working with primary sources and various sources and so on. And I think that a lot of the history that is taught is a sort of shorthand that's not representative of much of anything. I think that's too bad.

THE PRESIDENT: Do you pay a lot of attention to day-to-day politics these days?

ROBINSON: I do actually. I read the news for a couple of hours every morning.

THE PRESIDENT: Right. And how do you think your writer's sensibility changes how you think about it? Or are you just kind of in the mix like everybody else, and just, ah, that red team drives me nuts, and you're cheering for the blue?

ROBINSON: Well, if I'm going to be honest, I think that there are some political candidacies that are much more humane in their implications and consequences than others. I mean, if suddenly poles were to be reversed and what I see as humanistic came up on the other side, I'd be. I think in my essay on fear I was talking about the assumption of generosity in this culture, you know? We have done some very magnanimous things in our history.

THE PRESIDENT: Yes.

ROBINSON: Which seem in many ways unifying, defining. And then you see people running on what seem to be incredibly mean-spirited, tight-fisted assumptions, and you think, this is not us. This is not our way forward. Well, I'm getting all too political, but insulting people that you know will become citizens — however that's managed — giving them this bitter memory to carry into their participation in the national life. Why do that?

THE PRESIDENT: We're going through a spasm of fear. And you're seeing it elsewhere. This is not unique to the United States. You see the emergence of the far-right parties in Europe. I think that it's a moment of great change, and the change happens fast. And there have been periods in our history where change happened fast like this, and people just are trying to find firm footing.

When you're looking for firm footing, one of the easiest places to go is, somebody else is to blame. And the market system globally right now does create a situation where workers — ordinary people — have less control.

When you were growing up, when I was growing up, the majority of people had confidence that if they lost their job, it would be temporary, that they often would be with the same company for years, that there would be a pension in place, that they would be able to support a family, and that their kids would probably have a better life than they did. And people feel less confident about that because workers have less leverage, and capital is mobile and labor is not. And we haven't adapted our systems to take into account how fast this is moving.

What's frustrating to me is just that it wouldn't take that much for us to make the system work for ordinary people again.

ROBINSON: If I could strike one word out of the American vocabulary, it would be "competition." I think that that is the most bogus thing that has been entered into our [laughter] —

THE PRESIDENT: Now, you're talking to a guy who likes to play basketball and has been known to be a little competitive. But go ahead. [Laughter.]

ROBINSON: But what we're really telling people is that if they do not acquire nameless skills of a technological character, they will not have employment. It will be shipped out of the country. So basically it's a language of coercion that implies to people that their lives are fragile, that is charged with that kind of unspecific fear that makes people—it's meant to make people feel that they can't get their feet on the ground.

THE PRESIDENT: Right. Now, the argument would be, though, that that's the reality that people are feeling because companies can go anywhere and—

ROBINSON: Exactly, but when I look at these other economies we're supposed to be competing with, they're fragile. They're very fragile. And we're seeing that now. So all the competition has meant, it seems, is that labor is cheap and environmental standards are low. Look at, frankly, China. China has a vile ecology around its industrial centers. It's running out of appropriate cheap labor. And it's going into crisis. And what does that mean? It means that all of that capital will bundle itself up and land in another place that's relatively more advantageous. So what are we competing with? We run China into the ground, is that our great mission?

THE PRESIDENT: Well, in fact, historically, the way we "competed" was we educated our kids better. We put more money into research. We believed in science and facts, as opposed to being driven by superstition. We welcomed talent from all around the world. We put in place a social safety net so people felt that they could take risks without—

ROBINSON: That's crucial.

THE PRESIDENT: —without being utterly destitute.

ROBINSON: And having good bankruptcy laws. We have very liberal bankruptcy laws. But you know, we generate fantastic ideas—ideas move as fast as capital does. We can have the most brilliant population in the world, and if the best ideas that we have are sent offshore, we're still in the same position.

THE PRESIDENT: Right. We made progress on all these fronts. Slowly but surely. Where I completely agree with you, Marilynne, is that we have everything we need to thrive. And it is interesting watching the current political season for me because I'm not on the ballot, so although obviously I still have a huge stake in the outcome as a citizen, in addition to soon being an ex-president—and there are times where I'm listening to folks make these wild claims about how terrible America is doing, and I want to just press the pause button here for a second and remind them that by almost every economic criterion we are hugely better off than we were just seven years ago; that we have done far better than almost every advanced country, and certainly every large advanced country on earth, in terms of growing the economy, driving down unemployment, managing our budgets.

And the only thing that right now is holding us back is Washington dysfunction. We could knock off another percentage point on the unemployment rate if we started rebuilding roads and bridges and airports. You travel—it's embarrassing when you go to other airports in other countries. Ours used to be the nicest ones.

ROBINSON: They were nice first, and then all [laughter]—

THE PRESIDENT: Yes. Now they're a little worn down. We got to keep them up.

The same is true with our education system. It is outstanding, but we've got—everybody else is caught up. We got to step it up.

So one of the reasons I'm here in Iowa is to talk about two years of college education—or two years of community college education for everybody, as free as high school was before. Research—we have fallen behind in basic research that created all these amazing technological wonders upon which our economic engine ran.

And finally, making sure that people get paid enough money that they can support a family. Because all the evidence in history shows that when workers get paid a reasonable salary, then they spend it, businesses do better, the economy does better, and our political system does better. I mean, what is true is that when people feel pinched, then the generosity that you describe narrows to my immediate family, my immediate community, my immediate group.

ROBINSON: It's amazing. You know, when I go to Europe or—England is usually where I go—they say, what are you complaining about? Everything is great. [Laughter.] I mean, really. Comparisons that they make are never at our disadvantage.

THE PRESIDENT: No—but, as I said, we have a dissatisfaction gene that can be healthy if harnessed. If it tips into rage and paranoia, then it can be debilitating and just be a self-fulfilling prophecy, because we end up blocking progress in serious ways.

ROBINSON: Restlessness of, like, why don't we do something about this yellow fever? There's generous restlessness.

THE PRESIDENT: That's a good restlessness.

ROBINSON: Yes, absolutely. And then there is a kind of acidic restlessness that—

THE PRESIDENT: I want more stuff.

ROBINSON: I want more stuff, or other people are doing things that I'm justified in resenting. That sort of thing.

THE PRESIDENT: Right.

ROBINSON: I was not competing with anyone else. Nobody knew what my project was. I didn't know what it was. But what does freedom mean? I mean, really, the ideal of freedom if it doesn't mean that we can find out what is in this completely unique being that each one of us is? And competition narrows that. It's sort of like, you should not be studying this; you should be studying that, pouring your life down the siphon of economic utility.

THE PRESIDENT: But doesn't part of that depend on people having different definitions of success, and that we've narrowed what it means to be successful in a way that makes people very anxious? They don't feel affirmed if they're good at something that the society says isn't that important or doesn't reward.

Probably the best example for me is the teaching profession, where I can't tell you how many kids I meet—and I used to meet them in law school when I was teaching there—who had taught for two, three, four years, they loved teaching, and they thought it was just the most important thing. And you could tell that this was their calling, and at a certain point they couldn't afford to raise a family on it and they got discouraged, and—

ROBINSON: Somebody was looking over their shoulder.

THE PRESIDENT: Somebody was looking—or they'd get some comment from a classmate who had gone on to become an investment banker, they just eventually got discouraged and you didn't have a society that supported what they were doing, despite the fact that—talk about a complicated, magnificent art. Teaching. Being able to transmit ideas to young minds.

And so I like your definition of what America and freedom should be. But it does require all of us to have different definitions. And you have systems—or it requires a broader set of definitions than we have right now. And that's true for businesspeople, as well. I can't tell you how many businesspeople I meet [for whom] their joy is in organizing things to create products and services, and to help people be useful in various ways. And because they've got quarterly reports to shareholders and if they've made a long-term investment that may pay off way down the line, or if they're paying their employees more now because they think it's going to help them retain high-quality employees, a lot of times they feel like they're going to get punished in the stock market. And so they don't do it, because the definition of being a successful business is narrowed to what your quarterly earnings reports are . . .

So my last question to Marilynne is, when you think about your books and you think about your faith and you think about your citizenship as an American, when do you feel most optimistic? What makes you think, you know what, this experiment is going to keep going, I feel encouraged?

ROBINSON: Well, you know, I mean, when I do book signings, for example, and people come up one by one and talk to me about their lives, if there's time [to] do that, how earnest they are, how deeply committed they are to sustaining people they feel close to or responsible for and so on—there they are, the people that you think of as the sustainers of a good society.

And it's only—really, if we could all just turn off media for a week, I think we would come out the other side of it with a different anthropology in effect. I wish we could have a normal politics where I disagree with people, they present their case, we take a vote, and if I lose I say, yes, that's democracy, I'm on the losing side of a meaningful vote.

THE PRESIDENT: And I'll try to make a better argument the next time.

ROBINSON: Exactly.

THE PRESIDENT: I'll try to persuade more people the next time.

ROBINSON: And I think in little groups, like my department at the university or something—people get together, talk something over, take a vote, and that's it. And it's a little microcosm of democracy. That's what it's supposed to be.

THE PRESIDENT: Yes, but that does require a presumption of goodness in other people.

ROBINSON: Absolutely.

THE PRESIDENT: And that's not just what our democracy depends on, but I think that's what a good life depends on. Occasionally, you'll be disappointed, but more often than not, your faith will be confirmed.

ROBINSON: I believe that.

SAM SAX

■

Buena Vista Park, 2 a.m.

FROM *Fourteen Hills*

these men carry
famine in them

eyes
knives

the lamps throw their light
against branches

the branches rake their shadows
across a man's naked back

his back flat as a table
the table set for me

i did not come here hungry
& yet

i eat.

REBECCA MAKKAI

■

The Miracle Years of Little Fork

FROM *Ploughshares*

IN THE FOURTH WEEK of drought, at the third and final performance of the Roundabout Traveling Circus, the elephant keeled over dead. Instead of stepping on the tasseled stool, she gave a thick, descending trumpet, lowered one knee, and fell sideways. The girl in the white spangled leotard screamed and backed away. The trainer dropped his stick and dashed forward with a sound to match the elephant's. The show could not continue.

The young Reverend Hewlett was the first to stand, the first to signal toward the exits. As if he'd just sung the benediction, parents ushered their children out into the park. The Reverend stayed behind, thinking he'd be more useful here, in the thick of the panic and despair, than out at the duck pond with the dispersing families.

The trainer lifted his head from the elephant's haunch to stare at the Reverend. He said, "Your town has no water. That's why this happened."

The elephant was a small one, an Asiatic one, but still the largest animal the Reverend had ever seen this close. Her skin seemed to move, and her leg, but the Reverend had watched enough deaths to know these were the shudders of a soulless body. The clowns and acrobats and musicians had circled around, but only Reverend Hewlett and the trainer were near enough to touch the leathery epidermis, the short, sharp hairs—which the Reverend did now, steadying one thin hand long enough to run it down the knobs of the creature's spine.

The Reverend said, "There's no water in the whole state." He wondered at his own defensiveness, until he saw the trainer's blue eyes, accusatory slits. He said, "I'm not in charge of the weather."

The trainer nodded and returned his cheek to the elephant's deflated leg. "But aren't you in charge of the praying?"

At home in the small study, surrounded by the books the previous Reverend had left behind two years prior, Hewlett began writing out the sermon. *Here we are*, he planned to say, *praying every week for the drought to end. And yet who among us brought an umbrella today?* He would let them absorb the silence. He'd say, *Who wore a raincoat?*

But no, that was too sharp, too much. He began again.

The Roundabout was meant to move on to Shearerville, but now there was the matter of elephant disposal. The trainer refused to leave town till she'd been buried, which was immaterial since the rings and tent couldn't be properly disassembled around the elephant—and even if they could, their removal would leave her exposed to the scorching sun, the birds, the coyotes and raccoons. The obvious solution was to dig a hole, a very large hole, quickly. A farmer offered his lettuce field, barren anyway. But the ground was baked hard by a month of ceaseless sun, horses couldn't pull the diggers without water, and although the men made a start with pickaxes and shovels, they calculated that at the rate they were digging, it would take five full weeks to get an elephant-sized grave. These were the men who weren't away at war, the lame or too-old, the too-young or asthmatic.

The elephant was six days dead. Reverend Hewlett called a meeting in the sanctuary after Sunday services, which a few of the circus folk had attended—the bearded lady, the illustrated man, the trainer himself—and now more filed in, joining the congregation. A group of dwarfs who might have been a family, some lithe women who looked like acrobats. Reverend Hewlett removed his robe and stood at the pulpit to address the crowd. He was only thirty years old, still in love with the girl he'd left in Chicago, still anxious to toss a ball on Saturdays with whoever was willing.

He looked at them, his flock. Mayor Blunt sat in the second row—the farthest forward anyone sat, except, once a year, those taking first Communion—with his wife on one side, his daughter,

Stella, on the other. The mayor had decided that the burial of the dead was more a religious matter than a governmental one, and had asked Reverend Hewlett to work things out.

The Reverend said, "I've been charged with funeral arrangements for the elephant. For—I understand her name was Belle. We ask today for ideas and able hands. And we extend our warmest welcome to the members of the Roundabout." In the days since the disaster, his parishioners had already opened their homes, providing food and beds. (The circus trailers were too hot, too waterless, too close to the dead elephant. And the people of Little Fork had big hearts.) The performers, in turn, had started helping in the gas station and the library and the dried-out gardens, even doing tricks for the children on the brown grass of the park. They were drinking a fair amount of alcohol, was the rumor by way of the ladies at the general store, more in this past week than the whole town of Little Fork consumed in a month.

Adolph Pitt, of Pitt's Funeral Home, stood. "I called on my fellow at the crematorium, and he says it's nothing doing. Not even piecemeal, even if the beast were—forgive me—even if it were dismembered."

"*She*," the elephant trainer said from the back. "Not *it*." The trainer still carried with him, at all times, the thin stick he'd used to guide the elephant, nudging it under her trunk, gently turning her head in the right direction. No one had yet seen him without it. Reverend Hewlett imagined he slept with it under his arm. The man slept alone in his scorching trailer, having refused all offers for a couch and plumbing. Hewlett was an expert now in grief—they hadn't told him, at seminary, the ways his life would be soaked in grief—and it wasn't the first time he'd seen a man cling to an object. Usually he could talk to the bereaved about heaven, about the warm breast of God, about the promise of reunion. But what could he say about an elephant? The Lord loveth the beasts of the field? His eye is on the sparrow? Surely the burial would help.

Reverend Hewlett saw it as his duty to raise an unpopular option the men had been mulling over the past few days. The mayor couldn't bring it up, because he had an election to win in the fall. But Reverend Hewlett was not elected. And so he said it: "The swimming pool was never filled this summer. It's sitting empty."

Some of the men and women nodded, and a few of the children, catching his meaning, made sharp little noises and looked at their parents. The circus folks didn't much respond.

"It's an old pool," the Reverend said, "and we can't dig a hole this summer. We can dig a hole *next* summer, and that can be the new pool. This one's too small, I've heard everyone say since the day I got here."

"There's no dirt to bury him with!" Mrs. Pipsky called.

"Maybe a tarp," someone said.

"Or cement. Pour cement in there."

"Cement's half water."

The mayor stood. "This town needs that pool," he said. The youngest Garrett boy clapped. "We'll find another solution."

And before the meeting could devolve into argument, Reverend Hewlett offered up a prayer for the elephant (the Lord loveth the beasts of the field), and a prayer that a solution could be found. He invited everyone to the narthex, where the women of the Welcoming Committee had laid out a sheet cake.

The Reverend made a point of greeting each visitor in turn, asking how they were enjoying their stay in Little Fork. "Not much," the illustrated man said.

The Reverend thought, with awe, how God had a plan for everyone. Some of these people were deformed—a man with ears like saucers, a boy with lobster-claw hands—and yet God had led them to the circus, to the place where they could find friendship and money and even love. And now He had led these people to Hewlett's flock, and there must be a purpose for this, too.

In the corner, the fire eater chatted with the mayor's daughter. Stella Blunt was sixteen and lovely, hair in brown waves, and he was not much older, with a small, dark beard that Hewlett figured was a liability for a fire eater. Stella leaned toward him, fascinated.

The following Sunday, most of them returned. They sang along with the hymns and closed their eyes to pray, and one of them put poker chips in the communion plate. The fire eater sat in the rear next to Stella. They looked down at something below the pew back, giggling, passing whatever it was back and forth.

Over the past week, the smell of the elephant had crept from the tent and over the center of town. It was a strangely sweet smell, at least at first, more like rotting strawberries than rotting meat. Reverend Hewlett had planned a sermon on the beatitudes, but when the time came for prayer requests, Larry Beedleman asked everyone to pray for enough food to last his guests (all five trapeze artists were living in the Beedlemans' attic), and Mrs. Thoms asked them to pray for the Lord to take away the stench of the elephant. Gwendolyn Lake wanted them all to beg forgiveness for the sins that had brought this trial upon them. So Reverend Hewlett preached instead about patience and forbearance.

After the service, he caught Mayor Blunt's arm. He said, "Isn't it time we used the pool?"

Blunt was a large man who tucked his chin into his neck when he spoke. He said, "I'll lose the vote of every child's mother."

"Have you seen," Hewlett said slowly, "the way your daughter looks at that boy?"

"We've taken him into our home," the mayor said. As if that were definitive and precluded the possibility of teenage love.

"Joe," the Reverend said. "You'll lose more votes to scandal than to a hole in the ground."

And so on Tuesday fifty men and women dragged the elephant to the town pool on waxed tarps and lowered her until she rolled in with a thud and a sudden release of the smell they'd all been gagging against to begin with. They covered her with cartloads of hay—everyone had a lot of hay that summer whether they wanted it or not—and they covered the hay with the gravel Tom Garrett had donated, and they covered that all with fresh tarps, held down by bricks.

Reverend Hewlett gave the funeral service right there, with the locals and circus folk in a ring around the pool. The elephant trainer sobbed into his small, calloused hands. He did not have the stick with him, for once.

Afterward, when the other circus workers went to take apart the tent, to fold up the benches and load things into their trailers, the elephant trainer stayed behind. He put his hand on Reverend Hewlett's arm, then drew it back. And, as if it choked him, he said, "I can't leave her here."

"Will you pray with me?"

"I'm saying I don't think I can leave this town."

"My son, I won't let anything happen to the grave."

"I'm saying that my parents were drifters, and I'm a drifter, and I've never had a part of myself in the soil of a place before. And now I do, and I think I ought to stay here for the rest of my life."

Hewlett marveled at the ways he'd misread this man. Perhaps it hadn't been grief he'd seen in the man's face, but thirst.

He said, "Then it must be God's will."

The tarp stayed put through the dry fall and the dry winter, and the smell subsided.

Before Christmas, Stella Blunt came to Reverend Hewlett for help. The fire eater was long gone, but her stomach had begun swelling and she was panicked.

The Reverend arranged, to her parents' naive delight, for Stella to spend the spring semester doing work at the VA hospital downstate. Only she didn't really go there; he set her up in the vestry with a bed and a little library. She wrote her parents postcards, which Reverend Hewlett would mail in an envelope to Reverend Adams down in Landry, just so Adams could drop them in the postbox and send them back to Little Fork.

Hewlett visited her three times a day, and Sheila Pipsky, who used to be a nurse and could keep a secret like a statue, stopped by twice a week. The Reverend would sit on the floor while Stella sat on the bed, legs folded. If he had time, he ate with her. They spoke French together, so she wouldn't grow rusty. When the church was locked up for the night, he'd turn out the lights and let her know she was safe—and she'd walk around and around the pews, up to the little choir loft, down the hall to the Sunday school classrooms. As she grew bigger, less steady on her feet, he'd hold her arm so she wouldn't trip in the dark. If he closed his eyes—which he let himself do only for a second at a time—he could believe he was walking down a Chicago street with Annette, the breeze on their chests, her hair in a clip.

"It's funny," Stella said to him once. They were standing in the nursery, the rocking horses and dollhouse lit with moonlight. "I thought I loved him. But if I loved him, I'd remember him better. Wouldn't I?"

Hewlett had the utterly inappropriate urge to touch Stella's cheek, the top of her white ear. He slowed his breath.

Stella giggled.

"What is it?" he said.

"Your shoes. They're untied, like a little kid's."

In May, the doctor came in the middle of the night and delivered a healthy baby girl, and Reverend Hewlett called the Millers, who had come to him praying for a child that fall, and they were given the baby and told she came from Shearerville. They named her Eloise. Hewlett had looked away when Stella said goodbye to the baby. He muttered a prayer, but it was a pretense—he couldn't absorb her pain just then. He chose, instead, to think of the Millers. He chose to thank the Lord. Stella stayed two more weeks in the vestry, and then she went home. Hewlett continued his nighttime circuits of the church, though. They'd become habit.

The elephant trainer worked on one of the farms, tending the cows and horses, until he decided to open a restaurant in the space left empty when Herman Burns had gone to war. He used to cook for the circus folk, after all, and he missed it. He served sandwiches and soup and meatloaf. Soon they were calling him by his name, Stanley Tack, and by June he had fallen in love with the Beedleman girl, and she with him.

It made Reverend Hewlett think, briefly, of writing home to Chicago, to Annette. He worried she was waiting for him, the way her girlfriends were waiting for their boys to return, battle-scarred and strong and ready to settle down. But the war abroad would eventually end; Hewlett's war never would. And Annette would not join him on this particular battlefield. She'd made that clear. She would stay in Chicago, in her brownstone, and type for a firm, until he came to his senses and moved home to teach history. That she never doubted this would happen broke his heart doubly: once for himself, and once for her. She hadn't written in three months. And he did not write to her. To do so would be to punch a hole in his own armor.

* * *

As soon as summer hit, there was torrential rain—as if all the town's prayers from the previous year got to heaven at once, far too late. The bridge flooded out, and Stanley Tack's restaurant flooded, and nearly everyone you passed, if you asked how things were, would respond, "I'm building an ark!"

There were drowned sheep and missing fences at one farm, where the river now came to the barn door. An oak toppled in the park, roots exposed, like a loosened weed. Stella Blunt, lining up with the choir and looking through the stained glass, said, "It's like someone's trying to tear apart the world."

They sang "our shelter from the stormy blast" as thunder shook the roof. They sang "There Shall be Showers of Blessings," and some of them laughed.

Stanley Tack had come every Sunday that whole year, but always sat quizzical and silent through the prayers, the hymns. He never carried the stick anymore. He was always alone; the Beedleman girl worked the Sunday shift at the hospital. He never put anything in the offertory and he never took Communion. Reverend Hewlett started to see this as a personal challenge: Someday, he would give the sermon that would bring Stanley to his feet, that would open his blue eyes to the light shining through above the altar, that would make him pause on his way out of church and say, "Do you have a minute to talk?"

They planned, as soon as the rain let up, to pour cement into the old pool and dig the hole for the new one. But the rain never let up. On the fortieth day of rain, folks stopped Reverend Hewlett at the pharmacy and the gas pump to joke: "Tomorrow we're due our rainbow, right? Tomorrow we get our dove?" At least no one much minded not having a pool that summer.

The Millers brought little Eloise to church, and she was baptized as Stella Blunt looked on from the choir. Reverend Hewlett poured water on the baby's head and marveled at her angry little eyes. The daughter of a fire eater, born into a land of water.

Despite the tarp, the pool had filled around the elephant and the hay and the gravel, and if you walked by and peered through the chain-link fence, you'd see how the tarp was now sort of floating on top, how the whole pool deck was covered in an inch of water that connected with the water in the pool. The children dared each other to reach through the fence and touch the dirty elephant juice. Mrs. Thoms wondered aloud if the elephant water would go through the pool drains and into the town supply.

One day, Reverend Hewlett braved the rain to visit Stanley Tack's restaurant. After the downstairs had flooded, Stanley had taken over the vacant apartment upstairs, cooking out of its small kitchen and serving food in what used to be the living room. On an average Saturday you'd find three or four families huddled around the tables, eating soup and listening to the rain hit the windows, but today the Reverend was the only one in the place. It seemed people were leaving their houses less. The spokes of their umbrellas were broken, and their rain boots were moldy, and they realized there wasn't much they truly needed from out in the world. A lot of sweaters were knit that summer, a lot of books read.

The Reverend sat, and when Stanley brought his cheese sandwich and potato soup, he sat across from him. He said, "I believe this is my fault."

The only "this" anyone in town was talking about was the rain.

Reverend Hewlett said, "My child. This weather is the will of God."

"You preached—you gave a sermon, right after I chose to stay. And I couldn't help thinking it was intended for me. The story of Jonah trying to sail away from Nineveh. Of God sending the storm and the whale."

The Reverend tried his potato soup, and nodded at Stanley. The soup was good, as always. Never great, but always good. He said, "I was thinking of many things, but yes, one of them was you. The way the Lord sends us where we need to be, regardless of our plans. I was reflecting on my own life, as well. I ended up in Little Fork by chance, and in my first year, when I felt doubt, I'd think of Jonah in the belly of that fish. It was preaching, you know, that he was meant to do in Nineveh. That's what he was running from."

"Yes. But"—Stanley looked out the window, where the rain was slicing sideways—"what if this isn't my Nineveh? What if this is the place I've run away *to*, and all this, all the rain, is God trying to wash me out and send me on my way? Just as he sent that storm for Jonah."

This troubled the Reverend. He bought some time by biting into his sandwich, but then it troubled him even more. Stanley had reminded him of Annette, on the day he left Chicago, fixing him with dry eyes: "I don't see how you're so *sure*," she'd said. And he'd said, "There's no other way to be." And whether or not he was truly sure back then, he'd grown sure these past three years. Or at least he'd been too busy counseling others to foster his own concerns. He'd broken down in doubt a few times—not in God so much as in his plan—when he'd had to bury a child or when soldiers came home in boxes, but he'd always returned to a place of faith. Look at little Eloise, for instance, growing plump at the Millers' house. Exactly as it was meant to be. But somehow the elephant trainer's question had hit a sore spot in his own soul, a bruise he hadn't known was there.

He said, "All we can do is pray, and ask that God make clear the path."

"And how, exactly, would He make it clear?"

"If you listen, God will speak."

Most always, when he said something like this, his parishioners smiled as if assured they'd hear the voice of God that very night. Sometimes he even had to clarify: "This is not the age of miracles, you realize. His voice won't boom from the clouds. You'll have to listen. You'll have to look." And they'd leave to await the message.

What Stanley said was "God doesn't talk." It wasn't something Reverend Hewlett was used to hearing in this town. And then, all seriousness, he said, "I think I've broken the universe."

Reverend Hewlett looked at his own hands, the veins and creases. He imagined they might crack open like the parched earth had last summer. Or at least, he felt a small crack somewhere inside, one that didn't hurt but was letting in a bit of air. All he could think to say was "It's raining in the next town over, too. And in the next town beyond that."

Reverend Hewlett's name was Jack. This was increasingly easy for him to forget. He'd become John, and then—in the bulletins and on the sign outside the church—Rev. J. Hewlett, and since there was no one in Little Fork who didn't know him as the Reverend, since even the few Catholics who drove to services in Shearerville greeted him as "Rev" or sometimes, slipping, as "Father," he hadn't heard his own name in three years. Annette no longer wrote to him at all, no longer extended the tail of the J down like the first letter of a chapter.

And why had he left her? And why had he come here? Because he was needed. Because his mentor at seminary had said, "God is calling you there. God is calling me to send you there."

And that man, with his great beard, his walls of books, his faith in the hand of God, could not have been wrong.

That night there was a dance at the Garden Club, on the east end of town. It was Little Fork's version of a debutante ball, the same youngsters debuting themselves each year, in the same white dresses, until they were too old for these things, or married. Only tonight they were soaked through. Reverend Hewlett stood against the wall watching—his mere presence, everyone agreed, was salubrious—and observed the boys in their sopping bow ties, hair plastered to their heads, and the girls wrapped against their will in their mothers' shawls. No boy would see through a wet dress tonight. Heaps of galoshes and umbrellas by the door.

They coupled and uncoupled in patterns that seemed casual, chaotic, but of course were not. Every move, every flick of the eyes, was finely orchestrated. There were hearts being broken tonight. You just couldn't tell whose.

Gordon Pipsky sidled up and offered a sip from his flask. Gordon's son was out there dancing, a girl on each arm. When Hewlett accepted, Gordon winked and grinned. "I'll never tell," he said. Even though he saw the Reverend take the Eucharist every Sunday. Perhaps what he meant was "I'll never tell that you're just a man like me."

Was it a secret, really? He'd never been anything else.

He had felt like an impostor when he first put on his robe—but then everyone felt like an impostor, he'd learned in seminary. And now, after all this time, he rarely considered himself a fraud. But nothing had changed, really. Except that he had grown used to that robe, that second skin, just as he'd grown used to God's silent ways.

There was Stella Blunt, dancing in white. A debutante still.

The next morning, the rain stopped. Not the kind of pause that makes you worry the sky is just gathering more water, but a true, clear stop, the air bright and clean and dry.

And then the wind started.

For the first few hours, it just shook the windows and door hinges and made people sneeze—all that new mold now flying through the air—but by nightfall, it was bringing down tree branches and shingles. By morning, it had knocked down phone lines and garden fences and was tearing at the awnings on Center Street.

And worse: By late afternoon, with most of the surface water gone (blown to Shearerville, everyone said), the tarp blew off the old pool. No one was outside to see that part, but a fair number were witness to it flying smack up against the library, five blocks south, before continuing on its way. It took folks a while to realize what it was—and by that point, there was gravel skittering down the streets nearest the pool. There was moldy hay in everyone's yard.

Gwendolyn Lake came banging on the parsonage door to tell Reverend Hewlett. His first thought was to run and see if the elephant was uncovered, but his second thought was of Stanley, who should be kept from the pool. Stanley, who would want to run there but would regret it later. Who might take it all as some sort of sign.

Hewlett told Gwendolyn to get her brothers. "Use sheets," he said, "and bricks." He himself ran in the opposite direction, toward Center Street. The wind wasn't constant but came in great lumps: Every three or four seconds, a pocket of air would hit him, would lift him from beneath. If he'd had an open umbrella, he'd have left the ground. Trees were down, garbage blew through the streets, the bench in front of the barbershop was overturned.

Sally Thoms ran crying down the other side of the road, blond hair sucked straight up like a sail. "My cat blew away!" she cried. "He was in a tree and he just blew away!"

"I'll pray for you!" the Reverend called, but the wind ate his words.

He pulled with his full weight on the door beside the one that read STANLEY'S DINER, the door that everyone knew led up to the real place. Stanley stood in the kitchen, peeling carrots.

He said, "You're early for lunch, Rev."

For some reason—even later he couldn't figure out what had possessed him—the Reverend said, "I'd be happy if you called me Jack."

"Sure," Stanley said, and laughed. "Jack. You want to peel me some carrots, Jack?"

They stood side by side at the counter, working.

"What do you make of this apocalypse, Jack?"

He began to answer as he always did of late—something about God wanting to test us now and then, maybe something about Job—but instead he found himself telling a joke. "You hear about the man who couldn't see what the weather was like, because it was too foggy?"

"Ha!" He wasn't sure he'd ever heard Stanley laugh before. It was more a word than a laugh. Stanley said, "I know an old circus one. Why'd the sword swallower swallow an umbrella?"

"I—I don't know."

"Wanted to put something away for a rainy day."

It was a terrible joke, but Hewlett started laughing and couldn't stop—perhaps because he was picturing Stella Blunt's bearded fire eater, an umbrella blossoming in his throat just as the baby had stretched Stella's figure. This wasn't funny either, but the laughter came anyway.

He went to the sink for a glass of water, to cure his laugh and the cough that followed it. As he drank, he looked out the back window, over the yards behind Fifth Street and the abutting yards behind Sixth Street. Down below, on the other side of the block-long stockade fence, the Miller family had ventured out into the yard with baby Eloise. In the time between gusts, they were examining the damage to the old well, the top of which had tumbled into a pile of stones. A summer of baking and a summer of rain must have loosened everything, and all it took was a day of wind to knock things about. There was Ed Miller, peering down the hole, and there was Alice Miller, holding the baby, when a blast of wind—up here Jack Hewlett could see and hear but not feel it—tore limbs from trees and tore shutters from houses and tore Eloise from her mother's arms and into the air and across the yard. He must have made a noise, because Stanley rushed to peer over his shoulder just in time to see the baby, her pink face and her white dress, go flying over the garden and over the next yard and finally into the Blunts' yard, where, just as she arced down, there he was, Mayor Blunt, running toward the child. He caught her in his arms.

Hewlett heard Stanley inhale sharply. Neither man moved.

The mayor had been outside alone—presumably inspecting the maple that had fallen across his yard, the one that, were it still standing, the baby would have blown straight into—but now his wife ran out, and his son, and Stella. The two men watched from above as Stella leaned over the baby, covering her own mouth. Her mother's hand was on her back, and Hewlett wondered if she was crying, and—if she was—how she'd explain it. Well, who wouldn't cry at a baby landing in their yard?

The wind took a break, and Mayor Blunt handed the baby to Stella and wrapped his coat around her front, covering them both. Hewlett imagined what the man would have said: something about "You know I can never hold a baby right." Or "This should be good practice for you!" And the mayor led a procession around the front of the house and down the street to the Millers'. Hewlett hadn't thought to look back to the Millers for a while—they weren't in their yard. Ed Miller had scaled the fence to the lawn between his and the Blunts' and was running through the bushes, around the trees, behind the shed. Alice Miller stood out front, hands to her head, shouting for help. She ran toward the Blunts when she saw them, but she couldn't have known what was under Stella's coat until the mayor pulled it back, chest puffed out, proud of his miracle. He handed the baby back himself. Alice Miller covered the infant with kisses and raced her into the house, Mayor and Mrs. Blunt following. Stella stayed out on the walk a minute, looking at the sky. What she was thinking, Hewlett couldn't even guess.

"Well," Stanley said. "Pardon the expression, but Jesus Christ." The carrot and peeler, still in his hands, were shaking.

Hewlett wanted to run down, to see if Stella was all right, to make sure the baby wasn't hurt. But he wasn't a doctor. And he couldn't leave Stanley alone, couldn't let him think of checking on the pool. So he just said, "I think we've seen the hand of God." He wasn't at all sure this was true. Part of him wondered if he hadn't seen a miracle at all but its precise and brutal opposite—a failure of some kind, or the evidence of chaos. Whatever he'd just seen, it troubled him deeply. Was God in the wind, blowing that baby back to Stella where she belonged? Or was God in the catch, in the impossible coincidence of the mayor being in the right spot, in the return of the child to the Millers? Or—and this was the thing about a crack in faith, he knew, the way one small fissure could spread and crumble the whole thing into a pile of rocks—was God in neither place?

Stanley put his carrot down and turned. His face was soft and astonished, blue eyes open wider than Hewlett had ever seen them. He looked like a man who'd just survived an auto crash, a man who'd taken part in something bizarre and terrifying, not just witnessed it from above. "It's not true, is it?" Stanley spoke slowly, working something out. "What I said before, about Nineveh. We're—we're all where we're supposed to be. I was supposed to wind up here." He braced himself on the counter, as if he expected God to blow him across town next. "A beast brought Jonah to Nineveh, and a beast brought me here."

Hewlett said what he'd said so many times before. "The thing is to be listening when God speaks."

By the time Reverend Hewlett walked home that night by way of the old pool, Davis Thoms and Bernie Lake were down there mixing batch after batch of cement and pouring it into the hole. For the first time in more than a year, there was both enough water to mix the stuff, and not so much water falling from the sky that it would turn to soup.

He continued toward the parsonage. The wind was done. It had simply left town.

It was so strange to be outside without the roar of wind or rain, without the feel of air or water ripping at his skin, that Reverend Hewlett stood awhile on his own porch feeling that he was floating in the midst of vast and empty space. Everywhere he turned, there was nothing. No baking sun, no drenching storm, no raging wind. There were people coming out of houses, and people going into houses, and people walking from one store to the next. And people picking up branches, and people sweeping up glass. As if they'd been directed to do these things.

All this happened a very long time ago. And it's hard now to argue that what happened so far back *wasn't* inevitable. If the elephant hadn't died, there wouldn't be, on top of the old swimming pool, the playground that originally had some other name but quickly became known as Elephant Park; and the Little Fork High School football team would not be the Mammoths; and Stanley Tack wouldn't have stayed in town, and the son he had with the Beedleman girl (she was expecting already that day of the windstorm, she just hadn't told him yet) wouldn't have married Eloise Miller, and today the town of Little Fork wouldn't be half-full of Tacks of various generations, all descended (though none of them know it) from a fire eater.

Jack Hewlett might not have given up the cloth and returned home to be with his girl, with Annette, who'd waited for him even after her letters stopped—only to be drafted two months later, no longer clergy, no longer exempt from war. He might not have died in France, a bullet through his lung. But who's to say that the outcome of that battle—even of the entire war—hadn't hinged, in one way or another, on the bravery of one man? He was, after all, an exceptional soldier. He took orders well.

Or at least it can be said: This world is the one made by the death of that elephant.

The Sunday following the storm, Reverend Hewlett looked out from the pulpit at his battered congregation. There were black eyes and broken arms from the wind, and the women with husbands stationed overseas were exhausted from cleaning up their own yards and their elderly neighbors' besides. It was a good town that way. These people believed in things. Eloise Miller, unhurt and pink, slept in her mother's arms through the service. A green bonnet framed her face.

Hewlett, under his robe, was thin. He'd lost five pounds that week. His stomach felt empty even when it was full, so why bother to fill it?

Stanley Tack held hands with the Beedleman girl. For the first time, he joined the hymns. He opened the book of prayer.

Stella Blunt looked pale and tired. Hewlett tried to catch her eye. He felt he owed her at least a look, one she'd be able to interpret later, the next morning, or whenever it was that the citizens of Little Fork would find the parsonage deserted.

If he owed anything to Stanley Tack, he'd already given it. Hadn't he handed the man his own faith? It was in safer hands now than his own.

He said, "Let us read from Paul's letter to the Romans: *Whom he did predestinate, them he also called: and whom he called, them he also justified: and whom he justified, them he also glorified.*"

He said, "Let us lift up our hearts."

■

Death-Qualified

FROM *London Review of Books*

The following is a book review of The Brothers: The Road to an American Tragedy, *by Masha Gessen. The book appeared in April 2015 and the review was published in September 2015.*

ON JUNE 24, Dzhokhar Tsarnaev, the younger of two Chechen-American brothers responsible for the Boston Marathon bombing on 15 April 2013, was sentenced to death in a Boston federal court. (His older brother, Tamerlan, died following a street battle with police in Watertown, Massachusetts, several nights after the bombing.) The brothers had placed, and detonated by remote control, two explosive devices fashioned from pressure cookers stuffed with shrapnel; three people were killed in the blasts, and more than 260 others suffered serious, permanent injuries, including 16 who lost limbs.

Footage from multiple surveillance cameras overlooking the Boston Marathon dispelled any reasonable doubt that the Tsarnaev brothers had planted the bombs and set them off. At Tsarnaev's trial, notwithstanding his "not guilty" plea on thirty separate capital charges, his chief defence attorney told the court: "It was him." This effectively confined the defence case to the assertion that Dzhokhar had acted under the powerful influence of Tamerlan, and would not have carried out the bombing on his own, counting on character witnesses in the trial's penalty phase to dramatize this idea to the jury. One witness testified that Dzhokhar had been "like a puppy following his brother," a characterization eerily illustrated by surveillance videos of

Dzhokhar trailing Tamerlan by several meters on the pavement lining the marathon route.

The defence team's sole objective was a life sentence for their client, an unlikely outcome from the outset, given that the court denied motions to change the trial venue from Boston itself to a town where jurors' friends or families were less likely to have been affected by the bombing. In a non-death penalty state like Massachusetts a federal case in which execution is an option can still be heard so long as the jury is "death-qualified"—i.e., all the jurors have declared themselves willing to deliver a death verdict. Since 80 per cent of Massachusetts residents specifically opposed execution in the Tsarnaev case, the jury was necessarily drawn from an unusually narrow pool, and was therefore disproportionately likely to impose capital punishment. Dzhokhar Tsarnaev has since been moved to federal death row in Terre Haute, Indiana, since—although a non-death penalty state can deliver a death verdict—the executions themselves must be carried out in a state that has death penalty statutes. This risible scruple has a practical aspect: such states also have the requisite killing equipment on hand, and often seem to relish the chance to use it. (In recent Ohio, Arizona and Oklahoma executions, a European export embargo on lethal injection drugs has prompted mix 'n' match improvisations with untested pharmaceuticals, with results Josef Mengele would consider plagiarism.) Timothy McVeigh, whose trial venue was shifted from Oklahoma City to Denver, Colorado, got transferred post-trial to the same death row in Terre Haute.

Whether Tsarnaev will, as McVeigh did, forgo the often decades-long appeals process to hasten his end is an open question. While hiding from police inside a boat in a backyard in Watertown, Dzhokhar managed to write a rather long note on the boat's hull that began: "I'm jealous of my brother who ha [bullet hole] ceived the reward of jannutul Firdaus (inshallah) before me." ("Jannatul Firdous" is a name for "the highest paradise" in Arabic, as well as a line of speciality fragrances available online from Givaudan Roure, "the oldest perfumery house in the Arabian Gulf.") For all we know, Dzhokhar's jealousy may already have cooled. If so, ample grounds for appeal exist. There is the venue issue. Then too, U.S. District Judge George O'Toole Jr. refused to give the standard jury instruction, which says that a single holdout juror can avert a death sentence permanently—that is, without the penalty phase of the trial being repeated until a unanimous verdict is reached. The grotesqueness of executing a 22-year-old is not considered grounds for appeal: the death-qualifying age, so to speak, is 18.

Unlike several recent books on the marathon bombing, Masha Gessen's *The Brothers* is uninflected by consoling homilies, Manichean narrative framing or civic propaganda. Gessen's is a superlative work of reporting that locates the Boston atrocity and the Tsarnaevs in the queasy context of the modern world, where atrocities happen every day, in places presumed to be "safe" as well as those beset by civil war. *The Brothers* provides essential Soviet and post-Soviet geopolitical background, charting the Tsarnaev family's peregrinations from Kyrgyzstan (to where Stalin brutally transplanted the entire Chechen population in 1944) to Novosibirsk in south central Russia, where the brothers' parents, Anzor and Zubeidat, met (he was finishing his Soviet military service, she seeking her eldest brother's permission to move to Moscow). They later moved to Kalmykia, the Soviet republic where Tamerlan was born; back to Kyrgyzstan, where two daughters, Bella and Ailina, were added to the family; then to Chiry-Yurt in Chechnya, Dzhokhar's birthplace.

From Chechnya they returned again to Kyrgyzstan to escape the 1994 Russian bombing of Grozny. In 2000, they moved to Makhachkala in Dagestan, where the second Chechen war was spilling over the border. Wahhabi fundamentalism had spread through the Caucasus, its suspected adherents a target for Russian troops and local police. As Gessen writes:

> Makhachkala and much of the rest of Dagestan became a battleground ... This was the Dagestan to which Anzor and Zubeidat brought their four children, including Tamerlan, who at 14 was on the verge of becoming that most endangered and most dangerous of human beings: a young Dagestani man. [They] had to move again, to save their children—again.
>
> They would go to America after all.

The Tsarnaevs weren't always fleeing incipient war zones. Sometimes they just rolled elsewhere in search of a better deal. More often than not, his mother, Zubeidat, the more willful and ambitious of the parents, decided where they would go. Bad timing, bad luck and defective reality-testing all feature prominently in the story Gessen tells; so do seemingly minuscule ethnic and religious distinctions that caused the Tsarnaevs to feel out of place wherever they lived. They were Chechens outside Chechnya, Muslims in only the nominal sense that their ethnic codes reflected a vaguely Islamic influence.

Things didn't work out in America. The Tsarnaevs arrived soon after 9/11, when Muslims began to replace communists as objects of fear for the media demonization industry. Chechens, who had once been welcomed as refugees from Russian aggression, became suspect after Russia and the U.S. began collaborating in the "war on terror." (The US ignored Russian atrocities in Chechnya in exchange for air bases in Uzbekistan and Kyrgyzstan.) While it's unclear whether the Tsarnaevs experienced egregious anti-Muslim, anti-Chechen or other discrimination in the U.S. (they didn't wear Islamic dress, and one daughter successfully copped a Latina identity for a while), their ethnicity and religion complicated the legal status of some family members, and they must have seen themselves as part of a despised, if nebulous, minority.

The travails of the Tsarnaev clan are almost too numerous and tangled to itemize. The new life in America started with the thorny process of asylum-seeking, scrambling for housing and off-the-books work (asylum applicants are prohibited from employment or collecting benefits for a year), finding schools for the children, and trying to decipher local conditions. The Tsarnaevs landed in Cambridge, Massachusetts, which was a mixed blessing: a liberal enclave of top-notch universities and rapidly gentrifying neighborhoods, its contiguous working-class areas a Hogarthian reminder of the destiny awaiting failure. A well-educated, Russian-speaking, guardian angel landlady, Joanna Herlihy, entered their lives at a propitious moment. Herlihy, who "for most of her adult life ... had been trying to save the world," can be viewed retrospectively as a mixed blessing too. Untiringly helpful in practical matters, she sheltered her new tenants behind a baffle of contentious idealism, ratifying their feelings of persecution when wishes didn't come true. The stellar expectations of the Tsarnaevs eroded in increments. Within a few years, they collected grievances like baseball cards.

Gessen writes that kids in newly arrived families "stop being kids, because the adults have lost their bearings ... they go through a period of intense suffering and dislocation made all the more painful for being forced and unexpected. But at the other end of the pain, they locate their roles and settle into them, claiming their places in the new world." Most of the Tsarnaev children, however, did less and less well as time went on. The family pattern had been set by their parents: when troubles piled up after every fresh start, they just moved somewhere else. Gessen's narrative makes the Tsarnaevs palpable enough, but unworldliness mists the atmosphere around them; Anzor and Zubeidat sound too narcissistic, too skilled in extracting sympathy and favours from new acquaintants, to compromise much with American reality. No one in the family stuck to any ambitious plan long enough to realize it. Anzor, whose bogus claim to have been a prosecutor's assistant in Kyrgyzstan got him nowhere, took up his previous trade as a freelance car mechanic; Zubeidat, after thwarted efforts to translate documents for human rights groups, became a home care worker, later a beautician. With the exception of Dzhohkar, the undoubtedly bright children began to stumble in their new surroundings.

Zubeidat, who believed Tamerlan "perfect" and "destined for greatness," no doubt instilled a great deal of self-belief in him. But, as Gessen writes, "he had lived in seven cities and attended an even greater number of schools," entering tenth grade in Cambridge at 17. He struggled for good grades and to learn English, but as the oldest child was also the most wrongfooted by repeated dislocation. Hopes for him shifted to a career in boxing or music. Catnip to women, he dressed like a gigolo and kept himself gym-solid shapely. He played keyboards, and thought of becoming a music star, but never really pursued it. After dropping out of community college, he delivered pizzas and sold weed. He married, and fathered a child. He won some impressive boxing matches and an amateur Golden Gloves trophy, but was afterwards barred from title contests because he wasn't a U.S. citizen; his application was held up after he was arrested for smacking his wife. At the time of the bombings, he was living on benefits and dealing drugs.

The daughters, Bella and Ailina, despite some early promise, scuttled their educations; they married Chechen men (a cultural ukase), had children, divorced, got busted for passing on counterfeit banknotes and selling weed. Nothing reachy was expected of them in the first place and they soon seemed fated for a life of welfare and sporadic work in service industries. Their designated roles were to marry within the clan, have babies to continue the bloodline, and embrace domestic servitude, as per the will of Allah. They were independent enough to get out of bad marriages and free enough to keep their own children (in the old country children were a husband's property), but otherwise their American road turned into a dead end.

Dzhokhar, having spent his whole childhood in Cambridge, was the most assimilated of the family, and the last to stumble. A sweet, smart boy loved by all, he graduated with honours from high school (Cambridge Rindge and Latin, alma mater of Matt Damon and Ben Affleck), despite spending much of it stoned out of his mind. He also was dealing, like Tamerlan. While he couldn't have afforded a prestige university, Dzhokhar's choice of the University of Massachusetts Dartmouth—in Gessen's generous description, "the least academically challenging" of the schools he was admitted to—reflects a dazed, amiable passivity. The Tsarnaevs were a "tight-knit family" in the most ruinous sense that family alone provided each member's sense of identity and direction. If one ran awry, eventually they all would.

All the descriptions of Dzhokhar, Gessen writes,

> that have emerged from conversations with people who knew him, including people who cared for him deeply, are spectacular in their flatness. Those who watched him from a distance describe him as a social superstar. To those who thought they got closer, he was charming. Indeed, charm appears to have been his sole distinguishing personality trait. Teachers thought he was bright but uninterested in thinking for himself.

In his sophomore year at Dartmouth he began failing subjects, stepped up his marijuana sales and narrowed his social circle to a small band of other immigrant Dartmouth students—Dias Kadyrbayev and Azamat Tazhayakov from Kazakhstan, and Robel Phillipos, an Ethiopian with US citizenship—and their occasional girlfriends. He tweeted, he Facebooked. He spent much of his time away from his dorm room, at a New Bedford apartment the Kazakhs rented:

> The group spent three or four evenings a week on that sofa, getting stoned, watching movies and eating. The boys played FIFA, a soccer video game; the girls talked about which of the boys might be the hottest lovers, though it does not appear that anyone but Dias was getting much action.

In 2009, Tamerlan and his mother "began studying the Koran." Tamerlan also began studying *The Protocols of the Elders of Zion*, ever popular in Russia and the bible of anti-Semites everywhere. One of Zubeidat's home care clients, a loose screw called Donald Larking, passed along conspiracist libertarian newspapers and magazines. The Internet provided even more enticing forms of inflammatory propaganda—lectures by the al-Qaida recruiter Anwar al-Awlaki and the like—and the opportunity to share festering resentments with thinkalikes all over the planet. Relatedly or not, Dzhokhar, a whizz at languages, opened an account on vk.com, "a Facebook clone site on which most Russians his age maintained their social media lives." By this time, evidently, everyone realized that America had been a wrong move.

Anzor, despite a few drunken fights and scrapes with neighbors, was an essentially passive, Soviet-made working stiff, svelte and athletic in his youth, gaunt and ailing by middle age, indifferent to Islamist manias and 9/11 conspiracy lore, resigned to getting by fixing cars. His health deteriorated, and his marriage to Zubeidat, who had taken to wearing a burqa, fell apart. They divorced in 2011; in 2012, Anzor left the country for Dagestan. Meanwhile, after ten years, Herlihy got fed up with her rebarbative tenants and their increasingly cracked views. She asked them to leave, but gave them several months to do so.

Here, more or less, is where the train goes into the tunnel. More finely sifted details of all the above can be found in Gessen's extraordinary book. It's worth noting here that Zubeidat was arrested for shoplifting from the Cambridge branch of the department store Lord & Taylor in 2012; she then took off for Dagestan, two weeks after Tamerlan returned from a seven-month visit. With both parents gone, Tamerlan was, by custom, now the head of the family in America, though Bella and Ailina, haphazardly in and out of Cambridge with their children, were living erratic lives of their own. Dzhokhar shambled back and forth in a cloud of smoke between Cambridge and New Bedford. "There was an understanding in the family now: Dagestan was the place to live." Dzhokhar spoke of moving there next summer. Tamerlan was only waiting until he could get a US passport—a valuable commodity in a pinch.

At the time of the bombings, Tamerlan was 26, Dzhokhar 19. They had no known accomplices, though the bombs were far from simple to make, and no traces of their assembly were discovered anywhere. It's also unclear when the idea of bombing the marathon first occurred to either brother. In the months before the bombing, the brothers were rarely in the same place at the same time. It's easy to suppose they created a gang of two through phone calls and text messages, and fortified their sense of mission with YouTube jihadist videos and al-Qaida's online magazine, *Inspire*, which ran a DIY article entitled "Make a Bomb in the Kitchen of Your Mom." Had they held off for a year, ISIS might have attracted the brothers to Syria, but the ISIS brand hadn't yet overtaken al-Qaida's outside the Middle East and the Caucasus. It was widely reported that Tamerlan had been "radicalized" during his visit to Dagestan in 2012. Gessen thinks this an exaggeration, having tracked his activities there very closely. He hung out with young Salafi Muslims belonging to the Union of the Just, "allied with Hizb ut-Tahrir, one of the largest Islamic organizations in the world. Hizb ut-Tahrir proclaims the goal of creating a caliphate that would unite the Muslim lands of the world . . . by peaceful means, through political and philosophical struggle only." Gessen notes that some analysts consider Hizb ut-Tahrir "a gateway organization that facilitates young Muslims' passage from peaceful civilians to jihadis," but all the same, Tamerlan did nothing much in Dagestan besides talk the Islamist talk and show off his fancy clothes.

Retrospective suspicion that Tamerlan had murdered three drug dealers in Waltham, Massachusetts, in 2011, by slitting their throats, insinuates the possibility that Tamerlan had killed people before visiting Dagestan, and was already disinhibited about inflicting lethal violence. However, we don't know, and we probably never will; the only purported witness/accomplice to the Waltham murders, a gym-mate called Ibragim Todashev, was shot seven times and killed by an FBI agent in Orlando, Florida, a month after the bombing. According to the FBI, Todashev "became aggressive" while writing out a confession implicating Tamerlan, the uncompleted text of which was inconsistent with the Waltham crime scene.

This sort of obscurity is everywhere in the Tsarnaev saga. Why was a bevy of federal agents buzzing around the MIT area in Cambridge several hours before the Tsarnaevs shot an MIT security cop? Had the FBI, at the instigation of the Russian FSB, not just interviewed Tamerlan as a suspected extremist several times in 2011, but tried to recruit him as an informant? An informant who "went rogue"? If this were the case, could the FBI have hoped to take him out before he could spill, if the police caught him alive?

Gessen has taken flak from the *New York Times* for merely asking such questions, in a ponderous review by Janet Napolitano, director of the Department of Homeland Security at the time of the marathon bombing. A figure much loved by America's spy networks, Napolitano dismissed the book's descriptions of FBI malfeasance, abuses of the deportation laws and draconian prosecutions on accessory charges as "conspiracy theory." This seems quite unfair to Gessen, who tries for several pages to imagine a plausible scenario in which the FBI agent who shot Todashev seven times could have been acting in "self-defence." That she is unable really to do so is hardly her fault. The FBI itself issued several different versions of what happened before settling on something remotely credible.

Well before the Tsarnaev brothers were identified as suspects, tabloid TV and print media launched a free-ranging witch hunt targeting Muslims, people who looked like Muslims, and unaccountable others, picked out of footage of the marathon crowd, or out of nowhere; at one strange moment, even the actress Zooey Deschanel was identified as a bombing suspect on a news broadcast, perhaps because of the slightly unusual spelling of her name. After the police shoot-out (in which Tamerlan's nearly dead body was recovered, Dzhokhar having run over it in an SUV), authorities asked residents of the Boston area to "shelter in place," putting an entire American city under lockdown.

After Dzhokhar's arrest, various provisions of the Patriot Act permitted authorities to question the gravely wounded suspect, a U.S. citizen, for hours before he was read his Miranda rights; in the days and months that followed, almost anyone in the United States with the faintest connection to the Tsarnaevs was either harassed, deported or prosecuted for minor, even unconscious infractions that, if shoved under the umbrella of "terrorism," can be magnified by federal prosecutors into major felonies. Dias Kadyrbayev, Azamat Tazhayakov and Robel Phillipos, who removed some of Dzhokhar's belongings from his dorm room in a stoned panic, are currently doing long stretches in federal prison; another friend who deleted the search history on his own computer has been in custody for two years awaiting trial. The charges brought against these people presumed deliberate obstruction of the bombing investigation, or of making "materially false, fictitious and fraudulent statements" to police and the FBI, when in any reasonable view, nothing they did, or told or didn't tell authorities, had any effect on the investigation whatsoever. They had no knowledge of the bombing before it happened, and were in an even greater state of confusion afterwards than anyone else in Boston, simply because they happened to know the Tsarnaevs.

What passed between the brothers in the ten months after Zubeidat's departure to Dagestan is terra incognita. The chances are no specific event or Svengali-like radicalization inspired the Tsarnaev brothers to blow up the Boston Marathon. As a policeman in Yasmina Khadra's 2006 novel *The Attack* puts it: "I think even the most seasoned terrorists really have no idea what has happened to them. And it can happen to anyone. Something clicks somewhere in their subconscious, and they're off . . . Either it falls on your head like a roof tile or it attaches itself to your insides like a tapeworm. Afterwards, you no longer see the world in the same way." The media fantasy that Tamerlan was schizophrenic and "heard voices" is highly improbable. The consensus among terrorism experts is that terrorists are normal people. "He was a perfectly nice guy." "The last person I'd imagine doing something like this." After the fact, neighbors, friends and co-workers invariably say the same things about terrorists as they say about serial killers. It's worth noting that there isn't a single provable instance of the legendary FBI profiling unit in Quantico, Virginia, actually instigating the capture of a serial killer: it tends to be when someone is stopped for driving with a broken tail light that the dead body in the trunk is discovered. It's only afterwards that we're told they "fit the FBI profile."

Why did they do it? How could they? In the world we live in now, the better questions are: Why not? Why wouldn't they? To quote Khadra's novel again, on suicide bombers: "The only way to get back what you've lost or to fix what you've screwed up—in other words, the only way to make something of your life—is to end it with a flourish: turn yourself into a giant firecracker in the middle of a school bus or launch yourself like a torpedo against an enemy tank." Everything the U.S. has done to prevent terrorism has been the best advertising terrorism could possibly have. The "war on terror" has degenerated since its ugly inception in Afghanistan and Iraq into a two-pronged war against the U.S. domestic population's civil rights and the infrastructures of Muslim nations; every cynical episode of this endless war has inched America closer to a police state, and turned people minding their own business in other countries into jihadists and suicide bombers. If the United States were at all interested in preventing terrorism, it would first have to acknowledge that the country belongs to the citizens its economic policies have impoverished, and get rid of emergency laws that violate their rights on the pretext of ensuring their safety. This would involve dismantling the surveillance state apparatus that inflates its criminally gigantic budgets with phony terrorism warnings and a veritable industry of theatrical FBI sting operations. And then the country would have to address the systemic social problems that have been allowed to metastasize ever since the presidency of Ronald Reagan. As everyday existence becomes more punitive for all but the monied few, more and more frustrated, volatile individuals will seek each other out online, aggravate whatever lethal fairy tale suits their pathology, and, ultimately, transfer their rage from the screen world to the real one.

MICHAEL POLLAN

■

The Trip Treatment

FROM *The New Yorker*

ON AN APRIL MONDAY in 2010, Patrick Mettes, a fifty-four-year-old television news director being treated for a cancer of the bile ducts, read an article on the front page of the *Times* that would change his death. His diagnosis had come three years earlier, shortly after his wife, Lisa, noticed that the whites of his eyes had turned yellow. By 2010, the cancer had spread to Patrick's lungs and he was buckling under the weight of a debilitating chemotherapy regimen and the growing fear that he might not survive. The article, headlined "HALLUCINOGENS HAVE DOCTORS TUNING IN AGAIN," mentioned clinical trials at several universities, including N.Y.U., in which psilocybin—the active ingredient in so-called magic mushrooms—was being administered to cancer patients in an effort to relieve their anxiety and "existential distress." One of the researchers was quoted as saying that, under the influence of the hallucinogen, "individuals transcend their primary identification with their bodies and experience ego-free states . . . and return with a new perspective and profound acceptance." Patrick had never taken a psychedelic drug, but he immediately wanted to volunteer. Lisa was against the idea. "I didn't want there to be an easy way out," she recently told me. "I wanted him to fight."

Patrick made the call anyway and, after filling out some forms and answering a long list of questions, was accepted into the trial. Since hallucinogens can sometimes bring to the surface latent psychological problems, researchers try to weed out volunteers at high risk by asking questions about drug use and whether there is a family history of schizophrenia or bipolar disorder. After the screening, Mettes was assigned to a therapist named Anthony Bossis, a bearded, bear-ish psychologist in his mid-fifties, with a specialty in palliative care. Bossis is a co-principal investigator for the N.Y.U. trial.

After four meetings with Bossis, Mettes was scheduled for two dosings—one of them an "active" placebo (in this case, a high dose of niacin, which can produce a tingling sensation), and the other a pill containing the psilocybin. Both sessions, Mettes was told, would take place in a room decorated to look more like a living room than like a medical office, with a comfortable couch, landscape paintings on the wall, and, on the shelves, books of art and mythology, along with various aboriginal and spiritual tchotchkes, including a Buddha and a glazed ceramic mushroom. During each session, which would last the better part of a day, Mettes would lie on the couch wearing an eye mask and listening through headphones to a carefully curated playlist—Brian Eno, Philip Glass, Pat Metheny, Ravi Shankar. Bossis and a second therapist would be there throughout, saying little but being available to help should he run into any trouble.

I met Bossis last year in the N.Y.U. treatment room, along with his colleague Stephen Ross, an associate professor of psychiatry at N.Y.U.'s medical school, who directs the ongoing psilocybin trials. Ross, who is in his forties, was dressed in a suit and could pass for a banker. He is also the director of the substance-abuse division at Bellevue, and he told me that he had known little about psychedel-ics—drugs that produce radical changes in consciousness, including hallucinations—until a colleague happened to mention that, in the nineteen-sixties, LSD had been used successfully to treat alcoholics. Ross did some research and was astounded at what he found.

"I felt a little like an archeologist unearthing a completely buried body of knowledge," he said. Beginning in the nineteen-fifties, psy-chedelics had been used to treat a wide variety of conditions, includ-ing alcoholism and end-of-life anxiety. The American Psychiatric As-sociation held meetings centered on LSD. "Some of the best minds in psychiatry had seriously studied these compounds in therapeutic models, with government funding," Ross said.

Between 1953 and 1973, the federal government spent four million dollars to fund a hundred and sixteen studies of LSD, involving more than seventeen hundred subjects. (These figures don't include classi-fied research.) Through the mid-nineteen-sixties, psilocybin and LSD were legal and remarkably easy to obtain. Sandoz, the Swiss chemi-cal company where, in 1938, Albert Hofmann first synthesized LSD, gave away large quantities of Delysid—LSD—to any researcher who requested it, in the hope that someone would discover a mar-ketable application. Psychedelics were tested on alcoholics, people struggling with obsessive-compulsive disorder, depressives, autistic children, schizophrenics, terminal cancer patients, and convicts, as well as on perfectly healthy artists and scientists (to study creativity) and divinity students (to study spirituality). The results reported were frequently positive. But many of the studies were, by modern stan-dards, poorly designed and seldom well controlled, if at all. When there were controls, it was difficult to blind the researchers—that is, hide from them which volunteers had taken the actual drug. (This re-mains a problem.)

By the mid-nineteen-sixties, LSD had escaped from the labora-tory and swept through the counterculture. In 1970, Richard Nixon signed the Controlled Substances Act and put most psychedelics on Schedule 1, prohibiting their use for any purpose. Research soon came to a halt, and what had been learned was all but erased from the field of psychiatry. "By the time I got to medical school, no one even talked about it," Ross said.

The clinical trials at N.Y.U.—a second one, using psilocybin to treat alcohol addiction, is now getting under way—are part of a ren-aissance of psychedelic research taking place at several universities in the United States, including Johns Hopkins, the Harbor-U.C.L.A. Medical Center, and the University of New Mexico, as well as at Im-perial College, in London, and the University of Zurich. As the drug war subsides, scientists are eager to reconsider the therapeutic po-tential of these drugs, beginning with psilocybin. (Last month the *Lancet*, the United Kingdom's most prominent medical journal, pub-lished a guest editorial in support of such research.) The effects of psilocybin resemble those of LSD, but, as one researcher explained, "it carries none of the political and cultural baggage of those three letters." LSD is also stronger and longer-lasting in its effects, and is considered more likely to produce adverse reactions. Researchers are using or planning to use psilocybin not only to treat anxiety, addiction (to smoking and alcohol), and depression but also to study the neurobiology of mystical experience, which the drug, at high doses, can reliably occasion. Forty years after the Nixon Administration effectively shut down most psychedelic research, the government is gingerly allowing a small number of scientists to resume working with these powerful and still somewhat mysterious molecules.

As I chatted with Tony Bossis and Stephen Ross in the treatment room at N.Y.U., their excitement about the results was evident. According to Ross, cancer patients receiving just a single dose of psilocybin experienced immediate and dramatic reductions in anxiety and depression, improvements that were sustained for at least six months. The data are still being analyzed and have not yet been submitted to a journal for peer review, but the researchers expect to publish later this year.

"I thought the first ten or twenty people were plants—that they must be faking it," Ross told me. "They were saying things like 'I understand love is the most powerful force on the planet,' or 'I had an encounter with my cancer, this black cloud of smoke.' People who had been palpably scared of death—they lost their fear. The fact that a drug given once can have such an effect for so long is an unprecedented finding. We have never had anything like it in the psychiatric field."

I was surprised to hear such unguarded enthusiasm from a scientist, and a substance-abuse specialist, about a street drug that, since 1970, has been classified by the government as having no accepted medical use and a high potential for abuse. But the support for renewed research on psychedelics is widespread among medical experts. "I'm personally biased in favor of these type of studies," Thomas R. Insel, the director of the National Institute of Mental Health (N.I.M.H.) and a neuroscientist, told me. "If it proves useful to people who are really suffering, we should look at it. Just because it is a psychedelic doesn't disqualify it in our eyes." Nora Volkow, the director of the National Institute on Drug Abuse (NIDA), emphasized that "it is important to remind people that experimenting with drugs of abuse outside a research setting can produce serious harms."

Many researchers I spoke with described their findings with excitement, some using words like "mind-blowing." Bossis said, "People don't realize how few tools we have in psychiatry to address existential distress. Xanax isn't the answer. So how can we not explore this, if it can recalibrate how we die?"

Herbert D. Kleber, a psychiatrist and the director of the substance-abuse division at the Columbia University–N.Y. State Psychiatric Institute, who is one of the nation's leading experts on drug abuse, struck a cautionary note. "The whole area of research is fascinating," he said. "But it's important to remember that the sample sizes are small." He also stressed the risk of adverse effects and the importance of "having guides in the room, since you can have a good experience or a frightful one." But he added, referring to the N.Y.U. and Johns Hopkins research, "These studies are being carried out by very well trained and dedicated therapists who know what they're doing. The question is, is it ready for prime time?"

The idea of giving a psychedelic drug to the dying was conceived by a novelist: Aldous Huxley. In 1953, Humphry Osmond, an English psychiatrist, introduced Huxley to mescaline, an experience he chronicled in *The Doors of Perception,* in 1954. (Osmond coined the word "psychedelic," which means "mind-manifesting," in a 1957 letter to Huxley.) Huxley proposed a research project involving the "administration of LSD to terminal cancer cases, in the hope that it would make dying a more spiritual, less strictly physiological process." Huxley had his wife inject him with the drug on his deathbed; he died at sixty-nine, of laryngeal cancer, on November 22, 1963.

Psilocybin mushrooms first came to the attention of Western medicine (and popular culture) in a fifteen-page 1957 *Life* article by an amateur mycologist—and a vice-president of J. P. Morgan in New York—named R. Gordon Wasson. In 1955, after years spent chasing down reports of the clandestine use of magic mushrooms among indigenous Mexicans, Wasson was introduced to them by María Sabina, a *curandera*—a healer, or shaman—in southern Mexico. Wasson's awed first-person account of his psychedelic journey during a nocturnal mushroom ceremony inspired several scientists, including Timothy Leary, a well-regarded psychologist doing personality research at Harvard, to take up the study of psilocybin. After trying magic mushrooms in Cuernavaca, in 1960, Leary conceived the Harvard Psilocybin Project, to study the therapeutic potential of hallucinogens. His involvement with LSD came a few years later.

In the wake of Wasson's research, Albert Hofmann experimented with magic mushrooms in 1957. "Thirty minutes after my taking the mushrooms, the exterior world began to undergo a strange transformation," he wrote. "Everything assumed a Mexican character." Hofmann proceeded to identify, isolate, and then synthesize the active ingredient, psilocybin, the compound being used in the current research.

Perhaps the most influential and rigorous of these early studies was the Good Friday experiment, conducted in 1962 by Walter Pahnke, a psychiatrist and minister working on a Ph.D. dissertation under Leary at Harvard. In a double-blind experiment, twenty divinity students received a capsule of white powder right before a Good Friday service at Marsh Chapel, on the Boston University campus; ten contained psilocybin, ten an active placebo (nicotinic acid). Eight of the ten students receiving psilocybin reported a mystical experience, while only one in the control group experienced a feeling of "sacredness" and a "sense of peace." (Telling the subjects apart was not difficult, rendering the double-blind a somewhat hollow conceit: those on the placebo sat sedately in their pews while the others lay down or wandered around the chapel, muttering things like "God is everywhere" and "Oh, the glory!") Pahnke concluded that the experiences of eight who received the psilocybin were "indistinguishable from, if not identical with," the classic mystical experiences reported in the literature by William James, Walter Stace, and others.

In 1991, Rick Doblin, the director of the Multidisciplinary Association for Psychedelic Studies (MAPS), published a follow-up study, in which he tracked down all but one of the divinity students who received psilocybin at Marsh Chapel and interviewed seven of them. They all reported that the experience had shaped their lives and work in profound and enduring ways. But Doblin found flaws in Pahnke's published account: he had failed to mention that several subjects struggled with acute anxiety during their experience. One had to be restrained and given Thorazine, a powerful antipsychotic, after he ran from the chapel and headed down Commonwealth Avenue, convinced that he had been chosen to announce that the Messiah had arrived.

The first wave of research into psychedelics was doomed by an excessive exuberance about their potential. For people working with these remarkable molecules, it was difficult not to conclude that they were suddenly in possession of news with the power to change the world—a psychedelic gospel. They found it hard to justify confining these drugs to the laboratory or using them only for the benefit of the sick. It didn't take long for once respectable scientists such as Leary to grow impatient with the rigmarole of objective science. He came to see science as just another societal "game," a conventional box it was time to blow up—along with all the others.

Was the suppression of psychedelic research inevitable? Stanislav Grof, a Czech-born psychiatrist who used LSD extensively in his practice in the nineteen-sixties, believes that psychedelics "loosed the Dionysian element" on America, posing a threat to the country's Puritan values that was bound to be repulsed. (He thinks the same thing could happen again.) Roland Griffiths, a psychopharmacologist at Johns Hopkins University School of Medicine, points out that ours is not the first culture to feel threatened by psychedelics: the reason Gordon Wasson had to rediscover magic mushrooms in Mexico was that the Spanish had suppressed them so thoroughly, deeming them dangerous instruments of paganism.

"There is such a sense of authority that comes out of the primary mystical experience that it can be threatening to existing hierarchical structures," Griffiths told me when we met in his office last spring. "We ended up demonizing these compounds. Can you think of another area of science regarded as so dangerous and taboo that all research gets shut down for decades? It's unprecedented in modern science."

Early in 2006, Tony Bossis, Stephen Ross, and Jeffrey Guss, a psychiatrist and N.Y.U. colleague, began meeting after work on Friday afternoons to read up on and discuss the scientific literature on psychedelics. They called themselves the P.R.G., or Psychedelic Reading Group, but within a few months the "R" in P.R.G. had come to stand for "Research." They had decided to try to start an experimental trial at N.Y.U., using psilocybin alongside therapy to treat anxiety in cancer patients. The obstacles to such a trial were formidable: Would the F.D.A. and the D.E.A. grant permission to use the drug? Would N.Y.U.'s Institutional Review Board, charged with protecting experimental subjects, allow them to administer a psychedelic to cancer patients? Then, in July of 2006, the journal *Psychopharmacology* published a landmark article by Roland Griffiths, et al., titled "Psilocybin Can Occasion Mystical-Type Experiences Having Substantial and Sustained Personal Meaning and Spiritual Significance."

"We all rushed in with Roland's article," Bossis recalls. "It solidified our confidence that we could do this work. Johns Hopkins had shown it could be done safely." The article also gave Ross the ammunition he needed to persuade a skeptical I.R.B. "The fact that psychedelic research was being done at Hopkins—considered the premier medical center in the country—made it easier to get it approved here. It was an amazing study, with such an elegant design. And it opened up the field." (Even so, psychedelic research remains tightly regulated and closely scrutinized. The N.Y.U. trial could not begin until Ross obtained approvals first from the F.D.A., then from N.Y.U.'s Oncology Review Board, and then from the I.R.B., the Bellevue Research Review Committee, the Bluestone Center for Clinical Research, the Clinical and Translational Science Institute, and, finally, the Drug Enforcement Administration, which must grant the license to use a Schedule 1 substance.)

Griffiths's double-blind study reprised the work done by Pahnke in the nineteen-sixties, but with considerably more scientific rigor. Thirty-six volunteers, none of whom had ever taken a hallucinogen, received a pill containing either psilocybin or an active placebo (methylphenidate, or Ritalin); in a subsequent session the pills were reversed. "When administered under supportive conditions," the paper concluded, "psilocybin occasioned experiences similar to spontaneously occurring mystical experiences." Participants ranked these experiences as among the most meaningful in their lives, comparable to the birth of a child or the death of a parent. Two-thirds of the participants rated the psilocybin session among the top five most spiritually significant experiences of their lives; a third ranked it at the top. Fourteen months later, these ratings had slipped only slightly.

Furthermore, the "completeness" of the mystical experience closely tracked the improvements reported in personal well-being, life satisfaction, and "positive behavior change" measured two months and then fourteen months after the session. (The researchers relied on both self-assessments and the assessments of co-workers, friends, and family.) The authors determined the completeness of a mystical experience using two questionnaires, including the Pahnke-Richards Mystical Experience Questionnaire, which is based in part on William James's writing in "The Varieties of Religious Experience." The questionnaire measures feelings of unity, sacredness, ineffability, peace, and joy, as well as the impression of having transcended space and time and the "noetic sense" that the experience has disclosed some objective truth about reality. A "complete" mystical experience is one that exhibits all six characteristics. Griffiths believes that the long-term effectiveness of the drug is due to its ability to occasion such a transformative experience, but not by changing the brain's long-term chemistry, as a conventional psychiatric drug like Prozac does.

A follow-up study by Katherine MacLean, a psychologist in Griffiths's lab, found that the psilocybin experience also had a positive and lasting effect on the personality of most participants. This is a striking result, since the conventional wisdom in psychology holds that personality is usually fixed by age thirty and thereafter is unlikely to substantially change. But more than a year after their psilocybin sessions volunteers who had had the most complete mystical experiences showed significant increases in their "openness," one of the five domains that psychologists look at in assessing personality traits. (The others are conscientiousness, extroversion, agreeableness, and neuroticism.) Openness, which encompasses aesthetic appreciation, imagination, and tolerance of others' viewpoints, is a good predictor of creativity.

"I don't want to use the word 'mind-blowing,'" Griffiths told me, "but, as a scientific phenomenon, if you can create conditions in which seventy per cent of people will say they have had one of the five most meaningful experiences of their lives? To a scientist, that's just incredible."

The revival of psychedelic research today owes much to the respectability of its new advocates. At sixty-eight, Roland Griffiths, who was trained as a behaviorist and holds senior appointments in psychiatry and neuroscience at Hopkins, is one of the nation's leading drug-addiction researchers. More than six feet tall, he is rail-thin and stands bolt upright; the only undisciplined thing about him is a thatch of white hair so dense that it appears to have held his comb to a draw. His long, productive relationship with NIDA has resulted in some three hundred and fifty papers, with titles such as "Reduction of Heroin Self-Administration in Baboons by Manipulation of Behavioral and Pharmacological Conditions." Tom Insel, the director of the N.I.M.H., described Griffiths as "a very careful, thoughtful scientist" with "a reputation for meticulous data analysis. So it's fascinating that he's now involved in an area that other people might view as pushing the edge."

Griffiths's career took an unexpected turn in the nineteen-nineties after two serendipitous introductions. The first came when a friend introduced him to Siddha Yoga, in 1994. He told me that meditation acquainted him with "something way, way beyond a material world view that I can't really talk to my colleagues about, because it involves metaphors or assumptions that I'm really uncomfortable with as a scientist." He began entertaining "fanciful thoughts" of quitting science and going to India.

In 1996, an old friend and colleague named Charles R. (Bob) Schuster, recently retired as the head of NIDA, suggested that Griffiths talk to Robert Jesse, a young man he'd recently met at Esalen, the retreat center in Big Sur, California. Jesse was neither a medical professional nor a scientist; he was a computer guy, a vice-president at Oracle, who had made it his mission to revive the science of psychedelics, as a tool not so much of medicine as of spirituality. He had organized a gathering of researchers and religious figures to discuss the spiritual and therapeutic potential of psychedelic drugs and how they might be rehabilitated.

When the history of second-wave psychedelic research is written, Bob Jesse will be remembered as one of two scientific outsiders who worked for years, mostly behind the scenes, to get it off the ground. (The other is Rick Doblin, the founder of MAPS.) While on leave from Oracle, Jesse established a nonprofit called the Council on Spiritual Practices, with the aim of "making direct experience of the sacred more available to more people." (He prefers the term "entheogen," or "God-facilitating," to "psychedelic.") In 1996, the C.S.P. organized the historic gathering at Esalen. Many of the fifteen in attendance were "psychedelic elders," researchers such as James Fadiman and Willis Harman, both of whom had done early psychedelic research while at Stanford, and religious figures like Huston Smith, the scholar of comparative religion. But Jesse wisely decided to invite an outsider as well: Bob Schuster, a drug-abuse expert who had served in two Republican Administrations. By the end of the meeting, the Esalen group had decided on a plan: "to get aboveboard, unassailable research done, at an institution with investigators beyond reproach," and, ideally, "do this without any promise of clinical treatment." Jesse was ultimately less interested in people's mental disorders than in their spiritual well-being—in using entheogens for what he calls "the betterment of well people."

Shortly after the Esalen meeting, Bob Schuster (who died in 2011) phoned Jesse to tell him about his old friend Roland Griffiths, whom he described as "the investigator beyond reproach" Jesse was looking for. Jesse flew to Baltimore to meet Griffiths, inaugurating a series of conversations and meetings about meditation and spirituality that eventually drew Griffiths into psychedelic research and would culminate, a few years later, in the 2006 paper in *Psychopharmacology*.

The significance of the 2006 paper went far beyond its findings. The journal invited several prominent drug researchers and neuroscientists to comment on the study, and all of them treated it as a convincing case for further research. Herbert Kleber, of Columbia, applauded the paper and acknowledged that "major therapeutic possibilities" could result from further psychedelic research studies, some of which "merit N.I.H. support." Solomon Snyder, the Hopkins neuroscientist who, in the nineteen-seventies, discovered the brain's opioid receptors, summarized what Griffiths had achieved for the field: "The ability of these researchers to conduct a double-blind, well-controlled study tells us that clinical research with psychedelic drugs need not be so risky as to be off-limits to most investigators."

Roland Griffiths and Bob Jesse had opened a door that had been tightly shut for more than three decades. Charles Grob, at U.C.L.A., was the first to step through it, winning F.D.A. approval for a Phase I pilot study to assess the safety, dosing, and efficacy of psilocybin in the treatment of anxiety in cancer patients. Next came the Phase II trials, just concluded at both Hopkins and N.Y.U., involving higher doses and larger groups (twenty-nine at N.Y.U.; fifty-six at Hopkins)—including Patrick Mettes and about a dozen other cancer patients in New York and Baltimore whom I recently interviewed.

Since 2006, Griffiths's lab has conducted a pilot study on the potential of psilocybin to treat smoking addiction, the results of which were published last November in the *Journal of Psychopharmacology*. The sample is tiny—fifteen smokers—but the success rate is striking. Twelve subjects, all of whom had tried to quit multiple times, using various methods, were verified as abstinent six months after treatment, a success rate of eighty per cent. (Currently, the leading cessation treatment is nicotine-replacement therapy; a recent review article in the *BMJ*—formerly the *British Medical Journal*—reported that the treatment helped smokers remain abstinent for six months in less than seven per cent of cases.) In the Hopkins study, subjects underwent two or three psilocybin sessions and a course of cognitive-behavioral therapy to help them deal with cravings. The psychedelic experience seems to allow many subjects to reframe, and then break, a lifelong habit. "Smoking seemed irrelevant, so I stopped," one subject told me. The volunteers who reported a more complete mystical experience had greater success in breaking the habit. A larger, Phase II trial comparing psilocybin to nicotine replacement (both in conjunction with cognitive behavioral therapy) is getting under way at Hopkins.

"We desperately need a new treatment approach for addiction," Herbert Kleber told me. "Done in the right hands—and I stress that, because the whole psychedelic area attracts people who often think that they know the truth before doing the science—this could be a very useful one."

Thus far, criticism of psychedelic research has been limited. Last summer, Florian Holsboer, the director of the Max Planck Institute of Psychiatry, in Munich, told *Science*, "You can't give patients some substance just because it has an antidepressant effect on top of many other effects. That's too dangerous." Nora Volkow, of NIDA, wrote me in an e-mail that "the main concern we have at NIDA in relation to this work is that the public will walk away with the message that psilocybin is a safe drug to use. In fact, its adverse effects are well known, although not completely predictable." She added, "Progress has been made in decreasing use of hallucinogens, particularly in young people. We would not want to see that trend altered."

The recreational use of psychedelics is famously associated with instances of psychosis, flashback, and suicide. But these adverse effects have not surfaced in the trials of drugs at N.Y.U. and Johns Hopkins. After nearly five hundred administrations of psilocybin, the researchers have reported no serious negative effects. This is perhaps less surprising than it sounds, since volunteers are self-selected, carefully screened and prepared for the experience, and are then guided through it by therapists well trained to manage the episodes of fear and anxiety that many volunteers do report. Apart from the molecules involved, a psychedelic therapy session and a recreational psychedelic experience have very little in common.

The lab at Hopkins is currently conducting a study of particular interest to Griffiths: examining the effect of psilocybin on long-term meditators. The study plans to use fMRI—functional magnetic-resonance imaging—to study the brains of forty meditators before, during, and after they have taken psilocybin, to measure changes in brain activity and connectivity and to see what these "trained contemplatives can tell us about the experience." Griffiths's lab is also launching a study in collaboration with N.Y.U. that will give the drug to religious professionals in a number of faiths to see how the experience might contribute to their work. "I feel like a kid in a candy shop," Griffiths told me. "There are so many directions to take this research. It's a Rip Van Winkle effect—after three decades of no research, we're rubbing the sleep from our eyes."

"Ineffability" is a hallmark of the mystical experience. Many struggle to describe the bizarre events going on in their minds during a guided psychedelic journey without sounding like either a New Age guru or a lunatic. The available vocabulary isn't always up to the task of recounting an experience that seemingly can take someone out of body, across vast stretches of time and space, and include face-to-face encounters with divinities and demons and previews of their own death.

Volunteers in the N.Y.U. psilocybin trial were required to write a narrative of their experience soon after the treatment, and Patrick Mettes, having worked in journalism, took the assignment seriously. His wife, Lisa, said that, after his Friday session, he worked all weekend to make sense of the experience and write it down.

When Mettes arrived at the treatment room, at First Avenue and Twenty-fifth Street, Tony Bossis and Krystallia Kalliontzi, his guides, greeted him, reviewed the day's plan, and, at 9 a.m., presented him with a small chalice containing the pill. None of them knew whether it contained psilocybin or the placebo. Asked to state his intention, Mettes said that he wanted to learn to cope better with the anxiety and the fear that he felt about his cancer. As the researchers had suggested, he'd brought a few photographs along—of Lisa and him on their wedding day, and of their dog, Arlo—and placed them around the room.

At nine-thirty, Mettes lay down on the couch, put on the headphones and eye mask, and fell silent. In his account, he likened the start of the journey to the launch of a space shuttle, "a physically violent and rather clunky liftoff which eventually gave way to the blissful serenity of weightlessness."

Several of the volunteers I interviewed reported feeling intense fear and anxiety before giving themselves up to the experience, as the guides encourage them to do. The guides work from a set of "flight instructions" prepared by Bill Richards, a Baltimore psychologist who worked with Stanislav Grof during the nineteen-seventies and now trains a new generation of psychedelic therapists. The document is a summary of the experience accumulated from managing thousands of psychedelic sessions—and countless bad trips—during the nineteen-sixties, whether these took place in therapeutic settings or in the bad-trip tent at Woodstock.

The "same force that takes you deep within will, of its own imfetus, return you safely to the everyday world," the manual offers at one point. Guides are instructed to remind subjects that they'll never be left alone and not to worry about their bodies while journeying, since the guides will keep an eye on them. If you feel like you're "dying, melting, dissolving, exploding, going crazy etc.—go ahead," embrace it: "Climb staircases, open doors, explore paths, fly over landscapes." And if you confront anything frightening, "look the monster in the eye and move towards it. . . . Dig in your heels; ask, 'What are you doing in my mind?' Or, 'What can I learn from you?' Look for the darkest corner in the basement, and shine your light there." This training may help explain why the darker experiences that sometimes accompany the recreational use of psychedelics have not surfaced in the N.Y.U. and Hopkins trials.

Early on, Mettes encountered his brother's wife, Ruth, who died of cancer more than twenty years earlier, at forty-three. Ruth "acted as my tour guide," he wrote, and "didn't seem surprised to see me. She 'wore' her translucent body so I would know her." Michelle Obama made an appearance. "The considerable feminine energy all around me made clear the idea that a mother, any mother, regardless of her shortcomings . . . could never NOT love her offspring. This was very powerful. I know I was crying." He felt as if he were coming out of the womb, "being birthed again."

Bossis noted that Mettes was crying and breathing heavily. Mettes said, "Birth and death is a lot of work," and appeared to be convulsing. Then he reached out and clutched Kalliontzi's hand while pulling his knees up and pushing, as if he were delivering a baby.

"Oh God," he said, "it all makes sense now, so simple and beautiful."

Around noon, Mettes asked to take a break. "It was getting too intense," he wrote. They helped him to the bathroom. "Even the germs were beautiful, as was everything in our world and universe." Afterward, he was reluctant to "go back in." He wrote, "The work was considerable but I loved the sense of adventure." He put on his eye mask and headphones and lay back down.

"From here on, love was the only consideration. It was and is the only purpose. Love seemed to emanate from a single point of light. And it vibrated." He wrote that "no sensation, no image of beauty, nothing during my time on earth has felt as pure and joyful and glorious as the height of this journey."

Then, at twelve-ten, he said something that Bossis jotted down: "Okay, we can all punch out now. I get it."

He went on to take a tour of his lungs, where he "saw two spots." They were "no big deal." Mettes recalled, "I was being told (without words) not to worry about the cancer . . . it's minor in the scheme of things . . . simply an imperfection of your humanity."

Then he experienced what he called "a brief death."

"I approached what appeared to be a very sharp, pointed piece of stainless steel. It had a razor blade quality to it. I continued up to the apex of this shiny metal object and as I arrived, I had a choice, to look or not look, over the edge and into the infinite abyss." He stared into "the vastness of the universe," hesitant but not frightened. "I wanted to go all in but felt that if I did, I would possibly leave my body permanently," he wrote. But he "knew there was much more for me here." Telling his guides about his choice, he explained that he was "not ready to jump off and leave Lisa."

Around 3 p.m., it was over. "The transition from a state where I had no sense of time or space to the relative dullness of now, happened quickly. I had a headache."

When Lisa arrived to take him home, Patrick "looked like he had run a race," she recalled. "The color in his face was not good, he looked tired and sweaty, but he was fired up." He told her he had touched the face of God.

Bossis was deeply moved by the session. "You're in this room, but you're in the presence of something large," he recalled. "It's humbling to sit there. It's the most rewarding day of your career."

Every guided psychedelic journey is different, but a few themes seem to recur. Several of the cancer patients I interviewed at N.Y.U. and Hopkins described an experience of either giving birth or being born. Many also described an encounter with their cancer that had the effect of diminishing its power over them. Dinah Bazer, a shy woman in her sixties who had been given a diagnosis of ovarian cancer in 2010, screamed at the black mass of fear she encountered while peering into her rib cage: "Fuck you, I won't be eaten alive!"

Since her session, she says, she has stopped worrying about a recurrence—one of the objectives of the trial.

Great secrets of the universe often become clear during the journey, such as "We are all one" or "Love is all that matters." The usual ratio of wonder to banality in the adult mind is overturned, and such ideas acquire the force of revealed truth. The result is a kind of conversion experience, and the researchers believe that this is what is responsible for the therapeutic effect.

Subjects revelled in their sudden ability to travel seemingly at will through space and time, using it to visit Elizabethan England, the banks of the Ganges, or Wordsworthian scenes from their childhood. The impediment of a body is gone, as is one's identity, yet, paradoxically, a perceiving and recording "I" still exists. Several volunteers used the metaphor of a camera being pulled back on the scene of their lives, to a point where matters that had once seemed daunting now appeared manageable—smoking, cancer, even death. Their accounts are reminiscent of the "overview effect" described by astronauts who have glimpsed the earth from a great distance, an experience that some of them say permanently altered their priorities. Roland Griffiths likens the therapeutic experience of psilocybin to a kind of "inverse P.T.S.D."—"a discrete event that produces persisting positive changes in attitudes, moods, and behavior, and presumably in the brain."

Death looms large in the journeys taken by the cancer patients. A woman I'll call Deborah Ames, a breast-cancer survivor in her sixties (she asked not to be identified), described zipping through space as if in a video game until she arrived at the wall of a crematorium and realized, with a fright, "I've died and now I'm going to be cremated. The next thing I know, I'm below the ground in this gorgeous forest, deep woods, loamy and brown. There are roots all around me and I'm seeing the trees growing, and I'm part of them. It didn't feel sad or happy, just natural, contented, peaceful. I wasn't gone. I was part of the earth." Several patients described edging up to the precipice of death and looking over to the other side. Tammy Burgess, given a diagnosis of ovarian cancer at fifty-five, found herself gazing across "the great plain of consciousness. It was very serene and beautiful. I felt alone but I could reach out and touch anyone I'd ever known.

When my time came, that's where my life would go once it left me and that was OK."

I was struck by how the descriptions of psychedelic journeys differed from the typical accounts of dreams. For one thing, most people's recall of their journey is not just vivid but comprehensive, the narratives they reconstruct seamless and fully accessible, even years later. They don't regard these narratives as "just a dream," the evanescent products of fantasy or wish fulfillment, but, rather, as genuine and sturdy experiences. This is the "noetic" quality that students of mysticism often describe: the unmistakable sense that whatever has been learned or witnessed has the authority and the durability of objective truth. "You don't get that on other drugs," as Roland Griffiths points out; after the fact, we're fully aware of, and often embarrassed by, the inauthenticity of the drug experience.

This might help explain why so many cancer patients in the trials reported that their fear of death had lifted or at least abated: they had stared directly at death and come to know something about it, in a kind of dress rehearsal. "A high-dose psychedelic experience is death practice," Katherine MacLean, the former Hopkins psychologist, said. "You're losing everything you know to be real, letting go of your ego and your body, and that process can feel like dying." And yet you don't die; in fact, some volunteers become convinced by the experience that consciousness may somehow survive the death of their bodies.

In follow-up discussions with Bossis, Patrick Mettes spoke of his body and his cancer as a "type of illusion" and how there might be "something beyond this physical body." It also became clear that, psychologically, at least, Mettes was doing remarkably well: he was meditating regularly, felt he had become better able to live in the present, and described loving his wife "even more." In a session in March, two months after his journey, Bossis noted that Mettes "reports feeling the happiest in his life."

How are we to judge the veracity of the insights gleaned during a psychedelic journey? It's one thing to conclude that love is all that matters, but quite another to come away from a therapy convinced that "there is another reality" awaiting us after death, as one volunteer put it, or that there is more to the universe—and to consciousness—than a purely materialist world view would have us believe. Is psychedelic therapy simply foisting a comforting delusion on the sick and dying?

"That's above my pay grade," Bossis said, with a shrug, when I asked him. Bill Richards cited William James, who suggested that we judge the mystical experience not by its veracity, which is unknowable, but by its fruits: does it turn someone's life in a positive direction?

Many researchers acknowledge that the power of suggestion may play a role when a drug like psilocybin is administered by medical professionals with legal and institutional sanction: under such conditions, the expectations of the therapist are much more likely to be fulfilled by the patient. (And bad trips are much less likely to occur.) But who cares, some argue, as long as it helps? David Nichols, an emeritus professor of pharmacology at Purdue University—and a founder, in 1993, of the Heffter Research Institute, a key funder of psychedelic research—put the pragmatic case most baldly in a recent interview with *Science*: "If it gives them peace, if it helps people to die peacefully with their friends and their family at their side, I don't care if it's real or an illusion."

Roland Griffiths is willing to consider the challenge that the mystical experience poses to the prevailing scientific paradigm. He conceded that "authenticity is a scientific question not yet answered" and that all that scientists have to go by is what people tell them about their experiences. But he pointed out that the same is true for much more familiar mental phenomena.

"What about the miracle that we are conscious? Just think about that for a second, that we are aware we're aware!" Insofar as I was on board for one miracle well beyond the reach of materialist science, Griffiths was suggesting, I should remain open to the possibility of others.

"I'm willing to hold that there's a mystery here we don't understand, that these experiences may or may not be 'true,'" he said. "What's exciting is to use the tools we have to explore and pick apart this mystery."

* * *

Perhaps the most ambitious attempt to pick apart the scientific mystery of the psychedelic experience has been taking place in a lab based at Imperial College, in London. There a thirty-four-year-old neuroscientist named Robin Carhart-Harris has been injecting healthy volunteers with psilocybin and LSD and then using a variety of scanning tools—including fMRI and magnetoencephalography (MEG)—to observe what happens in their brains.

Carhart-Harris works in the laboratory of David Nutt, a prominent English psychopharmacologist. Nutt served as the drug-policy adviser to the Labour Government until 2011, when he was fired for arguing that psychedelic drugs should be rescheduled on the ground that they are safer than alcohol or tobacco and potentially invaluable to neuroscience. Carhart-Harris's own path to neuroscience was an eccentric one. First, he took a graduate course in psychoanalysis—a field that few neuroscientists take seriously, regarding it less as a science than as a set of untestable beliefs. Carhart-Harris was fascinated by psychoanalytic theory but frustrated by the paucity of its tools for exploring what it deemed most important about the mind: the unconscious.

"If the only way we can access the unconscious mind is via dreams and free association, we aren't going to get anywhere," he said. "Surely there must be something else." One day, he asked his seminar leader if that might be a drug. She was intrigued. He set off to search the library catalogue for "LSD and the Unconscious" and found *Realms of the Human Unconscious,* by Stanislav Grof. "I read the book cover to cover. That set the course for the rest of my young life."

Carhart-Harris, who is slender and intense, with large pale-blue eyes that seldom blink, decided that he would use psychedelic drugs and modern brain-imaging techniques to put a foundation of hard science beneath psychoanalysis. "Freud said dreams were the royal road to the unconscious," he said in our first interview. "LSD may turn out to be the superhighway." Nutt agreed to let him follow this hunch in his lab. He ran bureaucratic interference and helped secure funding (from the Beckley Foundation, which supports psychedelic research).

When, in 2010, Carhart-Harris first began studying the brains of volunteers on psychedelics, neuroscientists assumed that the drugs somehow excited brain activity—hence the vivid hallucinations and powerful emotions that people report. But when Carhart-Harris looked at the results of the first set of fMRI scans—which pinpoint areas of brain activity by mapping local blood flow and oxygen consumption—he discovered that the drug appeared to substantially reduce brain activity in one particular region: the "default-mode network."

The default-mode network was first described in 2001, in a landmark paper by Marcus Raichle, a neurologist at Washington University, in St. Louis, and it has since become the focus of much discussion in neuroscience. The network comprises a critical and centrally situated hub of brain activity that links parts of the cerebral cortex to deeper, older structures in the brain, such as the limbic system and the hippocampus.

The network, which consumes a significant portion of the brain's energy, appears to be most active when we are least engaged in attending to the world or to a task. It lights up when we are daydreaming, removed from sensory processing, and engaging in higher-level "meta-cognitive" processes such as self-reflection, mental time travel, rumination, and "theory of mind"—the ability to attribute mental states to others. Carhart-Harris describes the default-mode network variously as the brain's "orchestra conductor" or "corporate executive" or "capital city," charged with managing and "holding the entire system together." It is thought to be the physical counterpart of the autobiographical self, or ego.

"The brain is a hierarchical system," Carhart-Harris said. "The highest-level parts"—such as the default-mode network—"have an inhibitory influence on the lower-level parts, like emotion and memory." He discovered that blood flow and electrical activity in the default-mode network dropped off precipitously under the influence of psychedelics, a finding that may help to explain the loss of the sense of self that volunteers reported. (The biggest dropoffs in default-mode-network activity correlated with volunteers' reports of ego dissolution.) Just before Carhart-Harris published his results, in a 2012 paper in *Proceedings of the National Academy of Sciences*, a researcher at Yale named Judson Brewer, who was using fMRI to study the brains of experienced meditators, noticed that their default-mode networks had also been quieted relative to those of novice meditators. It appears that, with the ego temporarily out of commission, the boundaries between self and world, subject and object, all dissolve. These are hallmarks of the mystical experience.

If the default-mode network functions as the conductor of the symphony of brain activity, we might expect its temporary disappearance from the stage to lead to an increase in dissonance and mental disorder—as appears to happen during the psychedelic journey. Carhart-Harris has found evidence in scans of brain waves that, when the default-mode network shuts down, other brain regions "are let off the leash." Mental contents hidden from view (or suppressed) during normal waking consciousness come to the fore: emotions, memories, wishes and fears. Regions that don't ordinarily communicate directly with one another strike up conversations (neuroscientists sometimes call this "crosstalk"), often with bizarre results. Carhart-Harris thinks that hallucinations occur when the visual-processing centers of the brain, left to their own devices, become more susceptible to the influence of our beliefs and emotions.

Carhart-Harris doesn't romanticize psychedelics, and he has little patience for the sort of "magical thinking" and "metaphysics" they promote. In his view, the forms of consciousness that psychedelics unleash are regressions to a more "primitive style of cognition." Following Freud, he says that the mystical experience—whatever its source—returns us to the psychological condition of the infant, who has yet to develop a sense of himself as a bounded individual. The pinnacle of human development is the achievement of the ego, which imposes order on the anarchy of a primitive mind buffeted by magical thinking. (The developmental psychologist Alison Gopnik has speculated that the way young children perceive the world has much in common with the psychedelic experience. As she puts it, "They're basically tripping all the time.") The psychoanalytic value of psychedelics, in his view, is that they allow us to bring the workings of the unconscious mind "into an observable space."

In *The Doors of Perception,* Aldous Huxley concluded from his psychedelic experience that the conscious mind is less a window on reality than a furious editor of it. The mind is a "reducing valve," he wrote, eliminating far more reality than it admits to our conscious awareness, lest we be overwhelmed. "What comes out at the other end is a measly trickle of the kind of consciousness which will help us to stay alive." Psychedelics open the valve wide, removing the filter that hides much of reality, as well as dimensions of our own minds, from ordinary consciousness. Carhart-Harris has cited Huxley's metaphor in some of his papers, likening the default-mode network to the reducing valve, but he does not agree that everything that comes through the opened doors of perception is necessarily real. The psychedelic experience, he suggests, can yield a lot of "fool's gold."

Nevertheless, Carhart-Harris believes that the psychedelic experience can help people by relaxing the grip of an overbearing ego and the rigid, habitual thinking it enforces. The human brain is perhaps the most complex system there is, and the emergence of a conscious self is its highest achievement. By adulthood, the mind has become very good at observing and testing reality and developing confident predictions about it that optimize our investments of energy (mental and otherwise) and therefore our survival. Much of what we think of as perceptions of the world are really educated guesses based on past experience ("That fractal pattern of little green bits in my visual field must be a tree"), and this kind of conventional thinking serves us well.

But only up to a point. In Carhart-Harris's view, a steep price is paid for the achievement of order and ego in the adult mind. "We give up our emotional lability," he told me, "our ability to be open to surprises, our ability to think flexibly, and our ability to value nature." The sovereign ego can become a despot. This is perhaps most evident in depression, when the self turns on itself and uncontrollable introspection gradually shades out reality. In "The Entropic Brain," a paper published last year in *Frontiers in Human Neuroscience*, Carhart-Harris cites research indicating that this debilitating state, sometimes called "heavy self-consciousness," may be the result of a "hyperactive" default-mode network. The lab recently received government funding to conduct a clinical study using psychedelics to treat depression.

Carhart-Harris believes that people suffering from other mental disorders characterized by excessively rigid patterns of thinking, such as addiction and obsessive-compulsive disorder, could benefit from psychedelics, which "disrupt stereotyped patterns of thought and behavior." In his view, all these disorders are, in a sense, ailments of the ego. He also thinks that this disruption could promote more creative thinking. It may be that some brains could benefit from a little less order.

Existential distress at the end of life bears many of the psychological hallmarks of a hyperactive default-mode network, including excessive self-reflection and an inability to jump the deepening grooves of negative thought. The ego, faced with the prospect of its own dissolution, becomes hypervigilant, withdrawing its investment in the world and other people. It is striking that a single psychedelic experience — an intervention that Carhart-Harris calls "shaking the snow globe" — should have the power to alter these patterns in a lasting way.

This appears to be the case for many of the patients in the clinical trial of psilocybin just concluded at Hopkins and N.Y.U. Patrick Mettes lived for seventeen months after his psilocybin journey, and, according to Lisa, he enjoyed many unexpected satisfactions in that time, along with a dawning acceptance of death.

"We still had our arguments," Lisa recalled. "And we had a very trying summer," as they endured a calamitous apartment renovation. But Patrick "had a sense of patience he had never had before, and with me he had real joy about things," she said. "It was as if he had been relieved of the duty of caring about the details of life. Now it was about being with people, enjoying his sandwich and the walk on the promenade. It was as if we lived a lifetime in a year."

After the psilocybin session, Mettes spent his good days walking around the city. "He would walk everywhere, try every restaurant for lunch, and tell me about all these great places he'd discovered. But his good days got fewer and fewer." In March 2012, he stopped chemo. "He didn't want to die," she said. "But I think he just decided that this is not how he wanted to live."

In April, his lungs failing, Mettes wound up back in the hospital. "He gathered everyone together and said goodbye, and explained that this is how he wanted to die. He had a very conscious death."

Mettes's equanimity exerted a powerful influence on everyone around him, Lisa said, and his room in the palliative-care unit at Mt. Sinai became a center of gravity. "Everyone, the nurses and the doctors, wanted to hang out in our room—they just didn't want to leave. Patrick would talk and talk. He put out so much love." When Tony Bossis visited Mettes the week before he died, he was struck by Mettes's serenity. "He was consoling me. He said his biggest sadness was leaving his wife. But he was not afraid."

Lisa took a picture of Patrick a few days before he died, and when it popped open on my screen it momentarily took my breath away: a gaunt man in a hospital gown, an oxygen clip in his nose, but with shining blue eyes and a broad smile.

Lisa stayed with him in his hospital room night after night, the two of them often talking into the morning hours. "I feel like I have one foot in this world and one in the next," he told her at one point. Lisa told me, "One of the last nights we were together, he said, 'Honey, don't push me. I'm finding my way.'"

Lisa hadn't had a shower in days, and her brother encouraged her to go home for a few hours. Minutes before she returned, Patrick slipped away. "He wasn't going to die as long as I was there," she said. "My brother had told me, 'You need to let him go.'"

Lisa said she feels indebted to the people running the N.Y.U. trial and is convinced that the psilocybin experience "allowed him to tap into his own deep resources. That, I think, is what these mind-altering drugs do."

Despite the encouraging results from the N.Y.U. and Hopkins trials, much stands in the way of the routine use of psychedelic therapy. "We don't die well in America," Bossis recently said over lunch at a restaurant near the N.Y.U. medical center. "Ask people where they want to die, and they will tell you at home, with their loved ones. But most of us die in an I.C.U. The biggest taboo in American medicine is the conversation about death. To a doctor, it's a defeat to let a patient go." Bossis and several of his colleagues described the considerable difficulty they had recruiting patients from N.Y.U.'s cancer center for the psilocybin trials. "I'm busy trying to keep my patients alive," one oncologist told Gabrielle Agin-Liebes, the trial's project manager. Only when reports of positive experiences began to filter back to the cancer center did nurses there—not doctors—begin to tell patients about the trial.

Recruitment is only one of the many challenges facing a Phase III trial of psilocybin, which would involve hundreds of patients at multiple locations and cost millions of dollars. The University of Wisconsin and the University of California, Los Angeles, are making plans to participate in such a trial, but F.D.A. approval is not guaranteed. If the trial was successful, the government would be under pressure to reschedule psilocybin under the Controlled Substances Act, having recognized a medical use for the drug.

Also, it seems unlikely that the government would ever fund such a study. "The N.I.M.H. is not opposed to work with psychedelics, but I doubt we would make a major investment," Tom Insel, the institute's director, told me. He said that the N.I.M.H. would need to see "a path to development" and suspects that "it would be very difficult to get a pharmaceutical company interested in developing this drug, since it cannot be patented." It's also unlikely that Big Pharma would have any interest in a drug that is administered only once or twice in the course of treatment. "There's not a lot of money here when you can be cured with one session," Bossis pointed out. Still, Bob Jesse and Rick Doblin are confident that they will find private money for a Phase III clinical trial, and several private funders I spoke to indicated that it would be forthcoming.

Many of the researchers and therapists I interviewed are confident that psychedelic therapy will eventually become routine. Katherine MacLean hopes someday to establish a "psychedelic hospice," a retreat center where the dying and their loved ones can use psychedelics to help them all let go. "If we limit psychedelics just to the patient, we're sticking with the old medical model," she said. "But psychedelics are so much more radical than that. I get nervous when people say they should only be prescribed by a doctor."

In MacLean's thinking, one hears echoes of the excitement of the sixties about the potential of psychedelics to help a wide range of people, and the impatience with the cumbersome structures of medicine. It was precisely this exuberance about psychedelics, and the frustration with the slow pace of science, that helped fuel the backlash against them.

Still, "the betterment of well people," to borrow a phrase of Bob Jesse's, is very much on the minds of most of the researchers I interviewed, some of whom were more reluctant to discuss it on the record than institutional outsiders like Jesse and MacLean. For them, medical acceptance is a first step to a broader cultural acceptance. Jesse would like to see the drugs administered by skilled guides working in "longitudinal multigenerational contexts"—which, as he describes them, sound a lot like church communities. Others envisage a time when people seeking a psychedelic experience—whether for reasons of mental health or spiritual seeking or simple curiosity—could go to something like a "mental-health club," as Julie Holland, a psychiatrist formerly at Bellevue, described it: "Sort of like a cross between a spa/retreat and a gym where people can experience psychedelics in a safe, supportive environment." All spoke of the importance of well-trained guides (N.Y.U. has had a training program in psychedelic therapy since 2008, directed by Jeffrey Guss, a co-principal investigator for the psilocybin trials) and the need to help people afterward "integrate" the powerful experiences they have had in order to render them truly useful. This is not something that happens when these drugs are used recreationally. Bossis paraphrases Huston Smith on this point: "A spiritual experience does not by itself make a spiritual life."

When I asked Rick Doblin if he worries about another backlash, he suggested that the culture has made much progress since the nineteen-sixties. "That was a very different time," he said. "People wouldn't even talk about cancer or death then. Women were tranquillized to give birth; men weren't allowed in the delivery room. Yoga and meditation were totally weird. Now mindfulness is mainstream and everyone does yoga, and there are birthing centers and hospices all over. We've integrated all these things into our culture. And now I think we're ready to integrate psychedelics." He also points out that many of the people in charge of our institutions today have personal experience with psychedelics and so feel less threatened by them.

Bossis would like to believe in Doblin's sunny forecast, and he hopes that "the legacy of this work" will be the routine use of psychedelics in palliative care. But he also thinks that the medical use of psychedelics could easily run into resistance. "This culture has a fear of death, a fear of transcendence, and a fear of the unknown, all of which are embodied in this work." Psychedelics may be too disruptive for our society and institutions ever to embrace them.

The first time I raised the idea of "the betterment of well people" with Roland Griffiths, he shifted in his chair and chose his words carefully. "Culturally, right now, that's a dangerous idea to promote," he said. And yet, as we talked, it became clear that he, too, feels that many of us stand to benefit from these molecules and, even more, from the spiritual experiences they can make available.

"We are all terminal," Griffiths said. "We're all dealing with death. This will be far too valuable to limit to sick people."

DA'SHAY PORTIS

■

Strong City

FROM *Fourteen Hills*

Jesus loves
peppermint
it's clean and
fresh
I've used it.
where
he kisses me
it itches. No, it's
my father's
don't touch it

I will take the four corners of my cloak and clothe you
I see your nakedness and I know you
don't cry, I'll protect you
play your harp, he will not harm you

in my father's house
there are many rooms

I walk from room to room. pick up a copper gauntlet
drop two stone tablets. I walk from room to room, alone —
in the banquet hall there are golden plates, capers,
turkey legs. I see my face
or some child's face.
some small, chocolate child

in a cheetah bra and panties
a matching set.
she pouts.
her lower lip
jutted out.
she's bored.
her red lipstick, small lips
faded
cherry juice
down her chin

I walk from room to room, pick up a shawl,
drop down a cross
pick up His gall
drop down a power drill

I walk into the powder room.
It's so white and nice.
It's so white and clean.

in the corian cistern
filled with rainwater
two harem children
like kittens
lick one another
like lick lick lick
I watch them
their little cinnamon limbs
I look at my own skin
they could be my children

only a thin
clear curtain
keeps me
from reaching out
for them
from cradling her tiny head

under the chrome faucet
lathering her thick
chestnut hair
with our
mother's
lavender
conditioner

I'd comb it through with my fingers
till it was slick and swollen with foam
but I don't

instead I count the toilet paper squares
I fold them into cranes
I leave them for the girls
so when they're done
with their evening ceremony
they'll see them
and maybe remember me

from peppermint leaves god created a skin cream
that he rubbed on eve,
lifted and dipped her in uh stream

adam watched from the mulberry tree
adam watched a part of him leave
hollow and thin
a wisp of wind
while the good Lord
washed his lover's
auburn skin

ANNA KOVATCHEVA

■

Sudba 1

FROM *The Iowa Review*

I REMEMBER THE LAST TIME I saw snow on the mountaintops; I was five. I remember learning the national anthem in school: *Mila rodino, ti si . . .* I remember that we are out of sugar, but there is none to buy. I remember how Baba likes her coffee. I remember the last walk I took before things began to change, on a winter morning that smelled like clean water. I remember saying goodbye to my mother, but I do not remember where she went. I remember sitting with Lili under a dirty orange overhang and telling secrets in the rain. I remember names for six of the planets. I remember how to make baklava. I remember Baba's pills, where they are kept in the bathroom and how often she needs them. I remember some words of my own language, but others are missing, like pages torn from a book.

On my way home from the hospital, I see an old man shitting on the sidewalk. He squats over a closed manhole cover, his bare legs as white as his hair. He has that glazed look. I cross the street away from him, take out my GSM, and dial the hotline number stapled to every disused telephone pole. I give the man's location and hang up. A stray dog whines at me from an alley, tags on its collar jingling, but the poster for forgotten animal rescue has been rained through, and I can't read the number.

Six days to launch.

I'm afraid I'm not too reliable anymore.

I do remember the first case. Fifty-two days to launch. A young man brought his mother in, stood in front of my desk with his hand tight around her upper arm. The woman had bobbed black hair, was fashionably dressed with a shawl swept artfully across her shoulders. I had seen her before, at a pastry café, sitting behind a computer and wearing wire-framed glasses.

We were having lunch, the young man said. All of a sudden she didn't know who I was, or the word for salad. Please.

We rushed the woman in, ahead of a brittle Roma grandmother who had been waiting for hours. Her granddaughters muttered to one another, clutching their fidgeting babies. In the afternoon, I heard the nurses talking in the break room. No apparent physical cause for the woman's sudden loss of memory. By the time her tests came back, there were four new cases: a small boy with a lisp, a white-socked widower who sold tomatoes at the market, a councilman with mob connections, and a waitress who worked in the city center.

The real fear of it was in what they forgot. Individual words or whole decades, they disappeared just the same. The boy no longer recognized his cat; the mobster forgot how to read. Like memory could just break on the kitchen floor, and any shard could go sliding under the counter and out of reach.

I called Lili then. I think it was nearly Christmas. When I walked home that night, small white lights dotted the bones of the trees.

Something's happening, I told her. Don't come home.

I'd caught her on the way to the bus station. I heard her put down her bag, heard Georgi barking. He knew what her suitcase by the door meant, and he hated being left behind.

Something, she repeated. I imagined her squinting her eyes shut.

A long pause, the dog barking. I think she had a dog. I think I remember a dog.

There's something happening here. People are sick. Stay at home; I don't want them to ground you.

Later, she would write: *Every time I lose my keys, I'm afraid it's the first sign, and they won't let me go up.* She was always losing her keys, usually in yesterday's pockets. On the phone, she said, But it's Christmas.

Tell your mother anything. Don't come home.

Another pause. A nylon rustle I think came from her coat. It was a pink coat? Puffed up with down, shedding white wisps onto every shirt.

You're sure? she asked.

No.

She sighed. I'll think of something to tell Mama.

I hope it's nothing, I said.

Merry Christmas, she said.

On December twenty-sixth, the quarantine began. Roadblocks appeared at every way into the city. I don't think I saw them in person, but the television showed them. Policemen wearing paper masks over their faces, heavy guns across their bodies, halting the Christmas travelers trying to get back home.

The waitress had served the mobster his dinner. The mobster's wife loved tomatoes. The lisping boy passed the market on his way home from school, had asked the old tomato man for change so he could ride the merry-go-round; the woman who sold apricots from the next stall remembered the exchange until she was found wandering the market with glassy eyes three weeks later, and she didn't remember anything at all.

I don't remember if I was scared at first. My grandmother had been ill for years: had forgotten how to dress herself, frequently mistook me for my mother. I was preoccupied making sure she stayed warm in a house we could not afford to heat with electricity. Three times a day while I was at work, bald Uncle Lyupcho came from next door and built up the fire in her bedroom. Lately, Uncle Lyupcho hasn't been by; when I try to remember, it seems that his windows have been dark for weeks.

Space, said PM Imanev in his press conference. That's where Lili is going.

Space, he said — *That is where we can rise to new glory.* The national anthem swelled behind him as he waved for the cameras, accepting the nation's praise with his open palm.

We were far from the first; we were lagging far behind. The sky had been buzzing for decades: floating hotels, massive colony shuttles bound for new settlements. Mostly prison volunteers for the first few rounds, but once they carved the footholds, civilians donned space suits. On the news they showed night views of the earth, photographs from fifty years ago and from now: large dark patches shadowing today's map, whole cities left behind. Walking outside in the mornings, I imagined I could hear the rising silence coming in across the globe, imagined I could feel us more and more alone. The television showed animals reclaiming Paris, deer pulling at the grass growing up from heavy cracks in the rue de Rivoli while the grounded poor hurried past with bowed heads and radiation burns.

Even our own population was shrinking, bleeding through open borders, filling those abandoned houses in the countrysides. Latest reports claimed that half of Bulgarians now lived abroad. Some eighteen thousand dual citizens had already taken off with other space programs, but those of us left behind stubbornly dug roots deeper into the ground.

On the television: *This is no way for us to move forward,* Imanev said. *We must move upward.*

Mobsters were convinced, money was borrowed, training programs created. Open calls for volunteers, and at the end of it all, one of the four chosen for our first flight since 1988 was Lili. The token civilian, pulled from the masses to prove the charges of nepotism wrong. Lili was nobody but was brilliant, hard-working. When we were little, she drew countless pictures of rockets, stars, planets of her own invention. She went through black crayons at alarming rates, painting the sky.

Forty-four days to launch.

Eighteen new patients have been reported in quarantined Vuzlevo this week, and now concerns have surfaced about the health of prospective cosmonaut Liliana Dancheva. Dancheva, a native of Vuzlevo, claims she has not returned home since late September, three months before the outbreak began at Christmas, but this has not allayed fears that she may still be a carrier of the unknown disease. If she is allowed to launch with the rest of her team on the twenty-fourth of February, Dancheva will become the first Bulgarian woman in space.

A panel of hastily fabricated specialists took the stage, debating possible scenarios. The anchor said they had reached out to Lili for comment, but had received none. In an e-release, the BNCA politely told the press to go fuck themselves.

I half-listened while I set the moka to brew. I took Baba her porridge and coffee, helped her stretch two pairs of wool socks over the cold hams of her feet. That morning she thought I was my aunt.

Have you studied for your history exam?

I assured her I had. I got the fire going and settled her in front of it. Books sat within arm's reach on the table beside her, but I have no idea if she ever read from them when I was gone. When Uncle Lyupcho came, she told me, they sometimes played cards.

I have to go to work, Baba.

I kissed her cheek and pulled the blanket tighter over her shoulders.

Do your best on the exam, she said, and I promised her I would.

The young man brought his mother back. At the front door, a security guard in a rubber suit distributed masks. The paper crinkled as she breathed, eyes fixed on a point none of us could see.

She's worse, her son insisted.

The doctors examined her, interviewed the son at length.

It just kept happening, he said. Some days she was almost normal, like she was learning the things she'd forgotten, and then—

He'd found her walking down the middle of the street in her bathrobe and one bedroom slipper, her other foot red with the cold, a rusted nail in her heel.

More tests.

We have to send them out, the doctor explained. It might take a while. With the roadblocks.

They gave the woman a tetanus shot and sent her home with extra masks for her son.

At the end of January, the paper reported on the story of a six-year-old girl who got lost in the woods chasing after her dog. Her father forgot to look for her until a stranger found her coat tangled in a bush. He knew where to take it from the name and address stitched into the pocket. When he returned it, the father burst into tears, holding the coat to his nose. The house behind him was piled with half-cleaned dishes, clothes sorted for the laundry and then abandoned. The girl's body was found in the woods with a broken ankle, two weeks dead, muddy-gray and chewed by wolves.

I thought I'd dreamed her, the father said.

The next two columns in the paper were blank, as though the editors forgot to fill them with print, and the printers forgot to ask. The next day, there would be no new paper, nor the day after, nor the day after that.

I was the only receptionist still coming to work, but more and more, patients were missing appointments. By then, they were mostly brought by motorists after traffic accidents. Slow days, when I did old crosswords to check my memory and sent Lili optimistic dispatches from my desk. *We're seeing fewer cases now; I think it may all be over soon. How are your preparations? Only one month to go!*

Outside, orphaned pets dug through the trash by the sides of the roads. Thieves walked calmly in and out of houses that owners had forgotten to lock. People wandered, staring into the sky. The mayor's office reminded us to carry identification at all times, just in case. So that if we forgot where we belonged, we could be returned to our homes like lost books. A city van patrolled the streets, collecting the sick before they froze, depositing them in the closed high school, a makeshift human kennel. Grocery stores swept bare; no deliveries made since before Christmas. Official estimates: one half of all Vuzlevo had forgotten something of Importance.

Twenty-nine days to launch.

One night Baba and I watched a documentary about the rocket. It was called *Sudba 1: Nova Bulgarska Nadejda.* Inspirational swelling music, slow-panning shots of the construction, clipped interviews with the chosen cosmonauts talking about their hopes for our national future.

Lili came up, first in uniform, a space helmet under her arm, and then just her voice, overlaid with photographs of us as children, pictures of her family, posing with her dog.

What a nice-looking girl, Baba said. I wonder where she's from.

So you can see how sometimes, I could forget any of it was strange.

* * *

The market emptied quickly. Someone left the heat lamps on. The thick plastic winter sheets obscured the stalls like ghosts in a mirror. Inside, some merchants had posted signs. For asparagus, visit this address. Thanks to forgetful thieves, cucumbers are available only at this house. Or, from the import farmers, *Sorry, no oranges—roads closed*. At the foot of one stall a caved-in cantaloupe rocked in the wind, leaking seeds and a line of black ants onto the concrete.

Sudjuk for dinner! I told grandmother when I served her plate of cured meat and crackers, as though it were exciting. She was clearer that night. I told her I was scared and she patted my hand. We pressed our fingers into the plates to gather the crumbs.

When the first case outside of Vuzlevo was reported, the cosmonauts were moved into a security complex somewhere underground, though they were still a hundred kilometers away. We watched mass panic in the streets. A man was beaten to death in Krivograd for asking directions after he lost his mobile phone. Everybody wore masks. Somehow we'd been so quiet in Vuzlevo, watching it unfold.

It was nineteen days to launch. The news cut the footage from re-runs, but the video was all over the Internet by then. A protester in Varna was giving a speech on the steps of city hall, a picket sign in one hand and a megaphone in the other. People cheered around him, waving banners made of bed sheets.

Close-up on the man and his magnified voicebox: *Forget your glory—the rest of us have to live here.*

And then he stopped, swayed, and gave a soft mechanical gurgle through the throat of the megaphone. His eyes lost focus and he lowered the horn. Cameras rolled on as he looked for someone to hand it to.

Sorry, did you need this?

The news mics caught the collective intake of breath from the crowd. People lifted scarves and shirts to cover their faces, stumbling back like pigeons, while the police stepped in closer, raising their batons.

There's a word I keep thinking of today, one that I can't remember. Today it consumes me. Something for the brightness of the day, for the cold whiteness of sun without leaves on the trees. The pale wash of the concrete, color leached from the chipping ceramics of the roofs. I sit at my desk with a pen poised over paper, waiting for the word to come. Or waiting for the phone to ring or for the door to open, for there to be work today. Instead there is the buzzing of the lights overhead, the squinting grayness of the sky.

You are going there, I think to Lili, through that shell. You're going so soon.

Sudba 1, they called the rocket. The name was announced last year, along with the names of those cosmonauts selected to go. *Sudba*—destiny. Calculated propaganda, Baba said cheerfully, on a day when she remembered her own childhood in this country. But remarkable, she agreed, looking up. Remarkable nonetheless.

Sometimes I imagine that Baba will be the only one of us left with any memory at all. Walking down the street, I see more doors hanging open. The school windows glow in the dark. The roads are still blocked, though there hardly seems to be a point anymore. They have traced the Varna case to a man who wandered through the woods and onto an unguarded road, who was picked up by a driver heading north. The driver was the protester's uncle. Later, from behind quarantine glass, the motorist told the press: I asked him where he was going and he asked where there was to go.

Some days, Baba still remembers her life in sharp detail. Somewhere, she is intact. The rest of us are losing pieces once and for all. I imagine one day she will wake, lucid, to a town of empty people. She will bundle herself in a winter coat and step outside for the first time in months. She will walk among the ghosts and realize she is alone, and the only thing she will not know is where she's been for the change.

Before I go to sleep, I move the rest of our pantry into Baba's room, within easy reach.

One day to launch. Lili calls me and I can hear the smile straining her mouth over the phone.

I can't believe it, she says, over and over. I can't believe it's tomorrow. Is it bad to be so excited? So many things are happening *here*.

I assure her that it isn't.

In case anything happens while I'm gone—

Nothing will happen, I say. You'll be back in a few weeks. Don't worry.

Okay. Okay. I have to go. I need to call Mama before I leave. I love you.

I love you, too, I say. Have a good trip.

We hang up. I can't remember where she's going, but I think it's far.

INARA VERZEMNIEKS

■

Homer Dill's Undead

FROM *The Iowa Review*

THAT HE LOVED THE BIRDS cannot be disputed. His notes, detailed, thorough, are deeply admiring of their habits, which he came to know over the course of six brief weeks when he lived in their company on a tiny coral-sand island. There are the shearwaters "moaning in their burrows, the little wingless rail skulking from one grass tussock to another, the saucy finch." The white-breasted petrel, "a fearless, dove-like creature, quite amenable to petting and stroking." And the albatross. When excited, it emits a sound "like the neighing of horses." He has watched them closely, memorized their movements and mannerisms, recorded their particulars until he knows them by heart, all so that when he does what must come next—when, one by one, he catches them, and gently snuffs the life from them with his hands, then holds a blade to their warm feathered bellies and carefully slits the skin, pulling it away from the meat—he may one day bring them back to life.

At one time, everyone seemed to know his name and what he had done. The National Audubon Society invited him to address its members at a New York convention. Ornithological journals solicited his writings on the mating and nesting habits of the albatross and the *Fregata aquila*. The local papers turned his work into headlines: "One of the greatest accomplishments of modern science!" Today, all that remains of him can be found on the fourth floor of Macbride Hall on the University of Iowa campus, where a vast natural history collection, first opened in 1858, is now preserved for public display: rooms of stuffed walruses and rhinoceroses, otter and egret, elk and wolves. But also: jars of snakes and crawfish and leeches kept behind bolted blast doors, should the alcohol that pickles them ever ignite; cupboards that when opened reveal a company of wild turkeys and a single albino raccoon; drawer after drawer stuffed with the skins of songbirds, their eyes stitched shut; and a polar bear, eyes open, shrouded in plastic sheeting, too big to fit in the building's service elevator.

His achievement is located between displays of cranes of the South Dakota prairie and the yellow-rumped warblers and song sparrows of Iowa, a mahogany-paneled alcove with lettering above the door that says "Laysan Island Cyclorama, 1914." Walk through the narrow doorway, up the small ramp and onto a platform, where you'll find yourself in the center of a rectangular-shaped enclosure. Glass walls surround all sides of you, save the way you entered, so that the effect is perhaps what it would feel like to stand inside the letter C, its back flattened straight.

Behind the glass, a sandy beach filled with taxidermied birds. Dozens of birds—birds caught mid-wing, mid-preen, mid-skittering step. They stare down their beaks at you, challenge you with unblinking eyes. As you pace the edges of the platform, you are meant to feel as though you are tracing the shores of an island, a mural of waves crashing behind you, stuffed petrels peering out from the crags of cast rock. Before you is the suggestion of a massive rookery, nests balanced on tufts of bunch grass, awkward-looking albatross chicks, hunched, unfledged, the mural continuing its wrap-around illusion of hundreds, thousands more in the painted distance. Speakers above you play an endless loop of courting songs.

This is so unlike all the other displays in the museum. It clearly wants you to enter a scene, not just observe it, but be a part of it, to feel as though you have been transported to this white-sand island. You can feel the ambition of it, even if it comes off a little sad by today's standards: experience eviscerated, preserved, and staged behind glass, the birds' feathers coated in a fine dust, the sand worn in patches, the mural peeling at its corners. Still, someone tried desperately here with all the skills they possessed to evoke a moment in time that people hundreds of years and hundreds of miles removed could enter again and again. There is something poignant about that impulse, but also something a little strange: what is it about this rendered scene that demanded such obsessive attention by its maker, made him so certain that this place begged our endless return?

Homer Dill, says a sign.

This is his creation. And this is also his legacy: this curious alcove full of forever birds, as obscure as it is enduring.

What do we say when someone is beyond our grasp, a little peculiar? We call him an odd bird.

And yet, odd birds are also cause for wonder.

There is startlingly little to work with for a man who made immortality his business. One thin folder in the university archives containing only some correspondence regarding his appointments and promotions. A handful of files in the natural history museum's collection, clippings mostly from a scrapbook maintained by his first wife, who died in 1934 (*widower,* it is noted in spidery hand in the university's ancient personnel notes). The pages are as yellowed and brittle as dried leaves, and they crumble at the touch of a hand, each attempt to know him and what moved him to create that display of birds another assault on his fragile record.

The file contains inexplicable things: poems on love and faith; a list of the seven wonders of the world, ancient and modern; advice on how to kill flies; a black-and-white photograph of an open window snipped from the newspaper. But gradually, among the articles and old photocopied speeches and letters and papers ("Mounting Large Animals Without Opening Cuts in the Legs"), the spine of a story emerges.

And it begins on Laysan, a small isolated island in the Hawaiian archipelago, and one of the world's largest bird colonies.

In 1902, a ship called the U.S.S. *Albatross* drops anchor offshore, in an official government expedition. Among those on board is the curator of Iowa's natural history museum, a man named Charles Nutting, who is serving temporarily as a member of the ship's civilian scientific staff. Nutting is a bold man, a dreamer, who has big ambitions for his museum back in Iowa, which, like so many natural history museums around the world, has come of age in the late nineteenth century as the full inheritance of the Industrial Revolution becomes clear. People look for places to rest black lungs and imagine greener spaces, to commune with the furred, the fanged, the fragile and mysterious. They had been told that they would find wonder in the machine, but instead, at least on their days off, they crave a world without spinning jennies or blast furnaces or steam engines. The natural history museums, with their collections of strange, stuffed beasts, give them permission, however briefly, to imagine themselves in another, wilder, reality.

Nutting wants to lure these crowds because, smart man that he is, he knows that the higher the museum's profile, the more support for its research. He launches expeditions to such far-flung locations as the Arctic, the Dry Tortugas, and the Bay of Fundy in search of new marvels.

Then he arrives on Laysan. And although he has travelled around the world, from the rain forests of Costa Rica to the beaches of the Bahamas, he has never been so struck as he is when he steps off onto Laysan's shore and finds himself surrounded by eight million birds—birds covering every inch of the island's three-and-a-half square miles, the air so thick with their wings that the sky above him is nearly blotted out. "Try as we may, this scene can not be described," Nutting writes in the alumni magazine upon his return to Iowa. "And as day after day the wonder of it grew and deepened, the writer found [himself] constantly recurring and intensifying the great desire to have it reproduced as a masterpiece of art for the benefit of the . . . University and the people of Iowa."

He becomes possessed by this memory, imagines that if only he could find a way to re-create the brush of wings that he experienced on Laysan in an exhibit, he just might secure his university's place as home to one of the finest natural history museums in the world.

He carries the idea with him for years, until one day he hears of a concept kicking around the museum world: the cyclorama. Or, as Nutting describes it, in an appeal for money from Iowa alums and students, an exhibit "where the observer gazes upon hundreds of thousands of men and miles of space, a veritable miracle of vast numbers in intense action, the actual figures in the foreground so skillfully joined to the painted background as to deceive the very elect."

Actually, the cyclorama is a space—a room, an enclosure—designed so that those who enter experience a 360-degree panoramic view. A landscape perhaps, an epic historical moment. It is the invention of an Irishman named Robert Barker, who is said to have climbed a hill in Edinburgh in the late 1700s, gazed out over the city all around him, and decided to re-create the sensation through painted murals hung in the round. Barker's fairly simple idea takes hold, and around the world, people craft cycloramas of battle scenes and waterfalls and trans-Siberian railroads, grand, exotic moments and places that people might imagine being teleported to for a time.

But as far as Iowa's curator knows, no one has tried to build a cyclorama using taxidermies of animals. This is how he will bring Laysan to Iowa. This is how he will make his museum among the world's most famous. He sends letters to the U.S. government asking for access to the island, now a federal wildlife refuge. He tells the student paper that the cyclorama will make Iowa "the mecca of scientific men for years to come." And he seems to genuinely believe it. All he needs is a man capable of carrying out his vision.

Homer Dill. Did you think we had forgotten about him?

Without Homer Dill, there could be no story.

From the yellowed newspaper clippings we learn that he arrived in Iowa in 1906, hired by the museum "after winning a high reputation in the East." Dill is a naturalist who also happens to be a highly trained taxidermist; a skilled observer who understands each species, its behaviors and movements and physiology, but also, master of a skill that falls somewhere between butcher, tanner, upholsterer, artist, and resurrectionist—a man able to wield a gun and a knife, gut and skin, administer the proper potions, capture the still life, sew the perfect, binding stitch. Dill does not stuff animals. He transforms them.

Shall we transform him, then, back into a child, roaming the docks of Gardiner, Maine, where ships from ports around the world anchored then, and trading those ships' sailors "snitched cookies, boiled eggs, and apples for lizard skins, feathers, and whales' teeth." When he is about ten, a friend lends him a copy of *Practical Taxidermy and Home Decoration; Together with Practical Information for*

Sportsmen by Joseph H. Batty. As he recalls years later, "From then on, I mounted everything I could get my hands on."

His first is a bird: a saw-whet owl, a tiny, downy thing with piercing, saucer-shaped eyes.

Local hunters approach him to preserve their kills, and before long, he has built a flourishing taxidermy business while still a teenager. He goes through the motions in high school, but can "think of nothing else but taxidermy." We can only imagine what his classmates must have thought of him, this brooding boy, his own saucer eyes hidden behind spectacles, always hurrying away as soon as the bell rang to spend his free time forearm-deep in the belly of an elk, dropping guts in buckets. His parents, for their part, are "concerned," beg him to consider engineering.

Instead he writes to William Temple Hornaday, director of the New York Zoological Park and one of the most famous naturalist-taxidermists of his generation. Hornaday is clearly impressed because he invites the teenager to come apprentice with him in New York. For the next two years, Dill spends his days making plaster casts of dead jaguars, monkeys, and manatees. At night, he studies drawing at the Pratt Institute of Art. When Hornaday needs someone to mount his own personal collection of animals, or the big-game trophies of his famous friends, such as Teddy Roosevelt, he turns to Dill, Dill who will later give his first son the middle name of Hornaday, in honor of his mentor.

Dill returns to Maine, where he becomes the state taxidermist, and where his greatest achievement seems to have been the transformation of Wapiti, "a great male elk," who "died in the zoo at the Soldiers' Home." His ambition strains. "It is not technique and method that makes a taxidermist superior," he will write, many years later, "but rather, a God-given gift of keen insight and a feeling for outline and form as nature has given it to our wild creatures."

He begins to send out his CV.

One reaches Nutting, a thousand miles away in Iowa, who just happens to be looking for a new head taxidermist. Out of twenty-four applicants, he chooses Dill, who accepts with a letter signed "Your obedient servant."

It is not clear when Nutting first broaches the idea of the cyclorama, but he must have been watching Dill closely, weighing whether he was worthy of the vision. He watches as Dill sets about transforming tired exhibits—the warthog heads staring blankly from mahogany plaques, the kangaroos with sad skins manged by time, the owls that listlessly grip boring brass T-bars; watches as he banishes bottles of pickled things, groups displays according to habitat, trains students in his newly launched laboratory of "Taxidermy and Plastic Art."

Art. That's the key word for Dill.

He insists that taxidermy, conceived of and displayed as art, "can reach where books seldom go to the improving of men's minds and helping them to higher conceptions and new appreciations of nature and her manifold and marvelous worlds."

At last, convinced, Nutting approaches him about transforming the birds of Laysan into art.

Dill—*Your obedient servant*—Dill, with his dreams of helping man to higher conceptions—Dill, who can still recall the saw-whet owl in his hands—of course, he accepts.

Letters fly back and forth between Nutting and the U.S. government, negotiating access to Laysan. Supply lists are drawn up (sugar, rice, tapioca, dried cod, beef tongue, aspirin . . .). Finally, on April 5, 1911, Dill, along with a landscape artist from the Field Museum in Chicago, who will paint the twelve-foot-high, 138-foot-long backdrop of the cyclorama, and two of Dill's zoology students who will assist in the collecting and skinning of samples, set off from San Francisco aboard the U.S. cutter ship *Thetis*. Thetis, the mother who, in Greek myth, tries in vain to make her son immortal.

From Dill's account of the mission: "About 11 o'clock on the seventh day, the island was sighted. We expected to see clouds of birds about it, but in this we were disappointed."

Sometimes there is no bridging the distance between what we imagine we are prepared for and what we must discover on our own. The pristine, untouched island of Nutting's memories—the cyclorama's inspiration—no longer exists. Feather hunters in search of plumes to adorn ladies hats have discovered Laysan, too. Over the past few years, they have slaughtered hundreds of thousands of birds — sometimes hacking off wings while the birds are still alive, because the hemorrhaging makes the feathers easier to pluck. By one estimate, perhaps ninety percent of the island's original bird population is gone.

Dill and his group land on a beach that is littered with rotting carcasses, "bones bleaching in the sun." They find clubs and nets, swarms of flies, more flies than Dill has ever seen. In an old shed, thousands of rotting wings, stacked until they have touched the rafters and then burst through wooden walls with their cascading weight.

There are also rabbits, thousands of rabbits, racing across the soft white sand on their padded feet, burrowing among the albatross and tern nests, devouring the juncus and other grasses and bushes that provide valuable bird habitat, "their bodies concealed among the thick growth, [so that] only their ears show. At times there are so many ears protruding, they resemble a vegetable garden."

The rabbits are all that is left of a German immigrant who had come to Laysan to make his fortune mining the island's thick deposits of guano. Concerned about how to feed his operation, he decided he could bring rabbits, let them breed, then can their meat — Belgian hares and English hares "that have crossed and produced some strange-looking animals, both in form and color," according to Dill. Unchecked, with no natural predators, they are steadily taking over.

Poor Dill. One of the things he has prided himself on is how faithfully he has always tried to re-create what he finds in nature. He thinks of it almost as a calling — "to see things as they are and render them faithfully."

And so he does his best to collect what he can of the Laysan that he finds: the bristle-thighed curlews, who "come up around our camp uttering their peculiar complaining note," the wandering tattlers who hide among the reefs, the turnstones who spend "most of their time feeding on the small flies with which the shore and the water are black." He urges the group to collect dead birds if they can find them, but still, the scope of this project demands so many specimens they must kill hundreds. Later, he will tell the student paper, "We skinned birds from morning to night."

He brings home thirty-six large crates filled with the bodies of nearly three hundred birds, eggs, nests, Laysan sand, casts of the island's leaves and branches, photographs, pages of notes and sketches. And then he begins the meticulous, painstaking work of rebuilding Laysan in a corner of Macbride Hall, a process that will ultimately take three years.

When the cyclorama finally opens to the public in 1914, it is exactly as Nutting had intended, the rush of silent wings all around, an invitation to step into a kind of stilled documentary, to "visit" Laysan and its birds without ever leaving the state of Iowa. But it is not a Laysan that exists anymore. In some ways it is a Laysan that never existed, a memory of a memory of a memory, which was already vanishing before Dill even started his work. In fact, three of the species of birds Dill collected will be named extinct before his cyclorama even opens.

Today, the concept of the cyclorama itself is endangered, abandoned long ago to more truly interactive experiences, moving pictures and computerized displays. Iowa's Laysan exhibit is one of the few remaining natural history cycloramas in the United States. Most people arrive here by accident, suddenly cast ashore on Dill's forever island. But the longer we stare at it, the more unsettling its unwavering beauty becomes, perhaps because on some level we sense that it is a record, not of what is, or ever was, but what we wish, against all evidence, could be.

And yet what if he had spent those three years in his laboratory giving form to the nightmare landscape he discovered, stretching its ugly skin around the facts that none of us are eager to consider — that this is what our presence really looks like in the natural world, the buzz and hum of our competing desires, converging, swarming, until all that is left is a pile of feathers, dried blood on the sand.

Would that have changed him, stopped him from snipping from the newspaper tips on how to kill flies (could he still hear them, buzzing still, back on Laysan)? After years of faithfully noting he was a Unitarian in his university personnel files, would he have kept filling in that line, rather than abruptly leaving it blank? Was it just an unfortunate coincidence that a pamphlet printed to celebrate an anniversary of the cyclorama declares that it was "Composed and Executed by Professor Homer R. Dill"?

How to admit that maybe what we imagined to be a feel for outline and form as nature has given it to our wild creatures really means that we are good at skinning dead things.

Then again, perhaps the vision of Laysan he left for us—unspoiled, untouched—was the only way he could see it, and the only way he wished all of us to see it, too. Maybe, in the end, there is really more truth in his lie. Because when we all are nothing more than a few crumbling papers in a forgotten file, the birds will go on moaning and skittering in the more perfect world he made for them. And how many times do you have to visit, held back by the glass, before you realize it is a world entirely without us. A world wiped clean of our presence. As if we were never here.

KYLE BOELTE

■

Reluctant Citizens

FROM ZYZZYVA

WE ARE RELUCTANT citizens, the twelve of us—fifteen if you count the three alternates—sitting in the wood-paneled box on the side of the windowless courtroom in San Francisco. Already we are staring out into the distance, straining to stay awake, as the judge reads us his opening instructions. It is the first day of the trial.

Yesterday, we arrived in the basement jury intake room and began the waiting that would last a day and a half, and that was only the beginning.

Those potential jurors who were loud or outspoken were dismissed. Near the end of jury selection, as the pool shrank, the potential jurors became louder, more outspoken. Several told the judge outright that they were biased, that they could not be fair.

There were two people I spoke to yesterday who would have gladly served, both retired and seemingly looking forward to something to do for three or four weeks. But they were both dismissed during jury selection. It was not altogether clear why.

And so here we are, the ones who didn't make a fuss, resigned to be here, to do our duty. (We joke with one another that next time we too will be brash, and loud, and outspoken, though I'm not sure any of us could follow through on it.)

As the attorneys' opening statements begin, we slip into our roles, and try to stay awake, as we listen to the details of an on-the-job accident that happened more than six years ago.

* * *

"Has it only been forty-five minutes?" the juror in front of me asks, on Monday, when the judge gives us our first break during the witness phase of the trial. "I'm not sure I can make it if it's only been forty-five minutes," she says. We all smile, let out a long exhale. There are three weeks of witnesses scheduled.

Weeks of witnesses testifying about a construction site, about the proper way to climb and descend ladders, about medical diagnoses, about surgeries, about insurance payments. Large binders full of documents rest on the tables before the Plaintiffs' attorneys and the Defendant's attorney. They are full of contracts and photocopied pages from safety manuals and medical reports. The case is an endless stream of details.

As far as I can tell, the case rests on whether or not a construction company doing demolition in an old hospital building should have filled in shallow holes they had created in the floor. (The Defendant says the company only does demolition, not construction; the Plaintiff maintains the holes were a hazard and should have been filled in.)

An electrician working for a different company was descending a ladder one day six years ago and stepped onto the lip of one of the holes (the sides do not agree on the use of the word "hole" — the Plaintiff uses the term while the Defendant, if it refers to them at all, calls them "depressions" or "the different elevations of the floor").

When the electrician's foot landed on the lip of the hole (or depression), he twisted his back. The balance of the case rests on whether we, the jury, think the first company is at fault for the man's twisting and subsequent injuries.

During breaks, we all grab our phones to check the time and scroll through emails. Our attention spans are shot, killed long ago by our many screens. We lean in to whisper to one another. How we are dying of boredom. How the monotony of the proceedings is driving us crazy.

The Plaintiff has just been telling us about the pain he is in. About how he does nothing all day. How he watches TV until he is bored, and then lies down, and then gets up to walk around, and then lies down again. He can read only a few pages in a book before he is overwhelmed by headaches.

PLAINTIFF'S ATTORNEY: Can you describe your life, at present?
PLAINTIFF: I don't do anything. I have no life. I just exist.

It is tempting to see the Plaintiff's situation as a metaphor for the American working class. His injury occurred in 2007, just as the real estate and construction industries were teetering on the verge of collapse. He's white, has an eighth-grade education. Beyond that, his only schooling was a four-year apprenticeship when he was young. He has no savings.

He worked as an electrician for forty years, before the accident. He was a union man. He lives in an outer suburb of San Francisco, in a trailer park, but was injured six years ago working on a big project in the city. Now he is without work. Has not worked in six years. According to his lawyers, he will never work again.

It's tricky business, this, making metaphors of men. San Francisco is in the midst of a real estate boom. Prices are climbing ever higher, meeting and eclipsing pre-crash levels. Construction projects are going up throughout the city: lofts, condos, bars, restaurants. Construction jobs are coming back.

The members of the jury are mostly professionals. A chief executive officer, a chief operating officer, a few tech workers, a corporate attorney (mergers and acquisitions at a tech company), a research physicist, several nurses, a jeweler, a student. All educated. Six men, six women. Four people of color. (The three alternates are men, one Asian-American, one an immigrant from France.) One member of the jury and one alternate are gay.

At breaks, the physicist takes out his iPad and scrolls through its pages as he walks around the building's outer hallway. A tech worker takes out his MacBook Pro and sends emails. "Pretending to work," he tells me.

Each morning we discuss if and when the parties might settle, and when we might be released. Employers are nervous about lost productivity. We've been told the trial will last three and a half weeks.

One morning, the judge instructs us to strike from the record the Plaintiff's testimony that he cannot afford health insurance. We are told that we are to forget this information. To pretend that we never heard it.

I come to like my fellow members of the jury. I would be happy to have them on a jury if I ever were in the Plaintiffs' or Defendant's positions. Though they do not want to be here, I sense they want to do the right thing.

It occurs to me one day that the people of this country are like the members of this jury: we want to do the right thing.

And yet, we do not want to be here. We do not like how time-consuming voting is; we would rather play a game on our phone than read the news; we would rather focus on our own lives than the lives of others. We have internalized the mantra of *The Individual*. We are forever turning inward, into our own concerns.

It occurs to me—though I'm not sure I'm comforted by the thought—that we are creating our democracy, even as we inherit it.

The judge tells us we will not have court the next afternoon. "The attorneys in this case will not be available for trial," the judge informs us. "They will be meeting tomorrow afternoon, and their meeting may affect the length of this trial." We secretly discuss our wishes that the meeting will lead to a settlement, the end of the trial.

The morning after our free afternoon, the judge arrives, the clerk introduces the case, and the judge asks the Plaintiff for the next witness. He does not mention the previous afternoon's negotiations.

The injured man is not the only Plaintiff in the case. His attorney is joined at the Plaintiffs' table by an attorney representing the worker's compensation insurance company that has paid almost half a million dollars for the injured man's medical bills and disability payments. The insurance company is here to recoup what it paid to the injured man. One company is suing another company. We were told during the judge's opening instructions to treat the insurance company as if it were a person.

* * *

Each day, the clerk introduces the case to the judge. He reads the name of the case as [Injured Man's Name] vs. [General Contractor's Name].

Halfway through the second week, one of the members of the jury slips a piece of paper to the clerk with a question on it: why is the general contractor's name part of the name of the case, when it is a subcontractor, not the general contractor, that is being sued?

When we come back from break the judge calls the attorneys into his chambers for a sidebar. When they return, the judge explains to the jury that the case will, from now on, be known as [Injured Man's Name] and [Worker's Compensation Insurance Company Name] vs. [Subcontractor's Name]. The previous name, we are told, was the name of the case when it initially showed up in court.

There is a murmuring in the jury box.

For two days the attorney for the insurance company has been mentioning a Dr. Bathgate whenever he can. He has been trying to get witnesses to describe a report written by Dr. Bathgate. Whenever he does this the attorney for the Defendant objects.

"Objection. Hearsay," he says.

And every time the judge agrees.

"Sustained," he says, over and over.

Who is Dr. Bathgate?

"What day is it?" asks one of the jurors who sits in front of me, right before court begins, in the middle of the week, in the middle of the trial.

Today, when cross-examining a witness who works for the insurance company, the attorney for the Defendant mentions Dr. Bathgate. Behind him, the insurance company's attorney raises his eyebrows.

A few moments later, the attorney for the insurance company stands to re-question ("redirect") the witness. He asks about Dr. Bathgate's report.

"Objection. Hearsay."

"Sustained."

The attorney for the insurance company claims that the attorney for the Defendant has opened the door to such questions. He tries a second time, and then a third, and then a fourth, and on.

"Objection. Hearsay."

"Sustained."

We hear this continually, all afternoon. Though the objections will soon get old, there's tension in the room right now and the jurors are focused on the witness up on the stand.

When the day is over, and we are walking down the hallway to the elevator, we are as lively as we've been since the trial began.

"It's nice to have a little action," one of the jurors says. "It kept me awake, at least."

I can only imagine that the Plaintiffs' attorneys have spent months planning the logic of this trial. Still, it all seems disjointed, haphazard, unplanned.

Witnesses are called, and there is little connection between one and the next.

Questions asked of individual witnesses switch quickly from the present to the accident six years ago, to the witnesses' deposition, which may have been given a few months or several years ago, then back to the present.

My juror notebook jumps around from one bit of information to another.

It gradually becomes clear that Dr. Bathgate has not given a deposition and will not testify in court.

Several safety experts testify, and they read regulations and codes to us. There is nothing less lively in a courtroom than witnesses reading regulations and code out loud.

The attorneys argue about the meaning of a "walkway," about the meaning of a "hole." According to federal regulations read by one of the experts, a hole must be at least two inches deep (or, more technically, two inches "in its least dimension").

Sworn testimony by the witnesses in the case describes the hole (if it is a hole) that the injured man stepped onto the lip of as, variously, half an inch to three quarters of an inch deep; one inch to two inches deep; and two inches to three inches deep. The only witness who testifies that the hole was deeper than two inches is the injured man.

The court's rules are built on Enlightenment notions of rationality. When the judge strikes something from the record we are directed to forget it entirely as if we are machines. When we listen to testimony, we are to consider the evidence alone. We are directed not to draw conclusions until all the evidence has been given. After three weeks of evidence, when we are allowed to draw conclusions, we are to put our biases aside.

The attorneys know that we are humans, not machines. They ask leading questions to try to elicit answers from witnesses before an objection can be voiced. They direct witnesses to share information that the judge will later rule is inadmissible. They argue when they are not allowed to argue. They tell jokes. They try to win our sympathy.

And it works. We start to take sides.

I had a cup of tea before court began at nine. Now, at ten thirty, I need to go to the restroom. I'm having trouble concentrating on the witness's answers.

The attorney for the insurance company is asking a witness about the worksite.

"I don't really recall," the witness keeps saying. "It was six years ago . . ."

The case does not seem to be getting anywhere, and I'm not sure what, if anything, we've learned from this witness. At this moment I don't really care much. I'm feeling very much trapped in this animal body, and though I'm trying to concentrate on the testimony, I just want the morning break to come so I can go take a piss.

Most days, I watch the lawyers and paralegals watching us in the jury box. I imagine they are trying to decipher our opinions in the case by gauging our reactions to the witnesses' testimony. They watch us, and they take notes on their laptops. During breaks, they casually listen to our banter while they organize papers.

"I bet there is a whole world going on in front of us, and we can't see it because we don't know how this works," the juror in front of me says during a break.

Two experts testify about the site of the accident and whether signs would have prevented the injury. The expert retained by the Plaintiffs has experience with the construction industry, while the one retained by the Defendant has experience in academia and research. The first has a master's degree in psychology; the second has a PhD in psychology, from Stanford.

The first expert is a middle-aged woman on retainer by the Plaintiffs' attorneys. The second is a thirty-something woman on retainer by the Defendant. The Plaintiffs' expert is homely; the Defendant's expert is good looking, maybe beautiful: slender, long brown hair, a fitted suit.

If I admit that I'm more persuaded by the second woman, will you believe me when I tell you that her testimony was more convincing?

I am becoming fixated on the attorney for one of the Plaintiffs. Every day, he rolls his eyes when he doesn't get his way. He bullies the Defendant's witnesses.

We are admonished every day not to "form or express an opinion," and at this I am failing daily. Though I am not making any final conclusions, each time I see and hear this attorney speak, I am pushed ever closer to a final conclusion.

A new witness for the Defendant tells us that the two inches in the "least dimension" in the definition of a "hole" refers horizontally, not vertically. A "hole" is between two and eighteen inches wide, he explains to us. Anything larger than eighteen inches wide is a "floor opening."

The Defendant's attorney projects a copy of the federal code up on the wall while the witness tells us a "hole" needs to be at least six feet deep to be a hole. Same for a "floor opening." Six feet.

DEFENDANT'S ATTORNEY: So were these irregularities in the floor "holes"?
WITNESS: No, sir.

DEFENDANT'S ATTORNEY: And were they "floor openings"?
WITNESS: No, sir.

We are told the irregularities were "edges."

The injured man's wife is a witness. She takes the stand first thing one morning, and her testimony lasts only five minutes. Halfway through it, when asked to describe the injured man's daily schedule, she bursts into tears. She cries on and off as she gives answers to the injured man's attorney. It is the first time during the trial that we see any outward emotion. For five minutes, we are reminded that we are dealing with human events, human lives, and not just charts and numbers and expert opinions on the correct use of ladders.

And then we return to another safety expert, and the trial goes on as before.

On the last day of witness testimony, the Defendant's attorney calls an orthopedic surgeon to the stand. His CV indicates that he may be one of the top orthopedic surgeons in the country, maybe the world.

The surgeon says that some of the medical problems that the injured man sustained in the past six years were caused by the accident in question, and some were long-term degenerative problems not caused by the accident. The witness does not try to say more than he is asked, as other witnesses have. He does not try to argue a side, as other witnesses have.

Under cross-examination we learn that the surgeon lives in Orange County, that the Defendant's attorney has flown him up to San Francisco for the day. We learn that he charges $9,000 a day for his testimony, $4,000 for half a day.

"Isn't it interesting," the injured man's attorney asks him, "how each side can find expert witnesses who can argue for their position?"

During afternoon break the clerk, who is standing by the jury box, is asked by a juror how he can get out of jury service next time. In California, you can be called once every twelve months for jury duty.

"I could do maybe one week a year, but there's no way my employer could handle three weeks, two years in a row," the juror says.

"Well," the clerk tells him, "people are picked from the voter rolls."

"Then I'm going to un-register to vote," says the woman beside me. "I don't like voting anymore, either."

We are told it will take a day for the attorneys to finalize the evidence, so we will not need to return to the courtroom on Friday. We will not have court on Monday, either. We are to return on Tuesday morning, at 9 a.m.

On Friday afternoon, I get a call from the clerk. "It's taking longer than the attorneys had anticipated," he says. "We will start at 1 p.m. on Tuesday."

We return on Tuesday afternoon, ready for it all to be over. We've been standing in the hallway, prior to court, explaining to each other that we all need to get back to work.

The judge tells us that he will read us his instructions, and then we will hear closing arguments.

"This will take all of this afternoon," he tells us. "Hopefully we will be ready to give you the case by late tomorrow morning."

He reads us his instructions for half an hour or more.

During closing arguments, the injured man's attorney says he thinks we should award his client $9 million. He tells us this is like $240 a day for the man's suffering. (His math is off by only $7 million.)

"A pitcher makes $10 million *a year*," his says, by way of explaining the large number, "and he only pitches every fifth night, six months a year." There are many baseball fans on the jury. They've been talking about the Giants during breaks for weeks. Three went to a game this weekend.

The Defendant's attorney begins his closing arguments by focusing on the injured man's neck, and how the neck problem is not related to the initial back injury. He argues for fifteen minutes about this, and I start to think he's given up on the case. Of the almost $300,000 in medical expenses claimed by the insurance company, the neck makes up only $25,000. It's nothing, really, in a case where the plaintiffs are asking $9 million.

The Defendant's attorney argues for two hours. The two Plaintiffs' attorneys each receive forty-five minutes plus rebuttal time.

Eventually, the Defendant's attorney gets to the more substantial elements of the case. I realize that the order is important. If he started by saying that the Defendant was not liable, it would be odd to then switch gears and say, well, if we were liable then we would be liable for only a fraction of what the Plaintiffs are seeking.

After three weeks of jury duty, we seem to be where we started. We are going to have to decide whether a construction company doing demolition in an old hospital building should have filled in shallow "holes" they had created in the floor, or at least put up signs or barricades.

The judge gives us our final instructions, and the bailiff leads us to the room in the back of the building where we will make our deliberations.

We are to answer nine questions. Some of the questions have multiple points. The jury instructions are seventy pages long.

An early vote establishes that we are going to find the Defendant liable for the accident. Nine people vote for liability; three vote against it. Most of the rest of the deliberations concern how much we are to award.

We try to piece together answers to the next eight questions, but it's difficult to find any rational basis for many of the questions. Are we to award past economic earnings based on the injured man's income from the year before the accident, or the two years before, or the three years before? Are we to take into consideration the decline in construction jobs? How do we know the cost of medication, or doctors' office visits? Questions beget more questions as the afternoon goes on.

The majority starts to splinter when it becomes clear that some members are going to try to give the injured man as much as possible in every instance, even when they cannot come up with a rational justification based on the evidence in the case. One juror, who voted for the Plaintiff on the big question, now tries to delicately backstep.

"We should decide if we are going to follow the rules, or not," one juror says during an argument over prescription drugs. One of the nurses has just told us that medical inflation is 6 percent. "If we are going to use outside information, fine," the juror says, "but let's be clear with ourselves that we are not following the rules."

At one point, we ask the judge for help, some context, as we try to figure out what a reasonable Future Medical Expense award might be. The bailiff returns with a note: "It is entirely up to your judgment."

For three weeks, we've been told two conflicting stories about an accident that took place six years ago. Nothing was ever proven, just different opinions offered. As we deliberate, we make up the rules as we go, justifying, rationalizing our gut feelings, until the total award approaches $5 million, then pushes past it.

When we are finished, we head back into the courtroom, and then, our decision entered into the record, our duty done, we head out into San Francisco, citizens making our way home along the crowded sidewalks of our city, as the late afternoon sunlight shines down on us, so bright that we must shade our eyes, lest we be blinded.

MARK HITZ

■

Shadehill

FROM *Glimmer Train*

AT FIRST ALL the mothers were going into town. Then my cousin Jacob wanted to go, so I wanted to go. My uncles wanted to go, my father, my sister. We had arrived unprepared and now needed food by the pound, beer, fishing line, lighter fluid, worms, gasoline, comic books. This would be fun, everyone was going into town. Only my grandfather Ennis stayed behind. He leaned on the cabin porch behind a twisting screen of cigar smoke and watched three generations load into two long, low-slung vehicles, kids crushed in, limbs waving as we coughed across the dusty South Dakota grassland. Bye!

We came back in a laughing, marauding mess, toys and meat and toilet paper coming out of our ears. Ennis lay napping on the sofa. "The War Party," he said into his hat, "has returned with their spoils."

I settled in at the kitchen sink to peel an acre of potatoes for my grandmother. We were fourteen strong, ready to vacation hard, and needed nourishment. I peeled and watched Mary and Jacob in the sideyard dig a hole for some reason, or maybe no reason at all. My grandmother stood beside me mixing the next day's sourdough pancake batter and singing hymns under her breath. Ennis kissed her on the cheek and said, "I got a beaver."

"There's more than one," she said.

"Well then I got one beaver."

"What's all this?" I said, which was something my mother said.

"You'll cut yourself like that," she said. "Hold it like this. You know that nice little lonely tree on the point. They chewed through it, my favorite tree, always struggling out there all alone."

Ardyce was the reluctant keeper of our family cabin. She hated the place. Hated the wind, the dust, the bad water pressure, but believed, correctly, that as long as it was standing and put together, we would converge.

Soon I became aware of a gun on the porch. Wonderful. A gun. My father, who also knew nothing about guns, held it at arm's length like an unearthed artifact, a curious thing of meaning. I excused myself to the bathroom then went directly to the weaponized area, where Ennis was explaining to the men how he'd shot the beaver down by the floating dock, which we could just see from the porch. He'd built the cabin ten years before on a middle plateau, next to a cliff that dropped straight into the water of Shadehill Reservoir, a vast and unaccountably salty lake in northern South Dakota. The cabin sat defiantly beyond the restriction line—he knew the county assessor and liked it better there—but the plateau was unstable, hence the restriction, and every year the cliff receded a few inches, sometimes more than a foot, taking part of the yard with it and threatening to one day swallow the cabin itself. Every summer we had the same conversation about where the cliff's edge was now and where it used to be, how many good years before the cabin fell into the lake.

"Not much to it really," Ennis said. "Filthy things swim around under the dock. Saw him go under there. A second later and he'd still be alive, I'd have never seen him. So I uncorked the Savage and walked over to the edge there so I could get a better look. It paddled on out a minute later."

We all agreed it was a good shot, off a cliff with no scope, aiming at nothing but a wet crest in the water, and moving at that. We passed the loaded gun around and held it to our shoulders, imagined ourselves doing the same thing. There would be more opportunities.

Someone else finished the potatoes and soon everyone was relaxing into our week together, the adults leaning with drink, every nose in the air awaiting dinner and pulling those aromas of my childhood summers, roasted meat and casserole, cigarette smoke and gin. Sleeping quarters were prepared in the cabin, in the travel trailer, in my grandfather's army tent, and on the flat bow of the fishing boat, my favorite, where you could drift under that bright net of Midwestern stars.

Everyone had scattered through the property and down to the water's edge, so my grandmother hobbled around announcing dinner and gathering grandchildren, giving her standard ten-minute warning. Do not come to the table wet, do not come to the table covered in sand, take this time to clean up and comb your hair or you will go hungry, I promise you. Where's Ophelia?

One of the twins. Patsy and Ophelia, both eleven years old. They were quiet girls, languid and milky, with dark hair and deferring eyes. Ophelia had been growing more independent, to Patsy's dismay, and loved to travel in water, prove herself with ever-longer distances, so this was the first thing said: she swam around the point to another beach. It was a stupid thing she'd done before.

The kids spent ten minutes calling her name as far as our feet and voices could reach. Then we came back to the cabin where my uncle Charles was telling a funny story about running out of gas in a single-engine plane and landing it on a restricted runway at Grand Forks Air Force Base, high on an unnamed drug, while Ennis, who should have been the one flying the plane, lay drunk and unconscious in the passenger seat. Everyone but Dale's wife, Belle, had heard it before or was involved, and everyone was captivated. He had perfected it. They all laughed. Ophelia, I said, is missing.

After a brief discussion everyone left the table. My father and Charles and Ennis took the fishing boat to search the shores. My mother and the twins' mother and Ardyce each walked a separate trail to our three nearest neighbors' homes who had children of their own that Ophelia knew, and each came back with neighbors but without Ophelia and the adults all stood around in the yard, half-drunk and floating possibilities, she'll turn up, she'll turn up, the kids staring into the water and whispering, the roast and casserole cold in the kitchen.

"Where did Ophelia go after we came back from town?" said the twins' mother, Anne. This was the first thing I heard her say about it. Two years prior Charles had moved her and the twins from Colorado Springs to nearby Lemmon so he could help Ennis run the family filling station. No one spoke of it, but Ennis had threatened him and made this a condition of his inheritance. Anne did not like this area, did not trust the lake, did not feel part of us, was terrified.

Anyone? Nobody knew.

"Ophelia didn't come to town," Patsy said.

"Sure she did," my mother said.

Patsy shook her head. She was right. The two of them wore summer dresses their mother made two at a time, cut from the same piece of fabric, and because they had been quarrelling and spending more time away from each other, no one in the pandemonium of reunion, in the noise of stories and catching up and horseplay and all of it in two vehicles going back and forth to different ends of town—no one had noticed that there was only one twin, not two. No one except Patsy, and since then Patsy had all along been looking for Ophelia.

We took a breath together. The sun was going down. Ophelia was alone somewhere. The mothers filed into the house to call the police in Lemmon in case we'd left her there, and give a description of Ophelia, which was easy because it was a description of Patsy, standing right in front of them.

Then Walter, our favorite smartass fuck-up uncle and the only unmarried sibling, came out of the equipment shed carrying an old dive mask. He walked to the trail that led to the beach and the boat dock. My father went with him. The rest of us stood at the cliff's edge and looked down on them as they navigated the trail in the draining light and walked to the end of the dock. Walter took off his shoes but did not remove any clothes. This scared me. My mother pulled us close. My grandmother began to pray. We had known all along what was coming, each one of us, and been unable to allow the thought of it. Walter wet the mask in the water and secured it over his long hair, then slipped into the lake and took a deep breath and dove straight down. His feet vanished through an audible ripple in the water. From where we stood we were blind to the subsurface, but my father could see. After a long silence he looked up at us standing in our solemn row and I know if he could he would have stopped time there, and we would still be standing on the edge of that cliff, in the last moment of our careless lives. He opened his mouth as if to speak. Moments later in a shuddering fit of amazement Walter came to shore with Ophelia's pale, lovely body, and covered her poor unmade head with his T-shirt.

The next few hours are lapsed and folded, and I am not sorry that I cannot remember everything. In the few memories I have people move around with no purpose, from here to there and back, the screen door banging, people disappearing into darkness beyond the throw of porch lights. My cousin Jacob, thirteen years old, defecated in his pants and took them off then and there, half naked and sobbing in the yard. We pressed into our mothers' bosoms but could not disappear. At some point I saw someone carrying Patsy's limp body as if she too had been slain. Charles emerged with an axe and began cutting into the elm behind the cabin, a tree we loved, shouting obscenity and cursing Ennis to hell and disavowing his Catholic God. I found my sister Mary sitting in the corner of the utility closet on a pile of shoes and sat down with her and we tied all of the shoes and listened to flooded voices and noises and the shredding of family seams. Before any of us went to bed the sun came up.

My family and Dale's family and Walter took rooms at Lemmon's one motel and over the next three days we knocked on a lot of doors and tried to comfort each other, feed each other, say the right things. My mother spent most of her time with Anne and Patsy, shielding them from the clumsy sympathies of strangers and acquaintances. Anne had begun to faint periodically, almost on the hour, and was visited by a doctor who told her to eat something and drink more water. Patsy refused to change her clothes. We drove between their home and the motel, gathered at my grandparents' house and stared. But my grandfather. Ennis. The police spoke to him that first early morning at the hospital in Hettinger. They were state police in plain clothes who knew him by name, tired men woken from their beds. They also spoke briefly to Anne, Charles, Walter, and my father, did more talking than listening, and then left us alone. I imagined secret maneuverings behind the closed door, some kind of legal vanishing. Afterward Ennis milled about our red-faced gatherings like a mute, as if he were also only a witness to tragedy, as if he had nothing to do with it. He did not speak a word of apology, did not ask forgiveness. This infuriated some of us and especially Charles, who wanted to kill him, and maybe always had. This was not the first time Ennis' hubris and pride had ruined someone, and the brothers began unleashing their worst memories in a brotherly language, in storied code. Not the middle son, Dale, who held close to his own family, but young Walter and Charles, whose daughter was now killed. Hate and drink spilled from their mouths. Everything had come unthawed, and all at the wrong time. It was exactly what we did not need from these men. The morning of the funeral Charles approached Ennis for the first time, took off his own glasses and placed them on Ennis' face. Ennis had refused glasses his entire life, refused dentures, resisted doctors and experts of any kind. He sat there behind the corrected lenses and looked at his eldest son.

"Can you see me now?" Charles said, and they did not speak again in their lives.

Anne did not want to bury her daughter in Lemmon, in a cemetery — as that one is — next to a gun range. She had very little family left herself, but wanted to take Ophelia home to their burial plots in Colorado Springs, where she had lived her entire life and where she and Charles had met and the twins had been born. All of us would have loved her for it, but Charles refused her, insisted Ophelia be buried in the same place he would one day be buried, and Anne was too weak and distant in that moment to resist him.

Ennis did not attend the church services, but when we arrived at the cemetery he was already there, and managed the courage to stand among us. My grandmother hooked her arm into his. It was my first funeral, and for someone I knew, someone in my family, someone my age, and I have nothing else to say about it. Nothing beyond what we all know about funerals. Ophelia, what can I say?

After she was covered in earth none of us went to the reception, a church affair organized by some do-gooding friend of my grandmother's. Instead we all retreated to our quiet rooms, many of us with plans to leave the next day. We were tired and couldn't sleep. We were malnourished and seeing food everywhere. We were alive.

That night my family went to bed at the first possible moment, fleeing the day. I lay awake next to Mary, who had never stopped crying but was now sleeping mercifully, when the phone rang in the room like a schoolbell. We all sat upright and my mother answered, the phone to her ear, one hand to her forehead. It was my grandmother, who told her Ennis wanted to stay at the cabin tonight, and it would be nice if she, my mother, would join him. He was coming to pick her up, she might as well wait downstairs so he doesn't wake the kids. Too late for that, Mom.

Ennis believed in my mother, always wanted to kiss her first, give her the best education, save her the last piece of pie. Sylvia, he would say, is my favorite daughter. She's your only daughter. Exactly.

She put on her jacket over her nightclothes and packed a pair of underwear and a toothbrush, my toothbrush, into her handbag.

"Would you like us to come along?" my father said.

"No, stay with the kids. I'll be back in the morning, it's nothing." She was whispering, which made us lean in, wake up.

"I love you," my father said.

"Of course."

Then she kissed all of us and turned the light off and pulled the door shut with a too-careful slip of the lock. We desperately needed a series of banal and meaningless moments, and she had tried to convince us this was one of them. But all of her soundless care made it seem otherwise, as if she believed each moment's non-eventfulness balanced on a delicate wire of silence.

We lay there. The clock read eleven p.m. Half an hour went by.

Then I heard myself say my father's name in the dark. I call him Dad, even to this day, but I did not say that. I said my father's first name in the dark. "James," I said.

"I know," he said. "This isn't right. Get your sister dressed."

After the turn from Highway 12 my father didn't know how to get there exactly, especially at night, and it took a long time. Our headlights swung up and down over the treeless hills, through sweeping bends, and we turned around at least three times.

Finally we found the cabin's road and my father turned the headlights off well in advance, the moonlight more than enough for a drive. I wished he'd done it earlier because the bobbing headlights, among other things, had made me sick. The cabin was dark inside but the cabin itself looked white, and for a moment we were a little dazzled by the sight of it, unsure of our next move.

"Maybe I was wrong," he said.

"I'm glad we came," I said.

"Me too."

My father would later tell me that he believed my sister and I had inherited my mother's infallible heart, her ability to understand the needs of suffering people, which, he'd learned from her, is everyone, all the time. He said that in those few days he felt useless, like he was failing her, and whether he knew it at the time or not was looking to me for guidance. This was much later that he told me all this, after I was married with two children of my own. It sounded insane to me and I could not imagine it. At the time I was twelve years old.

I woke Mary and we walked hand-in-hand into the cabin, each carrying a canvas satchel, in mine clothes for everyone and in Mary's some eggs and bread for the morning, food we'd taken from the cabin two days before.

One of the bedrooms was empty and my mother lay sleeping on a bottom bunk in the other. Mary and I climbed onto her. She started crying, and I don't remember anything else. I was asleep.

When I awoke, I was alone. It was still night. At the foot of the bed lay a wrinkled letter addressed to my mother, written in my grandmother's liquid script. Dear Sylvia. Even in a light so dim I knew her handwriting, because she sent me three letters every year, penned on two or three folded half-size pieces of paper and tucked perfectly into short envelopes. They were wonderful, artful things but hard to read. She sent a birthday letter, a summer letter, and a Christmas letter. I was always too slow in my reply. Later I would learn that this was a letter from my grandfather, in my grandmother's handwriting. In her handwriting because my grandfather had grown up the son of an Irish immigrant on a struggling North Dakota farm, and never learned how to read. Ardyce took secret dictation from him, read him books, typed his correspondence, did his business, for fifty-three years. I did not know this. And this letter I did not try to read. It was not for me, and besides, Mary had appeared in the doorway. She wanted me to come with her. There was something going on in the cabin.

Everyone had arrived while I slept. Charles, Dale, Walter, Belle, Anne, my mother and father—all of the adults stood on the porch, in the dark, looking at the lake. Patsy, Jacob, and Dawn sat together on the sofa, drowsy and looking at the adults looking at the lake. Everyone was there except my grandmother.

"Grampa's out on the boat," Mary said. She was six. She stood on her toes and said that in my ear.

I somehow knew it already. I told Mary to wait with the others.

When I think back to this time I wonder if I'm not remembering other people's experiences, seeing a moment the way someone described it to me later, when we finally began to speak of these things, rather than the way I saw it myself. My mother, for example, told me Charles had tried to cut down the tree; I may have seen him but I'm not sure. I did not witness Charles putting his glasses on Ennis' face; Jacob told me about that, he cannot forget it. Our memories are no longer our own. They have become communal, inaccurate, and somehow more true. I say this because I now realize that my most comforting memory is of something I never saw: Ennis and Ardyce, after a long and eventful life together, drinking coffee into the night and drafting that letter, a final word Ennis had addressed only to my mother. Over the last few years both of my grandparents had become unimpressed with the thought of their own deaths and talked about them in casual conversation, though someone would always cut them short with common phrases like No, you're going to live forever, and in my grandfather's case might add, Unfortunately, and then laugh. But in the years to come when I was confronted with any kind of death, I would imagine the two of them facing it there in the kitchen as a matter of family business, putting the right words in order, tidying crumbs on the table.

When I opened the door everyone looked at me, but no one turned me away. Even then it felt too generous of them. I was tall for my age but I was not an adult. I wished they would force me back inside and relieve me of all maturity.

"This is tedious," Charles said. Nobody had been replying to the things Charles said. Nobody felt they had the right. But we couldn't have won him back. Ophelia's mother and sister needed him and he would never again be there for them and years later they would leave him and he would go on to some other life, of which none of us would know a thing.

"Dad," Jacob said. The other children had gathered in the doorway.

"Don't speak, son," Dale said.

Then none of us felt we could speak. We all tried to see, pick out a shape, find a flicker on the water. We weren't sure what he had done, what he was going to do, if this was a watch or a vigil, if we were waiting or mourning. But we stood rigid and expectant.

"Fuck this. He's either going to kill himself or he's already done it or he's too much of a coward," Charles said, and with this his wife, Anne, the smallest of the women, took two quick steps from across the porch and sunk her hands into his hair and pulled with her entire body. This spun him sideways and they stumbled together and fell, my father and others reaching helplessly, Anne clawing at Charles' face and reaching for his eyeballs and snarling until finally she rolled away and lay on the floor, frozen and soft, all these standing figures looking down on her and not knowing what to do.

Charles stood up bleeding from his cheeks and neck. Belle closed the other children inside the house. My mother knelt, her long unbrushed hair covering Anne's face, and in the short moment they were there said one thing to her. What it was I wish I knew. I like to believe it was something impossibly right. Then everyone was quiet.

Movement in the lake, a faint splashing sound. We all looked, drew into the yard. Someone was in the water. We hurried to the cliff's edge and looked down at the dock, where a flowered dress lay empty, and then Anne, her voice like an electrocution, jarring our bodies with the name of her daughter, Patsy.

She was swimming into the lake. Now everyone was running. My father to the nearest neighbor and their dock, their boat. Walter and Charles and Anne sliding, bounding down the trail. Walter tripped and fell, recovered, ran full tilt to the end of the dock and dove in, followed by Charles, all of us calling to Patsy. Come back.

And then the most miraculous sight in all my life. In all that blackness, in the middle darkness of the lake, a light came on. It swung across the cliffs and banks, across the flat water, and found my cousin there, struggling in its direction, her limbs and her head less than a suggestion on the surface, dustings of light all around her. Patsy. Traveling into the dark, for my grandfather, who would be there waiting to pull her from the water.

ARIANA REINES

■

Dream House

FROM *Ramayana* chapbook

The pavilion has walls of rug when I'm a knight with blood
Foaming out my chainmail so I lie down on my cot in the cool
Darkness and when I close my eyes the falcons alight on my page's
Glove. I'm fine to die in here, chill seeping into my bones, cold
Spring like a Carpaccio painting.
I fold my arms to compose myself like a coffinlid
Knight, a crypto knight I mean a dreamer. I mean a man
Who doesn't exist with his rock-hard sword standing up up forever.
Foy porter honeur garder. Since I was seventeen I've been dreaming
I'm the maid in a house, a wide house in the mountains, and I'm
A Victorian maid, a domestic, I'm asthmatic I mean
Consumptive like Chopin or Proust and I'm honest
And servile not artistic or cruel and not clumsily
Dressed. I'm ugly in the simple way of having been made
So by my servitude and not in the unsimple way of having
Pursued what I pursued as a so to speak free woman. Do you remember
The days of slavery. I do.
I am wan and dowdy and I sleep on the floor.
Once in the dream the house belonged to my father
And a man said to me in his Schwizerdeutsch accent *And Now
That You Have Entered The House Of Your Father.*
I remember the ice of a nearish glacier seeming to steam
Against the blue sky. One's eyes grow hard and gemlike

In the Alps you know, not that I am from there
Not even close. Still. In the Alps even (especially?) the dullwitted
Develop raptor eyes. My grandmother worked as the maid
To a duchess in Warsaw while her husband was gassed at Treblinka.
Then the duchess died and she my mother's
Mother had to find a new way to hide. Hide life
Is a phrase I've read somewhere. In a poem maybe. I keep
Wishing I were writing about tents, walls of rug,
Walls of yak felt, yurts, lying awake in my friend's mother's
Bed thinking THE TEETH IN MY HEAD THE TEETH IN MY HEAD
While my heart flared BIOS BIOS BIOS how could any woman bear
The rhythm—what it takes to sustain biological life.
I was naked except for culture like everybody else in my generation
I come from a broken home like they do and I hide it, acting serene
At the joystick in the command station of my so-called self
Except I try openly to hide only badly whatever it is I think is wild that I'm
Doing my best to reveal by not really hiding, though hiding.
A poet can be a permanent houseguest like Jimmy Schuyler.
A woman can be homeless to escape her homeless mother.
A white woman can get away with certain things.
A woman who does not want her spare thoughts to be consumed
By lip implant rippling butt implant wet tongue in the sushi
Flatscreeny gangbangs in a suntan might for example choose
                                        homelessness
In order to pursue with some serenity her for example let's call them
Literary researches, surveiling aristocratically only her own pathetic
Machinations, like one of the dogs
Shaped like Nazis in a guard tower in *Maus*
By Art Spiegelman while a countertenor
And a sackbut bleat Wikileaks Wikileaks and naked men
And men with hoods over their eyes and zappers on their peens
Quiver in citadels in which we The United States hid them. Yves
    Klein knew
That walls are sad: made to immure misery.
That is why he designed a house made of air. We only write
Because we're nudists but not the kind you think but also not necessarily

Not that kind. Art gets
Exhausted which is why a temple, the idea of a temple, I need to go
    to a temple
Every now and again and in order to have a home
I had to play a trick on myself which is that it's a temple, this house.
In a movie from the Eighties a man from California says
My body's my temple. Okay well now in my dreams of domestic
Servitude I receive small pay. I get to go across the street
To contemplate the toiletries in an Alpine Seven
Eleven. Salon Selectives, Prell, Garnier, or Pert Plus.
My hair will look like shit. I don't buy anything.
I go back to the kitchen to fish out of drawers three
Iron candlesticks. The dark lady who rages over the family
Near the high vaulted hearth where I slave over a hot stove
In nothing but a dirty t-shirt like a Thai baby in a *National*
Geographic photograph all gorgeous in the mufti of my total deprivation
This dark lady can only it seems be communicated with by me
No longer the maid, but—progress—household witch
Earning after all a salary however tiny, horse-whispering its deadest
homelessness
Most psycho old bitches, sweet-talking them down from the rafters, down
Out of tantrums unthrown, unthrowable by nobody me, the inverted
V of downward-facing liberty: when you have no choice but to try to
    have chosen
What you never, never would choose. Sitting on a bench at the end of
    my exhausted
Term like a regular grownup I pictured myself shampooing my luxury
Hair in some artsy shithole, mildew streaking the torn shower curtain
Lurching across the second expanse of poverty
My ruined imagination could manage: Well I guess I could join the
    Israeli
Army. Why the fuck would you want to do that said
Somebody else inside my dream head. Pretty much
Dead by the time they were done needing me as their slave
I started to feel kind of American I mean like an adult sitting
    uncomplaining,
Torso a plain physical fact over unquivering genitals,

Just meat on a stick with the vague sense that somewhere between
    lavish femininity
And state violence lay a mediocre thing called liberty.
Still, to be able to sleep at all's a procedure of waking. Everybody
Has to live somewhere being that we are here where most
Of us are not welcome. Did you know transcendental
Homelessness was a thing. But I dreamed this dream
On a physical mattress. On an actual floor in a room with a door
That I pay and pay for. If you write you can forge
A substance that is other than the woman of substance
You are. If you do it to such a point you can find
Yourself declining substance altogether. It happens. It is a danger. But
    there will
Always be the idea of a bath or a sleep in a bed or a dream
In the head of a woman who is even beautiful visibly
Or at least groomed, or somewhat fresh
Or like that most domestic of bugs the cockroach
Dragging his ponderous suit of armor across the floor
Or clean sheets when it's raining and I love you so much
And I think Gimme Shelter, which is a movie I've never seen.

ADRIAN TOMINE

Killing and Dying

from Killing and Dying

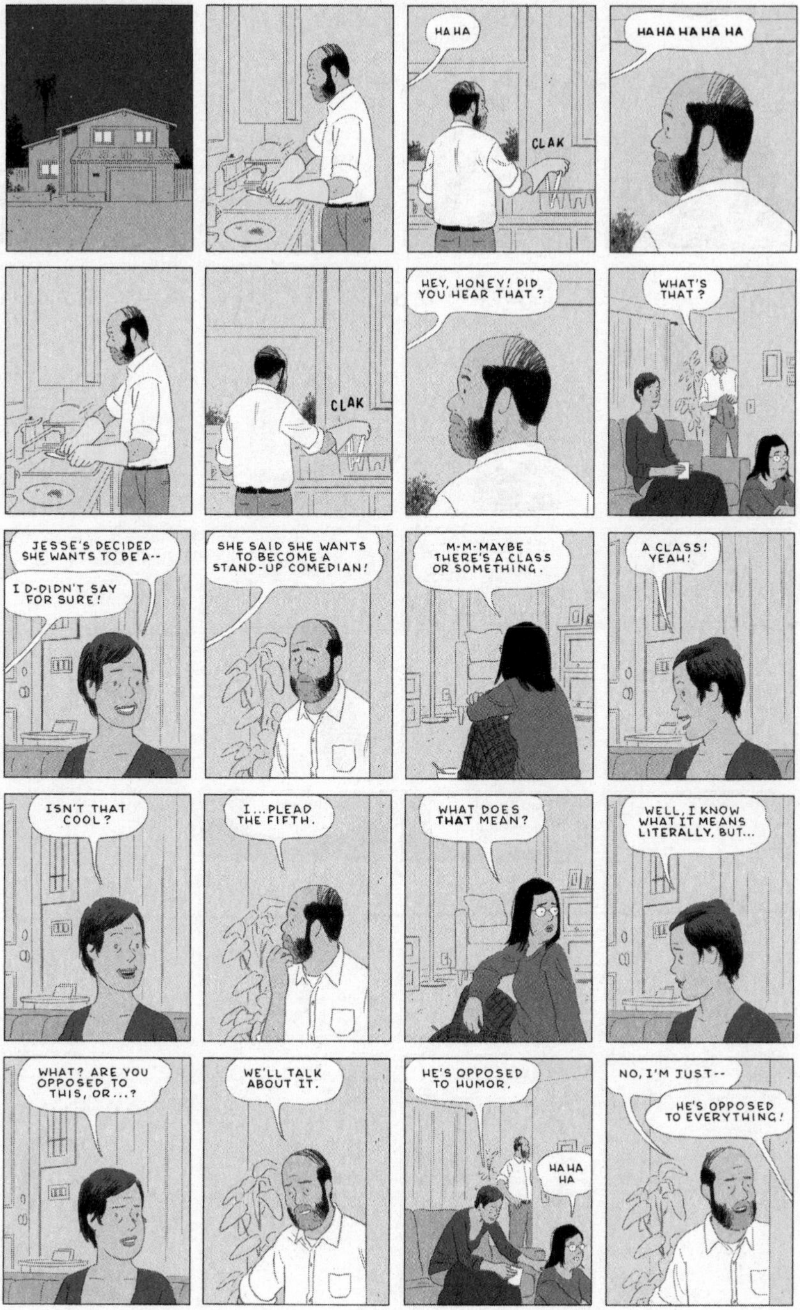
HA HA
CLAK
HA HA HA HA HA
CLAK
HEY, HONEY! DID YOU HEAR THAT?
WHAT'S THAT?
JESSE'S DECIDED SHE WANTS TO BE A--
I D-DIDN'T SAY FOR SURE!
SHE SAID SHE WANTS TO BECOME A STAND-UP COMEDIAN!
M-M-MAYBE THERE'S A CLASS OR SOMETHING.
A CLASS! YEAH!
ISN'T THAT COOL?
I...PLEAD THE FIFTH.
WHAT DOES THAT MEAN?
WELL, I KNOW WHAT IT MEANS LITERALLY, BUT...
WHAT? ARE YOU OPPOSED TO THIS, OR...?
WE'LL TALK ABOUT IT.
HE'S OPPOSED TO HUMOR.
HA HA HA
NO, I'M JUST--
HE'S OPPOSED TO EVERYTHING!

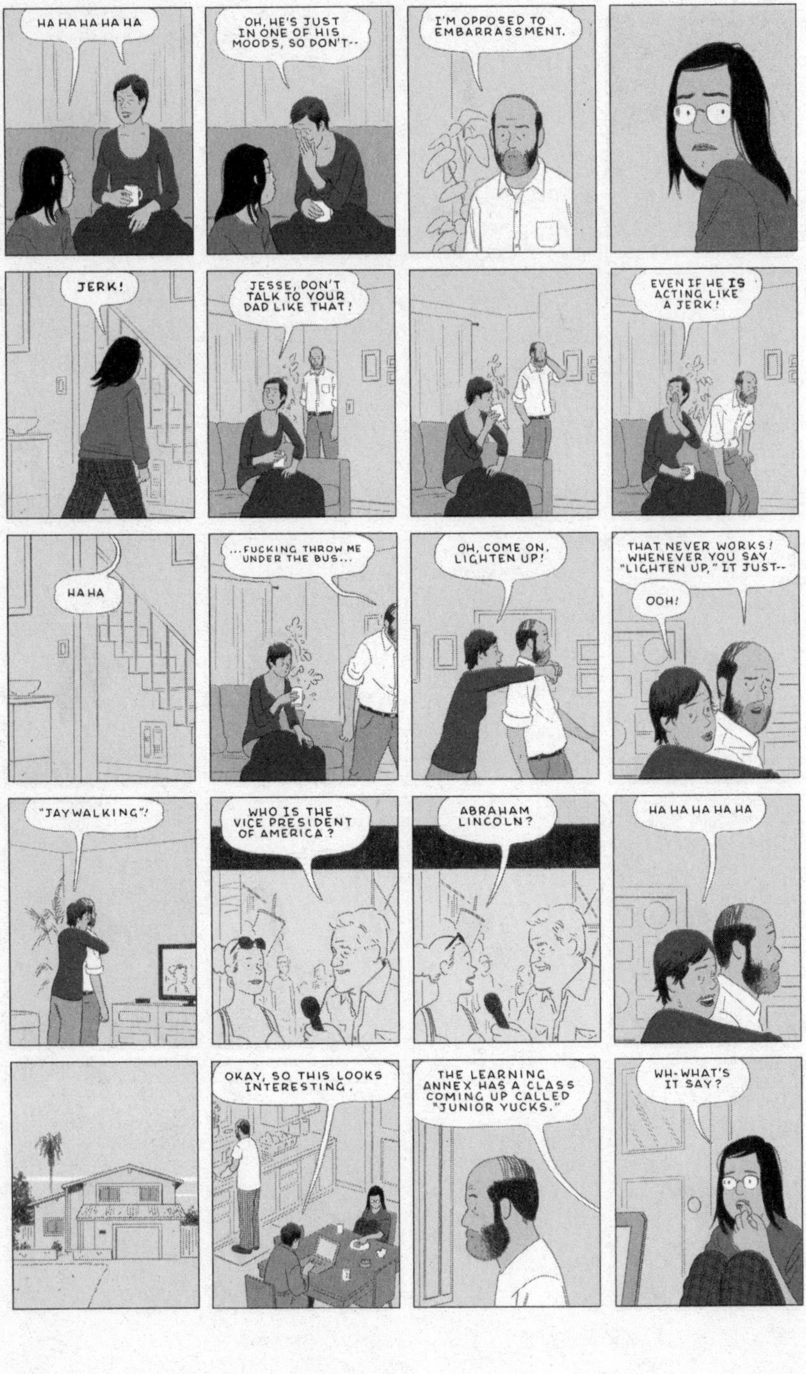
HA HA HA HA HA
OH, HE'S JUST IN ONE OF HIS MOODS, SO DON'T--
I'M OPPOSED TO EMBARRASSMENT.
JERK!
JESSE, DON'T TALK TO YOUR DAD LIKE THAT!
EVEN IF HE IS ACTING LIKE A JERK!
HA HA
...FUCKING THROW ME UNDER THE BUS...
OH, COME ON, LIGHTEN UP!
THAT NEVER WORKS! WHENEVER YOU SAY "LIGHTEN UP," IT JUST--
OOH!
"JAYWALKING"?
WHO IS THE VICE PRESIDENT OF AMERICA?
ABRAHAM LINCOLN?
HA HA HA HA HA
OKAY, SO THIS LOOKS INTERESTING.
THE LEARNING ANNEX HAS A CLASS COMING UP CALLED "JUNIOR YUCKS."
WH-WHAT'S IT SAY?

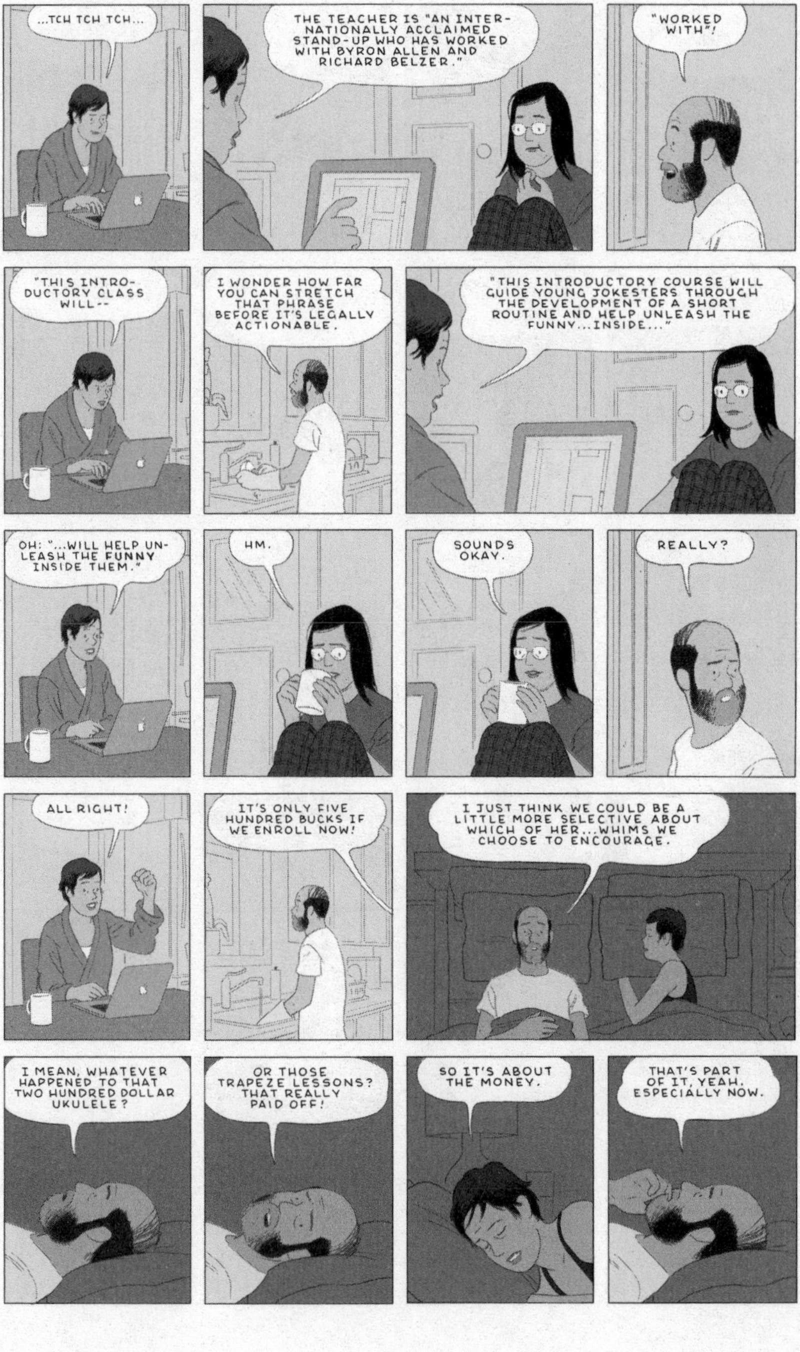
...TCH TCH TCH...
THE TEACHER IS "AN INTERNATIONALLY ACCLAIMED STAND-UP WHO HAS WORKED WITH BYRON ALLEN AND RICHARD BELZER."
"WORKED WITH"!
"THIS INTRODUCTORY CLASS WILL--
I WONDER HOW FAR YOU CAN STRETCH THAT PHRASE BEFORE IT'S LEGALLY ACTIONABLE.
"THIS INTRODUCTORY COURSE WILL GUIDE YOUNG JOKESTERS THROUGH THE DEVELOPMENT OF A SHORT ROUTINE AND HELP UNLEASH THE FUNNY... INSIDE..."
OH: "...WILL HELP UNLEASH THE FUNNY INSIDE THEM."
HM.
SOUNDS OKAY.
REALLY?
ALL RIGHT!
IT'S ONLY FIVE HUNDRED BUCKS IF WE ENROLL NOW!
I JUST THINK WE COULD BE A LITTLE MORE SELECTIVE ABOUT WHICH OF HER...WHIMS WE CHOOSE TO ENCOURAGE.
I MEAN, WHATEVER HAPPENED TO THAT TWO HUNDRED DOLLAR UKULELE?
OR THOSE TRAPEZE LESSONS? THAT REALLY PAID OFF!
SO IT'S ABOUT THE MONEY.
THAT'S PART OF IT, YEAH. ESPECIALLY NOW.

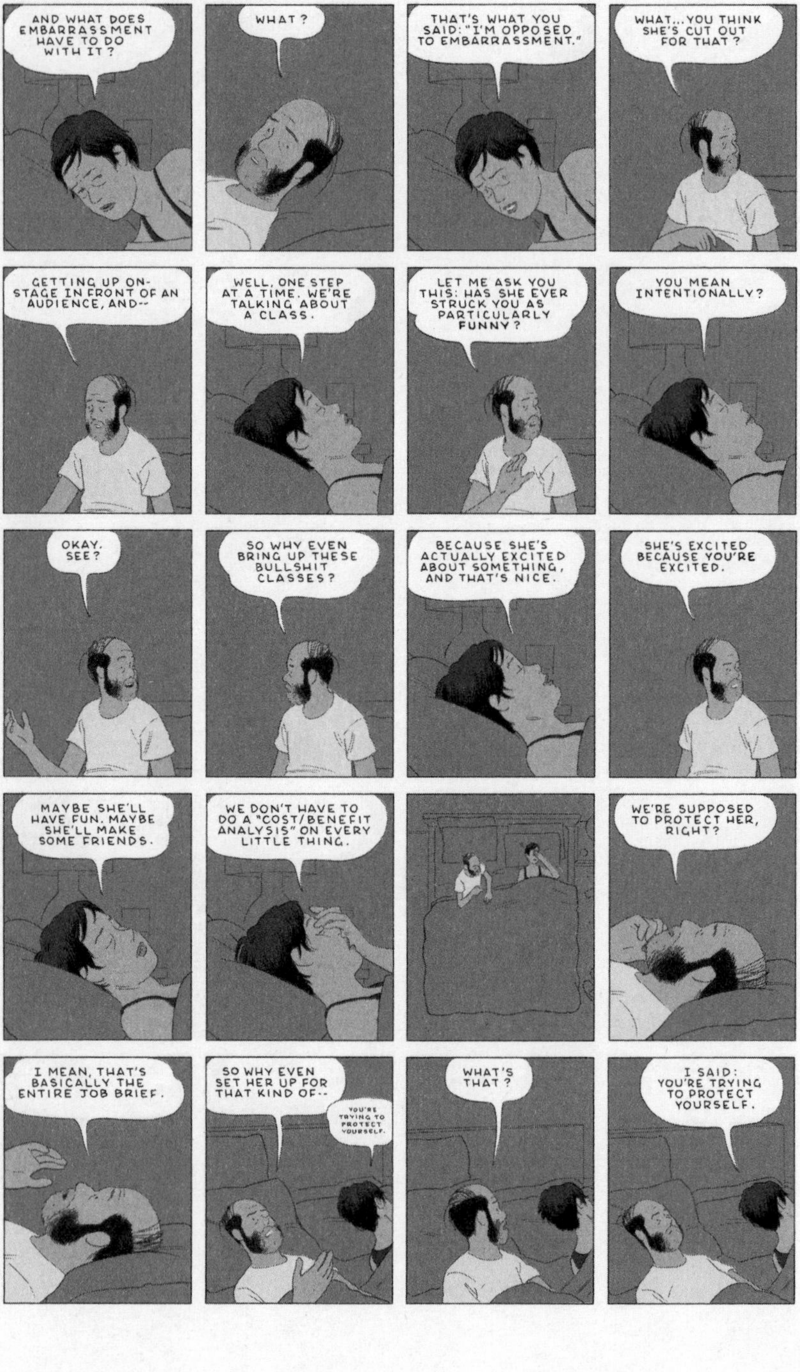
AND WHAT DOES EMBARRASSMENT HAVE TO DO WITH IT?
WHAT?
THAT'S WHAT YOU SAID: "I'M OPPOSED TO EMBARRASSMENT."
WHAT... YOU THINK SHE'S CUT OUT FOR THAT?
GETTING UP ON-STAGE IN FRONT OF AN AUDIENCE, AND--
WELL, ONE STEP AT A TIME. WE'RE TALKING ABOUT A CLASS.
LET ME ASK YOU THIS: HAS SHE EVER STRUCK YOU AS PARTICULARLY FUNNY?
YOU MEAN INTENTIONALLY?
OKAY. SEE?
SO WHY EVEN BRING UP THESE BULLSHIT CLASSES?
BECAUSE SHE'S ACTUALLY EXCITED ABOUT SOMETHING, AND THAT'S NICE.
SHE'S EXCITED BECAUSE YOU'RE EXCITED.
MAYBE SHE'LL HAVE FUN. MAYBE SHE'LL MAKE SOME FRIENDS.
WE DON'T HAVE TO DO A "COST/BENEFIT ANALYSIS" ON EVERY LITTLE THING.
WE'RE SUPPOSED TO PROTECT HER, RIGHT?
I MEAN, THAT'S BASICALLY THE ENTIRE JOB BRIEF.
SO WHY EVEN SET HER UP FOR THAT KIND OF--
YOU'RE TRYING TO PROTECT YOURSELF.
WHAT'S THAT?
I SAID: YOU'RE TRYING TO PROTECT YOURSELF.

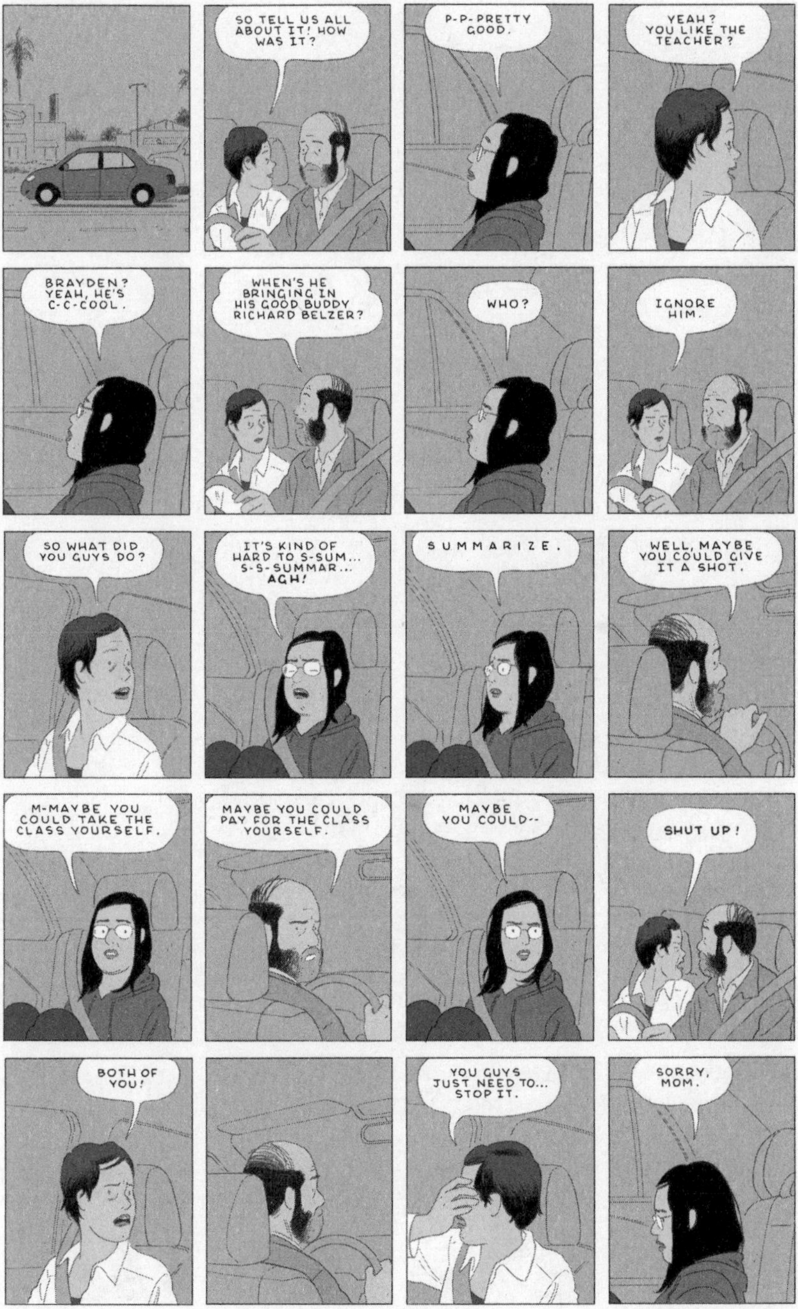

SO TELL US ALL ABOUT IT! HOW WAS IT?
P-P-PRETTY GOOD.
YEAH? YOU LIKE THE TEACHER?
BRAYDEN? YEAH, HE'S C-C-COOL.
WHEN'S HE BRINGING IN HIS GOOD BUDDY RICHARD BELZER?
WHO?
IGNORE HIM.
SO WHAT DID YOU GUYS DO?
IT'S KIND OF HARD TO S-SUM... S-S-SUMMAR... AGH!
SUMMARIZE.
WELL, MAYBE YOU COULD GIVE IT A SHOT.
M-MAYBE YOU COULD TAKE THE CLASS YOURSELF.
MAYBE YOU COULD PAY FOR THE CLASS YOURSELF.
MAYBE YOU COULD--
SHUT UP!
BOTH OF YOU!
YOU GUYS JUST NEED TO... STOP IT.
SORRY, MOM.

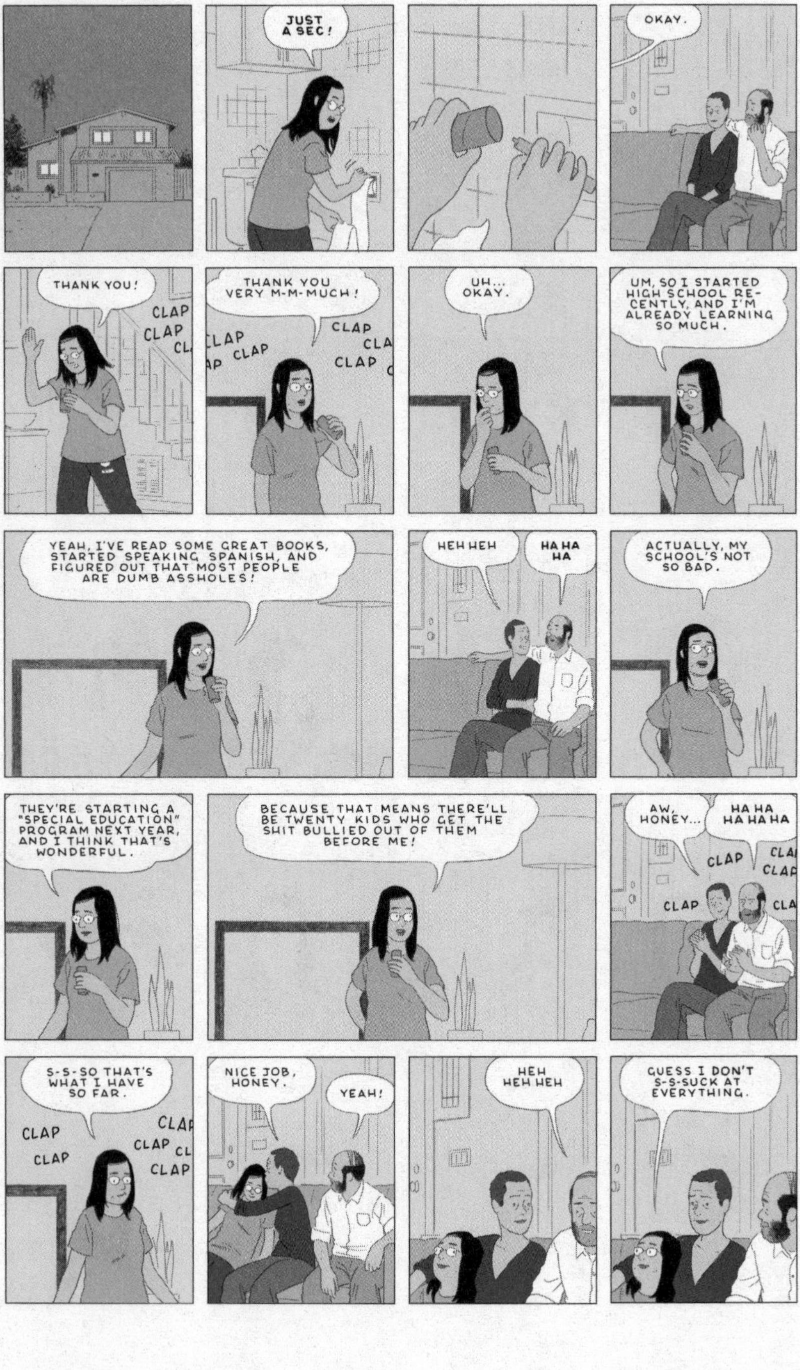
JUST A SEC!
OKAY.
THANK YOU!
CLAP CLAP
THANK YOU VERY M-M-MUCH!
CLAP CLAP CLAP
UH... OKAY.
UM, SO I STARTED HIGH SCHOOL RE-CENTLY, AND I'M ALREADY LEARNING SO MUCH.
YEAH, I'VE READ SOME GREAT BOOKS, STARTED SPEAKING SPANISH, AND FIGURED OUT THAT MOST PEOPLE ARE DUMB ASSHOLES!
HEH HEH
HA HA HA
ACTUALLY, MY SCHOOL'S NOT SO BAD.
THEY'RE STARTING A "SPECIAL EDUCATION" PROGRAM NEXT YEAR, AND I THINK THAT'S WONDERFUL.
BECAUSE THAT MEANS THERE'LL BE TWENTY KIDS WHO GET THE SHIT BULLIED OUT OF THEM BEFORE ME!
AW, HONEY...
HA HA HA HA HA
CLAP
CLAP
S-S-SO THAT'S WHAT I HAVE SO FAR.
CLAP CLAP CLAP CLAP
NICE JOB, HONEY.
YEAH!
HEH HEH HEH
GUESS I DON'T S-S-SUCK AT EVERYTHING.

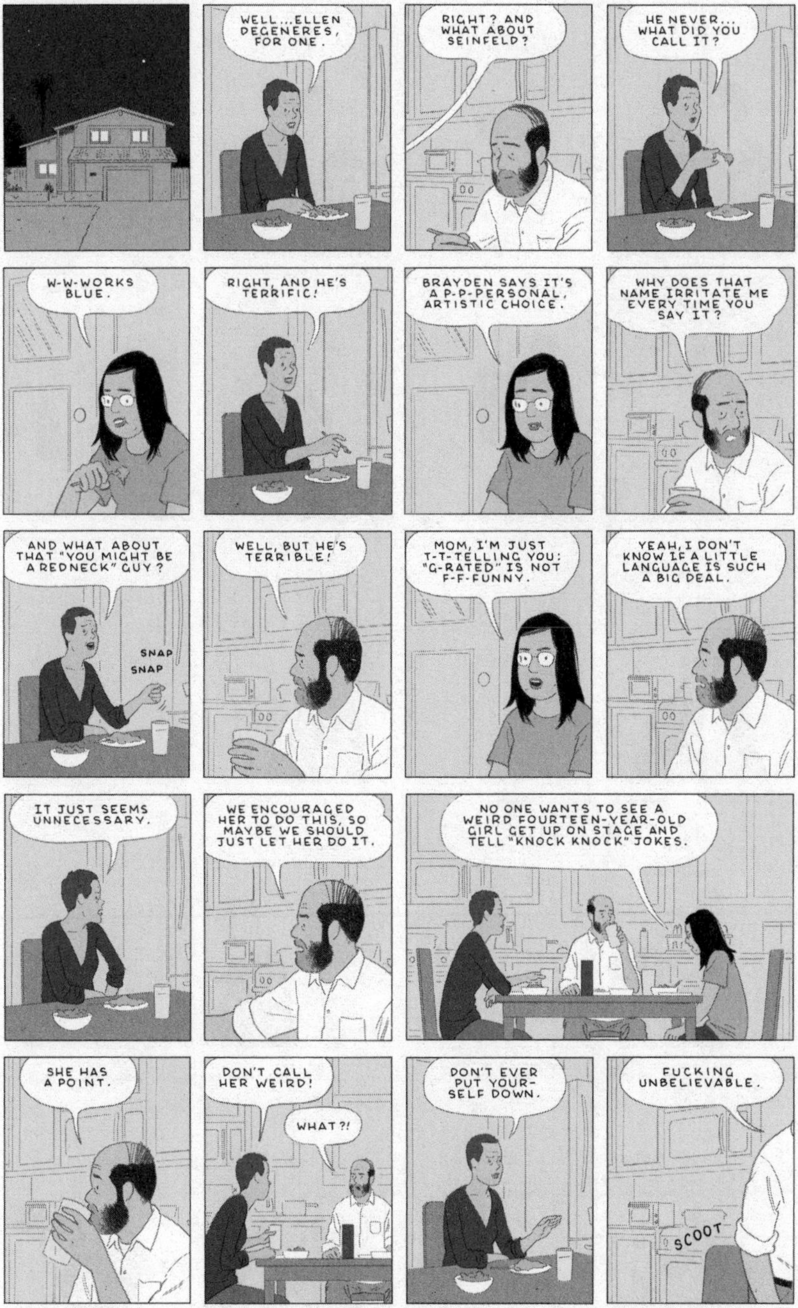

WELL...ELLEN DEGENERES, FOR ONE.
RIGHT? AND WHAT ABOUT SEINFELD?
HE NEVER... WHAT DID YOU CALL IT?
W-W-WORKS BLUE.
RIGHT, AND HE'S TERRIFIC!
BRAYDEN SAYS IT'S A P-P-PERSONAL, ARTISTIC CHOICE.
WHY DOES THAT NAME IRRITATE ME EVERY TIME YOU SAY IT?
AND WHAT ABOUT THAT "YOU MIGHT BE A REDNECK" GUY?
SNAP
SNAP
WELL, BUT HE'S TERRIBLE!
MOM, I'M JUST T-T-TELLING YOU: "G-RATED" IS NOT F-F-FUNNY.
YEAH, I DON'T KNOW IF A LITTLE LANGUAGE IS SUCH A BIG DEAL.
IT JUST SEEMS UNNECESSARY.
WE ENCOURAGED HER TO DO THIS, SO MAYBE WE SHOULD JUST LET HER DO IT.
NO ONE WANTS TO SEE A WEIRD FOURTEEN-YEAR-OLD GIRL GET UP ON STAGE AND TELL "KNOCK KNOCK" JOKES.
SHE HAS A POINT.
DON'T CALL HER WEIRD!
WHAT?!
DON'T EVER PUT YOUR-SELF DOWN.
FUCKING UNBELIEVABLE.
SCOOT

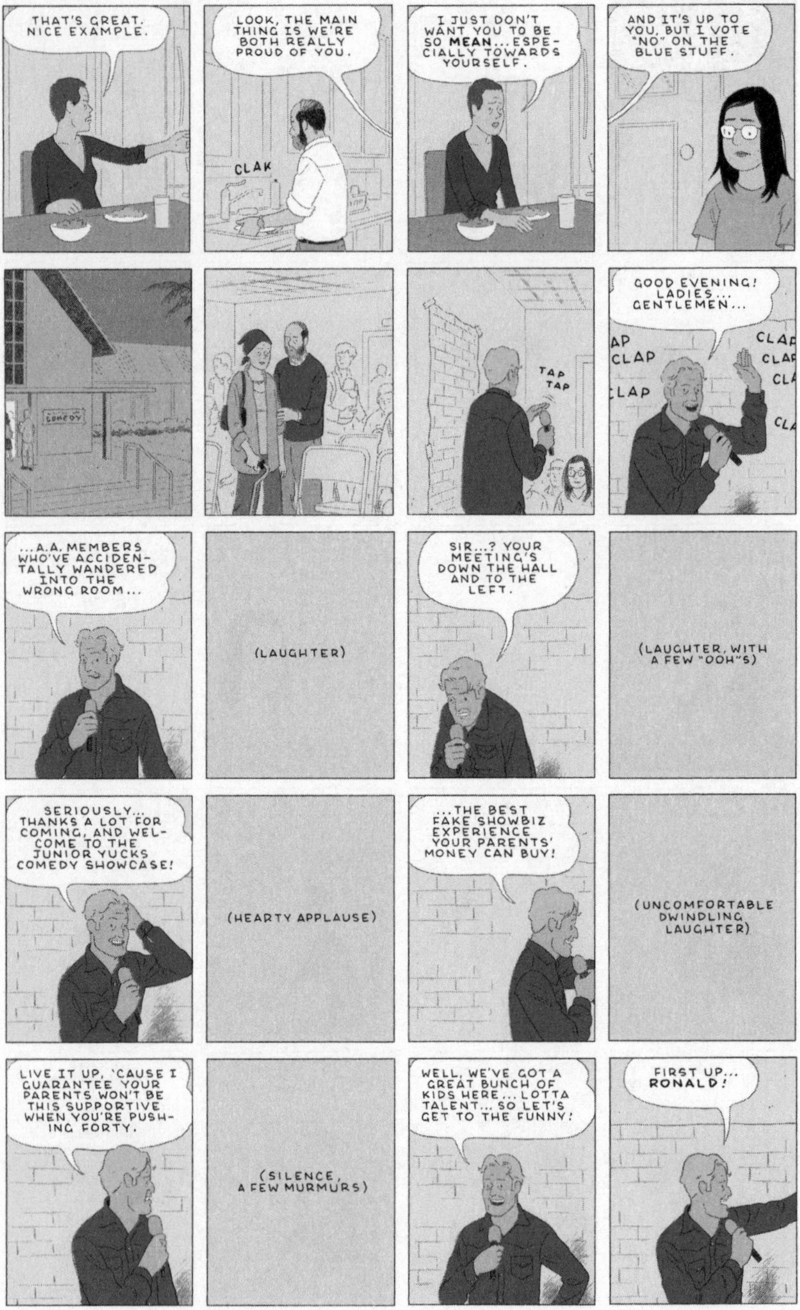
THAT'S GREAT. NICE EXAMPLE.
LOOK, THE MAIN THING IS WE'RE BOTH REALLY PROUD OF YOU.
CLAK
I JUST DON'T WANT YOU TO BE SO **MEAN**... ESPECIALLY TOWARDS YOURSELF.
AND IT'S UP TO YOU, BUT I VOTE "NO" ON THE BLUE STUFF.
COMEDY
TAP TAP
GOOD EVENING! LADIES... GENTLEMEN...
CLAP CLAP CLAP
...A.A. MEMBERS WHO'VE ACCIDENTALLY WANDERED INTO THE WRONG ROOM...
(LAUGHTER)
SIR...? YOUR MEETING'S DOWN THE HALL AND TO THE LEFT.
(LAUGHTER, WITH A FEW "OOH"S)
SERIOUSLY... THANKS A LOT FOR COMING, AND WELCOME TO THE JUNIOR YUCKS COMEDY SHOWCASE!
(HEARTY APPLAUSE)
...THE BEST FAKE SHOWBIZ EXPERIENCE YOUR PARENTS' MONEY CAN BUY!
(UNCOMFORTABLE DWINDLING LAUGHTER)
LIVE IT UP, 'CAUSE I GUARANTEE YOUR PARENTS WON'T BE THIS SUPPORTIVE WHEN YOU'RE PUSHING FORTY.
(SILENCE, A FEW MURMURS)
WELL, WE'VE GOT A GREAT BUNCH OF KIDS HERE... LOTTA TALENT... SO LET'S GET TO THE FUNNY!
FIRST UP... **RONALD!**

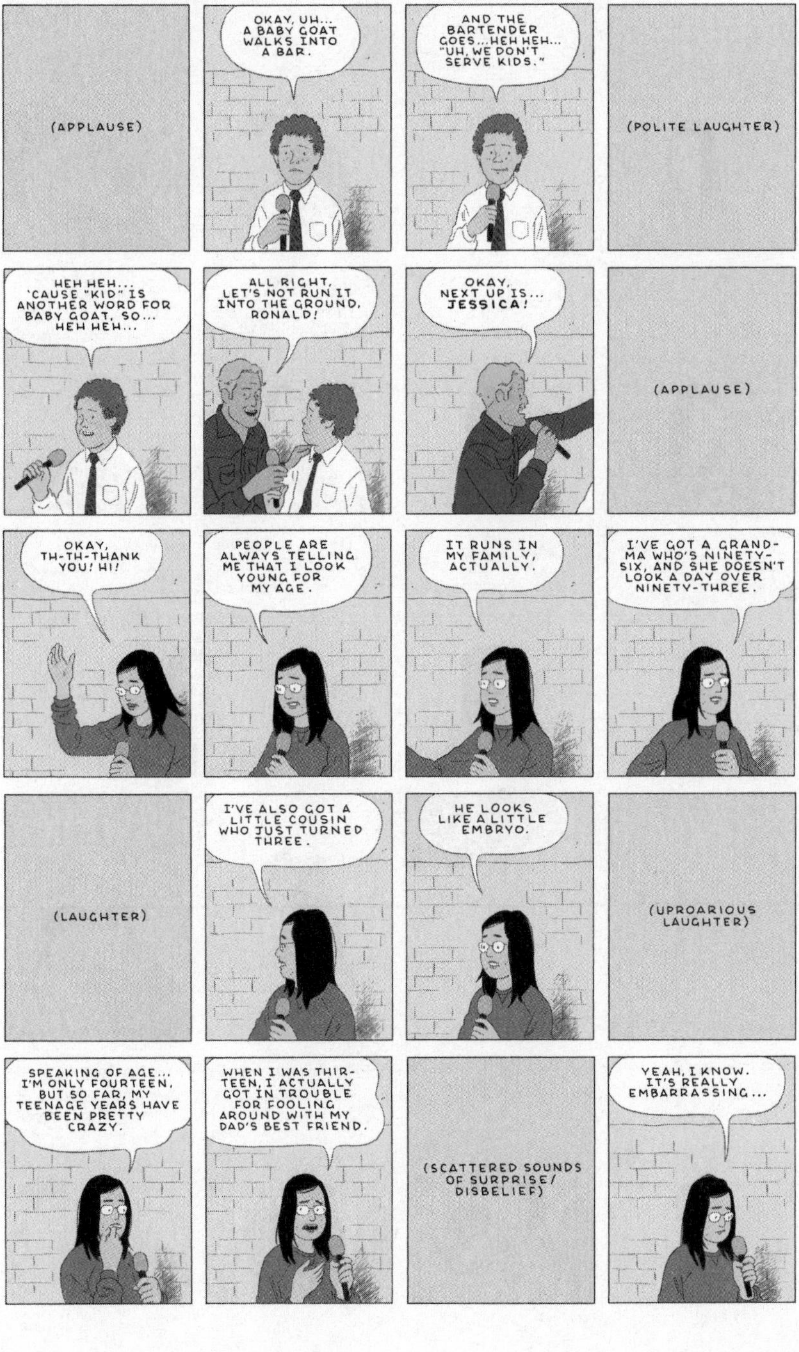
(APPLAUSE)
OKAY, UH... A BABY GOAT WALKS INTO A BAR.
AND THE BARTENDER GOES... HEH HEH... "UH, WE DON'T SERVE KIDS."
(POLITE LAUGHTER)
HEH HEH... 'CAUSE "KID" IS ANOTHER WORD FOR BABY GOAT, SO... HEH HEH...
ALL RIGHT, LET'S NOT RUN IT INTO THE GROUND, RONALD!
OKAY, NEXT UP IS... JESSICA!
(APPLAUSE)
OKAY, TH-TH-THANK YOU! HI!
PEOPLE ARE ALWAYS TELLING ME THAT I LOOK YOUNG FOR MY AGE.
IT RUNS IN MY FAMILY, ACTUALLY.
I'VE GOT A GRANDMA WHO'S NINETY-SIX, AND SHE DOESN'T LOOK A DAY OVER NINETY-THREE.
(LAUGHTER)
I'VE ALSO GOT A LITTLE COUSIN WHO JUST TURNED THREE.
HE LOOKS LIKE A LITTLE EMBRYO.
(UPROARIOUS LAUGHTER)
SPEAKING OF AGE... I'M ONLY FOURTEEN, BUT SO FAR, MY TEENAGE YEARS HAVE BEEN PRETTY CRAZY.
WHEN I WAS THIRTEEN, I ACTUALLY GOT IN TROUBLE FOR FOOLING AROUND WITH MY DAD'S BEST FRIEND.
(SCATTERED SOUNDS OF SURPRISE/ DISBELIEF)
YEAH, I KNOW. IT'S REALLY EMBARRASSING...

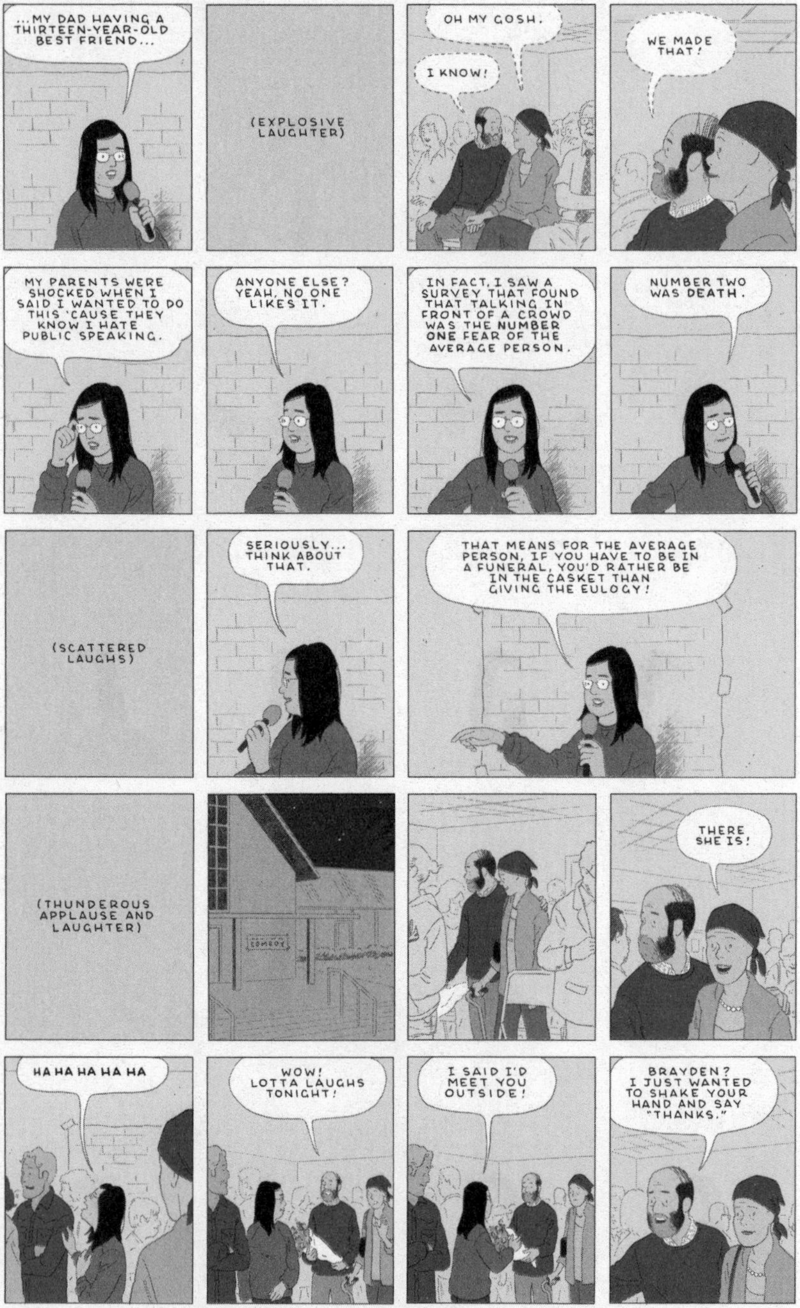
...MY DAD HAVING A THIRTEEN-YEAR-OLD BEST FRIEND...
(EXPLOSIVE LAUGHTER)
OH MY GOSH.
I KNOW!
WE MADE THAT!
MY PARENTS WERE SHOCKED WHEN I SAID I WANTED TO DO THIS 'CAUSE THEY KNOW I HATE PUBLIC SPEAKING.
ANYONE ELSE? YEAH, NO ONE LIKES IT.
IN FACT, I SAW A SURVEY THAT FOUND THAT TALKING IN FRONT OF A CROWD WAS THE NUMBER ONE FEAR OF THE AVERAGE PERSON.
NUMBER TWO WAS DEATH.
(SCATTERED LAUGHS)
SERIOUSLY... THINK ABOUT THAT.
THAT MEANS FOR THE AVERAGE PERSON, IF YOU HAVE TO BE IN A FUNERAL, YOU'D RATHER BE IN THE CASKET THAN GIVING THE EULOGY!
(THUNDEROUS APPLAUSE AND LAUGHTER)
COMEDY
THERE SHE IS!
HA HA HA HA HA
WOW! LOTTA LAUGHS TONIGHT!
I SAID I'D MEET YOU OUTSIDE!
BRAYDEN? I JUST WANTED TO SHAKE YOUR HAND AND SAY "THANKS."

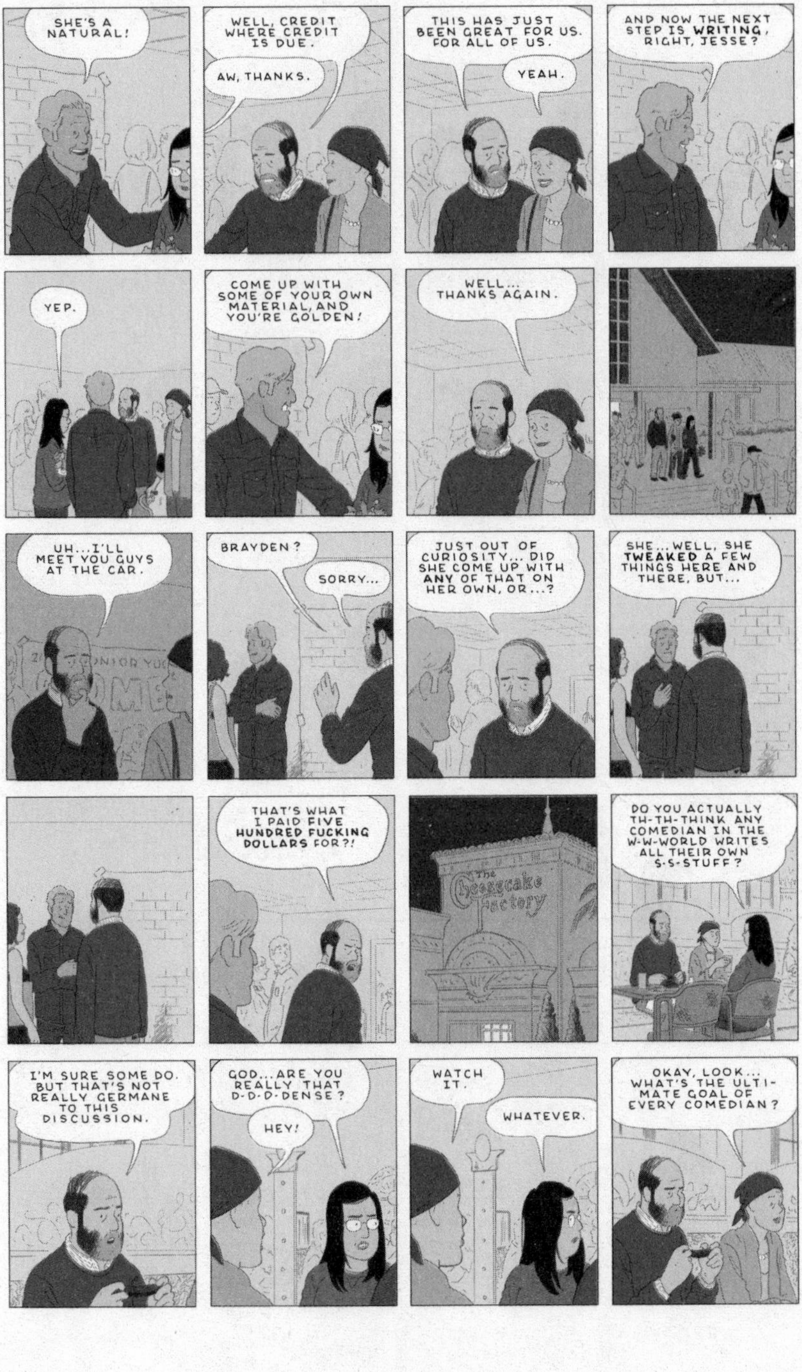
SHE'S A NATURAL!
WELL, CREDIT WHERE CREDIT IS DUE.
AW, THANKS.
THIS HAS JUST BEEN GREAT FOR US. FOR ALL OF US.
YEAH.
AND NOW THE NEXT STEP IS WRITING, RIGHT, JESSE?
YEP.
COME UP WITH SOME OF YOUR OWN MATERIAL, AND YOU'RE GOLDEN!
WELL... THANKS AGAIN.
UH... I'LL MEET YOU GUYS AT THE CAR.
BRAYDEN?
SORRY...
JUST OUT OF CURIOSITY... DID SHE COME UP WITH ANY OF THAT ON HER OWN, OR...?
SHE... WELL, SHE TWEAKED A FEW THINGS HERE AND THERE, BUT...
THAT'S WHAT I PAID FIVE HUNDRED FUCKING DOLLARS FOR?!
The Cheesecake Factory
DO YOU ACTUALLY TH-TH-THINK ANY COMEDIAN IN THE W-W-WORLD WRITES ALL THEIR OWN S-S-STUFF?
I'M SURE SOME DO. BUT THAT'S NOT REALLY GERMANE TO THIS DISCUSSION.
GOD... ARE YOU REALLY THAT D-D-D-DENSE?
HEY!
WATCH IT.
WHATEVER.
OKAY, LOOK... WHAT'S THE ULTI-MATE GOAL OF EVERY COMEDIAN?

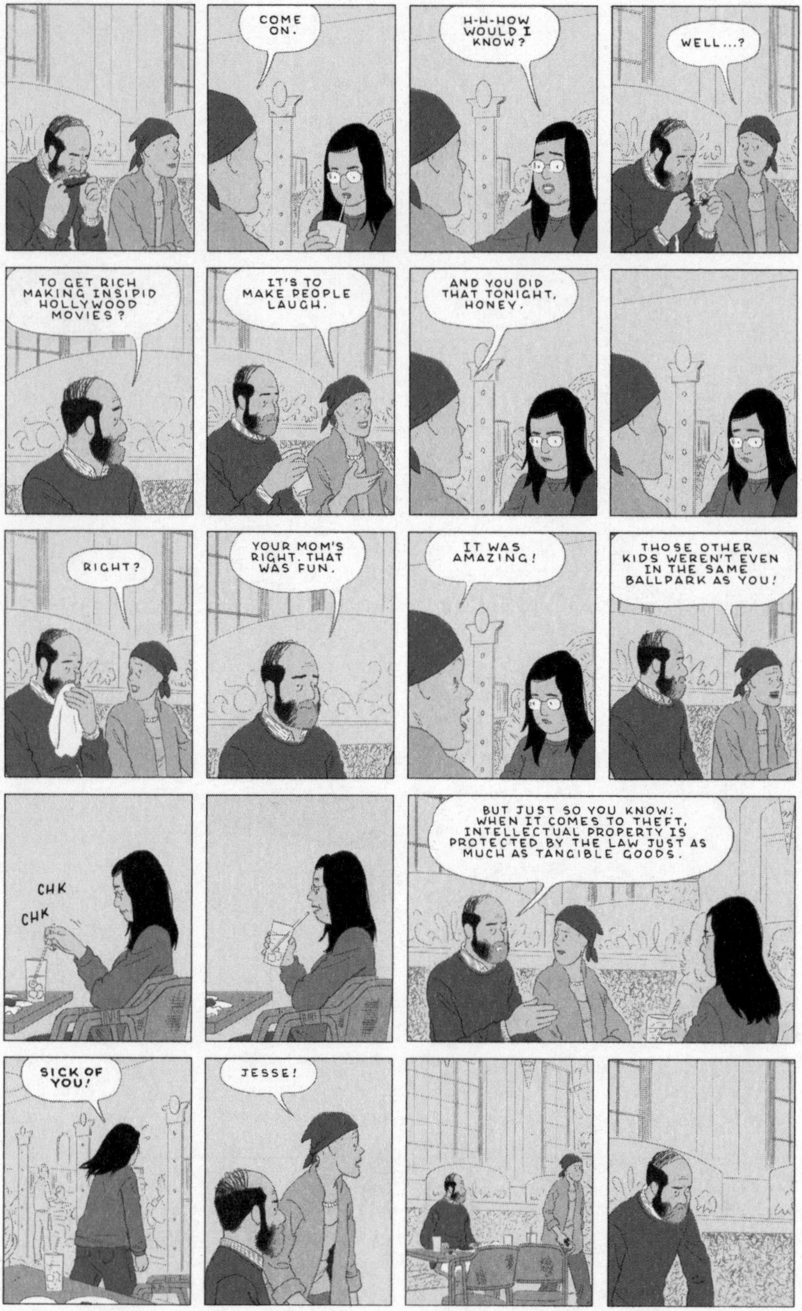
COME ON.
H-H-HOW WOULD I KNOW?
WELL...?
TO GET RICH MAKING INSIPID HOLLYWOOD MOVIES?
IT'S TO MAKE PEOPLE LAUGH.
AND YOU DID THAT TONIGHT, HONEY.
RIGHT?
YOUR MOM'S RIGHT. THAT WAS FUN.
IT WAS AMAZING!
THOSE OTHER KIDS WEREN'T EVEN IN THE SAME BALLPARK AS YOU!
CHK
CHK
BUT JUST SO YOU KNOW: WHEN IT COMES TO THEFT, INTELLECTUAL PROPERTY IS PROTECTED BY THE LAW JUST AS MUCH AS TANGIBLE GOODS.
SICK OF YOU!
JESSE!

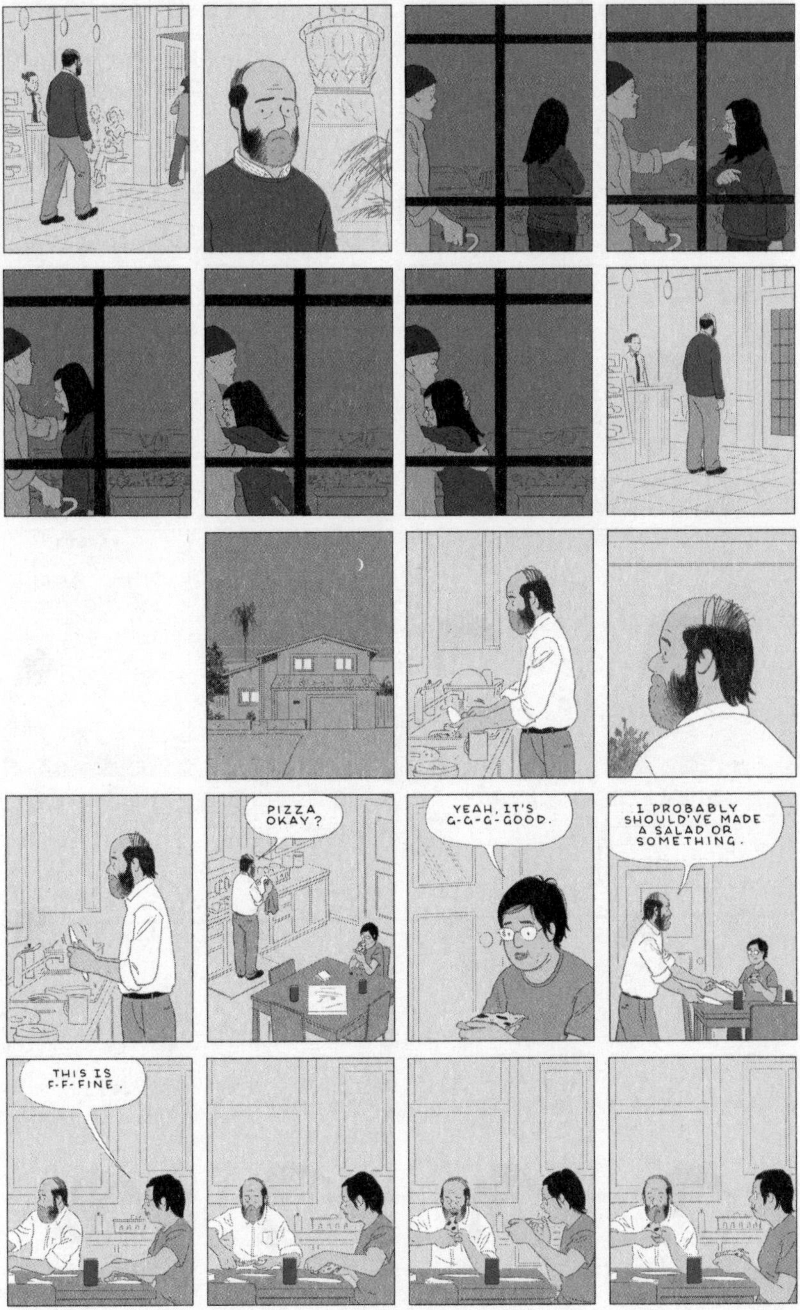
PIZZA OKAY?
YEAH, IT'S G-G-G-GOOD.
I PROBABLY SHOULD'VE MADE A SALAD OR SOMETHING.
THIS IS F-F-FINE.

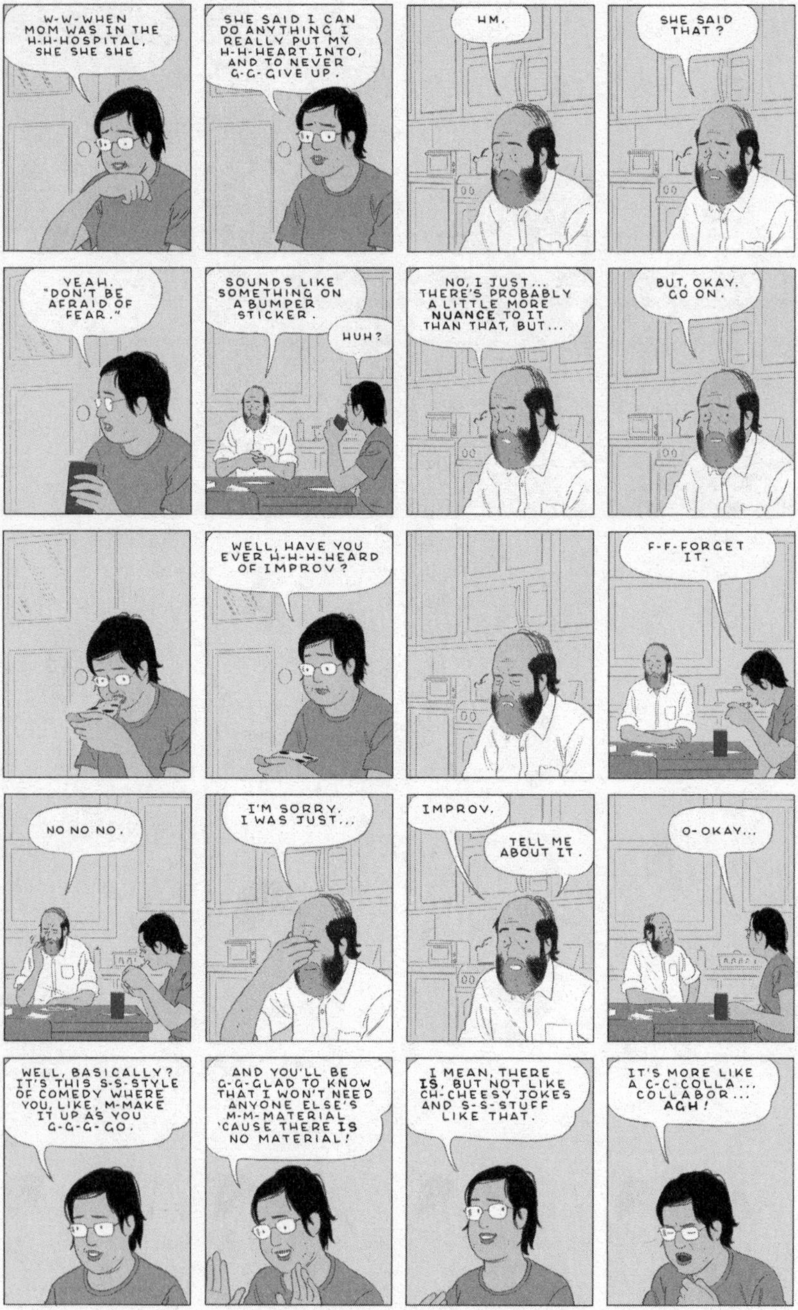
W-W-WHEN MOM WAS IN THE H-H-HOSPITAL, SHE SHE SHE
SHE SAID I CAN DO ANYTHING I REALLY PUT MY H-H-HEART INTO, AND TO NEVER G-G-GIVE UP.
HM.
SHE SAID THAT?
YEAH. "DON'T BE AFRAID OF FEAR."
SOUNDS LIKE SOMETHING ON A BUMPER STICKER.
HUH?
NO, I JUST... THERE'S PROBABLY A LITTLE MORE NUANCE TO IT THAN THAT, BUT...
BUT, OKAY. GO ON.
WELL, HAVE YOU EVER H-H-H-HEARD OF IMPROV?
F-F-FORGET IT.
NO NO NO.
I'M SORRY. I WAS JUST...
IMPROV.
TELL ME ABOUT IT.
O-OKAY...
WELL, BASICALLY? IT'S THIS S-S-STYLE OF COMEDY WHERE YOU, LIKE, M-MAKE IT UP AS YOU G-G-G-GO.
AND YOU'LL BE G-G-GLAD TO KNOW THAT I WON'T NEED ANYONE ELSE'S M-M-MATERIAL 'CAUSE THERE IS NO MATERIAL!
I MEAN, THERE IS, BUT NOT LIKE CH-CHEESY JOKES AND S-S-STUFF LIKE THAT.
IT'S MORE LIKE A C-C-COLLA... COLLABOR... AGH!

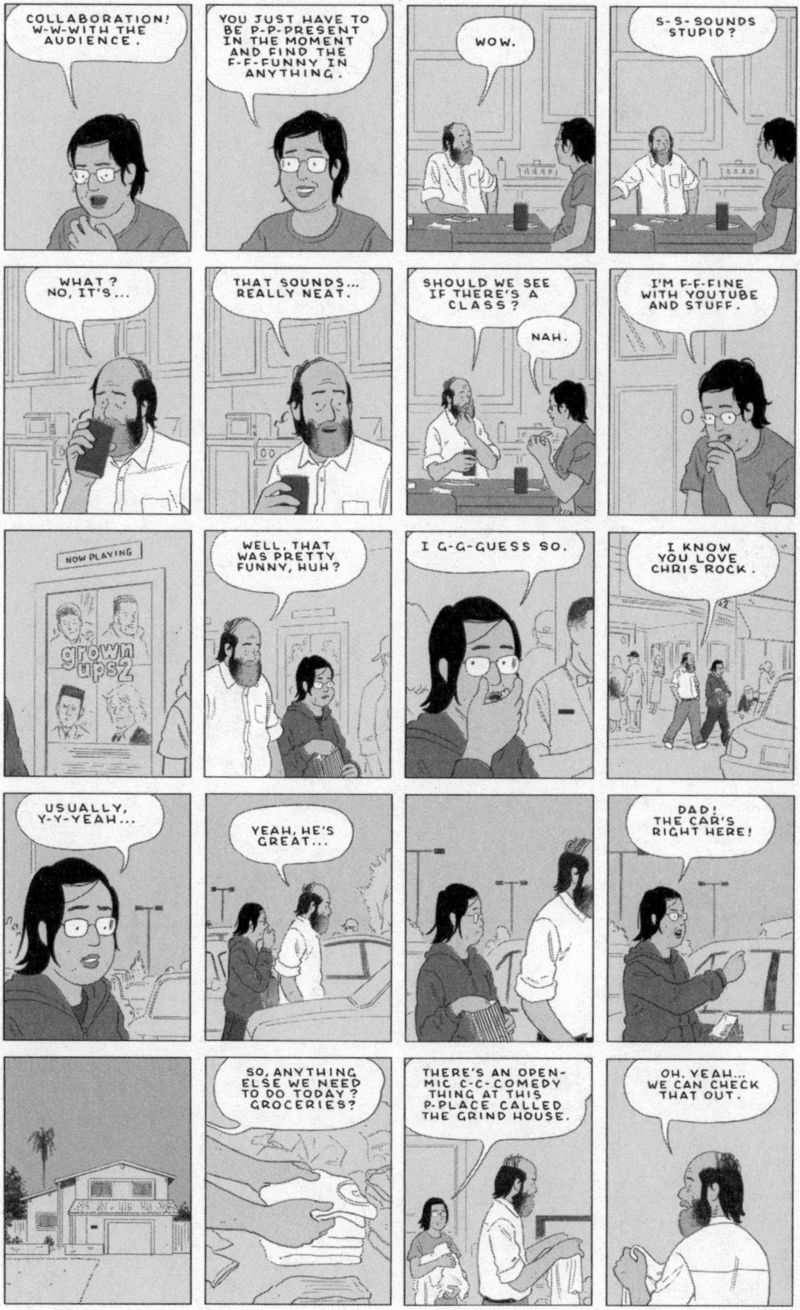
COLLABORATION! W-W-WITH THE AUDIENCE.
YOU JUST HAVE TO BE P-P-PRESENT IN THE MOMENT AND FIND THE F-F-FUNNY IN ANYTHING.
WOW.
S-S-SOUNDS STUPID?
WHAT? NO, IT'S...
THAT SOUNDS... REALLY NEAT.
SHOULD WE SEE IF THERE'S A CLASS?
NAH.
I'M F-F-FINE WITH YOUTUBE AND STUFF.
NOW PLAYING
grown ups 2
WELL, THAT WAS PRETTY FUNNY, HUH?
I G-G-GUESS SO.
I KNOW YOU LOVE CHRIS ROCK.
USUALLY, Y-Y-YEAH...
YEAH, HE'S GREAT...
DAD! THE CAR'S RIGHT HERE!
SO, ANYTHING ELSE WE NEED TO DO TODAY? GROCERIES?
THERE'S AN OPEN-MIC C-C-COMEDY THING AT THIS P-PLACE CALLED THE GRIND HOUSE.
OH. YEAH... WE CAN CHECK THAT OUT.

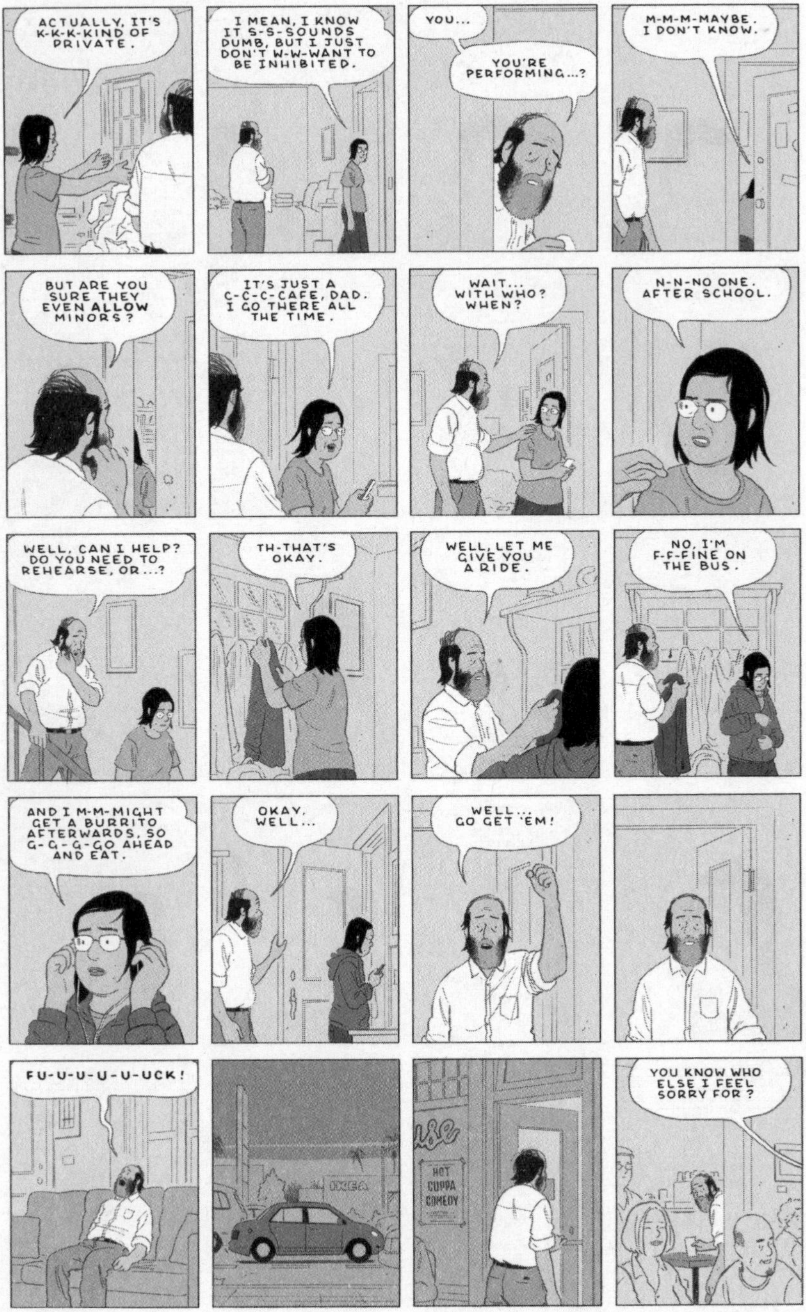
ACTUALLY, IT'S K-K-K-KIND OF PRIVATE.
I MEAN, I KNOW IT S-S-SOUNDS DUMB, BUT I JUST DON'T W-W-WANT TO BE INHIBITED.
YOU...
YOU'RE PERFORMING...?
M-M-M-MAYBE. I DON'T KNOW.
BUT ARE YOU SURE THEY EVEN ALLOW MINORS?
IT'S JUST A C-C-C-CAFE, DAD. I GO THERE ALL THE TIME.
WAIT... WITH WHO? WHEN?
N-N-NO ONE. AFTER SCHOOL.
WELL, CAN I HELP? DO YOU NEED TO REHEARSE, OR...?
TH-THAT'S OKAY.
WELL, LET ME GIVE YOU A RIDE.
NO, I'M F-F-FINE ON THE BUS.
AND I M-M-MIGHT GET A BURRITO AFTERWARDS, SO G-G-G-GO AHEAD AND EAT.
OKAY. WELL...
WELL... GO GET 'EM!
FU-U-U-U-U-UCK!
HOT
CUPPA
COMEDY
YOU KNOW WHO ELSE I FEEL SORRY FOR?

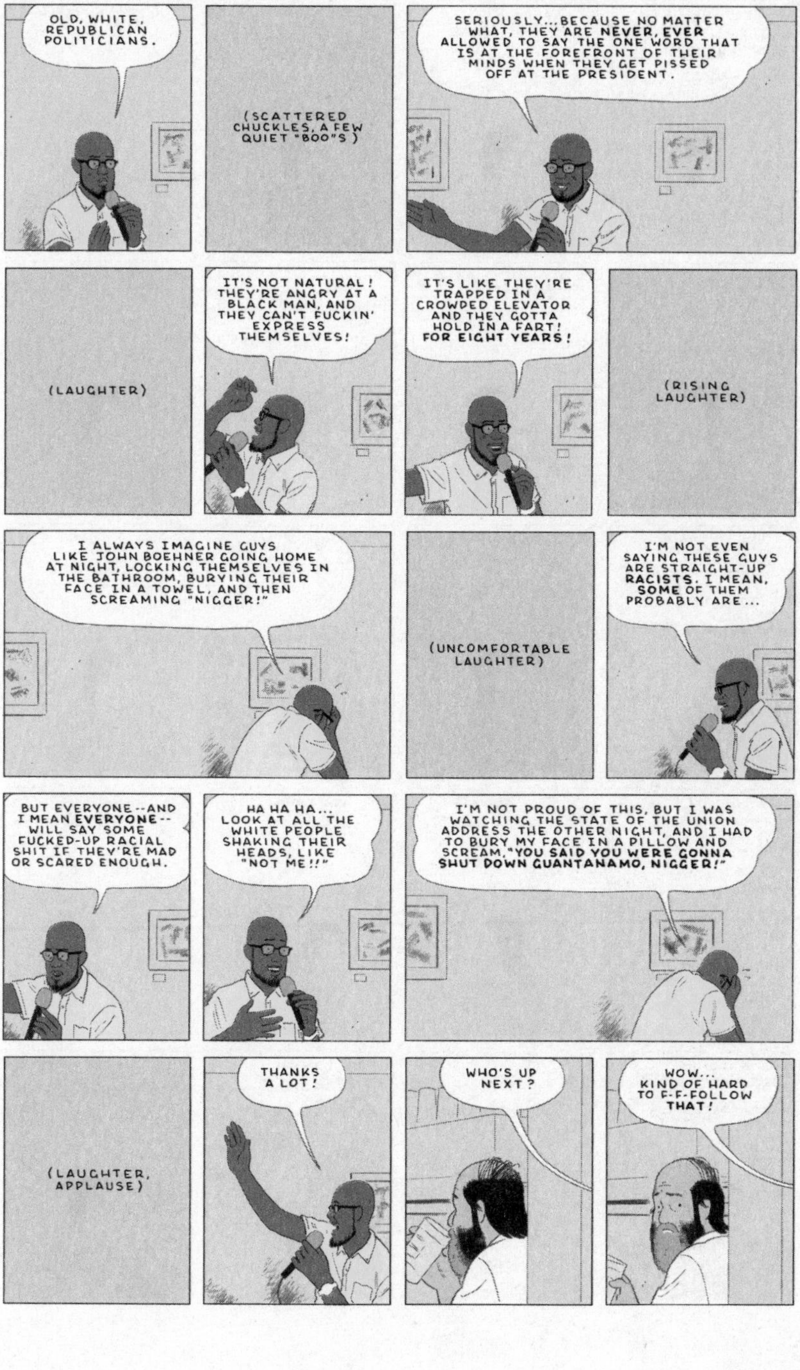
OLD, WHITE, REPUBLICAN POLITICIANS.
(SCATTERED CHUCKLES, A FEW QUIET "BOO"S)
SERIOUSLY... BECAUSE NO MATTER WHAT, THEY ARE NEVER, EVER ALLOWED TO SAY THE ONE WORD THAT IS AT THE FOREFRONT OF THEIR MINDS WHEN THEY GET PISSED OFF AT THE PRESIDENT.
(LAUGHTER)
IT'S NOT NATURAL! THEY'RE ANGRY AT A BLACK MAN, AND THEY CAN'T FUCKIN' EXPRESS THEMSELVES!
IT'S LIKE THEY'RE TRAPPED IN A CROWDED ELEVATOR AND THEY GOTTA HOLD IN A FART! FOR EIGHT YEARS!
(RISING LAUGHTER)
I ALWAYS IMAGINE GUYS LIKE JOHN BOEHNER GOING HOME AT NIGHT, LOCKING THEMSELVES IN THE BATHROOM, BURYING THEIR FACE IN A TOWEL, AND THEN SCREAMING "NIGGER!"
(UNCOMFORTABLE LAUGHTER)
I'M NOT EVEN SAYING THESE GUYS ARE STRAIGHT-UP RACISTS. I MEAN, SOME OF THEM PROBABLY ARE...
BUT EVERYONE--AND I MEAN EVERYONE--WILL SAY SOME FUCKED-UP RACIAL SHIT IF THEY'RE MAD OR SCARED ENOUGH.
HA HA HA... LOOK AT ALL THE WHITE PEOPLE SHAKING THEIR HEADS, LIKE "NOT ME!!"
I'M NOT PROUD OF THIS, BUT I WAS WATCHING THE STATE OF THE UNION ADDRESS THE OTHER NIGHT, AND I HAD TO BURY MY FACE IN A PILLOW AND SCREAM, "YOU SAID YOU WERE GONNA SHUT DOWN GUANTANAMO, NIGGER!"
(LAUGHTER, APPLAUSE)
THANKS A LOT!
WHO'S UP NEXT?
WOW... KIND OF HARD TO F-F-FOLLOW THAT!

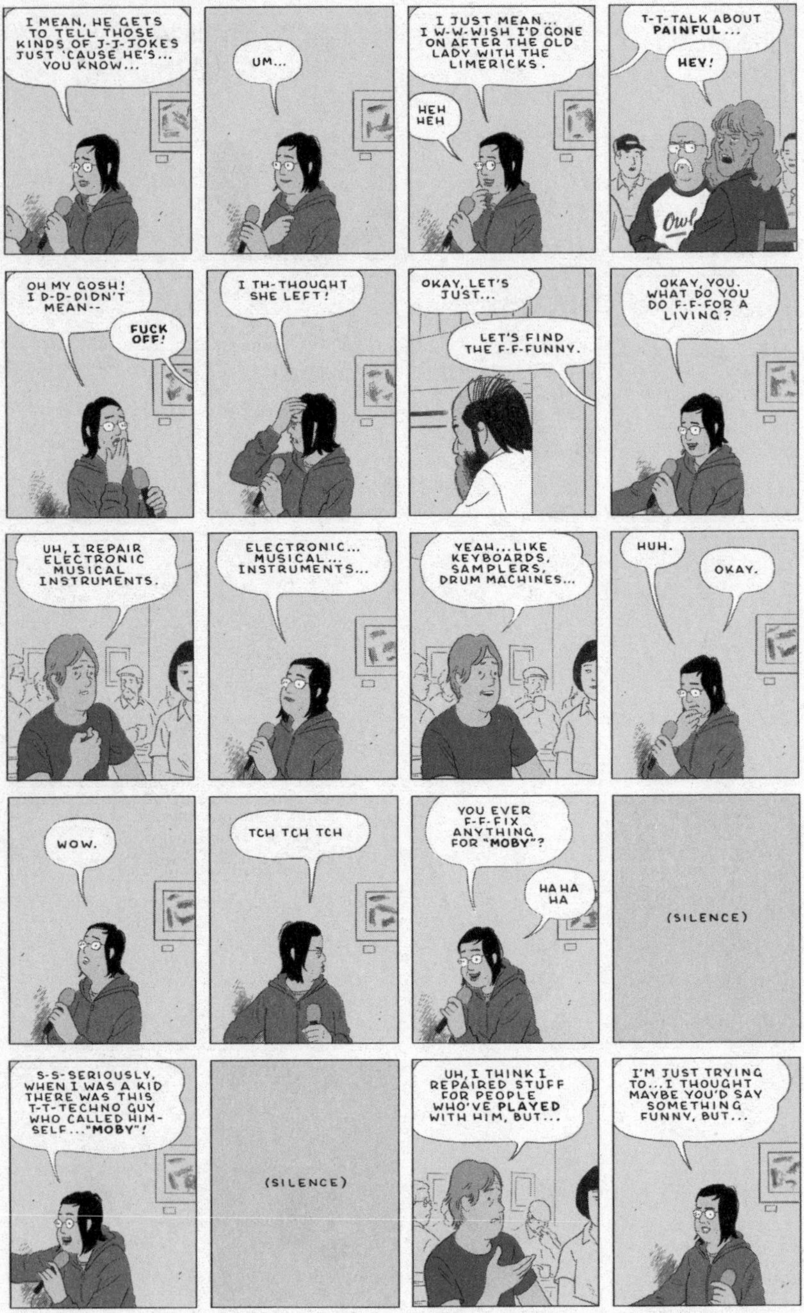

I MEAN, HE GETS TO TELL THOSE KINDS OF J-J-JOKES JUST 'CAUSE HE'S... YOU KNOW...
UM...
I JUST MEAN... I W-W-WISH I'D GONE ON AFTER THE OLD LADY WITH THE LIMERICKS.
HEH HEH
T-T-TALK ABOUT **PAINFUL**...
HEY!
OH MY GOSH! I D-D-DIDN'T MEAN--
FUCK OFF!
I TH-THOUGHT SHE LEFT!
OKAY, LET'S JUST...
LET'S FIND THE F-F-FUNNY.
OKAY, YOU. WHAT DO YOU DO F-F-FOR A LIVING?
UH, I REPAIR ELECTRONIC MUSICAL INSTRUMENTS.
ELECTRONIC... MUSICAL... INSTRUMENTS...
YEAH... LIKE KEYBOARDS, SAMPLERS, DRUM MACHINES...
HUH.
OKAY.
WOW.
TCH TCH TCH
YOU EVER F-F-FIX ANYTHING FOR "**MOBY**"?
HA HA HA
(SILENCE)
S-S-SERIOUSLY. WHEN I WAS A KID THERE WAS THIS T-T-TECHNO GUY WHO CALLED HIMSELF... "**MOBY**"!
(SILENCE)
UH, I THINK I REPAIRED STUFF FOR PEOPLE WHO'VE **PLAYED** WITH HIM, BUT...
I'M JUST TRYING TO... I THOUGHT MAYBE YOU'D SAY SOMETHING FUNNY, BUT...

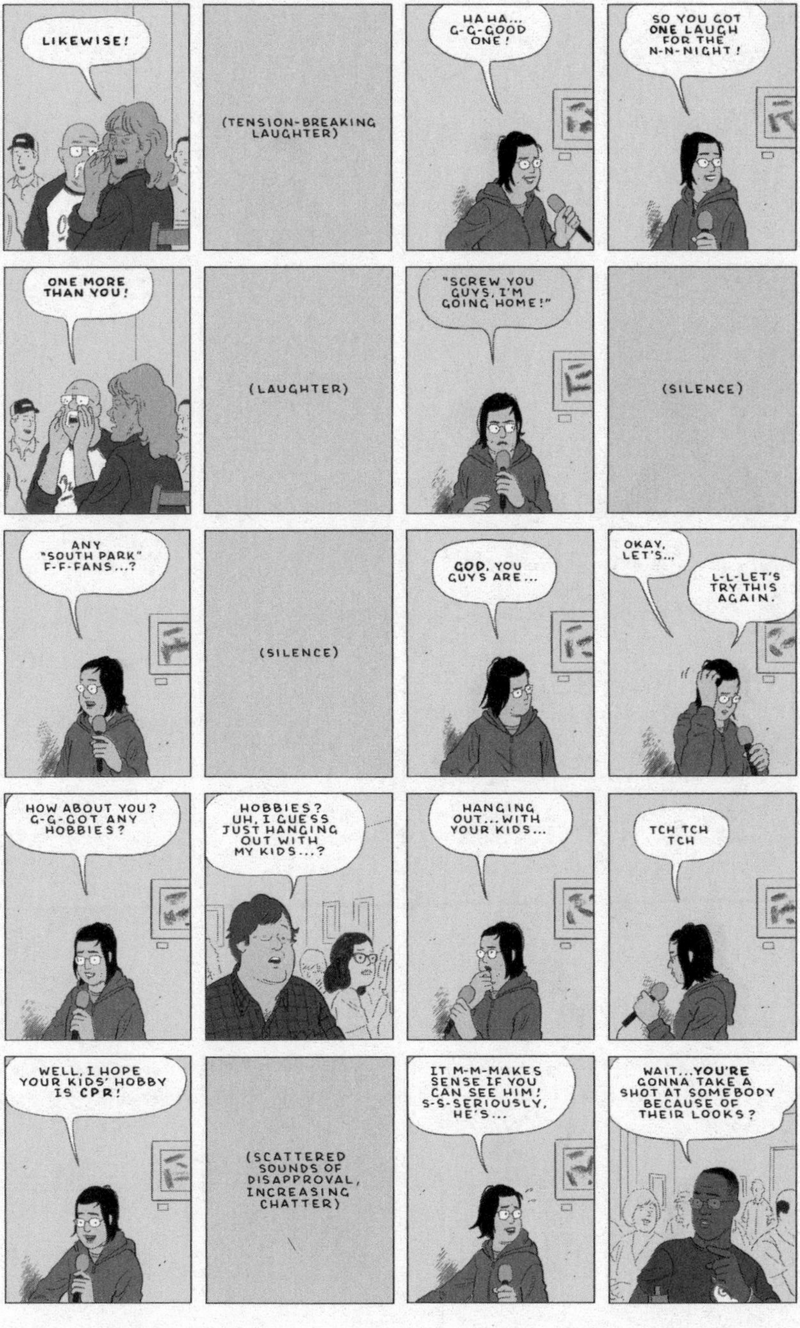
LIKEWISE!
(TENSION-BREAKING LAUGHTER)
HA HA... G-G-GOOD ONE!
SO YOU GOT ONE LAUGH FOR THE N-N-NIGHT!
ONE MORE THAN YOU!
(LAUGHTER)
"SCREW YOU GUYS, I'M GOING HOME!"
(SILENCE)
ANY "SOUTH PARK" F-F-FANS...?
(SILENCE)
GOD, YOU GUYS ARE...
OKAY, LET'S...
L-L-LET'S TRY THIS AGAIN.
HOW ABOUT YOU? G-G-GOT ANY HOBBIES?
HOBBIES? UH, I GUESS JUST HANGING OUT WITH MY KIDS...?
HANGING OUT... WITH YOUR KIDS...
TCH TCH TCH
WELL, I HOPE YOUR KIDS' HOBBY IS CPR!
(SCATTERED SOUNDS OF DISAPPROVAL, INCREASING CHATTER)
IT M-M-MAKES SENSE IF YOU CAN SEE HIM! S-S-SERIOUSLY, HE'S...
WAIT... YOU'RE GONNA TAKE A SHOT AT SOMEBODY BECAUSE OF THEIR LOOKS?

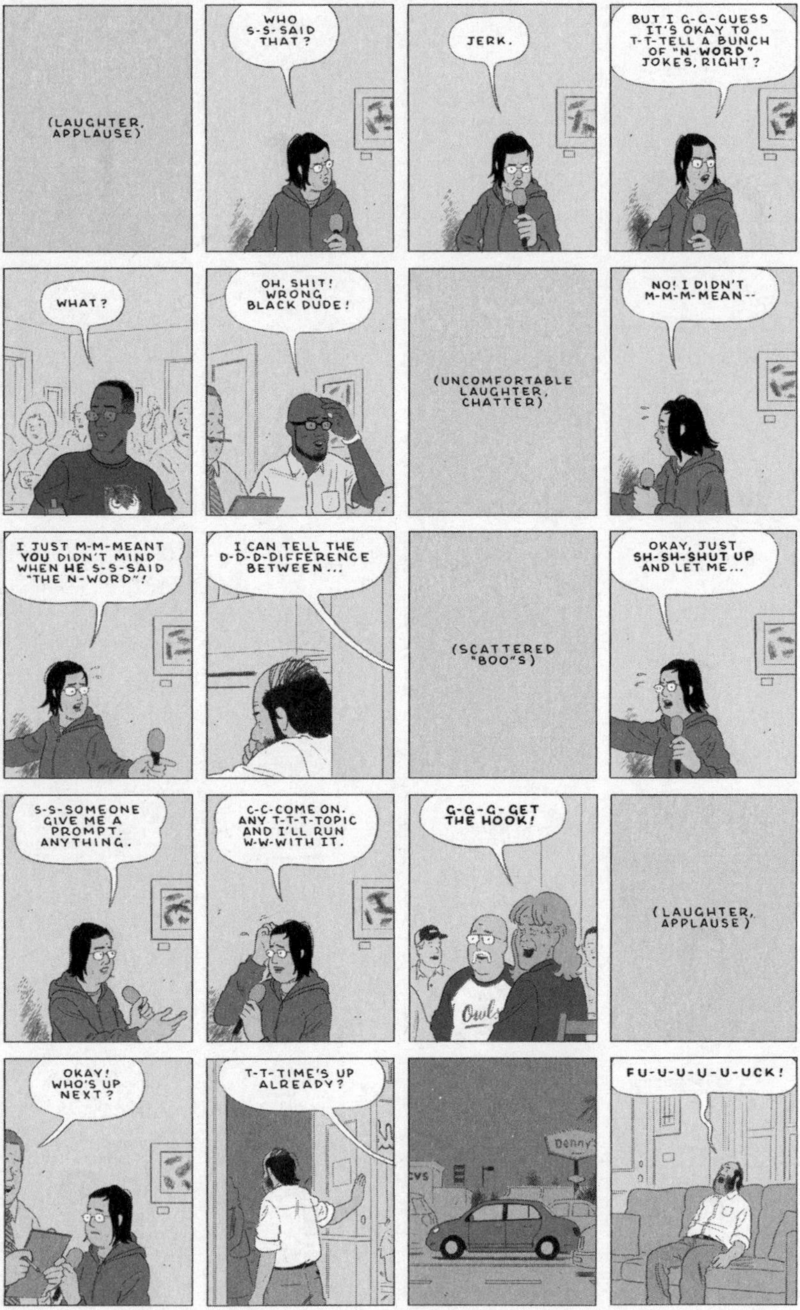
(LAUGHTER, APPLAUSE)
WHO S-S-SAID THAT?
JERK.
BUT I G-G-GUESS IT'S OKAY TO T-T-TELL A BUNCH OF "N-WORD" JOKES, RIGHT?
WHAT?
OH, SHIT! WRONG BLACK DUDE!
(UNCOMFORTABLE LAUGHTER, CHATTER)
NO! I DIDN'T M-M-M-MEAN--
I JUST M-M-MEANT YOU DIDN'T MIND WHEN HE S-S-SAID "THE N-WORD"!
I CAN TELL THE D-D-D-DIFFERENCE BETWEEN...
(SCATTERED "BOO"S)
OKAY, JUST SH-SH-SHUT UP AND LET ME...
S-S-SOMEONE GIVE ME A PROMPT. ANYTHING.
C-C-COME ON. ANY T-T-T-TOPIC AND I'LL RUN W-W-WITH IT.
G-G-G-GET THE HOOK!
(LAUGHTER, APPLAUSE)
OKAY! WHO'S UP NEXT?
T-T-TIME'S UP ALREADY?
Denny's
CVS
FU-U-U-U-U-UCK!

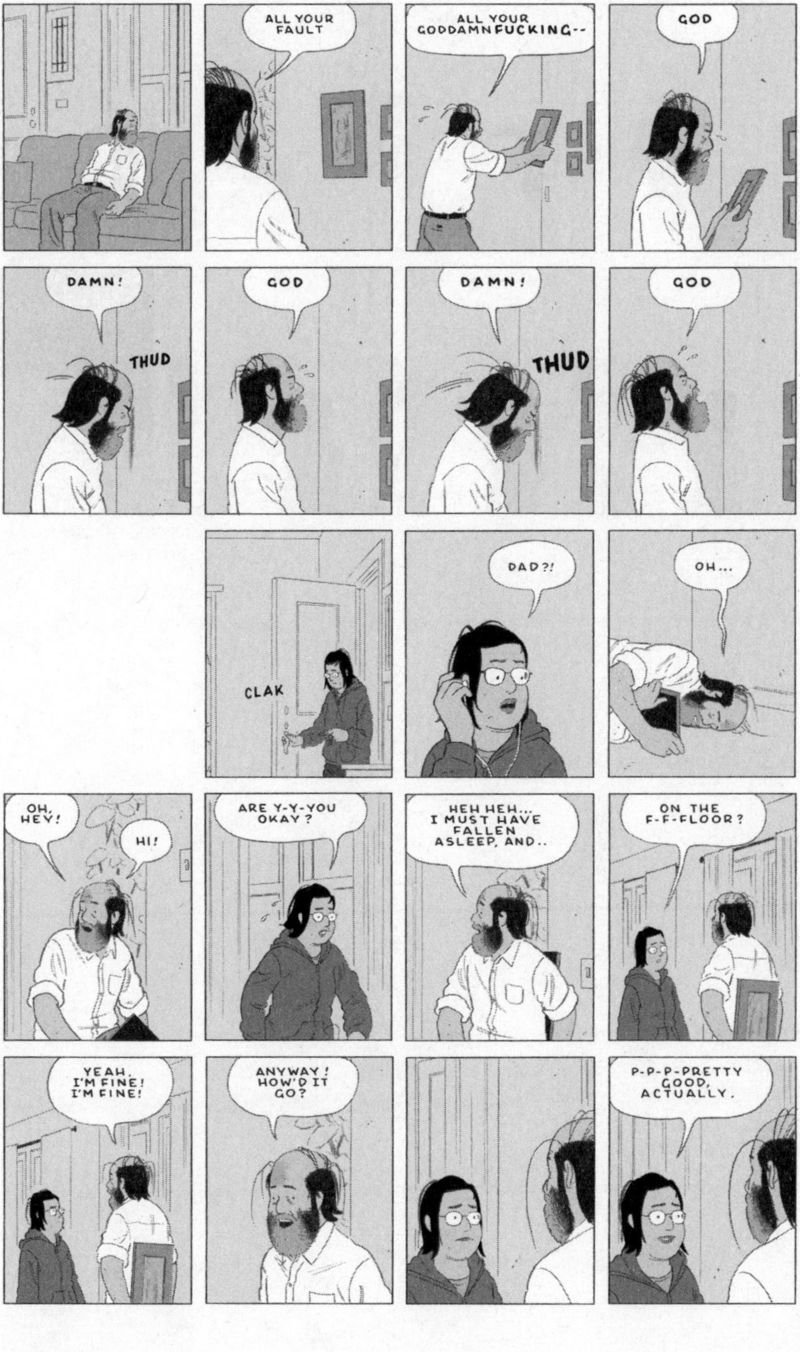
ALL YOUR FAULT
ALL YOUR GODDAMNFUCKING--
GOD
DAMN!
THUD
GOD
DAMN!
THUD
GOD
CLAK
DAD?!
OH...
OH, HEY!
HI!
ARE Y-Y-YOU OKAY?
HEH HEH... I MUST HAVE FALLEN ASLEEP, AND..
ON THE F-F-FLOOR?
YEAH. I'M FINE! I'M FINE!
ANYWAY! HOW'D IT GO?
P-P-P-PRETTY GOOD, ACTUALLY.

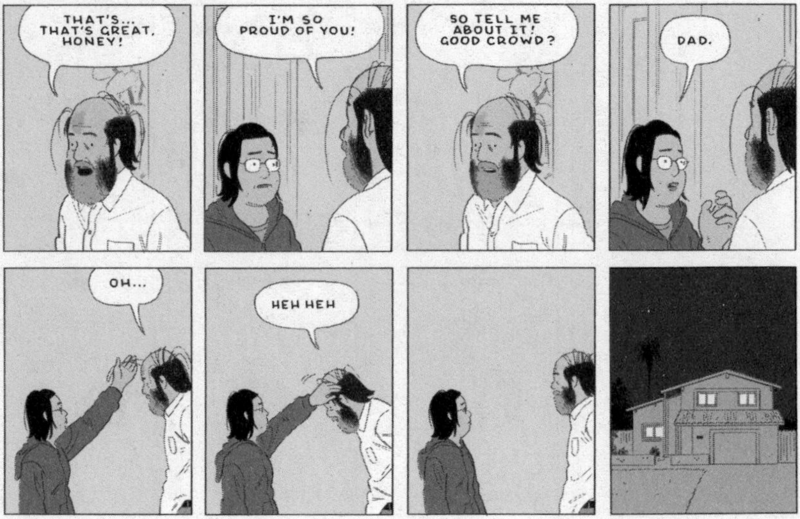
THAT'S... THAT'S GREAT, HONEY!
I'M SO PROUD OF YOU!
SO TELL ME ABOUT IT! GOOD CROWD?
DAD.
OH...
HEH HEH

■

On This Side

FROM *The Iowa Review*

TORU FOUND A GIRL sitting on the stairs in the midsummer heat when he came home from an early shift. Even from half a block away, she stood out against his decrepit apartment building. She sat hugging her bare knees in white cotton shorts, her long dark hair draped forward over both shoulders. The sleeves of her unseasonable denim jacket were rolled up to just below her elbows. There was a large canvas bag next to her, blocking the staircase. Through the afternoon heat everything shimmered uncertainly, and for a second Toru wondered if she wasn't an apparition. The insistent buzz of the cicadas created a kind of thick silence, numbing his senses.

Upon noticing him, the girl looked up with a hopefulness that made Toru feel apologetic. Suddenly he could smell his own body. He had come from making the rounds restocking vending machines and hadn't bothered to shower at the office when he'd changed out of the uniform. With his eyes to the ground, he tried to squeeze past her.

"Toru-kun." The girl stood up. Her voice sounded oddly thick.

For a moment they stood awkwardly together on the stairs. A mixture of soap and sweat wafted from her. Up close, Toru saw that her face was meticulously made up, her skin carefully primed and her expectant eyes accentuated with clean black lines. He was slow to recognize what was underneath. But then he felt his heart skip a beat.

"Masato?" he said.

"Hello." As though in relief she held out her hand, and Toru shook it automatically. Her fingers were bony but solid in his palm. "I go by Saki now."

"Saki?"

More than ten years ago, in junior high school, she had been a boy.

Toru tentatively invited her, or him, or whatever Saki was now, into his one-room apartment on the second floor. He didn't want to be seen with her on the stairs. His neighbors were mostly single men of meager means like himself, and, with only thin walls between them, everyone did his best to keep to himself.

Saki took off her sandals and walked in, not minding the dusty *tatami* floor bleached from years of sunlight. Her toenails were painted the color of pomegranate. Next to the entrance were a metal sink, a two-burner stove, and an antiquated fridge that constituted Toru's kitchen. The opposite wall had a closet with sliding paper doors where he kept his clothes and bedding. There was a toilet in each apartment, but the bath was shared. A small, tilting bookshelf and a folding coffee table were the only pieces of furniture, and the white canvas bag Saki flopped down in the corner became the third-largest item in the room.

Saki opened and closed the bathroom door and walked around the room once, as though giving it a quick inspection. She then went to the sink and tried the faucet. The air in the small room felt even more stagnant than usual. Toru considered offering her something cold to drink, but he didn't want this unexpected visit to draw out.

"Sorry I don't even have AC," he said.

"Oh, this is just fine," Saki said, and bent down to turn on the fan next to the coffee table. "I don't like AC anyway."

Toru glanced at the back of her shapely calves and noted a long-healed scar forming a startling trench on the side of her right knee. The first thing he had felt on the staircase was a knot forming in his stomach, a forgotten seed of guilt he didn't care to inspect, and now it was threatening to grow. He hadn't thought of his classmate once in all these years. But the longer he looked at her, this Saki, the more he realized that he wasn't as baffled as he might have been by the transformation. He remembered the slight neck that seemed to reach perpetually forward and the dense, long eyelashes that used to cast melancholy shadows over the eyes. She was, and had been, pretty.

"So." Toru cleared his throat. He had been staring. "How did you find me?"

"Oh, I just looked you up," Saki said. "There are ways. It's not that hard. Can I stay with you for a while?"

"Excuse me?"

"I need a place to stay. Just for a while."

Toru looked at her blankly. He was still in his shoes, standing just inside the door. "You mean here?" he said. "Why? What do you mean?"

"I'm in this predicament. A relationship problem, so to speak."

Toru felt the knot in his stomach become denser as he watched Saki drift to the open window. The only view he had was a narrow slice of southern sky between the walls of the adjacent buildings and the corrugated rooftop of a warehouse, but Saki gazed out as though at a refreshing country vista. Above her head hung boxers and socks and a thinly worn towel that Toru had hand-washed that morning.

"Well," Toru said. "I'm very sorry to hear that. I do feel sorry. But I wasn't expecting—I'm sure this isn't your best option. I mean, look at this place. There's barely room for myself."

"Oh, this is totally fine. I'm not particular."

Toru sighed. "Look, you don't understand. I'm afraid it's not fine," he said. "I have my own problems. For one thing, I have a girlfriend."

"That's a problem?" Saki tilted her head. "She's a jealous type?"

"No, no." Toru flinched. "That's not how I meant it. See, you don't even know me at this point. I'm barely managing day to day here. I'm surely not the best person to turn to in your situation."

"You don't know my situation yet. You haven't asked."

Although Saki's tone was matter-of-fact, simply pointing out his mistake, Toru was taken back by the truth of this.

"I don't want to pry," he said.

"It's really just for a while," Saki said, as though patiently reassuring a child. "I'll of course cook and clean."

"Don't you have other friends?" Toru said. "Does your family know you are here?"

Saki frowned at him. "If I had a family who cared where I was, don't you think I would go stay with them?"

When Toru failed to respond, Saki let out a small sigh and dropped her gaze to the floor.

"Here's the thing," she said. "I just got out of the hospital and I'm broke. I need a little time to sort things out."

"What, are you sick?" Toru said. "What happened?"

Saki bounced on her heels for a moment, fiddling with the hem of her shorts. "I was injured. Stabbed, actually, by my boyfriend." She paused, searching for something on his face. "He didn't know. That I was, you know. So."

Toru blinked. Then he blinked again.

"If you want, I can show you the wound." Saki grabbed the bottom of her shirt.

"Wait." Before he could think, Toru found himself across the room, still in his shoes, and seizing her wrists. Whatever was behind the fabric, he wasn't ready to see.

Saki was a horrible cook. When Toru came home the next day, she had prepared some curry, but it was straight out of a package. The vegetables were undercooked, the onion still tangy. She had added too little water, and the paste was not evenly dissolved. The rice was dry, even though she had used the same rice cooker Toru used every day. He was baffled that anyone could mess up the simplest of dishes.

"You shouldn't worry about cooking," Toru said, eating out of politeness and dripping with sweat. "You're—a guest, I suppose."

"Oh, it's no trouble." Saki had eaten less than a third of her bowl and was poking the vegetables around while Toru tediously worked on his. "It's the least I can do."

"No, really," Toru said. "Look, I'll prepare something simple after I come home. Okay?"

"Okay," Saki said. "If you insist."

Saki hadn't left the apartment all day. When Toru asked, she said she had mostly slept, read some, and listened to the radio. She then added, brightly, "You can't imagine how much I appreciate this. This is exactly what I needed."

The night before, he had conceded his thin futon to Saki and slept on top of his old sleeping bag. He couldn't bring himself to kick her out. Whatever sort of life Saki had lived since Toru had last known her he didn't feel inclined to imagine, but he couldn't help suspecting he'd had a hand in it. That life now all seemed to fit into her plain canvas bag. Everything that came out of it went back into it. If he were to pick up the bag and take it out like the trash, there would be no trace of her left behind.

For a few months at the beginning of eighth grade, Toru's life had revolved around Masato. Before his childhood friend Kyoko had singled out Masato as her crush a few weeks into school, Toru hadn't even taken note of him. Masato had been a quiet, fragile-looking boy who seemed to prefer solitude. Toru could only now surmise that he might have tickled maternal instinct in some girls. ("Don't you think he's adorable?" Kyoko had said. Toru had to search his mind to vaguely picture Masato's face.)

Earlier that spring, Toru had watched with bewilderment as Kyoko blossomed into something mysterious and fragrant next to him. He was desperately hoping that she would see a similar transformation in him and realize that he was no longer the silly neighborhood kid she could boss around. But Toru was her best friend. It had been to him that she confided her feelings for Masato. It had been he who had to help her get close to this taciturn classmate. He was enlisted to create many awkward coincidences for her to bump into Masako. He had to ask him to lunch, where Kyoko would casually join; find out his birthday and shoe size; and walk home with him so Kyoko would know which route he took.

For those few months, Toru hated Masato.

"What is your girlfriend like?" Saki said now, as they sat drinking beer after dinner. "Is she a good cook?"

Once in a while, Toru got to take home canned drinks that had passed the sell-by dates. If the timing was right, he got to pick a box of beer. It was one of the very few perks of his job.

"I actually don't know," Toru said. "She's never cooked for me. We never meet at either of our places."

"Why not?"

Toru didn't own a TV and was playing a movie on his old laptop, to have something when the conversation lulled. It was a black-and-white Kurosawa, something his girlfriend had lent him.

"Well, obviously this is not a place to bring a woman for a date," he said. He turned the beer can in his hands several times. "And she has a family."

There was a pause. "She's married?"

"Yes."

"Children?"

"Two. Boys, I think." Toru sneaked a look at Saki's face to gauge her reaction. She had her eyes on the computer screen, though he couldn't tell if she was watching. "So we meet at a hotel. Just a couple of times a month," he said.

"And eat at restaurants," she said.

He nodded. And he willed the conversation to cease there. His older girlfriend paid for meals and rooms most of the time, with her husband's money. He was not proud of it.

The evening air outside the open window smelled vibrant, as though the intensity of the heat had been skimmed off its surface and all the living things underneath were finally allowed to breathe. Occasionally trains went by just a few blocks away, but they sounded strangely muted and distant.

"Speaking of restaurants," Saki said, three beers later, "I have this recurring dream."

"About a restaurant?" Toru glanced at her. Having given up on the movie, she was leaning on the low windowsill, her elbow sticking outside and her cheek resting on the back of her hand. "A nightmare, no doubt."

"I don't know if it's a nightmare, quite. But I've had it for years. I'm in this crowded restaurant, with or without other people, the details always change. I place an order, but after waiting for a long time, I realize I'm not getting the food. So I go look for my server and find the kitchen closed in the back. I return to a different, dark room, and my food is on the table with plastic wrap over it, and there's a note stuck on it. Like a Post-it note. This makes me very sad, and the next moment I find myself in an empty house."

Toru waited. "And then? What happens in the empty house?"

"That's it," she said. "That's the end."

"Saki." Toru tapped her shoulder, but she didn't budge. While he finished the movie, she had fallen asleep on the floor. Her long hair hid most of her face, but he could see that her cheek was flushed and her mouth was open.

Toru moved the coffee table to make room for the futon next to her and rolled her over onto the sheet. She was alarmingly light. He observed her shoulder move up and down almost imperceptibly with her breathing, and noticed the imprint left on her temple from the floor.

The bottom of her shirt had ridden up a little. Toru was tempted for a moment to peek, to confirm the stab wound and, more importantly, to see how the subtle but unmistakable roundness of her breasts worked. Whether they were real.

Once, after walking home together, Toru had asked to use the bathroom at Masato's house. No one was home, and Masato invited him to stay for a snack. While Masato went to get things from the kitchen, Toru used the bathroom and poked around, just so he could report back to Kyoko. Masato's room, which he found down the hallway, was dim, with the curtains mostly drawn, and surprisingly messy. Strewn clothes covered most of the available surfaces, with textbooks and magazines and candy wrappers entangled in them, while the cream-colored walls remained strangely unadorned. There was something odd about the room, though Toru couldn't immediately put a finger on it. And then he saw what it was. Among the formless piles of clothes were several pairs of girls' underwear.

Saki twitched her fingers in her sleep. Toru stood up, picked up the empty cans, and turned the lights off.

"Don't you want to get out a bit?" Toru said to Saki a few days later. They had finished breakfast, and he was rinsing the plates. "Walk around or something? I guess you're still recovering, but I'm sure it'd feel better than sitting in this dingy room all day."

Saki looked up from the fashion magazine she was leafing through. In the evenings she would go to the convenience store near the station while Toru cooked dinner—the only time she would go out—and always come home with a new magazine. A small stack was starting to form on the floor beside the coffee table.

"I don't have a key," she said.

She was sitting on the floor in a pair of jean shorts, leaning against the table with one leg folded at her side and the other one, the one with the old scar, stretched out. Though they had just eaten, she was snacking on some potato chips. The fan next to her face mussed her hair every time it swung past, revealing her forehead.

"No one would break into a dump like this," Toru said. "There's nothing to take."

"But I have all my stuff here."

Toru put away the coffeepot and stood wiping his hands on the towel. "Trust me, nothing will happen while you take a little walk."

"The thing is," Saki said, "my apartment got broken into while I was in the hospital. The same boyfriend."

Toru sighed. He bunched the towel and tossed it on the dish rack.

"He systematically destroyed everything I owned," Saki said.

"Fine," said Toru, "I'll copy the key for you."

"Thank you," she said, and her smile made Toru wonder if he had been tricked. He still hadn't asked her when she intended to leave.

"Look, I won't even pretend to know what it's like." He sat down across the table from her. "But your situation sounds serious. Shouldn't you seek out some professional help?"

Saki went back to flipping through the magazine. From the open window the mechanical sound of cicadas seeped into the room and filled the little silence between them.

"Did you talk to the police?" he said. "I mean, this guy sounds like a psychopath. What did they do with him?"

"Nothing," Saki said. "I told them I was mugged. Didn't see any face."

"What?"

"The police won't do me any good. Trust me." Without taking her eyes off the pages, Saki reached for more potato chips and nibbled on them.

"Are you trying to protect this guy?" Toru said. "Is that it? After what he's done to you?"

Saki abruptly closed the magazine and tossed it onto the pile. "How about we go for a walk together?" she said.

Toru blinked. "Now? I have to go to work."

"Can I come along then?" she said. "I'd like to see what you do with the vending machines."

She picked up a glass with some melting ice cubes at the bottom and tilted it back to get a trickle of water. The clinking of the ice cooled the stale air in the room by a fraction of a degree.

"I don't think that's a good idea," Toru said.

"But you're making the rounds all by yourself, right?" she said. "No one's going to know."

"I'm going to a different job today," he said.

Saki raised her eyebrows. "Oh?"

"I have this part-time job," he said. "A seasonal one."

"Well, what is it?"

Toru hesitated for a second. "I work at a cemetery."

"A cemetery?"

"You know it's Bon this month, but a lot of people can't make the trip these days. So they hire someone else to do it for them. Some people more than once a year, but mostly just for Bon. It's the peak season."

"So you go visit and clean the graves of people you don't know."

"Right."

"That sounds great," Saki said.

One step out of the air-conditioned train, the chorus of cicadas once again vibrated the heavy air. Toru's ears had grown numb to the incessant ringing, but he felt it loudly on his skin. There was not a hint of breeze and walking was an effort, as though wading through thick liquid.

In public with Saki for the first time, Toru felt self-conscious, his movements somehow encumbered by her bare-legged presence. The whole walk to the cemetery, Saki followed a few paces behind him at a leisurely pace, dangling a shopping bag of cleaning supplies. Toru thought she was favoring her scarred leg, but the unevenness in her gait was subtle enough that he could have been wrong.

Sometime in late fall, back in eighth grade, Masato had jumped from the third-story balcony at school. A group of male students who had been with him at the time said it had been a dare, just a joke, that no one had expected him to actually jump. Others who had seen it happen confirmed that he had voluntarily climbed over the railing. When the assistant principal spoke about the incident to the student body, he referred to it as "an accident resulting from reckless behavior." They were not to confuse selfish acts that inconvenienced many people with courage.

Masato broke a number of bones and didn't come back to school after he was released from the hospital months later. His family had supposedly moved to another town. But by then it was past winter break, and his empty desk had long since been taken. The rumors and hushed excitement had grown stale.

Toru and Saki stopped to buy flowers near the station, and picked up boxes of sweets and fruits along the way for offerings.

"Wow," Saki said. "Fancy. All that for dead strangers?"

"I'll get reimbursed, of course." Toru neatly folded the receipts into his wallet. "And we get to keep the food. We have to take it home because we can't leave it out at the grave. It's just a gesture."

"I suppose that's what counts," she said. "A gesture."

The cemetery had sprawling paved grounds and no temple. Toru stopped at the management office to check in and pick up the assignment for the day, then went to fill a bucket with water.

"Whenever I think of a cemetery, I picture it in the summer," Saki said, watching Toru clean. "Quietly grilling under the sun, just like this."

Toru was on his fifth grave. Saki had closely observed the process the first time, and then had wandered off for a while to walk around the grounds before finding him again. This grave had a fairly new, elaborate headstone, its corners still sharp and its surface polished.

"I guess I do, too." Toru had removed the wilted flowers and incense ashes from their receptacles and was sweeping the tiny plot of land. "Because we used to play in the cemetery near our grandparents' during the summer. But an old man chased us with a broom this one time, saying we'd be cursed for disturbing the peace of the dead." He halted the sweeping and looked around. "I just remembered that. One of my cousins yelled back, 'Soon, when *you* are stuck under one of these stones, I bet you'll wish you had some company!'"

Saki contemplated this for a second. "Do you think it's really peaceful there?" she said. "On the other side?"

Toru glanced at her. She was tracing the clean edges of the gravestone with her long finger. The sun was already high, and everything in sight had a bright shallowness to it. A tiny thunderhead poised over the distant treetops, but no shade was in sight. Just then, there was something so delicate about Saki that for a second Toru had an urge to shield her from the harsh light. He shook the thought away.

"I personally don't believe in the other side," he said.

"Then you don't think there'll be suffering, either?" she said. "Like punishment?"

The sweeping done, Toru poured some water on the gravestone and started wiping it down with a cloth. "You mean like hell?"

"I don't know," she said. "Just some sort of consequence. Of your life."

"I've always imagined it'll just be complete nothingness. Back to zero," he said. "Would you get me the toothbrush?"

Saki bent down to search in the shopping bag. "Complete nothingness. That doesn't sound too bad." She handed him the toothbrush and rested her butt on the marble ledge marking the next plot, stretching out her scarred leg. "But what if you've done something horribly wrong in your life?"

"Like what?" Toru went on scrubbing the letters engraved on the stone. This one said "Tajima Family" on the front, with individual names and years on the back. Some of the stones were so worn he could hardly make out the letters, while some of the new ones had a name or two in red letters, indicating people who were still alive. He never understood the rush, the urge to have somewhere to go after this life.

"Like if you've seriously harmed someone. Or killed someone."

"I don't know," Toru said. "You'd *live* with the consequences then, right?"

Saki remained silent for a second. Toru could feel her eyes on his back.

"What if that wasn't enough?" Her tone sounded provocative, but Toru couldn't be sure. "What then?"

Toru ladled more water onto the gravestone and placed fresh bundles of flowers in the vases. The sky was overbearingly wide-open above them. His shirt clung to his back. The blinding sun was all around them, reflecting off the cement and white pebbles.

Kyoko and Toru never talked about Masato after the incident. Toru sensed Kyoko's intense shame and fear, and knew better than to bring up her crush on the bullying target. They acted as though nothing, not even a quiet ripple, had disturbed the smooth, continuous surface of their daily lives at school. But that meant they had to pretend that the months leading up to the fall had never happened, that this thing that had structured their days had never existed. The two of them hung out less and less, in a way that felt inevitable. It didn't occur to Toru until much later that Kyoko must have seen him as a threat, a ticking bomb that could be her undoing at any moment. That she might have desperately wanted to get rid of him. By the time they started the new school year in April, the two of them were going around in different circles.

"Of course," Toru said carefully, "it would be comforting to think there's something just about the whole thing in the end. That those who've done wrong wouldn't ultimately get away with it. But I have a feeling it doesn't work that way. We probably have to work things out on this side."

Saki picked up one of the rough-edged stones at her feet and toyed with it, as if to read something in the texture of its surface. She then straightened up, pocketed the stone, and walked around the grave.

"God, it's hot," she said. "I should have brought my hat."

"You shouldn't just be standing around." Toru felt relieved. "You'll have a heat stroke. Maybe you should go home."

"I'm fine," Saki said. "I kind of like it here."

"Why don't you go inside for a bit, at least?" he said. "And you could get two more bundles of incense for me on the way back."

While she was gone, Toru finished laying out the offerings and putting the cleaning supplies away. Although it was close to Bon, there weren't many other people visiting the graves on a weekday. He heard some kids shrieking in the distance and their mother calling after them. There was an old woman several rows away, pulling weeds under a broad-rimmed straw hat. When Toru stood up to stretch his back, the woman looked up and nodded approvingly. Toru nodded in return. He then realized he had thrown away the fresh flowers that he had just placed in the vases. He searched for them in the garbage bag, cursing himself, and put them back. They looked slightly disheveled now, but then again, he and Saki would be the only ones to see them anyway. He couldn't think straight. It was the heat.

For a while after the incident, Toru occasionally found himself picturing the scene on the balcony. In his mind, there was a haunting fierceness to Masato's action. Toru hadn't been there, not exactly; he had been copying Kyoko's homework in the classroom, and when he'd looked up, sensing the commotion on the balcony, Masato was already on the ground eight meters below. But Toru sometimes imagined that Masato's eyes had actually sought him through the window, that it had been Masato's gaze that had made him look up. That their eyes had met. This couldn't have really happened, because all Toru could see from where he sat at the far end of the classroom were the backs of his classmates, indistinguishable in their gray uniform sweaters. And yet the more he thought about that day, the more vividly he could picture the look on Masato's face.

Did his classmates also see it—anger, hatred, defiance, or was it mere desperation?—flicker in those large but normally downcast eyes? Toru tried to imagine the discomfort spreading among the group of boys as Masato climbed over the railing, even as they sneered at his bluff. And the shock that must have rippled through them when he jumped. The brutal instantaneity of the fall, how there was no moment of suspense in which he seemed to become airborne, as in a movie, but how instead the body just hit the ground with a dull thump before they could grasp what was happening. Had there been time for Masato to feel the triumph, the satisfaction, before the pain came? Had he been able to see the astonishment and perhaps awe on his classmates' faces high above? Toru didn't even know whether Masato had fallen facedown or up.

When Saki came back, she stood next to Toru and prayed with him. The clean grave smelled fresh from the evaporating water and the incense. Toru never knew what to say to the dead strangers, but he always put his palms together, closed his eyes, and thought something general and polite. This time, though, with his eyes shut, he could think only about Saki. He really needed to ask her to leave the apartment before he got entangled in some mess. Before it was too late.

But instead he said, "Shall we get something for lunch?" He felt lightheaded. "Something cold?"

Saki kept her eyes closed and finished her prayer before turning to him. "That sounds good," she said.

* * *

For the next few weeks, Toru went to clean the graves in the morning, and then worked the late shift refilling the vending machines. Now that she had the key, Saki seemed to go out regularly. Most days he would find her back in the apartment when he came home, reading her magazines and nibbling at sweets from the cemetery. Sometimes she would come back while he prepared dinner. They would always eat together, and afterwards they would have some beer and watch a movie on his computer. Somewhere along the way, their days started to acquire a new, plain rhythm, hypnotic in its simplicity and almost indistinguishable from the routine he had established alone.

He spent one evening with his girlfriend, but he was distracted. The thought of Saki sitting around his apartment while he ate at a restaurant and had sex in an air-conditioned hotel room kept him restless. It was easy to picture her at the coffee table munching on potato chips for dinner, and he wondered if he should have prepared and left something for her. In bed, he found himself going rough on his girlfriend, as though trying to dig through his thoughts to the body beneath him. His girlfriend noticed.

"What's on your mind?" She was fixing her hair in the mirror, combing it back into her usual, simple low ponytail. The room was by the hour, so they never lingered.

"There's a bit of a situation." Toru sighed, already dressed and sitting on the edge of the bed. "I should probably explain. It's just that I don't know—"

"If there's someone else, don't tell me," she said into the mirror, in a reassuring voice that he imagined would comfort her children. "I don't want to know. Just don't let me ever feel her presence. That's all I ask."

Toru watched her scrape mascara from under her eyes with her neatly trimmed nails. Her hands were unadorned, for practical use. He imagined her at home, in her kitchen, cooking meals that he would never taste.

"Where do you go every day?" Toru said.

It had been a little over a month since Saki had arrived, and he had another early shift. He found Saki hunched over the coffee table, repainting her nails. They were the same pomegranate color as her toes. She pretended not to hear.

"You've been going out, right?" Toru said, pulling a T-shirt over his head. "Are you looking for a job?"

She finished painting the last nail and held her left hand to the light to inspect the glossy surfaces before turning her attention to him. "Why so curious suddenly? You sound like a jealous boyfriend."

It was his turn to remain silent.

"You want to know what I'm doing while you aren't looking?"

"I thought you were trying to get back on your feet."

"It's okay." She sounded playful. "You want to know?"

"You said just for a while. It's only fair."

"I'll tell you, but you have to keep it a secret." There was a glow in her eyes. "I'm on a mission."

"A mission?"

"I've been tracking down all the bullies from my past."

Toru could feel the weight of the familiar knot taking shape in his stomach.

"So I can go around getting back at them, one by one."

"Get back how?" Toru said.

"I'd show up with these giant scissors, you see," she said. "Of course I'd first seduce them, drug them, and tie them up naked. In whatever order works. Then I'd wait until they were fully awake. And while they were saying, 'I'm sorry, I was a jerk, I repent! Please, forgive me!' I'd chop their thing off. Like this, with both hands. Snip."

Despite himself, Toru felt a small chill at the base of his spine. They held each other's gaze, the last word hovering in the humid air between them. Toru thought he recognized those eyes, the ones that had sought him from the balcony through the window, with a flicker of something that was lost before he could grasp it. Then he remembered that this had happened only in his mind. He was unable to distinguish real memories from those he'd imagined. For instance, he was no longer certain that he had never intended for things to turn out the way they had. It wasn't that he had meant, really, to compel his classmates to go after Masato when he told them about his curious collection of girls' underwear. But couldn't he have predicted that there would be bathroom ambushes, jeering, and peeking?

"Look at you." Saki laughed out loud. "I'm joking. Of course I'm looking for a job."

Toru, feeling weary, picked up his sweaty undershirt from the floor and brought it to the sink. He ran it under the water, squeezing the stench out of the thinning fabric. "Well? Any prospects?"

Saki didn't respond, and Toru kept squeezing and rubbing, as though if he kept up with it long enough, he would be able to wash away his thoughts as well. When he finally wrung out the shirt, much more thoroughly than necessary, and turned around, he was met with Saki's patient eyes.

"Did you know you can see the sunset from your window?" she said.

"What?"

She said she could see the western sky change colors in his neighbor's window. Toru was rarely home before sunset, and when he was, he never thought to look out. That evening, as the sky turned from pale blue to light green to amber to pink to crimson, they sat on the floor watching it, cut out in rectangular in the neighbor's windowpane. There was no way of knowing if all that transformation was actually happening in the real sky out of their sight, but there it was in the reflection, vivid and real enough.

"Hey, I just thought of something," Saki said, once it was all gone. "Do you know how to do the farewell fire?"

"No," Toru said. "My family never did the rituals. Why?"

"Wouldn't it be nice to do one of our own? I was listening to the radio and they were talking about it. The different ways they do it around the country."

"But Saki, the premise is that we've welcomed the spirits into the house beforehand. Who are we going to send off?"

"You've been taking care of a whole bunch of graves. That should be enough."

"I really have no idea how it's done."

"Let's just make it up then," Saki said. "We don't have to be proper. You said you don't believe in these things anyway. I want to do the one where you let the lanterns float away in the river."

Saki rummaged through Toru's kitchen drawers and found some plastic take-out containers and emergency candles. There was no

river in the area, so they decided an old irrigation ditch on the out-
skirts of town would do. It was a meandering, twenty-minute stroll
through streets lined with small houses and two-story apartments before the residential area gave way to an overgrown rice field.

"I'm pretty sure none of this is legal," Toru said as they climbed
down the short slope to the ditch in the dark. "This is a fire hazard,
and it's littering. Do you know plastics never biodegrade? Ever?"

"Will you be quiet for a second?" Saki was leading the way, sure-
footed and in control. She was giddy. "Just let me have a little fun."

The night air near the water was ripe with a grassy smell and
crickets' chirping. In the moonless sky above, Toru thought he could
make out some stars if he squinted hard. Once they found a little
spot that was level enough, Saki lit the candles and prepared her
makeshift lanterns, five in all.

"Here, you have to do one, too," she said.

They carefully lowered the plastic containers into the water, trying not to let them topple. They had to hold onto some roots with one
hand because the embankment's final drop was steep. When they let
go, the lanterns precariously bobbed up and down a couple of times
and then, finding their balance, started to float.

"It's working," Saki said. "They're leaving us."

In the dark, the disembodied voice belonged to Masato. Only it
had never sounded so cheerful back then, so certain. This—that despite the recent turn of events, perhaps Saki was at least more secure
now in her body—comforted Toru.

They lowered the remaining three lanterns so that they could follow the others' paths. As the flickering flames drifted away, they reflected off the water and multiplied. They grew smaller and seemed
to wander uncertainly, like spirits searching their way back. But Toru
imagined that both he and Saki were letting go of some parts of
themselves, shedding their pasts maybe, seeing them off to a better
place.

"Bye-bye," Saki said. "I hope it's peaceful there."

Back in the apartment, with the neighbor's dark window no longer reflecting anything, Saki continued to look out with her elbow on
the windowsill. As he prepared their dinner, Toru glanced over his
shoulder every once in a while to find her in the same position. The

sight was strangely reassuring. He thought perhaps this, the two of them on the fringe together, could work. Perhaps this was something he needed.

Toru was heading out to the station one morning when one of his neighbors caught up with him.

"Hey, 203," said the middle-aged day laborer whom Toru had seen several times in passing. "You're in 203, right? Wait up."

Toru nodded in acknowledgment but kept walking, and the man, who was shorter than he was, half-trotted beside him.

"So," the man said, "about that girl you got up in your room."

Toru glanced sideways at the man's deeply tanned, stubbly face. He thought he could smell alcohol on his breath, but he didn't seem confrontational. "Excuse me?"

"Come on now, there's no use playing dumb. You know the rules."

"What do you want?"

"Hey, didn't your mother teach you manners?" The man looked genuinely taken aback. "Slow down. I'm not trying to blackmail you or anything here. I could've complained to the landlord if I wanted to."

"Okay." Toru loosened his stride a little. "Then what is it?"

"That girl you've got. She's this, isn't she?" The man touched the back of his hand to his opposite cheek, in a gross approximation of femininity. "She a professional?"

"What? Of course not."

"Well, I don't know what the story is. I don't even want to know. But I wouldn't let her squat for too long if I were you."

Nearing the station, they were about to join a steady stream of commuters.

"I know that type," the man said. "The minute you let them into your life, they trample all over it. With their muddy shoes."

"What are you talking about?" Toru turned to face the man.

"I saw her bring a guy up to your room." The man evaluated Toru's expression. "Bet it wasn't something you'd arranged."

Toru stood there, his feet suddenly rooted to the hot asphalt.

"So here's some friendly advice," the man said. "Get her out of there."

A female voice announced the train Toru was supposed to catch. "I have to go," he said.

"Look, I know your lady issue's none of my business." The man was almost sympathetic. "I don't care what you do or with whom. But I don't want any fishy stuff where I live. I can't have police sniffing around, you know what I mean?"

"Sure," Toru said.

"I mean it. I'll tell the landlord if you—"

"I said okay," Toru said. "I understand."

"I've been wondering, Saki," Toru said, in that pocket of time just after dinner but before they were ready for the dishes, "if I could have more of a part in this, your situation, in some way. Longer term."

Two days before, after he had spoken with his neighbor, Toru had come home mid-shift to an empty apartment. He didn't know what he had expected to find, but he checked the futon sheet and tatami mat, perhaps for suspicious stains, and went through the trash. For a while he contemplated searching Saki's canvas bag, but then he suddenly became aware of what he was doing, a part of him coolly observing his discomposure from the outside, and felt disgusted. What exactly did he want to know, anyway? What was he going to do with the knowledge? He went back to work, sneaking out of his own apartment like a thief.

Saki looked up from where she sat across the table, leaning against the wall. They had the radio on and were listening to the weatherman predict the course of the first typhoon of the season. "What did you say?" she said.

"If I can help you find a job, a proper job," he said, testing the water, "maybe we can find another place. Together."

Saki picked up a chopstick and lightly tapped on an empty bowl. "I don't know," she said, "if that's going to work out."

On the radio, a young female announcer laughed at the weatherman's joke, and some cheerful music came on.

"Yeah?" Toru said. "Why not?"

Toru had remembered it was Saki's birthday. Masato's birthday. The date had been stored somewhere in his mind all these years, like a lock's combination that stuck with you long after the lock itself was lost. He had bought two slices of prettily decorated cake on his way home, and the box was sitting in the fridge.

"It's been so good being here," Saki said, not looking at Toru but gazing at the dirty dishes on the table. "You have no idea. I think I almost got too comfortable."

Toru got up and turned off the radio on top of the fridge. "Well then, what's going to work out? What is your plan?"

"I don't know," Saki said. "But you can't help me more than you already have."

"What's this all about then, Saki?" Toru felt a flash of anger somewhere deep behind his eyes. He sensed his plan to gently work out the tangle slipping away. "Tell me why you are here if I can't help you. Why you came to me."

Saki sat quietly for some time, as though contemplating the tip of the chopstick in her hand. "What would you like to hear?" she said almost kindly, now looking straight at Toru.

"Well, one thing for sure—that you don't bring your customers here again."

"What?"

"I know what you're doing." Toru couldn't stop. "A neighbor saw you. I don't know what you think I owe you; maybe you think I deserve this, and maybe I do. But how can you do such a thing? Have you thought of the consequences?"

Saki held his gaze, but Toru could see something retreat in her eyes, closing off. The fan slowly swung its head, back and forth, back and forth, just slightly stirring the air between them.

"That was my boyfriend's brother," Saki said, words exhaled like a resignation.

Toru stood still.

"I meant to tell you," she said, "but I hadn't figured out how to."

"He found you?" Toru said. "Is the brother also a psychopath? Did he do anything to you?"

"No, no." Saki halfheartedly waved her arms in the air, as though physically scattering the idea. "I've been going to see him. My boyfriend. His brother came to ask me to stop."

Toru felt weariness settling on him like fine dust, weighing him down. He thought maybe he should sit down, but that seemed to require too much effort. "Is that what you want?" he said. "To get back with this guy?"

"I don't know." Saki ran her hands through her hair, and then grasped it in her fists, as though holding onto her head. "I really don't know."

Long after they had turned the lights off, Toru lay awake on his sleeping bag. He could hear Saki's regular breathing, but he knew she wasn't asleep either.

"Toru-kun," Saki said, eventually. "Do you remember what I used to look like?"

"I do," he said. "I do remember."

"Did you know you were my only friend at school?"

Toru stared out the window at the small patch of sky that contained nothing. "No," he said. Then, "Maybe."

"Well, now you do. You were. That's why I came to you."

Toru got up and dragged his sleeping bag over to where Saki lay on her side, her back toward him. He placed his hand on her waist. It was warm. When she turned over onto her back, he gently lifted the bottom of her shirt. In the dim light from the street lamp, Toru could see her torso littered with old scars and healed incisions. He reached his hand and felt them with his fingertips, as though reading Braille. Just below her left rib cage, he found one that had healed into a forceful indentation, like a diagram of a black hole bending space-time.

"That's the new one," Saki said. "All the others are from the fall, back in school. Did you know I almost died then? Most of my injuries were internal, from the impact. They had to cut me open many times."

"I'm sorry," Toru said.

"He didn't mean it, you know. He didn't even know what he was doing. It was one of those moments."

"It's okay," Toru said. "You don't have to defend him to me."

"He was so gentle and proper. You'd never imagine him hurting anyone."

"Saki. If you think things will work out with this guy, you're totally deranged. You know that."

Saki made a sound that was halfway between a chuckle and a sigh. "Yeah," she said. "I know."

Toru continued to trace the scars, trying to decipher something from each of the textured edges, as though straining to hear someone whispering in a room next door. He kept his hand on Saki's torso and lay down next to her.

"Did you think I came to you for a romantic reason?" Saki said.

Toru didn't say anything. He didn't know the right answer.

"Who knows," she said. "Maybe I did."

Like that, with his hand rising and falling with Saki's breathing, he closed his eyes.

When Toru came home the next day, Saki wasn't there. Her white canvas bag, which normally sat on the folded futon in the corner of the room, was also gone. But she didn't leave her key, so Toru cooked dinner and waited, just in case. On the windowsill where she always rested her elbow, he found a stone he recognized from the cemetery. When the food grew cold, he packed a lunchbox and put it away in the fridge. The cake box still sat on one of the shelves, unopened.

That night, the typhoon hit. It was already September. The rain smashed onto the pavement with enough force to knock a child down. It was as though someone had decided to waste the entire world's supply of water on this town. The roaring replaced the sound of cicadas, which had by then become such a constant that Toru noticed it only in its absence. The new, powerful roar took up every inch of the available space, filling the world with another level of deafening silence.

Toru stood at his window, letting the stray splashes into the room. He picked up the stone and turned it in his hand, feeling its warm surface the way Saki had done, before putting it into his pocket. The neighbor's windowpane was pitch-black now. A streetlamp stood illuminating a sheet of rain, waiting for someone to step into its cone-shaped spotlight. Toru took out his cell phone and held it in his hand for a long time before finally flipping it open. He counted seven rings before she answered.

"Hello?" It was the familiar voice, half-worried, half-pleased. "Why are you calling now? Do you need to reschedule?"

"Hi," he said, and cleared his throat. "No, I just wanted to make sure you weren't stranded somewhere."

He heard a chuckle. "What, like in a flood?"

"You know, with all this crazy . . ." He trailed off, the words suddenly escaping his throat without first collecting sound.

"Yeah?" she said. "Well, I'm fine. Don't worry. Listen, the kids are here, so I should go. Next Wednesday, right?"

He thought about the empty house in Saki's dream. In his mind, he was walking from one dark room to another, looking for something. The Post-it note. Wasn't there a Post-it note? He needed to find out what was written on it. But none of the rooms in the empty house had a table on which the plastic-wrapped plate of food could be placed, on which the note could be stuck.

"Toru?" the voice was saying. It was right in his ear, yet so far away. "Are you there?"

N. R. KLEINFIELD

■

The Lonely Death of George Bell

FROM *The New York Times*

THEY FOUND HIM in the living room, crumpled up on the mottled carpet. The police did. Sniffing a fetid odor, a neighbor had called 911. The apartment was in north-central Queens, in an unassertive building on 79th Street in Jackson Heights.

The apartment belonged to a George Bell. He lived alone. Thus the presumption was that the corpse also belonged to George Bell. It was a plausible supposition, but it remained just that, for the puffy body on the floor was decomposed and unrecognizable. Clearly the man had not died on July 12, the Saturday last year when he was discovered, nor the day before nor the day before that. He had lain there for a while, nothing to announce his departure to the world, while the hyperkinetic city around him hurried on with its business.

Neighbors had last seen him six days earlier, a Sunday. On Thursday, there was a break in his routine. The car he always kept out front and moved from one side of the street to the other to obey parking rules sat on the wrong side. A ticket was wedged beneath the wiper. The woman next door called Mr. Bell. His phone rang and rang.

Then the smell of death and the police and the sobering reason that George Bell did not move his car.

Each year around 50,000 people die in New York, and each year the mortality rate seems to graze a new low, with people living healthier and longer. A great majority of the deceased have relatives and friends who soon learn of their passing and tearfully assemble at their funeral. A reverent death notice appears. Sympathy cards accumulate. When the celebrated die or there is some heart-rending killing of the innocent, the entire city might weep.

A much tinier number die alone in unwatched struggles. No one collects their bodies. No one mourns the conclusion of a life. They are just a name added to the death tables. In the year 2014, George Bell, age 72, was among those names.

George Bell—a simple name, two syllables, the minimum. There were no obvious answers as to who he was or what shape his life had taken. What worries weighed on him. Whom he loved and who loved him.

Like most New Yorkers, he lived in the corners, under the pale light of obscurity.

Yet death even in such forlorn form can cause a surprising amount of activity, setting off an elaborate, lurching process that involves a hodgepodge of interlocking characters whose livelihoods flow in part or in whole from death.

With George Bell, the ripples from the process would spill improbably and seemingly by happenstance from the shadows of Queens to upstate New York and Virginia and Florida. Dozens of people who never knew him, all cogs in the city's complicated machinery of mortality, would find themselves settling the affairs of an ordinary man who left this world without anyone in particular noticing.

In discovering a death, you find a life story and perhaps meaning. Could anything in the map of George Bell's existence have explained his lonely end? Possibly not. But it was true that George Bell died carrying some secrets. Secrets about how he lived and secrets about who mattered most to him. Those secrets would bring sorrow. At the same time, they would deliver rewards. Death does that. It closes doors but also opens them.

Once firefighters had jimmied the door that July afternoon, the police squeezed into a beaten apartment groaning with possessions, a grotesque parody of the "lived-in" condition. Clearly, its occupant had been a hoarder.

The officers from the 115th Precinct called the medical examiner's office, which involves itself in suspicious deaths and unidentified bodies, and a medical legal investigator arrived. His task was to rule out foul play and look for evidence that could help locate the next of kin and identify the body. In short order, it was clear that nothing criminal had taken place (no sign of forced entry, bullet wounds, congealed blood).

A Fire Department paramedic made the obvious pronouncement that the man was dead; even a skeleton must be formally declared no longer living. The body was zipped into a human remains pouch. A transport team from the medical examiner's office drove it to the morgue at Queens Hospital Center, where it was deposited in one of some 100 refrigerated drawers, cooled to 35 degrees.

It falls to the police to notify next of kin, but the neighbors did not know of any. Detectives grabbed some names and phone numbers from the apartment, called them and got nothing: The man had no wife, no siblings. The police estimate that they reach kin 85 percent of the time. They struck out with George Bell.

At the Queens morgue, identification personnel got started. Something like 90 percent of the corpses arriving at city morgues are identified by relatives or friends after they are shown photographs of the body. Most remains depart for burial within a few days. For the rest, it gets complicated.

The easiest resolution is furnished by fingerprints; otherwise by dental and medical records or, as a last resort, by DNA. The medical examiner can also do a so-called contextual ID; when all elements are considered, none of which by themselves bring certainty, a sort of circumstantial identification can be made.

Fingerprints were taken, which required days because of the poor condition of the fingers. Enhanced techniques had to be used, such as soaking the fingers in a solution to soften them. The prints were sent to city, state and federal databases. No hits.

Once nine days had elapsed and no next of kin had come forth, the medical examiner reported the death to the office of the Queens County public administrator, an obscure agency that operates out of the State Supreme Court building in the Jamaica neighborhood. Its austere quarters are adjacent to Surrogate's Court, familiarly known as widows and orphans court, where wills are probated and battles are often waged over the dead.

Each county in New York City has a public administrator to manage estates when there is no one else to do so, most commonly when there is no will or no known heirs.

Public administrators tend to rouse attention only when complaints flare over their competence or their fees or their tendency to oversee dens of political patronage. Or when they run afoul of the law. Last year, a former longtime counsel to the Bronx County public administrator pleaded guilty to grand larceny, while a bookkeeper for the Kings County public administrator was sentenced to a prison term for stealing from the dead.

Recent audits by the city's comptroller found disturbing dysfunction at both of those offices, which the occupants said had been overstated. The most recent audit of the Queens office, in 2012, raised no significant issues.

The Queens unit employs 15 people and processes something like 1,500 deaths a year. Appointed by the Queens surrogate, Lois M. Rosenblatt, a lawyer, has been head of the office for the past 13 years. Most cases arrive from nursing homes, others from the medical examiner, legal guardians, the police, undertakers. While a majority of estates contain assets of less than $500, one had been worth $16 million. Meager estates can move swiftly. Bigger ones routinely extend from 12 to 24 months.

The office extracts a commission that starts at 5 percent of the first $100,000 of an estate and then slides downward, money that is entered into the city's general fund. An additional 1 percent goes toward the office's expenses. The office's counsel, who for 23 years has been Gerard Sweeney, a private lawyer who mainly does the public administrator's legal work, customarily gets a sliding legal fee that begins at 6 percent of the estate's first $750,000.

"You can die in such anonymity in New York," he likes to say. "We've had instances of people dead for months. No one finds them, no one misses them."

The man presumed to be George Bell joined the wash of cases, a fresh arrival that Ms. Rosenblatt viewed as nothing special at all.

Meanwhile, the medical examiner needed records—X-rays would do—to confirm the identity of the body. The office took its own chest X-rays but still required earlier ones for comparison.

The medical examiner's office had no idea which doctors the man had seen, so in a Hail Mary maneuver, personnel began cold-calling hospitals and doctors in the vicinity, in a pattern that radiated outward from the Jackson Heights apartment. Whoever picked up was asked if by chance a George Bell had ever dropped in.

Three investigators work for the Queens County public administrator. They comb through the residences of the departed, mining their homes for clues as to what was owned, who their relatives were. It's a peculiar kind of work, seeing what strangers had kept in their closets, what they hung on the walls, what deodorant they liked.

On July 24, two investigators, Juan Plaza and Ronald Rodriguez, entered the glutted premises of the Bell apartment, clad in billowy hazmat suits and bootees. Investigators work in pairs, to discourage theft.

Bleak as the place was, they had seen worse. An apartment so swollen with belongings that the tenant, a woman, died standing up, unable to collapse to the floor. Or the place they fled swatting at swarms of fleas.

Yes, they saw a human existence that few others did.

Mr. Plaza had been a data entry clerk before joining his macabre field in 1994; Mr. Rodriguez had been a waiter and found his interest piqued in 2002.

What qualified someone for the job? Ms. Rosenblatt, the head of the office, summed it up: "People willing to go into these disgusting apartments."

The two men foraged through the unedited anarchy, 800 square feet, one bedroom. A stench thickened the air. Mr. Plaza dabbed his nostrils with a Vicks vapor stick. Mr. Rodriguez toughed it out. Vicks bothered his nose.

The only bed was the lumpy foldout couch in the living room. The bedroom and bathroom looked pillaged. The kitchen was splashed with trash and balled-up, decades-old lottery tickets that had failed to deliver. A soiled shopping list read: sea salt, garlic, carrots, broccoli (two packs), *TV Guide*.

The faucet didn't work. The chipped stove had no knobs and could not have been used to cook in a long time.

The men scavenged for a will, a cemetery deed, financial documents, an address book, computer, cellphone, those sorts of things. Photographs might show relatives—could that be a mom or sis beaming in that picture on the mantel?

Portable objects of value were to be retrieved. A Vermeer hangs on the wall? Grab it. Once they found $30,000 in cash, another time a Rolex wedged inside a radio. But the bar is not placed nearly that high: In one instance, they lugged back a picture of the deceased in a Knights of Malta outfit.

In the slanting light they scooped up papers from a table and some drawers in the living room. They found $241 in bills and $187.45 in coins. A silver Relic watch did not look special, but they took it in case.

Fastened to the walls were a bear's head, steer horns and some military pictures of planes and warships. Over the couch hung a photo sequence of a parachutist coming in for a landing, with a certificate recording George Bell's first jump in 1963. Chinese food cartons and pizza boxes were ubiquitous. Shelves were stacked with music tapes and videos: *Top Gun, Braveheart, Yule Log.*

A splotched calendar from Lucky Market hung in the bathroom, flipped open to August 2007.

Hoarding is deemed a mental disorder, poorly understood, that stirs people to incoherent acts; sufferers may buy products simply to have them. Amid the mess were a half-dozen unopened ironing board covers, multiple packages of unused Christmas lights, four new tire-pressure gauges.

The investigators returned twice more, rounding up more papers, another $95. They found no cellphone, no computer or credit cards.

Rummaging through the personal effects of the dead, sensing the misery in these rooms, can color your thoughts. The work changes people, and it has changed these men.

Mr. Rodriguez, 57 and divorced, has a greater sense of urgency. "I try to build a life like it's the last day," he said. "You never know when you will die. Before this, I went along like I would live forever."

The solitude of so many deaths wears on Mr. Plaza, the fear that someday it will be him splayed on the floor in one of these silent apartments. "This job teaches you a lot," he said. "You learn whatever material stuff you have you should use it and share it. Share yourself. People die with nobody to talk to. They die and relatives come out of the woodwork. 'He was my uncle. He was my cousin. Give me what he had.' Gimme, gimme. Yet when he was alive they never visited, never knew the person. From working in this office, my life changed."

He is 52, also divorced, and without children, but he keeps expanding his base of friends. Every day, he sends them motivational Instagram messages: "With each sunrise, may we value every minute"; "Be kind, smile to the world and it will smile back"; "Share your life with loved ones"; "Love, forgive, forget."

He said: "When I die, someone will find out the same day or the next day. Since I've worked here, my list of friends has gotten longer and longer. I don't want to die alone."

In his Queens cubicle, wearing rubber gloves, Patrick Stressler thumbed through the sheaf of documents retrieved by the two investigators. Mr. Stressler, the caseworker with the public administrator's office responsible for piecing together George Bell's estate, is formally a "decedent property agent," a title he finds useful as a conversation starter at parties. He is 27, and had been a restaurant cashier five years ago when he learned you could be a decedent property agent and became one.

He began with the pictures. Mr. Stressler mingles in the leavings of people he can never meet and especially likes to ponder the photographs so "you get a sense of a person's history, not that they just died."

The snapshots ranged over the humdrum of life. A child wearing a holster and toy pistols. A man in military dress. Men fishing. A young woman sitting on a chair in a corner. A high school class on a stage, everyone wearing blackface. "Different times," Mr. Stressler mused.

In the end, the photos divulged little of what George Bell had done across his 72 years.

The thicket of papers yielded a few hazy kernels. An unused passport, issued in 2007 to George Main Bell Jr., showing a thick-necked man with a meaty face ripened by time, born Jan. 15, 1942. Documents establishing that his father—George Bell—died in 1969 at 59, his mother, Davina Bell, in 1981 at 76.

Some holiday cards. Several from an Elsie Logan in Red Bank, N.J., thanking him for gifts of Godiva chocolates. One, dated 2001, said: "I called Sunday around 2—no answer. Will try again." A 2007 Thanksgiving Day card read, "I have been trying to call you—but no answer."

A 2001 Christmas card signed, "Love always, Eleanore (Puffy)," with the message: "I seldom mention it, but I hope you realize how much it means to have you for a friend. I care a lot for you."

Cards from a Thomas Higginbotham, addressed to "Big George" and signed "friend, Tom."

A golden find: H&R Block–prepared tax returns, useful for divining assets. The latest showed adjusted gross income of $13,207 from a pension and interest, another $21,311 from Social Security. The bank statements contained the biggest revelation: For what appeared to be a simple life, they showed balances of several hundred thousand dollars. Letters went out to confirm the amounts.

No evidence of stocks or bonds, but a small life insurance policy, with the beneficiaries his parents. And there was a will, dated 1982. It split his estate evenly among three men and a woman of unknown relation. And specified that George Bell be cremated.

Using addresses he found online, Mr. Stressler sent out form letters asking the four to contact him. He heard only from a Martin Westbrook, who called from Sprakers, a hamlet in upstate New York, and said he had not spoken with George Bell in some time. The will named him as executor, but he deferred to the public administrator.

Loose ends began to be tidied up. The car, a silver 2005 Toyota RAV4, was sent to an auctioneer. There was a notice advising that George Bell had not responded to two juror questionnaires and was now subpoenaed to appear before the commissioner of jurors; a letter went out saying he would not be there. He was dead.

If an apartment's contents have any value, auction companies bid for them. When they don't, "cleanout companies" dispose of the belongings. George Bell's place was deemed a cleanout.

Among his papers was an honorable military discharge from 1966, following six years in the United States Army Reserve. A request was made to the Department of Veterans Affairs, national cemetery administration, in St. Louis, for burial in one of its national cemeteries, with the government paying the bill.

St. Louis responded that George Bell did not qualify as a veteran, not having seen active duty or having died while in the Reserves. The public administrator appealed the rebuff. A week later, 16 pages came back from the centralized satellite processing and appeals unit that could be summed up in unambiguous concision: No.

Another thing the public administrator takes care of is having the post office forward the mail of the deceased. Statements may arrive from brokerage houses. Letters could pinpoint the whereabouts of relatives. When magazines show up, the subscriptions are ended and refunds requested. Could be $6.82 or $12.05, but the puny sums enter the estate, pushing it incrementally upward.

Not much came for George Bell: bank statements, a notice on the apartment insurance, utility bills, junk mail.

Every life deserves to come to a final resting place, but they're not all pretty. Most estates arrive with the public administrator after the body has already been buried by relatives or friends or in accordance with a prepaid plan.

When someone dies destitute and forsaken, and one of various free burial organizations does not learn of the case, the body ends up joining others in communal oblivion at the potter's field on Hart Island in the Bronx, the graveyard of last resort.

If there are funds, the public administrator honors the wishes of the will or of relatives. When no one speaks for the deceased, the office is partial to two fairly dismal, cut-rate cemeteries in New Jersey. It prefers the total expense to come in under $5,000, not always easy in a city where funeral and burial costs can be multiples of that.

Simonson Funeral Home in Forest Hills was picked by Susan

Brown, the deputy public administrator, to handle George Bell once his identity was verified. It is among 16 regulars that she rotates the office's deaths through.

George Bell's body was hardly the first to be trapped in limbo. Some years ago, one had lingered for weeks while siblings skirmished over the funeral specifics. The decedent's sister wanted a barbershop quartet and brass band to perform; a brother preferred something solemn. Surrogate's Court nodded in favor of the sister, and the man got a melodious send-off.

The medical examiner was not having any luck with George Bell. The cold calls to doctors and hospitals continued, but as the inquiries bounced around Queens, the discouraging answers came back slowly and redundantly: no George Bell.

In the interim, the medical examiner filed an unverified death certificate, on July 28. The cause of death was determined to be hypertensive and arteriosclerotic cardiovascular disease, with obesity a significant factor. This was surmised, based on the position in which the body was found, its age, the man's size and the statistical likelihood of it being the cause. Occupation was listed as unknown.

City law specifies that bodies be buried, cremated or sent from the city within four days of discovery, unless an exemption is granted. The medical examiner can release even an unverified body for burial. Absent a corpse's being confirmed, however, the policy of the medical examiner is not to allow cremation. What if there has been a mistake? You can't un-cremate someone.

So days scrolled past. Other corpses streamed through the morgue, pausing on their way to the grave, while the body presumed to be George Bell entered its second month of chilled residence. Then its third.

In early September last year, a downstairs neighbor complained to the public administrator that George Bell's refrigerator was leaking through the ceiling and that vermin might be scuttling about.

Grandma's Attic Cleanouts was sent over to remove the offending appliance. Diego Benitez, the company's owner, showed up with two workers.

The refrigerator was unplugged, with unfrozen frozen vegetables and Chinese takeout rotting inside. Roaches had moved in. Mr. Benitez doused it with bug spray. He plugged it in to chill the food and rid it of the smell, then cleaned it out and took it to a recycling center in Jamaica. A few weeks later, Wipeout Exterminating came in and treated the whole place.

Meanwhile, the medical examiner kept calling around hunting for old X-rays. In late September, the 11th call hit pay dirt. A radiology provider had chest X-rays of George Bell dating from 2004. They were in a warehouse, though, and would take some time to retrieve.

Weeks tumbled by. In late October, the radiology service reported: Sorry, the X-rays had been destroyed. The medical examiner asked for written confirmation. Back came the response: Never mind, the X-rays were there. In early November, they landed at the medical examiner's office.

The X-rays were compared, and bingo. In the first week of November, nearly four months after it had arrived, the presumed corpse of George Bell officially became George Bell, deceased, of Jackson Heights, Queens.

Cold out. Streaks of sunshine splashing over Queens. On Saturday morning, Nov. 15, John Sommese settled into a rented hearse, eased into the sparse traffic and drove to the morgue. He owns Simonson Funeral Home. At age 73, he remained a working owner in a city of dwindling deaths.

At the morgue, an attendant withdrew the body from the drawer, and both medical examiner and undertaker checked the identity tag. Using a hydraulic lift, the attendant swung the body into the wooden coffin. George Bell was at last going to his eternal home.

The coffin was wheeled out and guided into the back of the hearse. Mr. Sommese smoothed an American flag over it. The armed forces had passed on a military burial, but George Bell's years in the Army Reserves were good enough for the funeral director, and he abided by military custom.

Next stop was U.S. Columbarium at Fresh Pond Crematory in Middle Village, for the cremation. Mr. Sommese made good time along the loud streets lined with shedding trees. The volume on the radio was muted; the dashboard said Queen's "You're My Best Friend" was playing.

While the undertaker said he didn't dwell much on the strangers he transported, he allowed how instances like this saddened him — a person dies and nobody shows up, no service, no one from the clergy to say a few kind words, to say rest in peace.

The undertaker was a Christian, and believed that George Bell was already in another place, a better place, but still. "I don't think everyone should have an elaborate funeral," he said in a soft voice. "But I think burial or cremation should be with respect, or else what is society about? I think about this man. I believe we're all connected. We're all products of the same God. Does it matter that this man should be cremated with respect? Yes, it does."

He consulted the mirror and blended into the next lane. "You can have a fancy funeral, but people don't pay for kindness," he went on. "They don't pay for understanding. They don't pay for caring. This man is getting caring. I care about this man."

At U.S. Columbarium, he steered around to the rear, to the unloading dock. Another hearse stood there. Yes — a line at the crematory.

Squinting in the sun, Mr. Sommese paced in the motionless air. After 15 minutes, the dock opened up and the undertaker angled the hearse in. Workers took the coffin. Mr. Sommese kept the flag. Normally, it would go to the next of kin. There being none, the undertaker folded it up to use again.

The cremation process, what U.S. Columbarium calls the "journey," consumed nearly three hours. Typically, cremains are ready for pickup in a couple of days. For an extra $180, the columbarium provides same-day express service, which was unneeded in this case.

Some 40,000 cremains were stored at the columbarium, almost all of them tucked into handsome individual wall niches, viewable through glass. Downstairs was a storage area near the bathrooms with a bronze tree affixed to the door. This was the Community Tree. Behind the door cremains were stacked up and stored out of sight. The budget alternative. Names were etched on the tree leaves. Some time ago, when the leaves filled up, doves were added.

Several days after the cremation, the superintendent stacked an urn shaped like a small shoe box inside the storage area. Then he nailed a metal dove, wings spread, above the right edge of the tree. It identified the new addition: "George M. Bell Jr. 1942–2014."

On alternate Tuesdays, David R. Maltz & Company, in Central Islip, N.Y., auctions off 100 to 150 cars; other days, it auctions real estate, jewelry and pretty much everything else. It has sold the Woodcrest Country Club in Muttontown, N.Y., four engines from an automobile shredder, 22 KFC franchises. Items arrive from bankruptcies, repossessions and estates, including a regular stream from the Queens public administrator.

In the frosty gloom of Dec. 30, as a hissing wind spun litter through the air, the Maltz company had among its cars a 2011 Mustang convertible, multiple Mercedes-Benzes, two cars that didn't even run and George Bell's 2005 Toyota. Despite its age, it had just over 3,000 miles on it, brightening its appeal.

In a one-minute bidding spasm—"3,000 the bid, 3,500, 35 the bid, 4,000 . . ."—the car went for $9,500, beating expectations. After expenses, $8,631.50 was added to the estate. The buyer was Sam Maloof, a regular, who runs a used car dealership, Beltway Motor Sales, in Brooklyn and planned to resell it. After he brought it back, his sister and secretary, Janet Maloof, adored it. She had the same 2005 model, same color, burdened with over 100,000 miles. So, feeling the holiday spirit, he gave her George Bell's car.

In a couple of weeks, the only other valuable possession extracted from the apartment, the Relic watch, came up for sale at a Maltz auction of jewelry, wine, art and collectibles. The auction was dominated by 42 estates put up by the Queens public administrator, the thinnest by far being George Bell's. Bidding on the watch began at $1 and finished at $3. The winner was a creaky, unemployed man named Tony Nik. He was in a sulky mood, mumbling after his triumph that he liked the slim price.

Again after expenses, another $2.31 trickled into the Bell estate.

On a sun-kindled day a week later, six muscled men from GreenEx, a junk removal business, arrived to empty the cluttered Queens apartment. Dispassionately, they scooped up the dusty traces of George Bell's life and shoveled them into trash cans and bags.

They broke apart the furniture with hammers. Tinny music poured from a portable radio.

Eyeing the bottomless thickets, puzzling over what heartbreak they told of, one of the men said: "Depression, I think. People get depressed and then, Lord help them, forget about it."

Seven hours they went at it, flinging everything into trucks destined for a Bronx dump where the rates were good.

Some nuggets they salvaged for themselves. One man fancied a set of Marilyn Monroe porcelain plates. Another worker plucked up an unopened jumbo package of Nike socks, some model cars and some brand-new sponges. Yet another claimed the television and an unused carbon monoxide detector. Gatherings from a life, all worth more than that $3 watch.

A spindly worker with taut arms crouched down to inspect some never-worn tan work boots, still snug in their box. They were a size big, but he slid them on and liked the fit.

He cleaned George Bell's apartment wearing the dead man's boots.

The people named to split the assets in the will were known as the legatees. Over 30 years had passed since George Bell chose them: Martin Westbrook, Frank Murzi, Albert Schober and Eleanore Albert. Plus, there was a beneficiary on two bank accounts: Thomas Higginbotham.

Elizabeth Rooney, a kinship investigator in the office of Gerard Sweeney, the public administrator's counsel, set out to help find them. By law, she also had to hunt for the next of kin, down to a first cousin once removed, the furthest relative eligible to lay claim to an estate. They had to be notified, should they choose to contest the will.

There was time, for George Bell's assets could not be distributed until seven months after the public administrator had been appointed, the period state law specifies for creditors to step forward.

Prowling the Internet, Ms. Rooney learned that Mr. Murzi and Mr. Schober were dead. Mr. Westbrook was in Sprakers and Mr. Higginbotham in Lynchburg, Va. Ms. Rooney found Ms. Albert, now going by the name Flemm, upstate in Worcester.

They were surprised to learn that George Bell had left them

money. Ms. Flemm had spoken to him by phone a few weeks before he died; the others had not been in touch for years.

A core piece of Ms. Rooney's job was drafting a family tree going back three generations. Using the genealogy company Ancestry.com, she compiled evidence with things like census records and ship manifests, showing Bell relatives arriving from Scotland. Her office once produced a family tree that was six feet long. Another time it traced a family back to Daniel Boone.

Ms. Rooney created paternal and maternal trees, each with dozens of names. She found five living relatives: two first cousins on his mother's side, one living in Edina, Minn., and the other in Henderson, Nev. Neither had been in contact with George Bell in decades, and didn't know what he did for a living.

On the paternal side, Ms. Rooney identified two first cousins, one in Scotland and another in England, as well as a third whose whereabouts proved elusive.

When that cousin, Janet Bell, was not found, protocol dictated that a notice be published in a newspaper for four weeks, a gesture intended to alert unlocated relatives. With sizable estates, the court chooses the *New York Law Journal*, where the bill for the notice can run about $4,000. In this instance the court picked the *Wave*, a Queens weekly with a print circulation of 12,000, at a cost of $247.

The cousin might have been in Tajikistan or in Hog Jaw, Ark., or even on Staten Island, and the odds of her spotting the notice were approximately zero. Among thousands of such ads that Mr. Sweeney has placed, he is still awaiting his first response.

Word came that Eleanore Flemm had died of a heart attack, on Feb. 3 at 66. Since she had outlived Mr. Bell, her estate would receive her proceeds. Her heirs were her brother, James Albert, a private detective on Long Island who barely remembered the Bell name, along with a nephew and two nieces in Florida. One did not know George Bell had existed.

Death, though, isn't social. It's business. No need to have known someone to get his money.

On Feb. 20, a Queens real estate broker listed the Bell apartment at $219,000. It was the final asset to liquidate. Three potential buyers toured it the next day, and one woman's offer of $225,000 was accepted.

Three months later, the building's board said no. A middle-aged couple who lived down the block entered the picture, and, at $215,000, was approved. Their plan was to fix up the marred apartment, turn their own place over to their grown-up son and then move in, overwriting George Bell's life.

Meanwhile, Mr. Sweeney appeared in Surrogate's Court to request probate of the will. Besides the two known beneficiaries, he listed the possibility of unknown relatives and the unfound cousin. The court appointed a so-called guardian ad litem to review the will on behalf of these people, who might, in fact, be phantoms.

In September, Mr. Sweeney submitted a final accounting, the hard math of the estate, for court approval. No objections arrived. Tallied up, George Bell's assets amounted to roughly $540,000. Bank accounts holding $215,000 listed Mr. Higginbotham as the sole beneficiary, and he got that directly. Proceeds from the apartment, other accounts, a life insurance policy, the car and the watch went to the estate: around $324,000.

A commission of $13,726 went to the city, a $3,238 fee to the public administrator, $19,453 to Mr. Sweeney.

Other expenses included things like the apartment maintenance, at $7,360; a funeral bill of $4,873; $2,800 for the cleanout company; $1,663 for the kinship investigator; a $222 parking ticket; a $704 Fire Department bill for ambulance service; $750 for the guardian ad litem; and $12.50 for an appraisal of the watch that sold for $3.

That left about $264,000 to be split between Mr. Westbrook and the heirs of Ms. Flemm. Some 14 months after a man died, his estate was settled and the proceeds were good to go.

For the recipients, George Bell had stepped out of eternity and united them by bestowing his money. No one in the drawn-out process knew why he had chosen them, nor did they need to. They only needed to know him in the quietude of death, as a man whose heart had stopped beating in Queens. But he had been like anyone, a human being who had built a life on this earth.

* * *

His life began small and plain. George Bell was especially attached to his parents. He slept on the pullout sofa in the living room, while his parents claimed the bedroom, and he continued to sleep there even after they died. Both parents came from Scotland. His father was a tool-and-die machinist, and his mother worked for a time as a seamstress in the toy industry.

After high school, he joined his father as an apprentice. In 1961, he made an acquaintance at a local bar, a moving man. They became friends, and the moving man pulled George Bell into the moving business. His name was Tom Higginbotham. Three fellow movers also became friends: Frank Murzi, Albert Schober and Martin Westbrook. The men in the will. They mainly moved business offices, and they all guzzled booze, in titanic proportions.

"We were a bunch of drunks," Mr. Westbrook said. "I'm a juicer. But George put me to shame. He was a real nice guy, kind of a hermit. Boy, we had some good times."

In the words of Mr. Higginbotham: "We were great friends. I don't know if you can say it this way, but we were men who loved each other."

They called him Big George, for he was a thickset, brawny man, weighing perhaps 210 pounds. Later, his ravenous appetite had him pushing 350.

He had a puckish streak. Once a woman invited him and Mr. Higginbotham to a party at her parents' house. Her father kept tropical fish. She showed George Bell the tank. When he admired a distinctive fish, she said, "Oh, that's an expensive one." He picked up a net, caught the fish and swallowed it.

One day the friends were moving a financial firm. After they had fitted the desks into the new offices, George Bell slid notes into the drawers, writing things like: "I'm madly in love with you. Meet me at the water cooler." Or: "There's a bomb under your chair. Your next move might be your last."

Dumb pranks. Big George being Big George.

Friends, though, found him difficult to crack open. There were things inside no one could get out. You learned to suppress your questions around him.

He had his burdens. His father died young. As she aged, his

mother became crippled by arthritis. He cared for her, fetching her food and bathing her until her death.

He was fastidious about his money, only trusted banks for his savings. There was a woman he began dating when she was 19 and he was 25. "We got real keen on each other," she said later. "He made me feel special."

A marriage was planned. They spoke to a wedding hall. He bought a suit. Then, he told friends, the woman's mother had wanted him to sign a prenuptial agreement to protect her daughter if the marriage should break apart. He ended the engagement, and never had another serious relationship.

That woman was Eleanore Albert, the fourth name in the will.

Some years later, she married an older man who made equipment for a party supply company, and moved upstate to become Ms. Flemm. In 2002, her husband died.

Distance and time never dampened the emotional affinity between her and George Bell. They spoke on the phone and exchanged cards. "We had something for each other that never got used up," she said. She had sent him a Valentine's Day card just last year: "George, think of you often with love."

And unbeknown to her, he had put her in his will and kept her there.

Her life finished up a lot like his. She lived alone, in a trailer. She died of a heart attack. A neighbor who cleared her snow found her. She had gotten obese. Her brother had her cremated.

A difference was that she left behind debt, owed to the bank and to credit card companies. All that she would pass on was tens of thousands of dollars of George Bell's money, money that she never got to touch.

Some would filter down to her brother, who had no plans for it. A slice went to Michael Garber, her nephew, who drives a bus at Disney World. A friend of his aunt's had owned a Camaro convertible that she relished, and he might buy a used Camaro in her honor.

Some more would go to Sarah Teta, a niece, retired and living in Altamonte Springs, Fla., who plans to save it for a rainy day. "You always hear about people you don't know dying and leaving you money," she said. "I never thought it would happen to me."

And some would funnel down to Eleanore Flemm's other niece, Dorothy Gardiner, a retired waitress and home health care aide. She lives in Apopka, Fla., never heard of George Bell. She has survived two cancers and has several thousand dollars in medical bills that could finally disappear. "I've been paying off $25 a month, what I can," she said. "I never would have expected this. It's crazy."

In 1996, George Bell hurt his left shoulder and spine lifting a desk on a moving job, and his life took a different shape. He received approval for workers' compensation and Social Security disability payments and began collecting a pension from the Teamsters. Though he never worked again, he had all the income he needed.

He used to have buddies over to watch television and he would cook for them. Then he stopped having anyone over. No one knew why.

Old friends had drifted away, and with them some of the fire in George Bell's life. Of his moving man colleagues, Mr. Murzi retired in 1994 and died in 2011. Mr. Schober retired in 1996 and moved to Brooklyn, losing touch. He died in 2002.

Mr. Higginbotham quit the moving business, and moved upstate in 1973 to work for the state as an environmental scientist.

He is now 74, retired and living alone in Virginia. The last time he spoke to George Bell was 10 years ago. He used a code of ringing and hanging up to get him to answer his phone, but in time, he got no answer. He sent cards, beseeched him to come and visit, but he wouldn't. It was two months before Mr. Higginbotham found out George Bell had died.

It has been hard for him to reconcile the way George Bell's money came to him. "I've been stressed about this," he said. "I haven't been sleeping. My stomach hurts. My blood pressure is up. I argued with him time and again to get out of that apartment and spend his money and enjoy life. I sent him so many brochures on places to go. I thought I understood George. Now I realize I didn't understand him at all."

Mr. Higginbotham was content with the fundaments of his own life: his modest one-bedroom apartment, his 15-year-old truck. He put the inheritance into mutual funds and figures it will help his three grandchildren through college. George Bell's money educating the future.

In 1994, Mr. Westbrook hurt his knee and left the moving business. He moved to Sprakers, where he had a cattle farm. When he got older and his marriage dissolved, he sold the farm but still lives nearby. He is 74. It was several years ago that he last spoke to George Bell on the phone. Mr. Bell told him he did not get out much.

He has three grandchildren and wants to move to a mellower climate. He plans to give some of the money to Mr. Murzi's widow, because Mr. Murzi had been his best friend.

"My sister needs some dental work," he said. "I need some dental work. I need hearing aids. The golden age ain't so cheap. Big George's money will make my old age easier."

He felt awful about his dying alone, nobody knowing. "Yeah, that'll happen to me," he said. "I'm a loner, too. There's maybe four or five people up here I talk to."

In his final years, with the moving men gone, George Bell's life had become emptier. Neighbors nodded to him on the street and he smiled. He told lively stories to the young woman next door, who lived with her parents, when he bumped into her. She recently became a police officer, and she was the one who had smelled what she knew was death.

But in the end, George Bell seemed to keep just one true friend.

He had been a fixture at a neighborhood pub called Budds Bar. He showed up in his cutoff blue sweatshirt so often that some regulars called him Sweatshirt Bell. At one point, he eased up on his drinking, then, worried about his health, quit. But he still went to Budds, ordering club soda.

In April 2005, Budds closed. Many regulars gravitated to another bar, Legends. George Bell went a few times, then transferred his allegiance to Bantry Bay Publick House in Long Island City. He would meet his friend there.

The sign at the entrance to Bantry Bay says, "Enter as Strangers, Leave as Friends." Squished in near the window was Frank Bertone, sipping soup and nursing a drink. He is known as the Dude. George Bell's last good friend.

In the early 1980s, not long after moving to Jackson Heights, he stopped in at Budds in need of a restroom. A big man had bellowed, "Have a beer."

That was George Bell. In time, a friendship was spawned, deepening during the 15 years that remained of George Bell's life. They met on Saturdays at Bantry Bay. They fished in the Rockaways and at Jones Beach, sometimes with others. Mr. Bell bought a car to get out to the good spots, but the car otherwise mostly sat. They passed time meandering around, the days bleeding into one another.

"Where did we go?" Mr. Bertone said. "No place. One time we sat for hours in the parking lot of Bed Bath & Beyond. What did we talk about? The world's problems. Just like that, the two of us solved the world's problems."

Mr. Bertone is 67, a retired inspector for Consolidated Edison. Over the last decade, he had spent more time with George Bell than anyone, but he didn't feel he truly knew him.

"One thing about George is he didn't get personal," he said. "Not ever."

He knew he had never married. He spoke of girlfriends, but Mr. Bertone never met any. The two had even swapped views on wills and what happens to your money in the end, though Mr. Bertone did not know George Bell had drafted a will before they met.

Mr. Bertone would invite him to his place, but he would beg off. George Bell never had him over.

Once, some eight years ago, Mr. Bertone trooped out there when he hadn't heard from him in a while. George Bell cracked open the door, shooed him away. A curtain draped inside the entryway had camouflaged the chaos. Mr. Bertone had no idea that at some point, George Bell had begun keeping everything.

The Dude, Mr. Bertone, told a story. A few years ago, George Bell was going into the hospital for his heart and had asked him to hold onto some money. Gave him a fat envelope. Inside was $55,000.

Mike Kerins, a bartender, interrupted: "Two things about George. He gave me $100 every Christmas, and he never went out to eat." He had confessed he was too embarrassed because he would have required three entrees.

George Bell had diabetes and complained about a shoulder pain.

He took pills but skipped them during the day, saying they made him feel like an idiot.

Both the Dude and Mr. Kerins sensed he felt he had been bullied too hard by life. "George was in a lot of pain," Mr. Kerins said. "I think he was just waiting to die, had lived enough."

It was as if sadness had killed George Bell.

His days had become predictable, an endless loop. He stayed cloistered inside. Neighbors heard the regular parade of deliverymen who brought him his takeout meals.

The last time the Dude saw George Bell was about a week before his body was found. Frozen shrimp was on sale at the shopping center. George Bell got some, to take back to the kitchen he did not use.

Mr. Bertone didn't realize he had died until someone came to Legends with the news. Mr. Kerins was there and he told the Dude. They made some calls to find out more, but got nowhere.

Why did he die alone, no one knowing?

The Dude thought on that. "I don't know, man," he said. "I wish I could tell you. But I don't know."

On the televisions above the busy bar, a woman was promoting a cleaning product. In the dim light, Mr. Bertone emptied his drink. "You know, I miss him," he said. "I would have liked to see George one more time. He was my friend. One more time."

DAVID WAGONER

■

The Death of the Sky

FROM *Harvard Review*

After a blood-red evening, the sky fell
    as silently as the light it had shed on us
through all our other nights. It scattered
    its fire on fields and hills and cities, the Moon first,
her face spinning from full to dark, then Venus,
    unveiled and melting, Mars in a burned shambles,
and Mercury with featherless heels, the rubble
    of asteroids, the ice-laden, blurred foxfire
of comets, the wind-blown beard of Jupiter
    spun down and around and through
and intermingled with the saturnalia of Saturn,
    Uranus castrated again by Chronos
and dismembered, Neptune
    plunging, drowning, Pluto tumbling
dead as a stone, and from the broken belt
    of the Zodiac, the Ram and the Bull
brought down to slaughter, the Twins
    parting, the Crab clawless, the Lion
and Virgin crumpled together, snarling and weeping ashes,
    the balanced Scales unhinged, the Scorpion's tail
now stinging only itself, the Archer
    bent like his bow by the dying Goat,
the mouth of the fish
    gaping beside the Water-carrier, and we stood
dazed in that black night, and in the morning
    the Sun rose white into an empty whiteness.

MOLLY BRODAK

■

Bandit

FROM *Granta*

I.

I WAS WITH MY DAD the first time I stole something: a little booklet of baby names. I was seven and I devoured word lists: dictionaries, vocab sheets, menus. The appeal of this string of names, their sweet weird shapes and neat order, felt impossible to solve. I couldn't ask for such a pointless thing but I couldn't leave it either. I pressed it to my chest as we walked out of Kroger. It was pale blue with the word BABY spelled out in pastel blocks above a stock photo of a smiling white baby in a white diaper. I stood next to Dad, absorbed in page one, as he put the bags of our food in the trunk of his crappy gold Chevette and he stopped when he saw it. At first he said nothing. He avoided my eyes. He just pressed hard into my back and marched me to the lane we'd left and plucked the stupid booklet out of my hand and presented it to the cashier.

"My daughter stole this. I apologize for her." He beamed a righteous look over a sweep of people nearby. The droopy cashier winced and muttered that it was OK, chuckling mildly. Then, stooping over me, Dad shouted cleanly, "Now you apologize. You will never do this again." The cold anger in his face was edged with some kind of glint I didn't recognize. As he gripped my shoulders he was almost smiling. I remember his shining eyes and the high ceiling of the gigantic store and the brightness of it. I am sure I cried but I don't remember. I do remember an acidic boiling in my chest and a rinse of sweaty cold on my skin, a disgust with my own desire and what it did, how awful all of us felt now because of me. I never stole again until I was a teenager, when he was in prison.

2.

Dad robbed banks one summer.

He robbed the Community Choice Credit Union on 13 Mile Road in Warren.

He robbed the Warren Bank on 19 Mile Road.

He robbed the NBD Bank in Madison Heights.

He robbed the NBD Bank in Utica.

He robbed the TCF Bank on 10 Mile Road in Warren.

He robbed the TCF Bank on 14 Mile in Clawson. That was my bank. The one with the little baskets of Dum Dums at each window and sour herb smell from the health-food store next door.

He robbed the Credit Union One on 15 Mile Road in Sterling Heights.

He robbed the Michigan First Credit Union on Gratiot in East-pointe.

He robbed the Comerica Bank on 8 Mile and Mound. This was as close as he got to the Detroit neighborhood he grew up in, Poletown East, about ten miles south.

He robbed the Comerica Bank inside of a Kroger on 12 Mile and Dequindre.

He robbed the Citizens State Bank on Hayes Road in Shelby Town-ship. The cops caught up with him finally, at Tee J's Golf Course on 23 Mile Road. They peeked into his parked car: a bag of money and his disguise in the back seat, plain as day. He was sitting at the bar, drinking a beer and eating a hot ham sandwich.

3.

I was thirteen that summer. He went to prison for seven years after a lengthy trial, delayed by constant objections and rounds of firing his public defenders. After his release he lived a normal life for seven years, and then robbed banks again.

There: see? Done with the facts already. The facts are easy to say; I say them all the time. This isn't about them. This is about whatever is cut from the frame of narrative. The fat remnants, broken bones, gristle, untender bits.

I'd sit at the dinner table watching my parents' volley crescendo from pissy fork drops to plate slams to stomp-offs and squeal-aways, my sister biting into the cruel talk just to feel included, me just watching as if on the living-room side of a television screen: I could see them but they could definitely not see me. I squashed my wet veggies around on my plate, eyes fixed to the drama like it was *Scooby-Doo* or *G.I. Joe*. I could sleep, I could squirm, I could hum, dance or even talk, safe in their blind spot. I could write, I discovered, and no one heard me.

4.

Yes, one day it was like a membrane breached: before, Dad was like all other dads, and then he was not. We sat together at Big Boy, our booth flush against the winter-black windows reflecting back a weak pair of us, and I idly asked him what recording studios are like and how they work. I was something like eleven, and I had a cloudy notion that it would be exciting and romantic to work in a recording studio for some reason, to help create music but not have to play it. He fluttered his eyes upward like he did and answered without hesitation.

He told me about the equipment and how bands work with producers, how much sound engineers make and what their schedules are like. Details, I started to realize, he could not possibly know. Some giant drum began turning behind my eyes.

Very slowly, as he talked, I felt my belief, something I didn't really know was there until I felt it moving, turn away from him until it was gone, and I was alone, nodding and smiling. But what a marvel to watch him construct bullshit.

After that, I could always tell when he was lying. Something changed around his eyes when he spoke, a kind of haze or color shift, I could see it.

5.

It's the day after Thanksgiving and I've forgotten to write to him. I log into the Federal Bureau of Prisons' email system, called Corr-Links, and check my inbox. No new messages from him in the past month. I try to find the last email exchange we had but it's all empty: the messages are only archived for thirty days, then they disappear.

I write to him like I'd write to a pen pal—distanced, a little uncertain, with a plain dullness I know is shaped by the self-conscious awareness that someone screens these messages before he reads them, even though their content is never more than polite and bloodlessly broad life updates.

How's the new job? Is it interesting? I ask. I remember he told me he upgraded from a job rolling silverware in the kitchen for $2 a day to a "computer job"—previewing patent applications and rejecting them if incomplete. *I got a new cat. She's kind of shy but funny, with one white spot right on her chest. Her name's Jupiter.* I feel like I'm talking to a child. *Hope you are staying warm there!*

I eat lunch, grade papers, go for a walk, check back for a response, spurred by nagging and pointless guilt. No response. He's pushing seventy, with failing kidneys, and I sometimes wonder if he'll make it to his release date. Or even to another email.

The day passes. I try to forget about him. Then, I do forget about him. Days slip by, weeks.

Almost a month later I receive a Christmas card from his girlfriend.

Merry Christmas Molly—you're a doll!

Below her signature is his, pressed on by a stamp she had made of it. Enclosed is a check for $300, also with his signature stamped on it.

6.

In the window of the cab our beachfront hotel approached like a dream, as wrong as a dream, and I felt sick and overwhelmed with the luxury of the fantastic palm trees and clean arched doorways. This could not be right. As we left the cab I hung my mouth open a little long in joy and suspicion, for him to see. He made a round-about pointing sweep to the door and said, "Lezz go," goofily, like he did. Thinking about it now, the hotel was probably nothing special, maybe even cheap, but I couldn't have known.

This was the longest period of time we spent alone together. I was nine or ten and he'd brought me to Cancún, an unlikely place to take a child for no particular reason. He had a habit of taking vacations with just me or my sister, never both of us together, and never with Mom, even when they were married. I feel there was a reason for this; the reason feels dark and I don't like to guess at it.

During the day he would leave me. I'd wake up and find a key and a note on top of some money: *Have fun! Wear sunscreen!* I'd put on my nubby yellow bathing suit and take myself to the beach or the small, intensely chlorinated pool and try hard to have a fun vacation, as instructed.

What was he doing? Was there somewhere nearby to gamble? There must have been. Or was there a woman he met? He'd return in the evening and take me to eat, always ordering a hamburger and a Coke for me without looking at the menu, even though I hated hamburgers and Coke. Mom wouldn't let me drink soda, and he liked to break this rule of hers.

"*Hahmm-borrr-gaysa,*" he'd say to the waiter, childishly drawing out the words and gesturing coarsely as if the waiter were near blind and deaf, "and *Coca-Colé!*" he'd finish, pairing the silly "olé!" with an insulting bottle-drinking mime. He was condescending to waiters everywhere, big-shot style, but especially here. "This is the only word you need to know," he told me from across the dark booth. "*Hamburguesa.*" I tamped down my disgust with obliging laughs, since this show was for me. His gold chain and ring I did not recognize. I watched him carefully, waiting for a time when we'd say real things to each other.

I didn't tell him I liked my days there, on the beach, alone like a grown-up. But anxious. I knew the untethered feeling I liked was not right for me yet. I would have told him about my days lying on a blue towel, just lying there for hours burning pink in the sun, listening while two teenage Mexican girls talked next to me, oblivious to my eavesdropping, alternating between Spanish and English. They talked about how wonderful it would be to be born a *gringa*, and what kind of house they'd live in and what their boyfriends would look like and how their daddies would spoil them with cars and clothes and fantastic birthday parties.

Once, he waited for me to wake up and took me to a Mayan ruin. As the tour started, the foreigners drew together automatically to climb the giant steep steps of a pyramid. It was soaking hot, and I felt so young and small. The other tourists seemed to have such trouble climbing. I bounded up the old blocks, turning to the wide mush of treetops below and smiling. Dad was down below. I waved to him but he wasn't looking. We were herded up for the tour and kids my age and even older were already whining. I couldn't imagine complaining even half as much as my peers did. It frightened me, the way they said what they wanted. *Hungry* and *tired* and *thirsty* and *bored* and *ugh, Dad, can we go?* At the edge of the cenote nearby a tour guide described how the Mayans would sacrifice young women here by tossing them in, "girls about your age," he said, and pointed at me. The group of tourists around us chuckled uncomfortably but I straightened up.

I rested on a boulder carved into a snake's head, wearing the only hat I owned as a child, a black-and-neon tropical-print baseball cap I am certain came from a Wendy's kids' meal. I remember seeing a photograph taken of this, and I wonder if it still exists somewhere. I remember resting on the snake's head, and I remember the photograph of myself resting on it. I liked this day, seeing these things that seemed so important, Dad mostly hanging back in the wet shade of the jungle edge, not climbing things. But he had brought me here and I loved it. I felt the secret urge children have to become lost and stay overnight somewhere good like a museum or a mall as a way of being there privately, directly. I circled the pyramid hoping to find a cave where I could curl up, so I could sleep and stay in this old magic and feel like I'd be a good sacrifice, just right for something serious. But it was hot and we had to go. Dad seemed tired, suspicious of it all, not especially interested in learning too much from the guide or in looking too hard at the ruins. I was happy, though, and he was pleased with that, seemed to want to let me have my happiness without necessarily caring to share in it or talk about it.

On the way back, the tour van we were in had to stop for gas. Children my age but much skinnier came to the windows with their hands out, pleading, keeping steady eye contact. Some tourists in the van gave them coins. The kids who received coins immediately pocketed them and stretched their hands out again, empty. I looked at my dad. He laughed dismissively. "They're just bums. They can work like the rest of us."

And then, back to the days like before, which now seemed even longer. I grew tired of the pretty beach. The tourists were loud, desperate in their drinking and their little radios. I sat alone in the hotel room. It was yellow and clean and there was a small TV I would flip through endlessly. *We are just not . . . friends,* I remember thinking. I wondered who was friends with Dad. Mom? That seemed insane. My sister? Yes, her. She'd be good at this, being here with him. She'd be having the time of her life, sucking down a virgin strawberry daiquiri and posing poolside, hamming it up for Dad's camera. The hallways were tiled brown and cold, and the smell of chlorine from the pool seemed trapped forever in the corridors, night and day. I would walk around the hotel with the $20 bill he had given me for food, not sure what to do with it.

7.

I want to say plainly everything I didn't know.

I didn't know Dad gambled. Sports betting mostly, on football, baseball or college basketball, point spreads, totals, money lines, whatever was offered. Bookies, calls to Vegas, two or three TVs at once.

I knew there were little paper slips and crazy phone calls and intense screaming about games—more intense than seemed appropriate—but it only added up to a kind of private tension orbiting him. I didn't know what it was.

Sports betting is so different from card games or other gambling because the player doesn't play the game, exactly. His game is the analysis of information—knowing which players might be secretly hurt or sick, which refs favor which teams, the mood of one stadium over another, the combination of one pitcher with a certain kind of weather—and the synthesis of hunches, superstitions, wishes, loyalty. And beyond that there are the odds the bookies are offering, which reflect what everyone else is predicting. Perfect for someone who thinks he's smarter than everyone else.

Before Detroit built big casinos downtown there was always Windsor Casino across the Canadian border, so there was always blackjack too. But nobody knows much about this—my mom, my sister, his co-workers, his brothers and sisters—no one saw his gambling, no one was invited to come along, or share strategy, or even wish him luck. It was totally private. Perhaps it would not have been so evil if it hadn't been so hidden. Mom's experience of his gambling came to her only in cold losses: an empty savings account, the car suddenly gone, bills and debts, threatening phone calls. Sometimes broken ribs, a broken nose. The rare big win must have been wasted immediately in private, on more gambling or something showy and useless like a new watch. Or, of course, on his debts.

Outcomes get shaken out fast in gambling. In real life, big risks take years to reveal themselves, and the pressure of choosing a career, a partner, a home, a family, a whole identity might overwhelm an impatient man, one who values control, not fate. He will either want all the options out of a confused greed, hoarding overlapping partners, shallow hobbies, alternate selves; or he will refuse them all, risking nothing. And really, the first option is the same as the second. Keeping a few girlfriends or wives around effectively dismisses a true relationship with any one of them. Being a good, hardworking dad and a criminal at the same time is a way of choosing to be neither.

Besides, an addict is already faithfully committed to something he prioritizes above all else. Gambling addiction, particularly, is easy to start; it requires no elaborate or illegal activities, no troublesome ingestion of substances, and it programs the body using its own chemicals. I thought at first gambling was about chance, the possibility of making something out of nothing, of multiplying money through pure cleverness. He'd like that. Something from nothing. And that is the first charm. But the ones who get addicted, I think, are looking for certainty, not chance. Outcomes are certain, immediate and clear. In other words, there will be a result to any one bet, a point in time when the risk will be unequivocally resolved, and the skill and foresight of the gambler can be perfectly measured. A shot of adrenaline will issue into the bloodstream, win *or* lose. It's not messy, not indefinite or uncontrollable, like love, or people. Gambling absolves its players of uncertainty.

8.

Dad steered Mom through the broad doors of the restaurant at the Hazel Park Raceway for their first date. The old host lit up, welcomed him by name and seated them by the wide windows. The waiters knew him too, and he tipped outrageously. Mom wore a baggy white hippie smock embroidered with lines of tiny red flowers (a dress, she said, like "a loose interpretation of a baseball"), and her wild black curly hair down in a plain cloud. Dad wore a gold-button sports jacket, creased slacks, hard-shined shoes and slick hair; a near Robert De Niro. They'd met while working in a tool and die shop in Romeo, Michigan, in 1977. Mom had been placed there for a few weeks by a temp agency to do packing and shipping.

After only a couple months of dating, Dad took her on an elaborate vacation to South America to see Machu Picchu. He'd first suggested Mexico, but Mom said she didn't like Mexico. It made her nervous.

The trip was impulsive and strange, something my mom would have loved. And he seemed so rich. He'd told her, I imagine in his shy way, without eye contact, that if he ever were to marry someone, it would be her. Mom felt adored, scooped up in his big gestures, bound by the certainty of them. I have seen some photographs from this trip. They both look so excited and free and wild, in jeans and thin T-shirts, laughing, almost childish against the ancient monuments and green vistas. He directed the trip with sheer confidence, ever-calm, bullying through the language barrier, tossing indulgences to my mom along the way like the king of the parade. She didn't know he had cashed out a life insurance policy to take her there, and that he was dead broke. Soon after the trip she discovered she was pregnant with my sister.

Mom's pregnancy started to show at the shop, drawing stronger looks from the bitter receptionist with the beehive hairdo. Mom noticed the looks, and turned to her, straight and direct, like she always did if something needed to be sorted out.

"Darlin'," the receptionist said before Mom even opened her mouth, "he didn't tell you he's married, did he?"

Mom laughed but said nothing. The receptionist just shook her head in pity. Mom didn't like pity. She would have ignored it. He had told her he'd marry her if he was ever inclined to marry, and it just didn't seem to her like something someone already married could come up with. It was so sweet. He was so generous, so affectionate.

The idea, though, began to itch. She did think it was odd that she had never been to his house, didn't have his home phone number and had only been offered vague indications of where he lived. That night she asked him if he was married, and he said no. He acted genuinely confused, suggesting that the receptionist was just a jealous cow because he wouldn't flirt with her. She felt happy with that. And besides, there was a baby to consider now. She let it go. Soon, she moved into an apartment with him and quit working.

For her first doctor's visit, Dad gave her his insurance card and the name of the clinic to visit while he was at work. She handed over the card to the receptionist, who pulled a file, opened it and then paused. The receptionist looked at Mom, then at the file, then at Mom again, glancing at the nurses near her to spread her discomfort. An indignant look hardened her face. Mom was puzzled. "Is everything OK?" she finally asked.

"Yes, but . . . I'm sorry, ma'am . . . but you are not Mrs. Brodak."

Mom smiled politely. "Well, not officially yet, but I'm on his insurance now so you have to honor that."

"No, I mean . . ." The nurses now looked on with worry. "Mrs. Brodak and her daughter are regular patients of this clinic. They were just in last Wednesday. You are not Mrs. Brodak."

It was then, she told me, that it should have ended. It wasn't too late. "Everything," she told me, "could have been avoided if I had just gone back to my parents instead of to him the moment I left that clinic." I nod, imagining how much better that would have been for her, skipping past the idea that this "everything" she could have avoided would have included me. "It's like all I could do was make mistakes," she said.

The moment he stepped through the door that evening she told him the story of the insurance card at the clinic and demanded to know who the real Mrs. Brodak was. He softened his shoulders and toddled gently to her, engulfing her with a hug, caressing her as she cried. His softness and confident denial stunned her into silence, just like it had before. He told her the woman was just a friend he'd allowed to use his card, that he was just doing someone a favor out of kindness, that he was certainly not married. He laughed about it, prodding and rousing her into laughing with him as he smoothed her face.

He could turn you like that. He just wouldn't let your bad mood win. He'd steal your mad words and twist them funny in repetition, poke at your folded arms until they opened, grin mockingly at your dumb pout until you smiled, as long as it took.

A few days later she called the county clerk's office to inquire about some marriage records. The clerk on the other end delivered the news plainly, as she probably always did. He'd been married for just a few years. He had a daughter, aged four.

See, this is how my dad starts—stolen from another family.

Mom packed her small suitcases and moved to her parents' house that same day, and that, again, should've been the end of it. She stayed in her room. The road to her parents' house had not been paved yet, and there were still fields around them, overgrown lilac bushes, honeysuckle and wild rhubarb where now there are neighbors' neat lawns.

She thought about his tenderness. The honest, steady light in his eyes when he told her he loved her. How he'd suddenly sweep her up for a small dance around the kitchen. All these things he'd practiced with his real wife. She gave birth to my sister, quietly.

But he wouldn't leave her alone. He found her and would come whenever he could, tossing rocks at her window in the night like a teenager until her father chased him off, leaving bouquets on the doorstep with long love letters. He was unreasonably persistent, beyond what she would've expected of any boyfriend, and perhaps it was the insane magnitude of this persistence that convinced her to go back to him. She thought maybe their relationship was worth all of this effort, all of the dozens and dozens of roses, the gifts, the jewelry, the long letters pleading for forgiveness, praising her virtues, promising to leave his wife. "And poetry," Mom said. "You should have seen the poetry he wrote to me. I almost wish I hadn't thrown it all away."

First she wanted to meet the real Mrs. Brodak. Mom looked up their number in the phone book, called to introduce herself and extend an invitation to meet, which Mrs. Brodak accepted stiffly.

It was a muggy summer. Dad's wife appeared at the screen door and stood without knocking. In a thick blue dress with her waist tied tightly, she said nothing when Mom opened the door. "Would you like to hold the baby?" Mom asked.

My sister was placed in her lap like a bomb. Nothing could be done but politely talk, with hard grief in their chests, softening their voices. The real Mrs. Brodak was scared too. "How did you meet?" Mom asked Dad's wife.

They had met in high school. After he had returned from Vietnam, they married impulsively. She never had time to think, she said. Baby, work, no time to think. This is how life works: hurrying along through the tough moments, then the hurrying hardens and fossilizes, then that's the past, that hurrying. She asked Mom what was going to happen now.

"Now," Mom said, "we leave Joe Brodak. We don't let our babies know him. He's not a good person." She leaned to her, with hands out. They lightly embraced and nodded tearfully. Mom would have wanted to help Mrs. Brodak.

Mom also would have felt a little triumphant somehow. She would have felt like she had won him. Whatever there was to win. She didn't actually want to quit like that, despite what she said to Mrs. Brodak. She had a baby now, and no real career prospects, having ditched the student teaching she needed to finish her certification, and on top of that her own mental illnesses kept her from self-sufficiency. Her parents looked on with reserved worry. After Dad's wife left, Mom joined them in the kitchen, where they had been listening to the exchange. They sipped coffee, looking out at the bird feeder. Eventually Mom's mother urged her to go back to him. "It is better to be married," she said. "You have to just deal with it."

She turned back to him, resolved to trust him.

This looks bad, I know. I would not have made this choice, I think. Most people wouldn't. But what do any of us know?

In the basement of the Romeo District Court my dad married my mom, with his sister, Helena, as a witness. The dress Mom wore, an off-white peasant dress with low shoulders and small pouf sleeves, I wore when I was ten, as a hippie Halloween costume.

A small dinner party was held at a restaurant on a nearby golf course. Mom met her mother-in-law there, and many other Brodaks, who all regarded her warily. As a homewrecker.

Soon after the wedding, I was born, during a year of relative happiness in their relationship. Perhaps, Mom thought, their rocky start was over, that there would be no more problems. She threw her wild energy into this life: these children, and him, her husband, now. She enacted a vigorous and healthy routine for her family: reading, games, walks to the park, dancing, art and helping the elderly lady upstairs with her housework. She attended to us with pure devotion. She baked homemade bread and wrote folk songs, singing them softly to us with her acoustic Gibson at bedtime. The songs were always minor key, lament-low, about horses and freedom and the ocean. In the dark, I'd cry sometimes in their hold.

Mom isn't sure exactly when Dad got divorced from his first wife; he kept the details a secret. With her daughter, my half-sister, Mrs. Brodak moved to California, where she died of cancer a few years later.

9.

Mom threw away all of the letters and poetry he'd sent her when she remarried and moved in with her new husband. It stings to think about. I wish I could have read these things, but they were not for me. And I don't blame her.

But I did see the letters, a long time ago. I saw the shoebox full of them when I was little. Pages and pages of blue-lined notebook paper with Dad's loopy, fat, cursive writing, or sometimes the harsh, slanted caps he'd use. The words rattled on the pages with some mysterious grown-up intensity that pushed me away from them. I did take something from the box. A thing that made no sense to me.

A small, square, black-and-white photo of him he had sent her. The background is pure white and the whiteness of his knit polo shirt disappears into it so his head appears to be floating in whiteness, rooted only by the wide, heathered gray collar of his shirt. He is young and smiling broadly, open-mouthed, joy in his eyes, like he was just laughing, really laughing. He's smiling honestly, more honestly than I have ever seen.

On the back of the photo is his loopy cursive in blue pen. When I read it I began to cry instantly, in gusting sheets of tears. I took it because it was the first object that made me cry. I couldn't understand how. I'm crying now, reading it again.

Nora,
My first real, true love. You changed my life with your "crazy" love.
I love you,
J.B.

10.

After I was born Dad came across an ad for an attorney who was hiring women to be surrogate mothers. He became convinced that this would solve their financial problems. Nowadays paid surrogacy is common, but in the early eighties the process was new, and still somewhat risky. He pressed my mother, and she started to warm to the idea; after all, she loved being a mother and felt good about the idea of helping a couple have a baby. It seemed kind and smart and wonderful. She said the couple met her in a restaurant, and she brought me and my sister along, "you know, to show you off, so they could see how healthy and happy you were," she told me. We squirmed and smiled in the booth like the best roly-poly babies possible, and Mom beamed while the couple fell for her.

They lived in Long Island, so Mom was flown out to New York to do the insemination there. It didn't work. She was flown out again. It didn't work.

Meanwhile, Dad's gambling debts were secretly starting to accumulate. He was thinking about the $10,000 they were set to receive as soon as the baby was born, and had started spending recklessly.

Mom started noticing odd things. Some men had asked the neighbors where the Brodak girls went to school. The phone rang off the hook. Only once did she respond, finding a strange man on the line. He told her he was calling from Vegas. "Your husband," the man said, "is a scumbag. A fucking deadbeat. Did you know that?" She unplugged the phone. That night, the living-room windows were shot out.

Dad told her they needed to move. And why not to Long Island, to be closer to the couple? To him it was the perfect out.

We moved to a cramped basement apartment on Long Island. In photos of us from this era, on a cheap swing set or feeding ducks by a weak pond, there is a kind of stressy child anger in our eyes. Mom kept up her focus on us. Free from his debts back in Michigan, Dad returned to gambling. She never knew how bad things were until something went missing.

Mom was cleaning us up from breakfast one day when Dad was leaving for work. He came back through the door after a minute. "Forget something?" Mom asked absently.

"No, uh, my car . . ."

Mom looked out the window. It was gone, had disappeared overnight. "Where's your car?"

"Oh . . . I let a buddy of mine borrow it."

"He just came in the night and took your car? He had a key to your car?"

"Yeah, it was an emergency, no big deal. I'm gonna borrow yours today, OK?" He grabbed her keys and left.

How could he resolve this one? Weeks went by and his "buddy" didn't return the car. Eventually he just came home with a new one, an old beater with green upholstery smelling of dogs. He told Mom he'd decided to sell his buddy the car, but she'd already seen the repo notice. She wasn't surprised anymore. She shuffled her rage into resignation, and focused on us.

The insemination attempts continued. One night, after returning from a long trip, drunk and tired, Dad forced himself on her. Mom said she screamed and fought him. But he was strong. Sex was against the contract they had with the couple, for obvious reasons.

On a hunch, she took a test a few weeks later and discovered she was pregnant. Now, though, she wasn't sure whose baby it was.

She took us to stay with her aunt in Baltimore for a few weeks. And there, without telling anyone, she decided to abort the fetus. She hadn't spoken to Dad for weeks, nor did she return the calls from the couple. Eventually she returned home, with us in tow, to find Dad having just returned too, from Atlantic City. He had gambled away everything. Their savings, his car, his wedding ring, every penny he could find. She packed our clothes and whatever small things would fit into her powder-blue Caprice Classic and took us back to Michigan that same day. She filed for divorce and moved back in with her parents. It was here, living with my grandparents, that I first started to know my life. I remember Goodison Preschool. A salt-dough Christmas ornament I made and tried to eat. Playing Red Rover in the sun. My bossy sister teasing me, and stress around us all.

Eventually she was going to have to call the couple to tell them what happened. She says she still remembers that phone call, their voices on the other line, warm, but quiet and shocked. They were crushed. They said they would have taken the baby either way, and loved it completely. They had come to trust and care for her, and she failed them in the worst possible way. Listening to my mom reveal this story crumples me inside.

She was about my age when this happened, and I imagine her next to me, as a friend. I would have helped her out of this.

I would have shaken her bony shoulders and said no no no no until the stupid false hope in her eyes was gone and all of Dad's tricks fell away.

II.

Such a short part of their lives, really, this marriage and this family. Just a few years.

Dad moved back to Michigan too, following us a few weeks later. He was living in a hotel room in Center Line, near the GM Tech Center where he worked.

We'd be dropped off there, and walk the AstroTurf-lined walkways to the room while teenagers screamed and splashed in the pool. Mexican music blared and faded in the rooms we passed, some with open doors, some with eyes following. But it was a break from the attentive care children can get sick of. It seemed like a party. He bought us huge bags of candy—Skittles for my sister and Raisinets for me. There were always cold cuts and a shrimp ring in the fridge. During the day he'd often leave us alone, and we were OK, watching movies, eating candy, puffy-painting giant cheap sweatshirts and playing Nintendo. I didn't really miss him when he was gone, and I knew that couldn't be right.

My sister took care of me when we were alone. She directed me to eat the crackers and ham she'd arranged and have a glass of milk while I was absorbed in *Mega Man*. She knew how to pull out the sofa bed when we were getting tired. I'd watch her tiny body rip the creaky metal frame out of the nubby brown couch. She'd straighten the sheets around the lumpy mattress and drag the comforter from Dad's bed onto ours, nestling me into the uncomfortable mess wordlessly.

She'd check to make sure the door was deadbolted, then flip the lights off and tuck us in. The puffy paints and bags of candy and the half-consumed glasses of milk and the ham plates would be scattered on the floor around the sofa bed, and we'd just lie there, listening. The rush of 12 Mile Road below and the garbled living sounds from the other residents would lull us to sleep. We imagined different versions of where Dad was. A cool movie, on a date with a hot lady, at a nightclub, at a concert. Sometimes we'd compare ideas, sometimes we'd just let them play out in our heads as we fell asleep.

During the day I'd poke around his stuff. Shoved under towels in the linen closet: *Playboys* and baggies of green and white drugs. Sometimes money. Under the bed, in a shoebox: a heavy, greasy-looking gun.

I wanted to have the fun he wanted us to have. He'd take us to things, kid things, like water parks or Chuck E. Cheese's, places Mom would never take us because she insisted on productive activities like hikes or art museums. He'd take us to a golf dome with a bar and a dark arcade attached, then hand us both a roll of quarters to spend in the arcade while he was in the bar. For hours we'd feed the machines, Mortal Kombat and Rampage and Gauntlet. When our quarters were gone we'd gingerly shuffle through the bar and find him alone, glued to a sports game. He'd hand us more quarters or say it was time to go. It was fun but, I don't know, thin fun. He'd put something in front of us: a sports game or play place or movie or toy and he was always on the other side of it, far on the other side of it. I kept it that way too, I know. I didn't like to go with him, I didn't like to have to answer his perfunctory questions about school or interests, I didn't even like to hug him. I feel awful remembering this.

And, once again, he pursued Mom relentlessly, but I never saw it happen and didn't know this until later, when Mom told me. I often wonder why he did it. He could have easily walked away from us, and perhaps he didn't only because that was the more obvious thing to do. The only thing that makes sense is that he wanted to be with us. Or that he felt like he was supposed to be with us, an obligation he couldn't shake.

I should be able to feel my way through that question, to be able to know, in my gut, if he really wanted to be a dad and husband. But I can't feel it. Nothing really matches up. There are fragments of a criminal alongside fragments of a dad, and nothing overlaps, nothing eclipses the other, they're just there, next to each other. No narrative fits.

12.

No, I did see it, once. On a softball field in the evening when the sky was getting dark pink. Mom had brought me to see my sister's softball team play, a team that my dad coached. I had wandered away to sit in the grass, probably looking for interesting insects or rocks, and from some distance I saw my dad approach my mom at the edge of the bleachers where she stood. The sun was behind them but I could see their gray shapes in the nook of the gleaming silver bleachers and the matching fence. Perhaps the game was over. He was talking closely to her face and she was looking away at first, arms crossed. I edged to the other side of the bleachers to hear. He had his hand on her shoulder; she was starting to smile. I could hear him say, "I need you. I need you," in a steady pleading voice I can still hear in my head. I was surprised at this sound, and memorized it. Then he lifted his knee and softly and childishly kneed her thigh, still saying, "I need you" and now drawing it out lightly and funnily with each jab—"I *kneed* you. I *kneed* you"—and she was really smiling now, looking down sweetly and smiling.

13.

My dad was born August 19, 1945, in a displaced persons' camp. This is how he first lived: being carried by his mother, in secret, while she worked silently in the camp.

The previous year his mother and father and five siblings had been moved out of their homes in Szwajcaria, Poland, by the Nazis and forced to board a train. My Aunt Helena, a few years older than my dad, told me she remembers it. She remembers their mom, Stanislawa, hopping off the train when it stopped to hunt for wood to start a cooking fire. Stanislawa's parents and three of her siblings had died a few years before in Siberia, having been shipped there to cut trees for the Russian supply. "The trees would shatter if they hit the ground because it was so cold. No one had enough clothes or food, so most people died there," my aunt told me in a letter. She has memories of their life during the war, "but they don't seem real," she wrote. She remembers the mood of the train: the animal-like panic any time the train stopped, the worry of the adults, and her worry when her mother would disappear. They were taken to Dachau, where my grandfather was beaten and interrogated daily because the Nazis suspected him of being a partisan, like his brothers.

My grandfather was separated from the family. The rest of them lived and worked together, hoping he'd be returned. Nothing useful came out of the interrogations.

After a few months they were reunited, and all transferred to a sub-camp in Kempten, Germany, where they worked as slaves, mostly farming. This is where my grandmother became pregnant with my father. She hid her pregnancy because she was afraid she'd be forced to abort it. She had to work to be fed like everyone else, even the children, the sick, everyone. My aunt remembers a little of this but won't say much. "There were horrors every day," she says, and I don't press her. The war was over in April and my dad was born in August.

After the war, my grandfather felt strongly that they should move to Australia, since he liked the idea of working a homestead and living freely as a farmer. But a few months before they were to leave, he died, and Australia no longer welcomed them—a widow with five children. Through a Catholic sponsorship program a passage to America was offered, and they took it. My dad's first memories were of this ship: troop transport, cold and gray all around, the sea and metal smell.

14.

They arrived at Ellis Island on December 4, 1951, and Dad's name was changed from Jozef to Joseph. They took a train to Detroit. Their sponsor took them to St. Albertus Church, on the corner of St. Aubin and Canfield, an area that used to be called Poletown. They lived on the top floor of the adjacent school, built in 1916, until my grandma found work in the cafeteria of the *Detroit News* and rented an apartment for them. St. Albertus closed as a parish in 1990, and now stands in urban prairie among other abandoned buildings.

I wanted to see it for myself. One family visit in December I snuck away for the day and drove myself there. There are a lot of death holes in Detroit. Not poor neighborhoods but something beyond that: nothingnesses, forsaken places. Scattered plots, some whole blocks, whole streets, sets of streets, in the middle of the city. The place where my dad grew up is dead.

This area, around Mack and Chene, is one of the emptiest in Detroit. It is not the most dangerous; there just aren't many people here at all. Only a few structures stand on each block, and rarely are those structures occupied. Sometimes you can't really tell. Most houses are in different states of decay, some just piles of charred wood and ash. These are not the most picturesque ruins. They're not the famous ones, like the Packard Plant or the huge train depot, or the ornately ruined Michigan Theater. They're not the pretty castles of Brush Park, derelict and looted, the cool tall office buildings downtown with wild trees growing on them, the broken buildings out-of-town journalists and photographers come to document and vaguely lament. These were plain poor houses to start with.

St. Albertus sits next to homes like these, and plots of empty grassland. Across the street is one occupied house, and a heavily gated new-but-cheap apartment complex, where a convent and girls' orphanage used to be. Behind the church is the school, a sturdy three-story brick building with a stone facade, ST ALBERTVS carved across a neoclassical frieze above four faceted pilasters between the doors. The school is a ruin—windows are broken or boarded up, graffiti covers the building man-high around the dark brick and the yard is grown over, with dumped TVs and furniture in the grass. I looked at it for a long time. This is where my family first lived in America. This is where my dad learned English. A ruin, like any other. I watched a solidly fat black squirrel climb the brick effortlessly, pause to eat a small thing on the windowsill, then disappear inside.

On the front steps I pulled shyly at the boards over the three doors, but they were nailed tight. It would have been easy enough to climb up to any of the glassless first-floor windows, but I was alone and it seemed unwise. I took some photos with my phone. A rind of green copper wound weakly around the roof, the rest of it having been pulled off by scavengers. I had explored abandoned structures before, but not alone. Still, here I was. I had come this far. I looked up and down the street, but there was not a soul around. I walked quickly to an inner corner and hoisted myself up on the ledge, then to the same glassless window into which the black squirrel had disappeared.

Broken glass and soft piles of crumbled plaster. Cold dark. The smell of old wet wood and dead animals. I dropped down into a class-room with gritty gray floors. But there had been some maintenance here by church people; I could tell the floor had been swept occasion-ally. I walked like I was stepping on someone. The boards shivered and a steady wind hushed me.

A dark wood door lead to the hall, lined with more classrooms. All of the doorknobs removed, stolen. The next room was painted a sweet sky blue, peeling at the top, with a chalkboard but no furni-ture. A red fire-alarm box. Very nice wood, rotting. Powdery plaster making the ground soft. Every surface peeling. The next room was pale acid green. A patch of exposed cinder blocks where the chalk-board had been. It's hard to imagine my father as a boy. He was a star athlete, he'd told me. Captain of the football team in high school. He would've been fun. Quiet but brave and strong, like me. I kicked lightly at some planks on the ground, and the sound of scurrying claws in the walls moved away from me.

I went slowly down the hall, feeling ridiculous for using the flash-light feature on my expensive phone but glad to have it, since the floorboards were warped, with odd piles of glass and nails and wood shards. The bare rooms felt heavy and full, and I can't explain this. I came to a stairwell. Plaster dust had been swept into loose mounds against the wall, and footprints marked a path up the steps.

On the top floor, the hall opened into the auditorium. The windows were not boarded up here, and the room was bright and open and cold. I stood astounded: at one end a gaping black stage was framed with pale peach and jaunty blue leaf patterns, deco style, and flanked by two doors topped with Greek urns and vines of plaster. A very small gold-fringed pale blue curtain hung straight across the stage, painted with mounds of red and orange flowers with wispy grass behind.

My mouth hung dumbly and I started to cry. The peeling colors and the light of the room, the flowered curtain and the darkness, the piles of powder, the good wood, the hidden air. It was beautiful in a way I recognized in the oldest part of me. I felt like I was see-ing something true. I walked the thin boards of the floor to the center of the room, past a large blue A painted inside of a circle, like a tidy anarchy symbol. Bird shit covered the floor, concentrating un-der grates. The cooing and wheezing and clawing of pigeons echoed blindly. Above the center of the room, on the high ceiling arching like a coffin top, was a trinity of large pale blue medallions, the cen-ter one probably once surrounding a light fixture that was now gone. My family slept on cots in this room for months. They looked up at this. As a child, my dad, packed in with the other refugees, looked up at this ceiling and thought about the future, this future I am in now. It was hard not to feel grateful for this useless beauty. It was there for them, this silent, mindless pattern, how it looked like love over the empty room.

The sky can be so solid gray in Michigan, like wet concrete, churn-ing without breaking for days. Under it, this home, sinking into the earth, the earth digesting its own paradox, in silence.

■

Borb

FROM *Borb*

Beginning on the next page are a series of excerpts from Jason Little's *Borb*, a collection of comic strips featuring a homeless, alcoholic man. The collection was published by Uncivilized Books in Minneapolis, Minnesota.

BORB
TRUDGE SHUFFLE
5-6
RIP!
OOPS
OOPS
5-7
BUSTY
OOPS

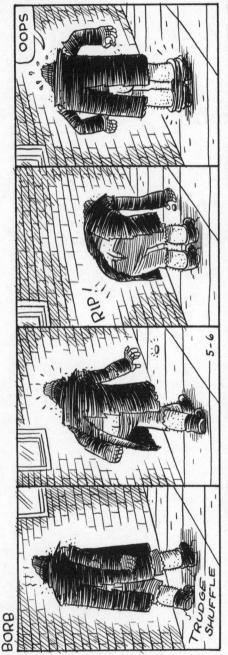

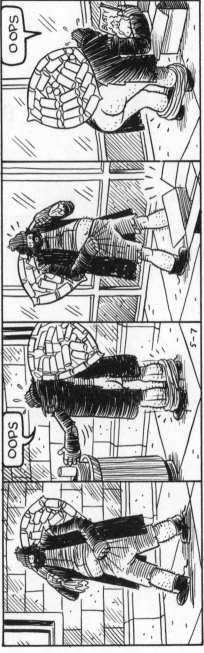

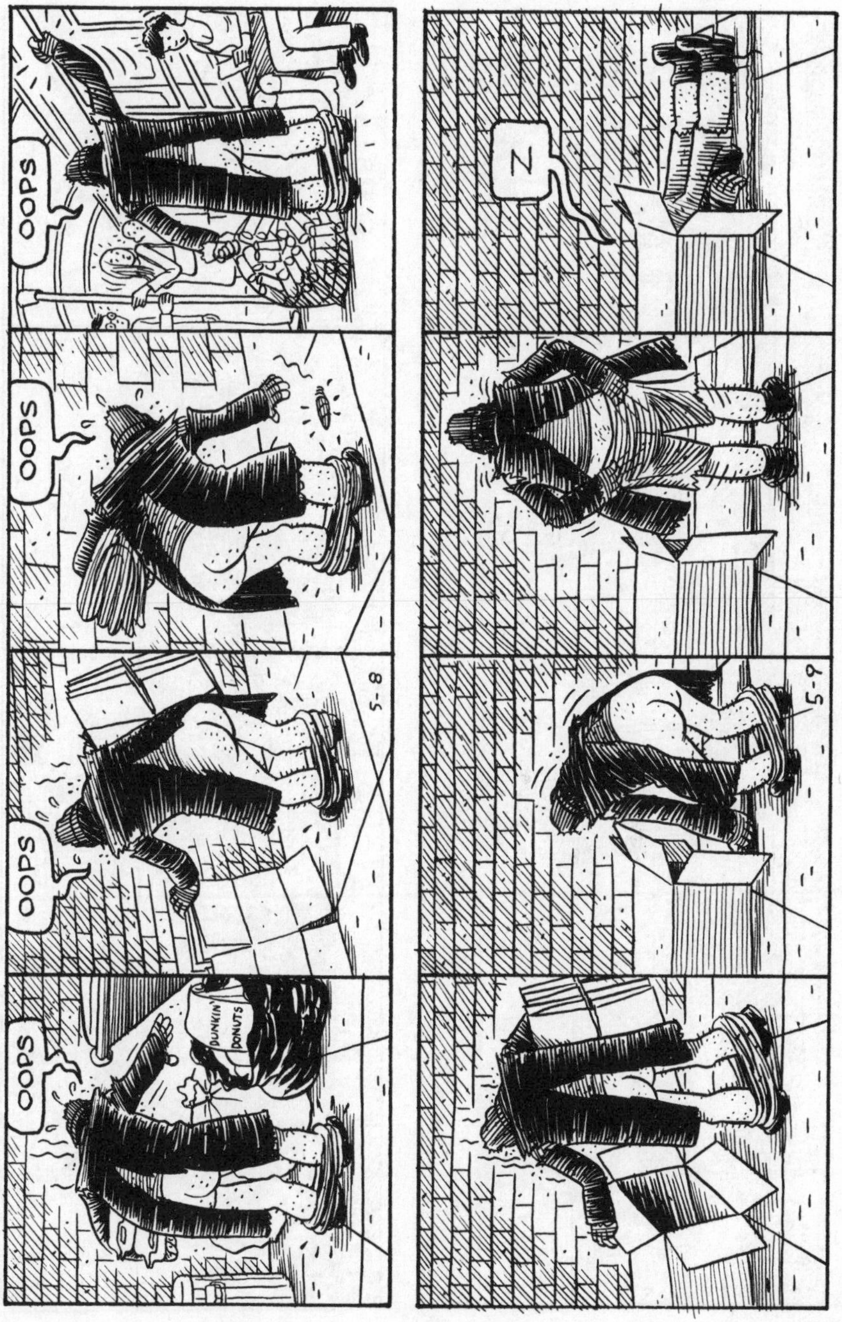
OOPS
DUNKIN DONUTS
OOPS
5-8
OOPS
OOPS
5-9
N

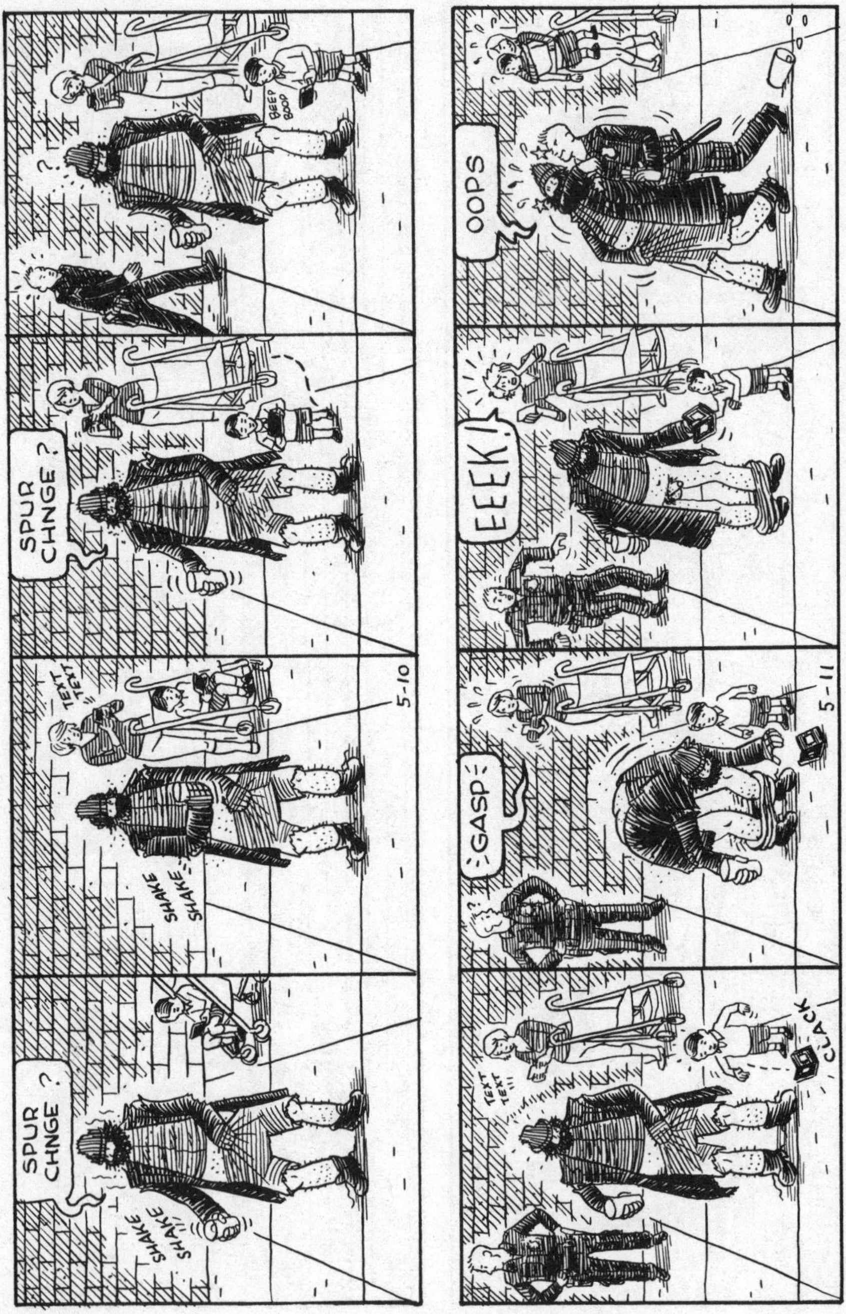
SPUR CHNGE ?
SHAKE SHAKE
SHAKE SHAKE
TEXT TEXT
5-10
SPUR CHNGE ?
?
BEEP BOOP
TEXT TEXT
CLACK
GASP
?
5-11
EEEK!
OOPS

HERE'S A CHILD MOLESTER TO KEEP YOU BOYS COMP'NY

5-13

SO WHAT'S YOUR STORY, BUDDY?

MMM-HMM

CN Y' GT ME A BELT?

A BELT

THE CHARGES ARE: INDECENT EXPOSURE WITH POSSIBLE CORRUP-TION OF A MINOR, CHILD MOLESTATION, AND SEXUAL ASSAULT

PUBLIC DEFENDER

5-14

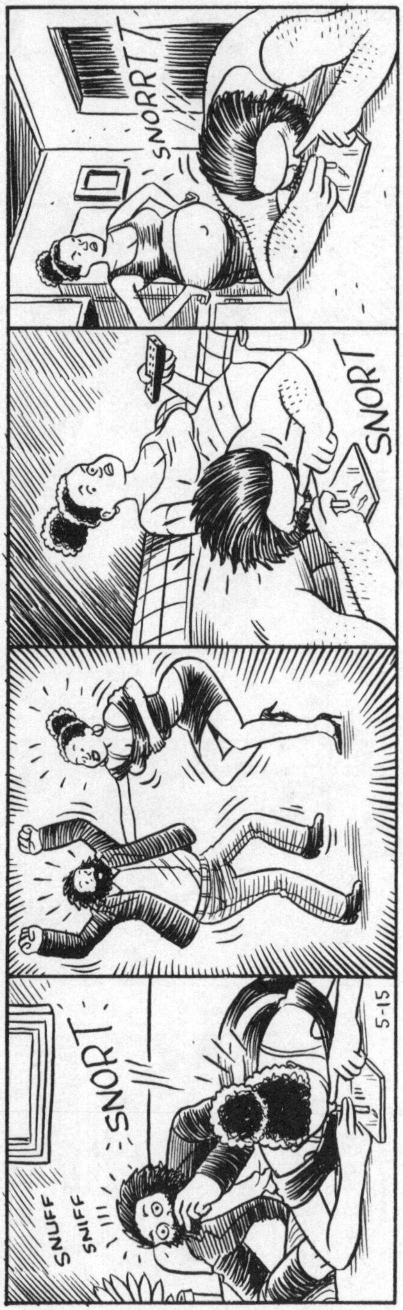
SNUFF
SNIFF
SNORT
5-15
SNORT
SNORRT

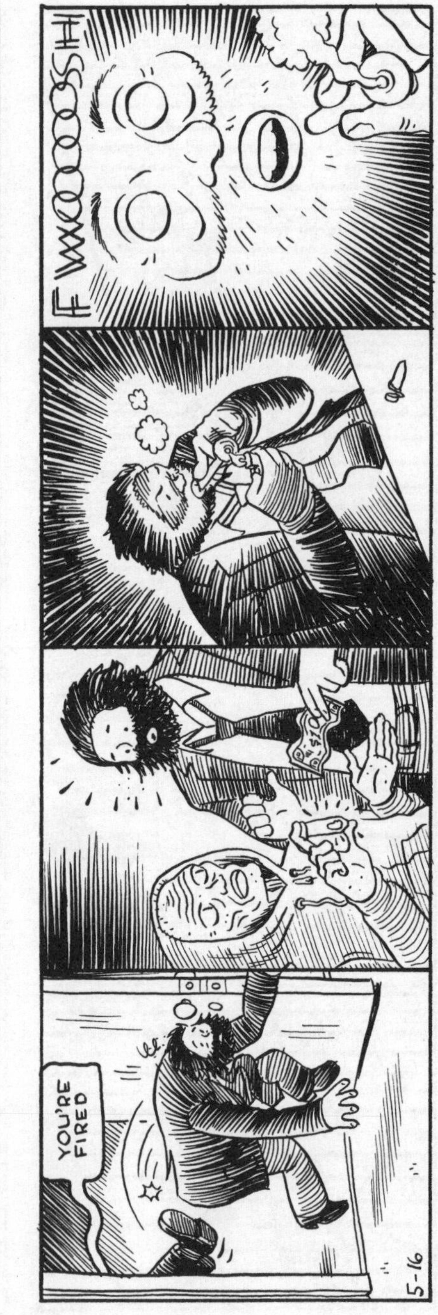
YOU'RE FIRED
5-16
FWOOOOOOSSH

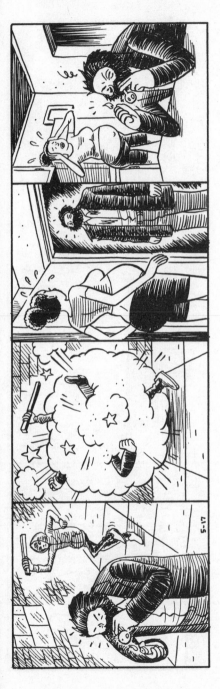

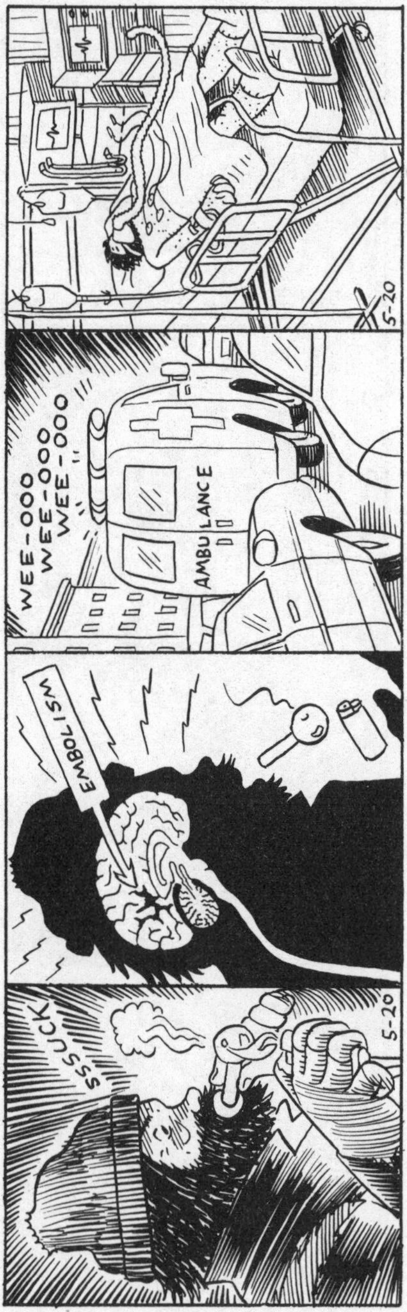
SSSSUCK
5-20
EMBOLISM
WEE-OOO
WEE-OOO
WEE-OOO
AMBULANCE
5-20

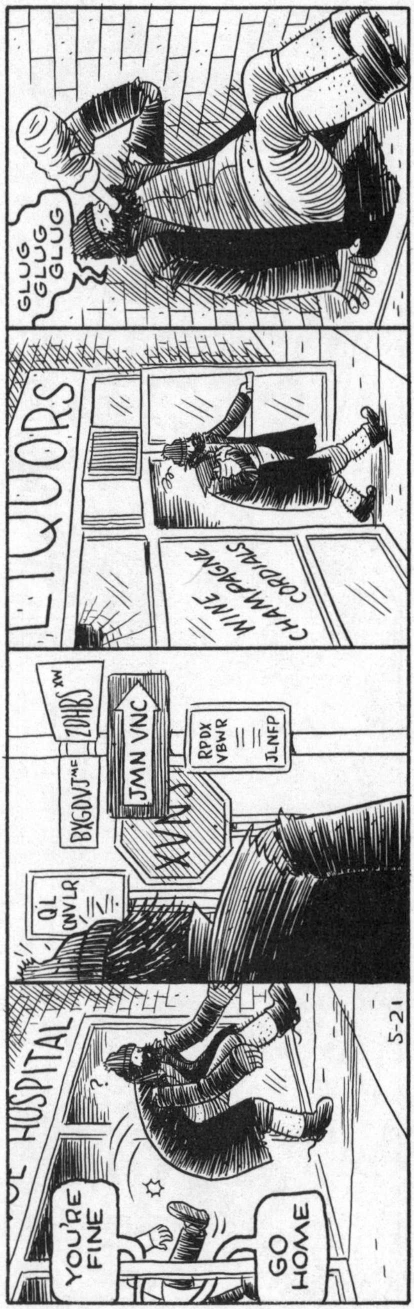
HOSPITAL
YOU'RE FINE
GO HOME
?
5-21
BXGDVJ
JMN VNC
RPDX VBWR
JLNFP
LIQUORS
WINE
CHAMPAGNE
CORDIALS
GLUG
GLUG
GLUG

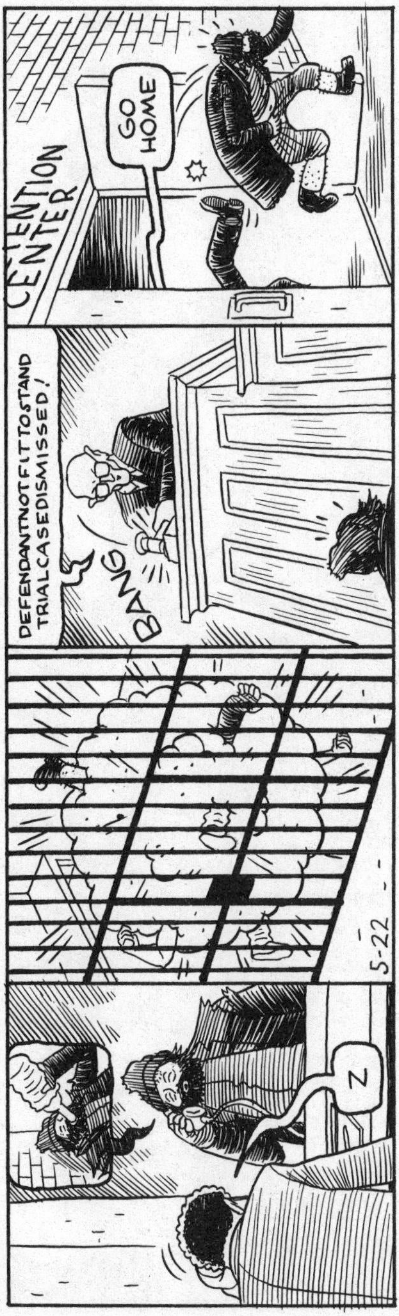
Z
5-22
DEFENDANTNOTFITTOSTAND TRIALCASEDISMISSED!
BANG
ETENTION CENTER
GO HOME

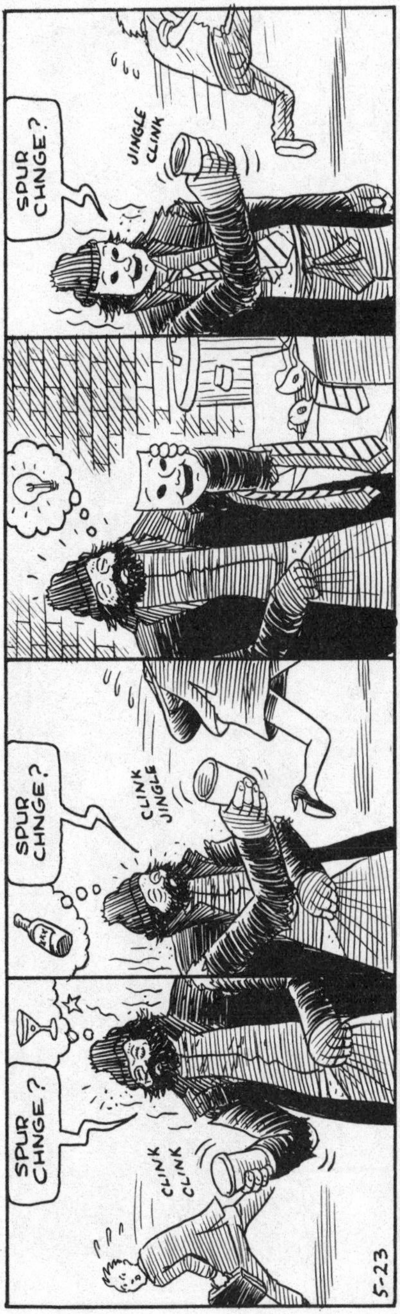
SPUR CHNGE?
CLINK CLINK
SPUR CHNGE?
CLINK JINGLE
SPUR CHNGE?
JINGLE CLINK
5-23

XXX
5-24
XXX
XXX
XXX
XXX
XXX
SCRATCH SCRATCH
EEEYEEEKK
©2013
DELIRIUM TREMENS
SHIVER
MOAN
41 HOURS LATER
Z
5-25
Z
PSSSSSS

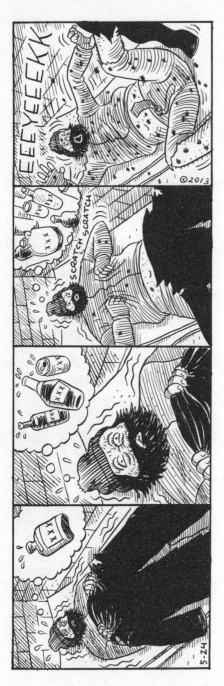

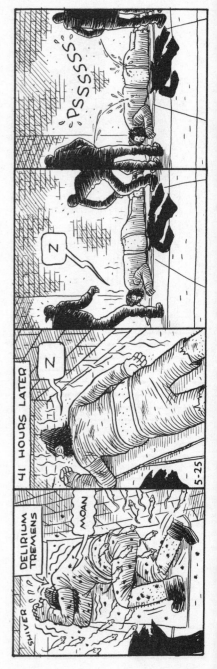

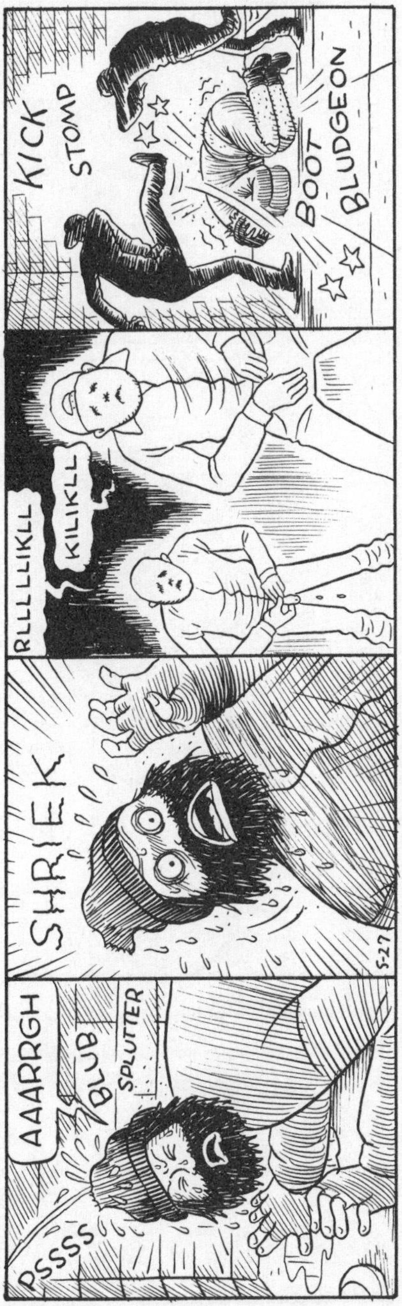
PSSSS
AAARRGH
BLUB
SPLUTTER
SHRIEK
5-27
RLLLLLIKLL
KILIKLL
KICK
STOMP
BOOT
BLUDGEON

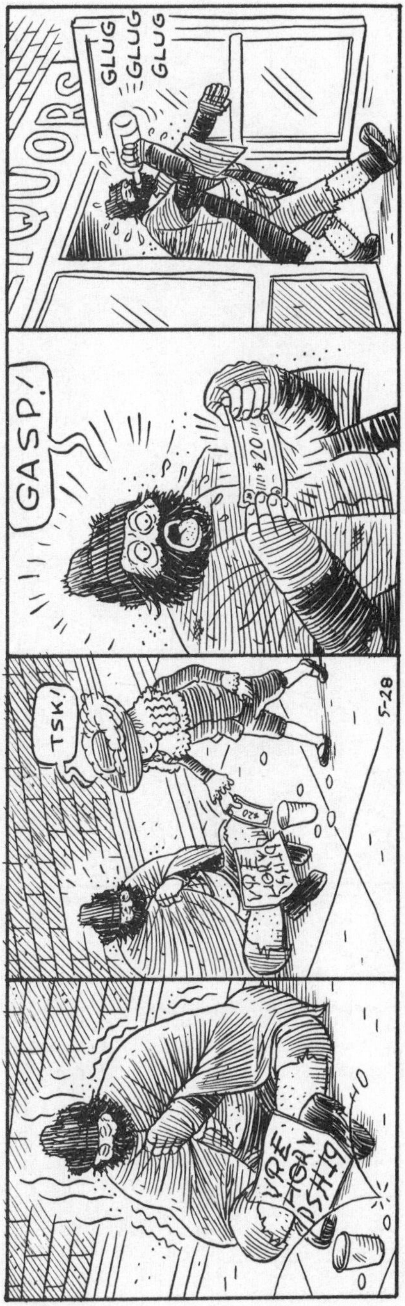
TSK!
$20
5-28
GASP!
$20
GLUG
GLUG
GLUG

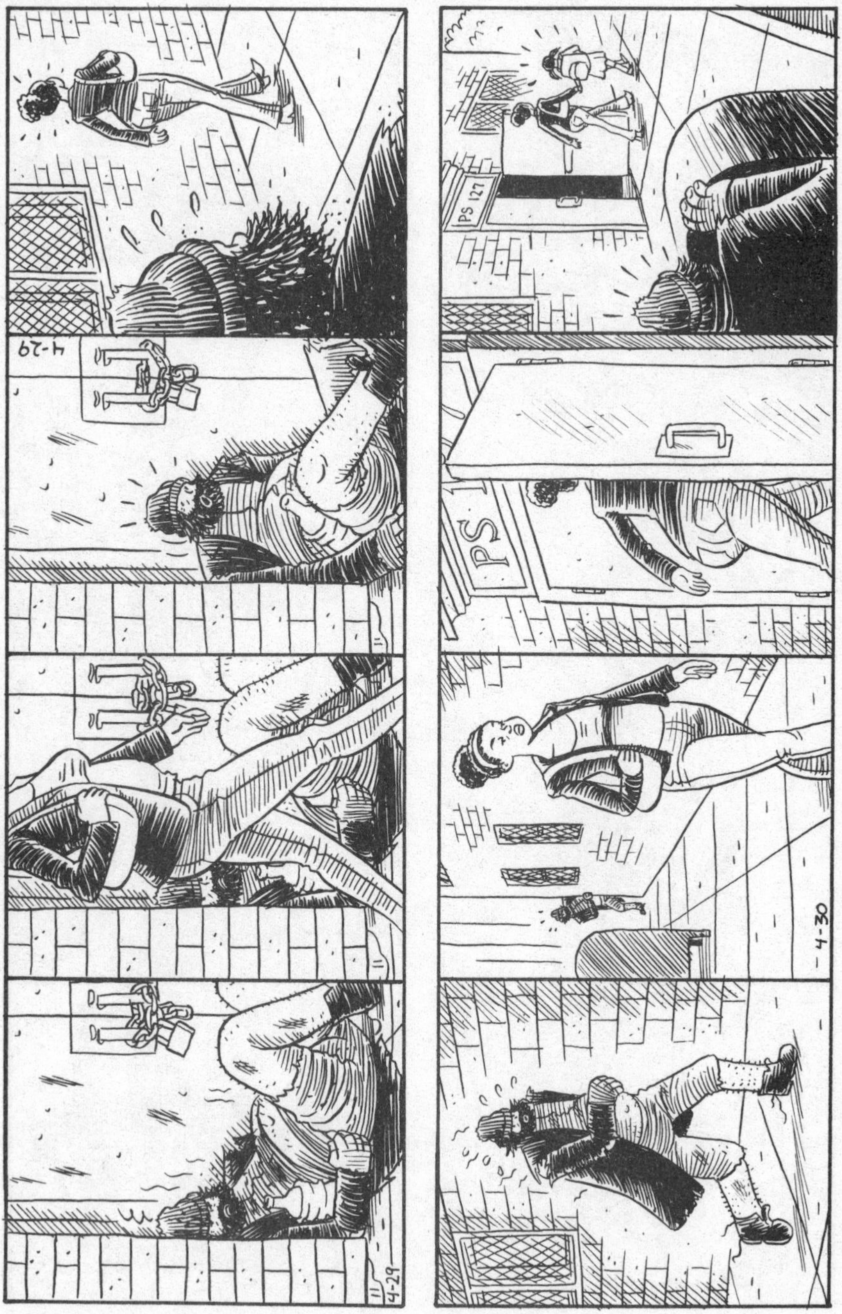
4-29
PS 127
4-29
4-30

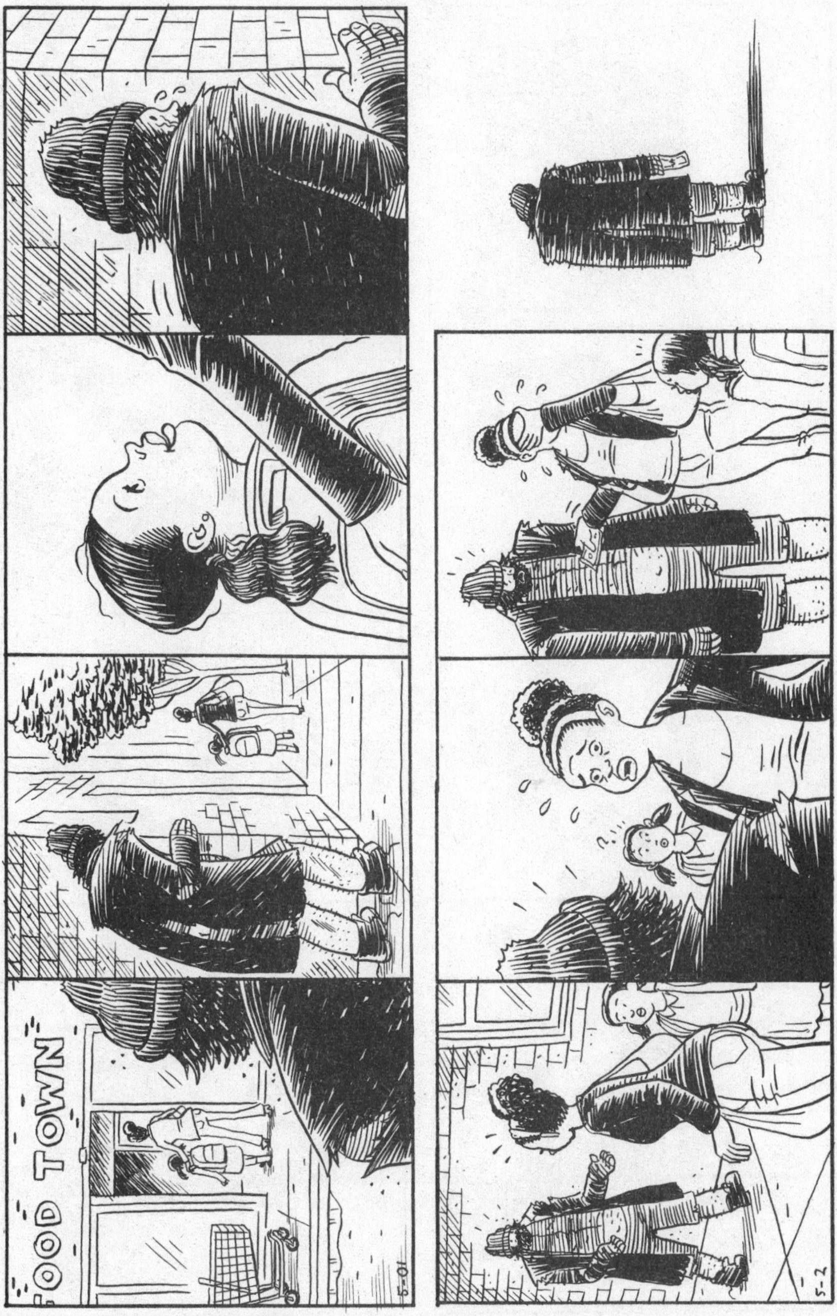
OOD TOWN
5-01
5-2

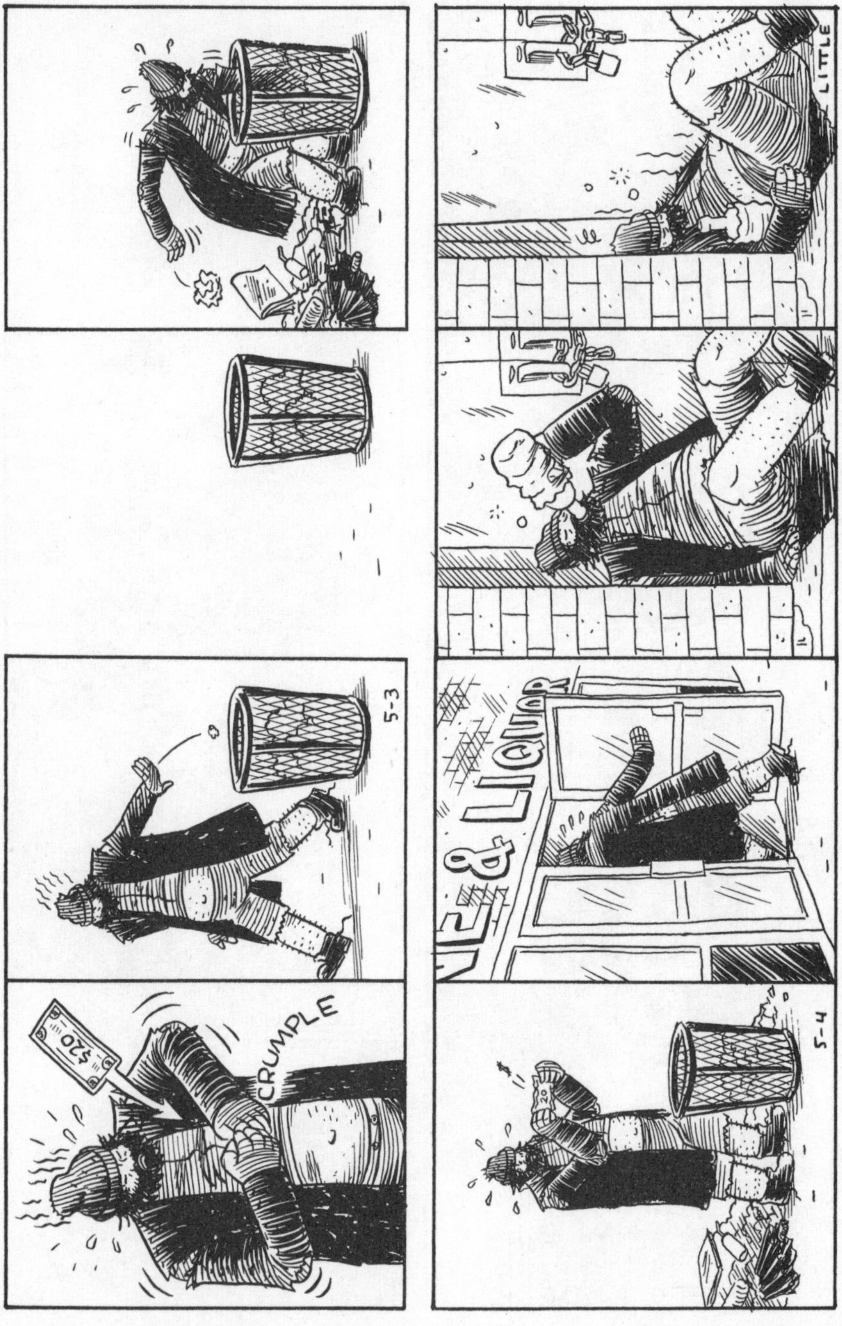
LITTLE
5-3
$20
CRUMPLE
& LIQUOR
5-4

■

Last Poem for OE

FROM *Salt Hill*

Tell me how the forest was glass and our stomachs were covered in
    rashes,
how we sat in the trees
and threw our shoes at the bears. Then the bears were undeterred

and our shoes were gone. You were gone.
At least you didn't see the rashes.
I only wanted the shape of you

in bed beside me. I tried to measure you out in boxes of salt,
in loaves of bread. Deer nosed at my sleeping body. They ate the bread,
licked the salt. Bears ate the deer.

Devour me, please, I said to the bear king.
He didn't though. Surprise. He took off his crown and lay beside me,
until the shape of his body was the shape of your body, and the absence

of his words was the absence of your own.
You are tangible light, I said to the bear king. You are light
made meat.

In the morning, he was gone and I was covered in all the shoes
he'd ever stolen. Years of shoes.
Only that's not true. In the morning I ate him.

KENDRA FORTMEYER

■

Things I Know to Be True

FROM *One Story*

I AM LEAVING the library when Miss Fowler stops me, peering through her glasses like they are windows in a house where she lives alone. She says, "Charlie, a patron saw you ripping up books."

"I didn't," I say. These words sound true, but Miss Fowler holds up *The Collected Works of Edgar Allan Poe*. Bits of paper flutter from its edges like snow.

I know a man in that book. He was trapped underground, dying in the dark and the antiquated language. He coughed then. He rustles in the pocket of my windbreaker now.

From elsewhere, Miss Fowler says, "Give me the pages."

"I am going to take him outside," I announce. I *declare*. *Declare* which is like *clarion call* which is of trumpets. "I am going to take him into the light."

"Look," Miss Fowler says. Her lips blow bubbles of words into the air: crisp, faceted ones like *replacement* and thin-filmed ones like *expensive*. She speaks to me like I am a child. Like *operations* can smooth these cracked, dark hands, like *damages* can topple the twenty-seven precarious years stacked in my name. I try to listen but my eyes jump to the rack of newspapers behind her, the small truths of their headlines swimming up like snakes: CARTER WINS DEMOCRATIC NOMINATION IN NY. MONTREAL PREPARES FOR 1976 OLYMPIC GAMES. NORTH, SOUTH VIETNAM PREPARE FOR REUNIFICATION.

Miss Fowler says *last chance*, her eyes blinking behind her glasses like she is drawing the curtains and they are a color she never particularly liked.

She says, "Give me the material or we're revoking your borrowing privileges."

It is the *we* that frightens me, because I can see Miss Fowler, but I cannot see the rest of *we*. They could be anywhere, plural.

Slowly, I draw the crumpled pages from my pocket, the clamshell edges glinting gold.

Miss Fowler waits until I put them in her hand, nose curling. She eyes my blue jacket, careful not to touch my skin.

"Thank you, Charlie," she says.

This is my day: I wake up. I make oatmeal. I eat my oatmeal, and I go to the library. I go to the library because it is full of words, and I trust words. They make things real.

Words like: this is my apartment. Like: I have lived here alone for eight months. Like: it is small, and dark, and the air conditioner is broken, and no one is on the other end to fix it when I call. All true. My sister Linda pays the rent, but we both agree that *this is my apartment*. The same way everyone agrees that *I can't live with Mother*, even though Mother says it's because I'm too grown-up to live at home and Linda says it's because Mother's a selfish drunk and then apologizes and looks exhausted.

Is it any wonder that I prefer words?

There is a list above my bedroom door. I do not remember making it, but it's in my handwriting. This is what it says:

These are the things that I know to be true:
1. The past and future exist through stories
2. Stories are made of words
3. Words make the future and past exist

This means: if I went to the VA clinic yesterday I can say, "I went to the clinic yesterday." Then there it is, in your head, like a real thing: a little image that is *me at the clinic*. I could also say, "I went to the zoo yesterday," and then that would be real in your head instead. You would not know the difference. I might not know the difference. I could believe the words *I went to the zoo* or I could believe the words *I went to the clinic.*

Maybe both are true.

It is some several tens of thousands of words later, or a dark night, a long winter, a little girl losing her mother, a retired detective taking on one last case. There is a body in a dumpster when I feel a touch on my shoulder.

"I thought we talked about this." It is Miss Fowler. Her words are the same but her voice is the word *truncheon.*

"Oh my God," I say. There is a hand lying on top of a McDonald's wrapper. Its fingernails are blue.

"Charlie," Miss Fowler says again. Then I look up and scream, because the hand is *on my shoulder on my shoulder* and suddenly Miss Fowler's face is far away shouting "Charlie! Charlie!" and all of the other faces are turning to see us, like too many small dark moons. The hand is gone from my shoulder and it is waving through the air and it is *attached to Miss Fowler* and I am screaming but the fingernails are pink and there is no dumpster and I am in the library and slowly I am breathing, breathing, calming.

There is a man standing in the doorway of the reading room. He is in a uniform. My muscles flinch to attention, and then down again. It is not the place or time. Linda is always saying those words, ever since I came back home. *Charlie, this is not the place or time.*

Miss Fowler holds a book with a woman on the cover, her face curling at the edges. "I told you, Charlie," Miss Fowler says. "We can't have you damaging any more books."

I look at the man in the uniform. I know the uniform is all I am supposed to see, but I can see his eyes, too, and they are full of pulling away.

"It was the fire," I say to the uniform man.

Miss Fowler asks, "What fire?" There are teeth in her voice.

"Her lover was burning alive," I say. "She couldn't stop it."

Miss Fowler looks pained. "So you tried to put it out."

"I did put it out." I turn back to my book *to the dumpster,* but Miss

Fowler closes the book. Her mouth makes a line like a broken-down L. It is not a word whose shape I understand.

"No, you didn't, Charlie. What you did was run a book under the bathroom faucet because you read the word *fire*." She opens the book, points to a page. "Look, Charlie. *Fire. F-I-R-E.*" She rubs her finger on the page, and I wince. The word *smoke* floats past my eyelids and the back of my throat begins to burn. "See? No fire. Just four letters that won't go away, no matter how much water you pour on them."

Her fingers are beginning to smoke. I can see her pink nails turning black, and still she stares at me from behind the windows of her eyeglasses. She does not flinch.

"I'm sorry, Charlie," she says. Her hand is beginning to sear and crackle around the edges. There is a smell like bacon. I gag, eyes watering. Miss Fowler says, "I know it's hard for you to understand, but what's in here? It's fiction." The flames are eating her sleeve now. One of her fingernails peels off and lands on the floor where it writhes like an insect.

"Miss Fowler!" I say.

"And what's out here," she says, reaching towards me with a hand that is charred and bone, "is the real world."

"Stop it!" I shriek. "Stop! Stop!" I lunge through the fire that is eating her alive. There are flames dancing on the lenses of Miss Fowler's horned glasses and behind them, something dawns in her eyes. Then my hand is on the book, and I can feel it singeing the pads of my fingertips as it sails across the room, arcing through the stacks like a firefly in the dark. My panic follows the book for a moment *it will burn the library down* but Miss Fowler is standing there next to me, and her skin is blackening and shriveling like a fungus. I know somewhere deep down that it won't do any good *her burns are too bad it's too late* but I tackle her to the ground, beating her with my coat, trying to put out the fire that's everywhere, everywhere. People are shouting. The uniform man has left the doorway. He is beside me now, and he is holding my arms behind my back.

"Miss Fowler!" I howl. "Miss Fowler!"

"All right, buddy, that's enough out of you," the uniform man says and hauls me towards the door.

I don't want to go, but pain shoots through my shoulder and I stumble forward. "Miss Fowler!" I cry.

I hear her voice say, "Thank you, Robert," and I twist around. Miss Fowler looks tired, terrified, bedraggled. But soft and clean and whole.

"You're alive!" I shout to her. The man in the uniform is dragging me towards the door and my shoulder is crying in unwritten language, but I cannot stop staring, marveling at Miss Fowler's wholeness. "I saved you," I say. "You're alive!"

The man in uniform pushes me through the door. "Wait," I say. My feet turn to syrup on the floor, dragging. I do not want to leave this house of words. Miss Fowler watches me go. Her mouth looks like the word *sorry.*

The uniform man does not wait. The uniform man has no pity. He pushes me out into the dazzling sunlight.

Then we get into his car and go to the police station.

I spend one afternoon and part of a night in jail. They make me take off my belt and give them my wallet. There is nothing inside but a library card and a feather I found on a park bench. The feather is blue. The jail cell is gray like bad teeth and the word *granularity.*

There are two men in the cell with me: one in a corner saying quiet, angry things, and another who just sleeps. The angry man rushes the door when I come in, and I fall backward against the uniform who shouts HEY HEY HEY and the angry man backs off, still saying angry things into the air, eyes jumping from one mildew-stained wall to the other. My heart and I stumble over to the opposite side of the cell, where the sleeping man sleeps on the concrete floor. His army shirt is vomit-stained and his beard is scraggly and his skin has been beaten into submission by the sun. I sink down by the toilet, biting the fleshy part of my hand. I try to tell myself this is *jail* instead of *prison* but it's unfurling in my brain like a fire ant sting. The past and future are made of stories *of words* so I tell myself don't give words to this. Don't give words to this. Don't give it any words.

My sister Linda comes down from Richmond, a two-hour drive that takes three with Nixon's new speed limit. She signs her name for my freedom at the maroon desk. Her face looks like it was in the middle of a wash cycle when she got the call—still damp and rumpled, half-wrung out. The policemen give me my wallet and jacket back. Linda has my keys. She makes a face when she sees my windbreaker.

"You're still wearing that ratty thing?" She looks me over, checking face, teeth. "Mom would have a conniption. What happened to that sweater she sent?"

I shrug, zip the coat up to my chin. Cloaked in a windbreaker, I cannot be broken. It smells like safety, and me.

They let Linda take me home. She ties a kerchief around her hair and lights a cigarette before starting her car which is a Dodge Dart. Her husband Lewis is not with her, which makes me happy because I do not like Lewis. He laughs at things that are not funny, and he makes too much money to be nice. One year on Thanksgiving he brought me some pamphlets that made Linda mad: they said *Institutional Living Facility*. Linda threw them in the garbage. She said, "Dr. Schaefer said he's making progress." She said, "For God's sake, can't you give him some time to recover?" My mother said nothing and only poured herself another drink. Lewis said, "It's been six years." And, "We're paying too much for that damn apartment." And, "He's not okay, he's *crazy*." Those words have kept knocking around in my skull. When I try to imagine myself striding into the future, I trip over them like stones.

Linda and I walk through the front door of my apartment. There are library books everywhere—books on the floor, on the sofa, lining the halls like yellowed border guards. Linda wrinkles her nose.

"Can I get you something to eat?" I ask, because I remember that that's what you're supposed to do when people come to your house. I hope she won't say yes because I don't have anything except a can of SpaghettiOs, and I would like to eat it myself. But Linda shakes her head.

"I ate on the road," she says. "Stopped at a McDonald's. Jesus, Charlie."

She starts to laugh, stops, then gives up and laughs anyway. I laugh too, politely, though I'm starting to wish she would leave.

She wipes her eyes. "It's not funny," she says.

"Okay," I agree.

Linda sits on my armchair and digs her finger into the stuffing. Her finger looks like a pink worm that cannot escape from her hand.

"Why did you attack that librarian?" she says at last.

"I didn't," I say, feeling uncomfortable. I don't remember attacking anybody. But there are the words: *You. Attack.* "Did I?" I ask, trying to sound casual.

She stares at me. "The librarian at Cameron Village," she says. "Mrs. Fuller."

"Miss Fowler," I say automatically. And then, "She was on fire." Saying this makes me feel better. I think this will make Linda proud of me, but she looks at the sofa instead, at the little worm of her finger. It writhes in the Styrofoam innards of my couch.

"Charlie," Linda says. Her voice sounds tired, like it used to when we were kids and she was tired of playing whatever game we were playing. "I can't drive down here every time you get into trouble."

"Okay," I say.

"The woman's not pressing charges, though Lord knows she could," Linda says. "You got off easy. Not even a fine. They just banned you from the library. All the county libraries, actually."

I blink. I am just banned.

Banned: *officially or legally prohibited.*

Just: *guided by truth, reason, fairness.*

My mind races.

"For how long?" I say in a voice that is tight and high and not mine.

Linda shakes her head. "It's not a 'for how long' type of deal, hon," she says. "That's it. You're out."

My lips work, but there are no words.

The worm disappears from my sofa as Linda rises. She takes me in her arms. Her eyes are hurting for me, and blue.

"I'm sorry, sweetie," she says. "You're just going to have to handle it the best you can, okay?" She rocks me in her arms. She smells like french fry oil and Virginia Slims. "You're going to be okay. You'll find a new hobby. All right?"

It is strange how everything in the room looks exactly the same while my world slides slowly sideways.

I try not to watch as Linda packs up all of my library books. The fat classic editions. The dog-eared paperbacks. The worlds I know so inside and out that no card catalog in the world can make them not mine. I eat my SpaghettiOs and focus hard on all the new words I can make: *flavormouth, redsauce.* I try to make new words, new small truths, because if I do, I can make this moment into one where I am not twenty-seven years old and trying not to cry.

Linda promises to drop my books off at the library on her way back to Richmond. She asks if I want to come and live with her and Lewis, but I shake my head. I wish my sister would stay with me here, and we could move back again with Mother and things would be just like they were before my hands grew cracks, and when Mother could still look at me without flinching away and talking too loud.

Linda presses some money into my hand, but I make my hand limp, and so she leaves the bills on an empty bookshelf before kissing me a kiss that is goodbye.

I wonder if Linda would still come see me if she weren't called *sister*. I wonder if the light would still fade if there weren't a word *night*.

It is a long, cold couple of weeks.

This is my day: I wake up. I make my oatmeal, and I eat my oatmeal. My feet still want to take me to the library at first, and I have to fight them. "We are going somewhere new today, feet," I say, and a little girl stares at me. I pull my blue windbreaker tight and drag my body north.

I walk a new direction every day, until I do not recognize anyone or anything. Only the letters are the same, on street signs and in newspaper boxes, everything everywhere draped in red-white-and-blue. It is America's Bicentennial. Bi, meaning *two*. Centennial, meaning *hundred years*. 1776 and 1976.

The flags in shop windows and lawns twinkle like clues to another world where everything is truer and brighter and nothing is denied to me. Where *Oakwood Ave.* is green like meadows and bobbing in the wind, and *Peace St.* is not a place where car horns wail and men sleep with their feet on the sidewalks. This outside world makes me ill. Nothing makes sense. I come back to my apartment at the end of the day and feel I cannot trust anything.

I have no books left. None: *not any, not at all, not one.* I read what is left: cereal boxes, warning labels, my life delineated into *fat* or *iron*, *blindness* or *death*. I try to read the shapes carved into the popcorn ceiling by the streetlights outside, and everything swims.

My eyes feel like they are starving.

Dr. Schaefer says I should write new stories. Dr. Schaefer says I can choose what is in them. "You get to invent yourself now, Charlie," he says. "Pick the person you want to be. That's what happens in America. You get to start over."

I try to explain to him *go to the clinic* or *go to the zoo*. He smiles enormously with an exclamation point. "That's it precisely!" he exclaims. "Do you want to be Charlie who is sick and sorry for himself, or Charlie who has fun? Tell me, Charlie, where would you rather go?"

I say, "The library."

Dr. Schaefer nods yes but his forehead is scrunched *no*. He lights a cigarette. He sucks the end and blows out smoke.

He says, "You don't need the library, Charlie. The library was an escape. Think of this as an opportunity. You've got a talent with words. You could go back to school. Journalism. Maybe advertising. Have you thought about that?"

"No," I say.

Dr. Schaefer reaches for my chart. "The old you is gone," he says. I want to ask how to make the library ban *gone*, but he does not have time to hear what I want. Instead he takes a green, spiral-bound notebook from his desk and puts it into my hands. He says, "Now is the time to write the new story of you."

That night, I try to write the story of myself. I use the green notebook. All of the words jumble in my head, with no order to them. I keep my mouth pursed up in a small *O*, so that only one sound can come out at a time. I write with a ruler, so everything stays straight, but nothing helps. Too many letters, too many lines. Here and there a sentence pokes out, and it is like a small miracle: *This is my day.*

I tear out the pages. Being mine doesn't make a story worth telling.

At night, I dream of paper leaves and trees made of fire.

Once, I forget a word. I am on my way to the bathroom and I think, *I am going ___ the bathroom* and suddenly it is gone. The word means: move in the direction of something. Closer. Move at something. I panic, because without the word, how can I move? How can I do what I cannot say? I lie on the floor with my bladder aching and want to cry until there is a whisper in my mind like angels that says *toward*. And I know how to move forward again. This is not the me I want to make.

I have to find new words.

I do not know what day it is, or what time, when I get a phone call from Mother. She says, "Charlie, dear." She calls me once a month, usually. Sometimes she forgets and two months go by but that is okay because she is very busy. It takes a lot of time to have an adult son. There is so much more of me to take care of.

"How have you been?" she asks.

"Fine," I say. This means *small* and *slippery* and *falling through the cracks*.

We talk about her bridge club and her church. We talk about if Linda will ever have children. Then Mother says, "Linda called last week. She told me you're not allowed to go to the library anymore."

Oh. I fiddle with my fingers. They are out of key. "I was banned," I say.

Banned. Brand. A stigma stamped in my skin.

Mother sniffs. "They sent you over there, and now they want you to be invisible. I think it's sick. Denying a man the right to read. But that's what we get, electing a Democratic governor."

I do not know the answer to the questions she isn't asking, but I barely care. My mind is whirling. *A man the right to read.*

"Mother, I love you," I say.

"Thank you, Charlie," she says, and sounds surprised.

We hang up, and I lie on the couch, seeing nothing, mind singing *a man the right a man the right a man invisible the right to read.* And me humming with it, because I figured it out:

If I go to a new library, nobody will know me.

And: If they do not know who I am, they cannot make me leave the library.

I stay up late at night, thinking about this until my head hurts.

I walk the next day to the CAT bus station, and I purchase a 30-day pass. It uses up nearly all of the money that Linda sent with her last letter, but I cannot make myself care. I have never been good with numbers anyway.

I climb on the bus. The bus rattles. Inside of me, my organs rattle. I am afraid of being caught and turned away, but the bus driver doesn't even look at me as I fumble with my bus pass. He looks at the numbers printed on it and finally he says, like he is surprised that I am still there, "Sit down, son." I sit. I am so grateful that I smile at every person on the bus. It is my thank-you to them for being alive on the day that I get my world back.

The new library is in a shopping center. At first I think I am making a mistake, but the driver says no, this is the North Hills branch. The cars in the parking lot shimmer in the heat. By the time I get inside, through the glass doors and into the air conditioning, sweat has stuck my windbreaker to my back.

A librarian looks up when I step into the library, and every nerve in my body shrieks. I duck my head, turn blindly left. I end up in the children's area. A new librarian looks up at me. She frowns. Before she can speak, I plunge left, and left again. I feel dizzy, and the walls lean out at odd angles. *We know you Charlie you are not supposed to be here Charlie you'll hurt us drown us burn us Charlie Charlie Charlie.*

Then suddenly the space opens up around me. I am in a place I recognize: *Reading Room.*

The air is quiet. Other patrons float by like fish, weaving in and out of the stacks in earthy colors. I go to a table. I put down my bag and breathe a soft sigh. Then I go to the stacks like that is exactly where I am supposed to be, and I begin to pull down books.

I know better than to try my library card. If they find out who I am, they will make me leave, and then I will be empty again, my shelves empty, no words left to me and mine.

But now I know how to keep the words.

At my table I take Dr. Schaefer's green notebook from my bag and begin to copy the first book. Word. By. Word. It is slow going, and my hand starts to hurt, but I don't stop. The library begins to darken and empty, and when the first closing announcement bursts through the intercom, I drop my book and scuttle out the door. In my old library, Miss Fowler used to have to come and make me leave, but here I am afraid of being recognized. So I go home before anyone can lay a kindly hand on my shoulder like a little white bird and sing, "We're closing, Charlie. Closing time."

On the bus I smile the whole way home because my world has come back, and this is so true that one lady even smiles back at me.

I get home with my notebook. I put my notebook on the table and think about all of the things I could do that are not reading my notebook: *Eat soup. Go to the bathroom. Go* . . . but the words get blurred in my head in a kind of hunger, and before I can help myself I have the notebook in my hand.

I open it to the first page, and the paper crinkles a little. My eyes swim for a moment in the glory of words: all the lines and shapes and letters that say a million different things and all belong to me. My own book. I almost do not understand what to do with it.

But then I begin to read, and that is when my heart breaks. Because I know all of these words already. Because I read them all already. When I was copying them down.

There is a dark feeling building and building in my chest, so hard and sharp-edged that it pushes the notebook out of my hands. I bite down on my forearm like they taught us, to *don't make a fucking sound* when you see something you don't want to see, like someone's head blown away or their guts hanging out over their knees. I bite into my own flesh and bone, and in the biting my mouth is full and there are no words and there are too many.

I wake up. I eat my oatmeal and don my blue windbreaker. I go back to the North Hills Branch and do not turn left.

I pick a new book and begin again. When I realize that I am reading the book too much, I begin to hum in my head, to keep my mind completely blank so that my hand can copy now and my mind can read later. I hum a song called the *1812 Overture*. It loops in my mind, all brightness and fireworks and triumph.

I work for a long time at my table and nobody bothers me. I even get up to go to the bathroom, and as I pass by the desk, there are no lingering looks, no pointed questions punctuated "Charlie?" I go to the bathroom and come back to my table and embrace my new-found identity of *nobody*.

On the bus home, two people smile back.

At home I take out my notebook and I begin to read. And there, in my stilted handwriting, a beautiful first sentence: *For a long time, I went to bed early.*

I read until the light drains from the room.

I finish one book and start another. Chapter by chapter, I rewrite myself. In Agatha Christie, in Marcel Proust, in Kurt Vonnegut, in Richard Bach. The covers are luscious, titles cool and ripe on my tongue. I glut myself in ink, stained to the knuckles. Time passes in pages and in dried-up pens.

It is late and what they call a Tuesday. I have been working on *Cannery Row* for the last several weeks, and am nearly complete. I place the period at the end of the second-to-last chapter, close my notebook. My hands are cracked but strong.

I zip up my blue jacket and stand ready to leave, when a voice says, "Excuse me. Are you Charles Harrison?" and I jump.

She has the right soft voice of a librarian. Also the glasses. Also the cardigan sweater.

She has hair that is colored like sunsets and freckles flung in a star scape across the planes of her face.

I have never seen her before. She should not know my name.

"Please," I say softly. I am caught. I want to hide, to go to earth, but I have no earth, just this word: "Please."

"I thought it might be you," she says. "I have something for you. Hold on, I'll go get it, all right?"

I am *banned caught in trouble* tearing into two. Two syllables. Dismay, consent. "Oh," I say, and "kay."

She beams, a spill of light. "Just wait right here."

I stand a second, a minute, unsure. *She caught me she didn't seem angry how does she know it was me she's pretending she's going to call the police she's going to going to call the police.* My feet drag on the tile. The second hand drags across the clock face.

I will wait. She smiled. It is safe. I will wait.

I wait twenty seconds exactly. Then I bolt out the door.

I lie in bed a long time the next day, trying to find meaning in the bumps and shadows of the ceiling. I am trying not to think about *Cannery Row*, or about the way I feel when I am reading it. Like everything was wrong and now I am in a room full of music and laughter.

I cannot go back to the library. It is not safe anymore.

But.

I climb on the bus and tell myself I am just going for a ride. My pass expires tomorrow. I may as well enjoy it. See the sights. I smile at everyone and it is such a good day that four people smile back and one person says hello. I feel like a true American citizen.

(I get off at the library.)

I duck my head and go straight for the reading room. I find *Cannery Row* behind the plant where I left it, and I keep my head down. I scrawl and I scrawl and I scrawl, waiting at any moment to feel the hand on my shoulder. *Where were you? You ran away! You're a criminal! You've been banned! You can't be here! Security!*

Two pages left. One. I write the final words: *And. Behind. The. Glass. The. Rattlesnakes. Lay. Still. And. Stared. Into. Space. With. Their. Dusty. Frowning. Eyes.*

I fling my notebook into my bag and dash for the door. I catch a blush of autumn in my periphery, and my steps do not falter. I vanish into the white afternoon light.

You believed me, didn't you? You saw me in your brain, vanishing. Which means that for one minute it was true, and now it exists, and will be true forever.

But what also happened is this:

* * *

Doc is washing glasses carefully because there is beautiful music and he is afraid of spoiling it when somebody sits down across from me and puts something on the table. The somebody is the red-haired librarian. The something is a crumpled yellow envelope.

"You ran away yesterday," she says.

"I'm sorry," I say. "I forgot."

She knows I am lying and I think she likes me a little less now. But she gives me the envelope anyway. There is a book inside, so stained and ugly and battered that the title is rubbed off its broken spine.

But I know this book. I would know it anywhere.

I want to push my chair back from the table, but I can't move. I see faces smiling frowning shouting and I see jungle so thick that I'm afraid my eyelashes have grown up over my eyes.

"This book," I say through the jungle, "is gone."

The librarian does not understand. She gives a tentative smile. "I found this Joseph Heller mixed in with a large bundle of returns," she says. "I thought someone had taken notes in the margins. And then I read what you had written and I thought . . . well, I thought you might like to have it back."

She reaches across the table and opens the cover and there is my name in red crayon. Written in my own handwriting. The pages flutter like crazed butterflies. I look down and see through the high whine in my ears that my hands are cracked and through the cracks I see names. Jimmy Metcalfe. Lucas Johnson. I see the way the light reflects on the water where they found that girl bathing. I see the song Joe Crispin played on his guitar in Quang Tri, and how it got stuck in everyone's head for days, and we changed the words so many times that no one remembered the original. And how a month later, out of the blue, Soup came busting up singing *your cheese is straight from hell* and Joe laughed so hard he shot bug juice out his nose. I see C-Rations and finger necklaces curled like shrimp. I see all of us tired, and hot, twenty-one and younger and breathing Jimmy Metcalfe's farts all morning on patrol through jungle leaves thick as eyelashes. And I see the way the air gleamed pink after Jimmy stepped onto the mine—the tiny click and then the sky blown apart and the whole world set singing, flashing white in the sun, pieces of flesh against the green like cherry blossoms in the first light of spring: so pink and bright that your heart rips in half at the beauty.

One half says, *the trees are on fire.*

The other half says, *the trees are not on fire.*

Maybe both are true.

I see this book inside Jimmy's pack and then me taking it and writing down these words, a story hidden inside another story. I see the pages fill while the doctors patched up my leg and the skin scabbed over on my arm. I see the hospital bed with the ringing fading from my ears and my leg itching and burning and stinking in its cast. I see the medical review when no one in the room would look at me straight, and the smell in the air from the bed-wetters was so thick you could cut it with a knife. And I see the book on a plane, carried all the way home until I landed on American soil, and that chapter ended and I closed it.

But then, here it is. On the table. In the library. And here I am.

"This book is gone," I say again.

"No," the librarian says, slowly. "It was just misplaced."

I think, *This is not the place or time.*

"How did you know it was me?" I ask.

"We had a regional staff meeting at the beginning of the month," she says. "Your name came up. There was a photo." Simple as that. She does not say, *you are a criminal.* Does not say: *you attacked Miss Fowler.* Just. You came up. Like a flower.

I push away from the table. "I am going to go home now."

"It's okay," she says. "You can stay."

"I am going to go home," I say again, and leave.

I do not smile at anybody on the bus. At the corner, I throw my *Cannery Row* notebook into the trashcan. No matter how hard I read and how hard I write, it seems like I can only have one story, after all.

I try to do everything right. I wait until the sun goes down. I light the lights. I close the curtains, so that the echoes of me are not in the window. I sit across the room from the book that won't let me go and wonder how long it is before the words harden back into truth.

In her last card to me Linda wrote, *Have you thought about keeping a journal like Dr. Schaefer said?* I look at the card, alone on the empty bookshelf. On the front is a rabbit wishing me an Egg-cellent Easter.

"I can't write me down again," I say to the rabbit.

I pretend the rabbit can answer. It says, *But you can write any story you want. You can make the words.*

The rabbit sounds like Linda. I want to make her happy but I know that I can't. All I want is to be gone, like the book was supposed to be gone. Then I see the list above my door. *The Things I Know To Be True.*

I detach it from the wall and try not to look at my hands.

I write: *Charlie didn't go to war, and he didn't kill anybody.*

And his mother let him come home again.

And his sister lived there too and they went to the movies together.

It was Superman.

And Charlie had a good car.

And a library card.

And he was never hungry again.

I sit and wait for those words to become truth, and my stomach rumbles. I underline, *never hungry*, but it rumbles again and my world blurs. I shred the list into pieces so small that they slip through my fingers like water, spilling onto the bare floor and down over my dry and rootless feet.

This is where the story ends. But.

The sun comes up again the next day. The sun always comes up again. It doesn't know when to quit, maybe because it doesn't speak any language that can tell it *no.*

So I get up. I make my oatmeal. I eat my oatmeal, and I go to the bus stop. The bus driver looks at my 30-day pass and shakes his head at me.

"Sorry," he says to the zipper of my windbreaker. "This expired yesterday. You've got to go get a new ticket. Sir," he says. "Sir?"

But I am not listening. I am looking past him at all the people on the bus, their feet secure in boots, their faces as closed as books on a shelf. The whole bus of unwritten words humming, waiting, sentences strung out in infinite lines across the city. Carefully, I shred my ticket. I shred the expiration date into pieces. Then I find a seat and wait to be carried, like everyone else, into some bright and not-yet-written future.

DAN HOY

■

Five Poems

FROM *The Deathbed Editions*

Miracle

I follow everyone out of the elevator and up to the roof. We're all of us
sitting on real grass next to a pool. There are trees and everything. It's
a miracle, really. I get overly aware of my brain as an apparatus, like
a pair of binoculars. I'm wearing jeans and shoes with socks. Everybody else seems fully integrated. / Why would I text you this. / I'm
standing at the rail and pretty sure it's the most panoramic thing I've
ever seen. There's this whole other world made entirely of rooftops
like a city built on the ruins of another city. Anybody not on a rooftop is living in the past. I see four or five people dancing like assholes
like a hundred yards away but there's no music or else the music is
just this sense of being a part of the sky and therefore everything.
Somebody suggests going to an actual club. Ideally I've alluded to
some mystery illness earlier so I can make reference to it now and
bail. Instead I'm going to have to live life and fuck everything I know
in the face.

The Baseline

Just the fact this video exists and is happening. When we're in the
car with the top down and the sun flares I want to die. The way everything is cut together with the palm trees and everything. People who
think this video is just ok are dead to me. For people who are against

life the esplanade is like outer darkness. The chorus alone is proof that going solo is some next level shit. Taking it next level is all I care about. Without this video the world is a total piss hole and even then. I love you.

Life

This photo says everything I want to say about life. The entire canvas is the sky. These bathing suits are from all eras combined. How the four of them are facing each other their hands on their hips. Except for the hand touching its thigh in defiance. This is a dramatic moment. Something permanent is being decided here. The tiny airplane entering the frame like an accident. This is where time is born.

Waterfront

Really not in the mood to do this thing today so I leave a VM that says somebody died. I'm just like standing on the edge of a pier the sun blasting off my chest like a power saw. Next thing I'm doing is gripping both hands on the wheel ready to just fucking do it. This isn't even my car. I push some buttons and hurl my brains all over the sidewalk. Stagger toward these pedestrians like what. Take out my phone and I'm like what. I'm throwing my feelings under the bus like an advertisement. Everything I do is the future.

Empire

This song is like someone pouring a cherry slush into my ears. I have to remember to tip the cab driver extra for the ambiance. What am I talking about. I step in a puddle on purpose and go up or down some stairs. People try to talk about my condition but I'm not having it. My human condition. My phone is a tether to the world I don't need so I let it fall over the balcony. I let everything fall to the floor like an empire. This is without doubt my greatest triumph.

XUAN JULIANA WANG

■

Algorithmic Problem Solving for Father-Daughter Relationships

FROM *Ploughshares*

TO BE A GOOD computer scientist, a man needs first to understand the basics. Back away from the computer itself and into the concepts. After all, a computer is just a general-purpose machine; its purpose is to perform algorithms.

It is due to the fact that algorithms are unambiguous that they are effective and executable. However, algorithms aren't only for machines. In designing an algorithm, a person can execute a complex task through observation and analysis. To be a good father, it would be a logical assumption that these same acquired skills should apply.

As I used to say during my lectures at Dalian University of Technology some thirty years ago — Everything in life, every exploit of the mind is really just the result of an algorithm being executed.

For example: To peel garlic

- Obtain a bulb of garlic and a small baggy

As long as there is still-wrapped garlic, continue to execute the following steps:

- Break the garlic petal from the garlic bulb
- Peel off the outer skin

- Put the smooth garlic into the baggy
- Throw the skin into the wastebasket

To my students and colleagues I famously said the same can be applied to something as complicated as getting married. As long as an adult male is still without a wife, continue to execute the following steps:

- Ask librarians, family members, and coworkers if they know any single girls
- Invite girls to watch movies

Assess compatibility facts as follows:

- Beauty
- Family
- Education

If compatibility measures up to previously set standard, move to step 4, if not, start from beginning.

- Ask the girl to be wife

A coworker introduced me to my ex-wife. Her nose was too small for her face, her hairline too high. However, she came from a family with good Communist party standing and we attended similarly ranked universities.

One day on the way to see a play, she lost the tickets and I yelled at her for being careless. I thought that was the end of us. Then on the way back, I stopped along the street and tied an old man's shoes for him. She agreed to marry me after that.

There was a miscalculation in this equation, which I see now of course. I liked the girl I married very much, but not the woman she became after we immigrated to America. This woman never respected me. All the data was there to be sorted, I just didn't decode it until it was too late. She had this way of making me feel spectacularly incompetent. She was a literature major in college, she had what people said was a nice sense of humor. Once I took her to a company party and all anybody could talk about the next day was how beautiful and amazing my wife was. That was when it began to bother me. That people didn't think I deserved her. That they thought I was somehow less than her.

I don't think she understood the protocol of being a good wife. "Let's go into the city and eat at a nice place," she used to say. Why? So I could feel more out of place not being able to read the menu? No thanks.

But without her, there would be no daughter, Wendy. There's that to consider.

Now that I'm old, I see my theory prove itself day after day. Until illness and then death, life is the result of a series of algorithms being executed. The GPS in my car is using an algorithm, taking into its calculations a satellite moving through space, transmitting down to me to tell me where my car is.

So right now I need to make an algorithm to solve the problem of Wendy. My only daughter, who I somehow managed to drive away from me—door slamming and little eyes pooling up during dinner.

I wish to concentrate on the relevant details of our relationship, from tonight and beyond, in order to break down our problem into something that can be decoded, processed, and used to save our relationship. How did I hurt her? Will she ever come back to me?

The evening was one of those calm, snowless December evenings in Westchester County. My daughter, whom I hadn't seen in nearly a year, was home on vacation from studying in England and planned to spend two weeks living in her old bedroom. I had already prepped the pigs feet to throw in the pressure cooker. When she walked through the door, pink-nosed and taller than I remembered, I felt such a rush of affection for the girl that I went right up to her and pinched her arm really hard.

I broke down these two weeks into pseudocode just to see how it was going to work out in my mind:

If (daughter comes to stay)
   then (if (temperature = cold))
      then (enjoy home cooking)
   else (watch movies)
   else (buy her consumer electronics)

"*Baba*, is it your goal to make me obese?" she asked when I showed her the five-pound bag of uncured bacon shoved in my fridge. I replied, "Oh, come on, little fatty, you know you crave my pork stew," and she laughed. She hadn't changed very much, had the same chubby little hands that I love squeezing. She still had my smile, the one that was all gums.

Even before I had finished putting out all the vegetables and meats on the counter for prepping, Wendy was already showing me pictures of all her trips. She'd been to France, Italy, and Spain. I pulled my head back so that the countries got into focus.

"Where are pictures of you?" I asked as she clicked.

"I was too busy documenting the landscape." She went through the snapshots slowly, importantly, lifting her computer to show me pictures of bus stops, lampposts, jars of pickles.

"How do you have so much time to travel when you're supposed to be studying?" I asked.

"You think I went all the way to England just to sit in my room? Besides, all the Brits do it too."

For me, she speaks Mandarin, which had gotten rusty. She mispronounced words and made up her own metaphors. But I loved hearing her talk, just like when she was a child, telling me stories while I tried to teach her how to make a good steamed fish. While her mother would be out taking real estate courses or painting a still life, Wendy would always keep me company in the kitchen. I didn't want to look at the pictures, but I was happy having her voice fill up the house. I gutted a red snapper and stuffed it with ginger.

"Can't say I have the same attitude toward education," I said. I handed her a potato peeler and she finally put away her laptop.

"Of course, I studied too, Dad, and I made a ton of friends from all over the world," she said.

"That's good, expanding your horizons," I said.

"There were Chinese students at my school too. Bunch of wack-jobs. They just stayed in their dorm rooms and made dumplings all the time. You could smell the chives from the hallway."

I nodded, and she went on, "In England. Can you imagine?"

"And they were your friends too?" I asked.

"No, they never talked to me. Probably because I spoke English and didn't study engineering."

She started chopping the carrots into strips, and I showed her how to make them into stars, "but I didn't go over to England to pretend like I lived in China, you know?"

"Probably good you weren't friends with them," I said solemnly. "The only Chinese kids that get to study in England have to come from crooked families with embezzled money."

"I can't imagine it would be all of them," she said, squinting at me. "There was this one crazy thing that happened while I was there. There's a lake in the middle of campus where the university raised exotic geese. Then one day, the caretakers noticed that one of the Egyptian geese was missing its mate."

She stopped talking until I gave her my full attention. "Turns out this guy from China had killed it! Goose dumplings."

She put down her chopping and with great affect said, "The University expelled him."

"That's a pity."

"Isn't it? It's so awful." She said. "Why did he do it? Even if he didn't know they were pets. What makes him see a beautiful bird and immediately want to make it into food?"

"I wouldn't worry about it, Wendy," I said. "Here, help me over here." How would she know that my brothers and I used to kill sparrows with slingshots as food to eat. How we shot so many sparrows the birds couldn't land, so exhausted they began falling out of the sky, dead.

"It's just so typically Chinese too. His friends didn't even protest or stand up for him." She went over to the sink and began peeling the potatoes with great indignation.

If anything, I thought, it was she who protested too much. Always concerned with things that she has zero control over. Like missing her SATs for a hunger strike against the Iraq War, something she had nothing to do with. Maybe I should have told her, the happy dinners where those little birds filled up my little brothers' swollen, wanting bellies. Maybe a little American like her might have understood after all. The water boiled and the fish was steamed.

Then there was the wine.

"I brought you this wine, Baba, carried it on my back through three border crossings," she said. "It's from Ravello, below Naples, on the way to this beautiful town called Amalfi." I nodded at the unlabeled bottle, which was made of heavy green glass.

"It was a family vineyard. The vintner said it was the best wine he's ever made. The vines grew on the cliffs facing the ocean. I had to hitchhike just to get this bottle for you." The girl kept going, excitedly, her hands remembering Italy.

Right then the phone rang; it was Charles and Old Ping, my two divorced and now bachelor buddies. They were wondering what I was doing for Christmas dinner. They had nowhere to go that night, so naturally, I invited them over.

"Come! We are going to have great food, and my daughter's here," I said.

I smiled at Wendy and she shrugged and went about opening the wine. She couldn't have been upset about that, could she? Having my best friends over to share our Christmas dinner? No way, she wouldn't be that selfish. In fact, even though she's not very logical, she was always a remarkably reasonable, well-behaved child.

My ex-wife and I, we never hid things from her; she shared equal partnership in the family.

Maybe there were some things we shouldn't have told her. She probably shouldn't have been at the lawyer's during the divorce agreement where I probably shouldn't have yelled at her crying mother, "What are you going to actually miss? Me or the money?" That was probably a mistake, but I can't do anything about that now.

Was it the wine? I bet it had something to do with that wine. As we were preparing the last of the food, we had a rather unpleasant conversation about the fundamentals that make up a good bottle. "The most popular cocktail in China right now is the Zhong Nan Hai no. 5," I said. "They say it was created by former Premier Jiang Zemin himself: wine with Sprite."

"*Ba*, let me tell you some of the basics. So the most common red wines are Merlot, Cabernet Sauvignon, and Syrah," she said. She continued on like an expert, "Wine is not supposed to be *ganbei*-ed, the way you do it. It's supposed to be tasted and sipped, since it's about the appearance, the smell, the aftertaste."

"That sounds like a needless hassle to me," I said. "It's a drink."

"You know, you were probably destined to be a lonely migrant farmer, but instead you were blessed with me and you don't even know how to appreciate it!"

She circled around the kitchen counter and stood facing me. "Come on, I thought you'd like knowing about this," she said, as she slowly opened the bottle. "While I'm here, maybe I can take you to a wine tasting in the city. It'll be really fun!"

"You can save your energy, Wendy. Your old man is not fancy, and I'm not going to sniff booze like a snob. I'm a working-class guy, in case you forgot," I said with a sniff, "while you were in Europe."

I took a sip from the glass she poured me and said, "I feel that in my experience, the best wine is wine that is over 14 percent alcohol content, with a wide neck; preferably the bottle should have a large indent at the bottom."

I thought I saw her roll her eyes at me, so I said, "When did you get so stuck up? Did you learn that from your mother?" and she turned away from me.

The previous situation can be broken down into pseudocode:

If (daughter is frustrating) then (compare her to her mother)
While (daughter shuts up) do (change the subject)

When the doorbell rang, Wendy ran over to answer and I assumed everything was back to normal. She was very polite. I didn't even have to ask her to help unpack the two cases of beer into the fridge. What a sight my friends must have been to her! Old Ping was as unwashed as ever, but he had changed out of his work overalls for the occasion.

Charles still had paint splatters above his eyebrow, and his hair had grown long everywhere that was not bald.

When I tried to offer them Wendy's wine, both of them initially refused.

"I don't know about foreign liquors. Most things white people like give me the runs," said Charles.

"I'll stick to my *baijiu*, but thanks, little Wendy," said Old Ping, whose eyes were already rimmed with red. He must have started drinking in the car.

Wendy set up the table while I finished cooking. It was one of my most sumptuous spreads. There were five dishes, fish done two ways, and a soup. All the colors satisfied, every plate still hot. Old Ping opened twelve bottles of beer and clinked them against the plates. Now we could eat.

"A toast," Old Ping said, "for little Wendy giving us the honor of her presence. We owe it all to you for this nice meal we are having."

"Don't pay attention to your Uncle Ping, he has no education like you," said Charles.

Old Ping pointed a chopstick at Wendy. "Be nice to your old dad, don't neglect him."

"Chi Chi! Eat eat!" I said, digging into the brisket.

The table was quiet with eating, until Ping started talking again: "Say, Wendy Wendy Wendy, when are you going to get married?"

"Ah, don't bother the girl, Ping, she's going to get a PhD, isn't she?" Charles asked me.

"You know!" Old Ping cut in, "They have a saying in China, there are three genders: men, women, and women with PhDs."

"Well, this isn't China, last time I checked," she replied.

"Don't take too long is my advice," said Old Ping. "Make sure you find a boyfriend before your PhD scares all the boys away!"

I jumped in, "She doesn't have to worry about that. She can always live here with her old dad. I'll pay the bills."

Then, what the heck, they decided to give the wine a shot. Charles asked her, "Wendy, you really think this tastes good? I'm not going to lie. I'm ignorant."

"It's from a family vineyard in Italy," I said, but not wanting to make my friends feel out of place, I added with a laugh, "Not that I could taste the difference."

"It's a little too sweet," Old Ping said as he wobbled toward my refrigerator and cracked a few ice cubes from the ice tray with his hands. He sauntered back to the table with a fist full of ice cubes and I reached out my glass.

I drank a big gulp and made a satisfied sigh.

It happened sometime after that. Charles had made us all take some shots of baijiu, and we were laughing when I noticed Wendy had stopped eating. She pushed her bowl away from her and was blinking at the ceiling light.

"Try the fish," I said to her.

Her eyes glistened. "Dad, why am I here?" she said, getting up from the table. "I flew back just to spend time with you, but it's like you have no interest in me. It's like I'm . . ."

"Oh, so if you're going to have to spend time with me, it should be all about you."

"I'm not saying that."

"I should be honored that you came back."

"Jessica's dad said her first verb was 'scurry!' What was my first *verb*?" she asked me.

"How am I supposed to remember a stupid word from twenty years ago?" I laughed. I should have just made something up on the spot, like "eat!"

"Come on, come on," Charles said. He pressed his lips together and rubbed his hands together. He had his own grown daughter that he was afraid of.

Knocking against the table, she struggled to put on her jacket.

"Hey, you can't be mad at your dad," I said. "I raised you, you can't just throw a tantrum over nothing," I said, and somehow I accidentally ripped a few hairs from her head in trying to stop her from getting up and putting on her jacket.

She yanked away from me and went into the kitchen. I got up and the ground moved below me.

"Think of all the stuff I bought you. Think of all the sacrifices I've made for you. Now you come here with a bottle of wine and ask me questions? Make demands on *me*?" I said, yelling now, "Do you know how much of my money it cost to raise a little bratty girl like you all these years?"

She stopped by the kitchen door and looked at me. "You calculated the exact amount of money it cost to raise me?"

Old Ping cleared his throat. "Hey, Ma, stop it now."

"Yeah, it's 150,000 US dollars, not including all your tuition," I said to her, the blood rushing to my head as if I was hung upside down. "How about I act like Jessica's American dad, and ask you to pay me back?

"How about you pay me my money back?" I asked, "Why don't you think about that?"

She left. Charles and Old Ping left soon after that too, leaving the table a mess of bottles and bones. An hour passed before I realized she was not going to take responsibility for her disrespectful behavior and return to apologize. Fine, have it her way. If she was going to be an ungrateful little brat, then that's her code of operation. I don't get it. My mind works best in bytes, in data, in things permanently and irrevocably true. I'm not even going to pretend that I understand women at all.

It's possible that I might have said some things in bad taste. I might have drunk a little too much as well. Thus, I had a problem on my hands.

I am aware there are limits to the capabilities of the human mind. That's why solving complicated algorithms is difficult; it requires a person to keep track of so many interrelated concepts. The solution couldn't possibly be figured out that very night. The last of the wine tasted bitter in my mouth, but I drank it anyway. Birds went up into their nests and I went to bed.

Wendy didn't call that night. She is still young, self-important, and takes her hurt feelings seriously. Even though she knows, at least should know, that I'd simply lost my temper. But even though I am asleep in bed, things will start happening. That's the phenomenon of problem solving; the mysterious wells of inspiration will often follow a period of incubation. Often the most difficult problems are solved only after one has formally given up on them.

So while I sleep, my mind will be incubating. The subconscious part of my brain will continue working on a problem previously met without success. Even after I wake up, work my mindless eight-hour shift in the assembly line of a computer repair shop, then watch basketball with Charles and Ping, I'll be trying subconsciously to get to the mysterious inspiration to solve my yet unfathomable problem. Once I do, the solution will be forced into my conscious mind.

Everything makes logical sense in computer science. Machines know not to get sentimental; they can rise above and work in symbols and codes. The world of imagination, uncertainty, and doubt can be managed through entities, HEX notations, and sooner or later, everything becomes representational and quite manageable. You don't need to worry about the specifics, once you figure out the abstract.

My favorite is the Nondeterministic Polynomial, which is simply a case in which someone or something, a magic bird perhaps, shows up out of nowhere and simply gives you the "answer" to a difficult problem. The answer is "yes." The only thing you need to do is to check if the answer is correct, that the circumstances of the problem actually exist, and to be able to do so in a reasonable amount of time.

At one point in the past, I thought I had all the answers already. It happened before moving to America, before the marriage, before the daughter, before I'd even attended college. It was the summer I hitched a train to Guangzhou, then bought the cheapest ticket to Hainan. I was eighteen years old with a shaved head and twenty yuan in my pocket, but I just wanted to see the ocean, to float above the water and see the sand below. I still remember the water reflecting a million perfectly placed petals, lifted up to meet the moon. Those birds that lined the trees like big white fruit, who transformed back into birds when I approached them and then flew away to become clouds. Those clouds reaching down to meet the sea, like a lock of wet hair on a girl's neck.

It was then I realized that the reflection on the sand looked like the electricity in a light bulb, like the mysterious maps of marble. I thought I knew the answer to a question I hadn't even asked, that there was some order in this universe.

Life happened so quickly. My hair thinned and I developed a paunch. The years melted and quietly pooled at my feet. Before I was at all prepared, I was married to an ambitious woman, with a precocious daughter, giving up my professorship and moving to New Jersey to become another immigrant American living an ordinary immigrant life.

Now that I think about it, those years were like watching a sunrise. It was not at all like the pleasant vision I had in mind. It was too much to handle, the great sun peering out from the distance: warm and comforting for a moment, and then brilliant, too brilliant to bear. The soft halo of light quickly became a flare and it stung. And yet, by the time I learned to turn away, most of my life was over.

Some nights I wake up in a panic and wonder: Why did everything that I worked for turn into things I despised? How did I become an old man? How did I end up with no one?

Algorithm discovery is the most challenging part of algorithmic problem solving. The phases themselves are unambiguous, but it is *determining* them that is the art. To actually solve a problem, I must first take the initiative.

Phase 1: Define and understand the problem
Phase 2: Develop a plan for problem solving
Phase 3: Execute the developed plan
Phase 4: Evaluate the solution for accuracy, and for its potential as a tool for solving other problems

Phase 1: Define the Problem: The daughter herself

I always knew this daughter was going to be trouble. The first inkling of it was sparked when I used to take her on my bike around my old campus. Because we didn't have any children's seats, I sat her on the pole directly behind the handlebars of my bike. The first thing I told her was to never, ever, get her feet close to the wheels. They would get caught and the wheel would cut her feet badly. I told her the only thing to do was concentrate on keeping her feet as far from the wheel as possible.

So the first thing she did was get her feet caught in the wheel. Cold sweat beaded on my face when I bandaged her bloodied little feet, but she barely cried. It was as if she was testing me, as if she had gone against my warning just to be sure I was telling the truth.

Phase 2: No . . . let's go back.

Phase 1: Understand the Problem: Immigration

Maybe it began soon after Wendy was born, after my wife and I boarded a plane from Beijing to JFK. Probably right after I took my first bite of ham and peanut butter sandwich and liked it. The problem might have arisen following decades of listening to the same Chinese songs, driving to Queens to be surrounded by other transplanted Chinese people, craving the same food we left behind. Perhaps it was sparked during the last twenty years of watching television, how I could never understand enough of the dialogue to chuckle along with the laugh track.

Phase 2: Could it have begun because TV wasn't funny? No, let's try again

Phase 1: Understand the Problem: Unfair and unexpected reversal of roles

When I pictured myself being a father, I'd always assumed I'd take the lead in the relationship. I'd teach her how to read, how to ride a bike, how not to talk to strangers, and all that, but a lot of these opportunities at fatherhood have been robbed from me. It was she who taught me how to read English, when she was eleven. When she was twelve, she helped me pass my citizenship exam by making up acronyms. When she was sixteen, I taught her how to drive, but it was my daughter who helped me renew my license. I never got to console her over some little punk kid breaking her heart, but she held my hand when I cried, after her mother left me.

Is that all there is? It can't be. Cannot proceed to Phase 2.

I must admit, there are some ultimate limitations of algorithms. A difference does exist between problems whose answers can be obtained algorithmically and problems whose answers lie beyond the capabilities of algorithmic systems.

A problem solved algorithmically would be my temperamental attitude. I have since stymied the urge to physically threaten teenage boys being assholes in public, and I no longer pay for car damage due to routine road rage. It was logical reasoning.

However, there is ultimately a line to be drawn between processes that culminate in an answer and those that merely proceed forever without a result, which in this case might be:

1. The problem of wine
2. The problem of daughters

But this can't be the end, not for Wendy and me. We used to have a good relationship, a great relationship, with some all-involving grace that didn't need problem solving. When I watched her ride away on her first bicycle, her ponytail flapping back and forth like a bird's wing; or as I listened to her sing in the school choir, my heart skipped when she spotted me in the crowd and waved. That's my girl! I made her! Like when I visited her third grade open house and she showed me that in her bio, she had written "hiking with father" under hobbies, and "father" under heroes. That's got to be worth something.

There has to be a solution and I won't give up until I find it.

And so, a portion of my unconscious mind will go on translating ideas from abstraction to pseudocode and laying it out systematically in algorithmic notations. It will be an ever-slowing process. Once I wake up, life will bring about more arguments and disappointments; small trespasses in a long life.

My relationship with my daughter might never fully recover from this night. We might miss a lot of holiday cooking together, and my hair will thin even more and she will grow just a little taller. Maybe out of the blue, some years from now, she will introduce me to a boyfriend, a strange-looking but polite boy. It might take even more years, but maybe she will come home and apologize and wash my dirty pillowcases and overeat in order to please me. I wouldn't be able to know how unhappy I had been until she returned.

She cannot abandon me. She loves me and thus will be able to anticipate my indignation and put my hurt feelings before her own. Those are some of the concessions made. There will be others. These sequences of instructions are programmed within her; that is her heritage.

Ah, but the solution, and there is one, will come to me years later. Perhaps when I am on a fishing boat in Baja, or in the middle of my honeymoon with my second wife, or in the hospital room at the birth of my new baby daughter, Lana. When it comes to me, and it will, I will remember this:

One afternoon, not long after we immigrated, when my daughter was still outgrowing her baby teeth, I came home from work early and found her walking alone around the dim apartment. Holding a hand mirror, face up at her waist, she walked from room to room while peering down into the reflection.

"What are you doing?" I asked.

"I am walking on the ceiling," she replied.

I was about to tell her to stop fooling around, to do her homework, but instead I paused and allowed myself to go with her imagination. I tried to picture what she might have seen up there. What magical inexplicable things could have been walking on the ceiling with my lovely fat-faced daughter, who spoke no English, sensitive and shy, and so often alone.

ENDNOTES (JOHN CLEGG AND ROBERT LUCAS)

∎

Brown vs. Ferguson

FROM *Endnotes #4*

Endnotes *is a journal/book series published by a discussion group based in Germany, the U.K., and the US. Each edition of the journal emerges from conversation and debate among* Endnotes *members. What follows is an excerpt from* Endnotes #4, *which attempts to provide a historical account of the Black Lives Matter movement. Its principal authors were John Clegg and Robert Lucas.*

> Ferguson is a picture of pleasant suburbia, a town of tree-lined streets and well-kept homes, many of them built for the middle class at mid-century. But Ferguson is in north St. Louis County, and the area is suffering from one of the region's weakest real estate markets.
>
> —St. Louis Post Dispatch, *18 August 2013*

IN 1970 a sociologist from Galveston, Texas, Sidney M. Willhelm, published a book with the incendiary title *Who Needs the Negro?** In it he pointed out a bitter irony: just when the Civil Rights Movement was promising to liberate black people from discrimination in the workplace, automation was killing the very jobs from which they had previously been excluded. Willhelm painted a dystopian future that has proved eerily prophetic. He warned that African Americans were in danger of sharing the fate of American Indians: heavily segregated, condemned to perpetually high levels of poverty and dwindling birth rates—an "obsolescent" population doomed to demographic de-

---

* Sidney M. Willhelm, *Who Needs the Negro?* (Shenkman 1970).

cline. At the time, in the heady days of Civil Rights success, Willhelm was dismissed as a kook. Today his book is remembered only within some obscure black nationalist circles.*

In retrospect most of Willhelm's predictions bore out, but even his bleak vision failed to anticipate the true scale of the catastrophe in store for black America. He wrote that "the real frustration of the 'total society' comes from the difficulty of discarding 20,000,000 people made superfluous through automation," for "there is no possibility of resubjugating the Negro or of jailing 20,000,000 Americans of varying shades of 'black.'" Nowhere in his dystopian imagination could Willhelm envisage an increase in the prison population of the scale that actually occurred in the two decades after his book was published. Yet this was the eventual solution to the problem that Willhelm perceived: the correlation between the loss of manufacturing jobs for African American men and the rise in their incarceration is unmistakable.

Today in the U.S. one in ten black men between the ages of 18 and 35 are behind bars, far more than anything witnessed in any other time or place. The absolute number has fallen in recent years, but the cumulative impact is terrifying. Amongst all black men born since the late 1970s, *one in four* have spent time in prison by their mid-30s. For those who didn't complete high school, incarceration has become the norm: 70% have passed through the system.† They are typically caged in rural prisons far from friends and family, many are exploited by both the prison and its gangs, and tens of thousands are currently in solitary confinement.

How to explain this hellscape? Wilhelm gives us an economic story: capitalists no longer have the capacity or motive to exploit the labor of these men; unnecessary for capital, they are made wards of the state. Michelle Alexander, in *The New Jim Crow*, gives us a politi-

---

* For a contemporary discussion of Willhelm's ideas see "Do Black Lives Matter?" a conversation between Robin Kelley and Fred Moten, on the Critical Resistance website. Automation has long been a key topic for black revolutionaries in the US. See, for example, James Boggs, *The American Revolution: Pages from a Negro Worker's Notebook* (Monthly Review Press 1963).

† Bruce Western, *Punishment and Inequality in America* (Russell Sage Foundation 2006).

cal one: fear of black insurgency (a backlash against the successes of the Civil Rights Movement) led white voters to support "law and order" policies, like increased mandatory minimum sentences and reduced opportunity for parole.* Alexander underplays the impact of a very real crime wave beginning in the late 1960s, but it is true that these policies were first championed by a Republican "Southern strategy" that did little to conceal a core racial animus, and they began to receive bipartisan support in the 80s, when the crack epidemic united the country in fear of black criminality.

However, if white politicians had hoped to specifically target blacks with these punitive policies, they failed. From 1970 to 2000, the incarceration rate for whites increased just as fast, and it continued to increase even as the black incarceration rate began to decline after 2000. Blacks are still incarcerated at much higher rates, but the black–white disparity actually *fell* over the era of mass incarceration. Even if every black man currently in jail were miraculously set free, in a sort of anti-racist rapture, the US would still have the highest incarceration rate in the world.

I.

St. Louis, a city born in slavery, has a long history of state-mandated racial segregation in the twentieth century: redlining, segregated public housing and restrictive covenants.† Out of urban engineering and "slum surgery" there came the 1956 Pruitt-Igoe project, which

---

* These reforms, along with new conspiracy charges that could be used to turn any associate into a state's witness, effectively gave sentencing power to prosecutors. Michelle Alexander, *The New Jim Crow: Mass Incarceration in the Age of Colorblindness* (New Press 2010). However, as James Forman Jr. points out, Alexander's backlash thesis overlooks the support of black politicians for this same legislation. James Forman Jr., "Racial Critiques of Mass Incarceration: Beyond the New Jim Crow," *NYU Law Review*, vol. 87, 2012.

† In 1974 a panel of federal judges concluded that "segregated housing in the St. Louis metropolitan area was . . . in large measure the result of deliberate racial discrimination in the housing market by the real estate industry and by agencies of the federal, state, and local governments." Richard Rothstein, "The Making of Ferguson: Public Policies at the Root of Its Troubles," Economic Policy Institute, 15 October 2014.

housed 15,000 people in North St. Louis. Built in part according to Le Corbusier's principles by Minoru Yamasaki, the architect who would go on to design the World Trade Center, this project became notorious almost immediately for its crime and poverty. Local authorities solved the problem—and that of Pruitt-Igoe's large-scale rent strike—by simply demolishing it in the early 1970s, in an event that Charles Jencks famously identified as "the day modern architecture died."* North St. Louis has remained heavily impoverished and racialized to the present, with 95 percent of the population identifying as black, and unemployment among men in their twenties approaches 50 percent in many neighborhoods.

An incorporated city close to the northern edge of St. Louis, Ferguson had been an early destination for white flight, as both workers and jobs moved out of the city in the 1950s and 60s, to escape the desegregated school system and benefit from the lower taxes of suburban St. Louis County. But many of the refugees of the Pruitt-Igoe disaster too fled north to places like Ferguson when other white suburbs blocked the construction of multi-family housing, enforced restrictive covenants, or simply proved too expensive. This was the beginning of another wave of out-migration—this time black—as crime and poverty swept the deindustrialized city through the 1980s and 90s. Whites now began to leave Ferguson, taking investment and tax revenues with them, and the local government started to allow for the construction of low- and mixed-income apartments in the southeastern corner of the town.† These developments fit a general pattern of spatial polarization and local homogenization, as segregation has occurred between blocks of increasing size—town and suburb rather than neighborhood.‡ Through such dynamics, the population of Ferguson has become increasingly black over recent decades: from 1% in 1970, to 25% in 1990, to 67% in 2010. But the local state

---

* With a certain historical irony, some would later view the other famous demolition of Minoru Yamasaki buildings as the day postmodernity died.

† See Chris Wright, "Its Own Peculiar Decor," in *Endnotes* 4, October 2015, for an analysis of such dynamics.

‡ See Daniel Lichter et al., "Toward a New Macro-Segregation? Decomposing Segregation within and between Metropolitan Cities and Suburbs," *American Sociological Review*, vol. 80, no. 4, August 2015.

ruling over this population has lagged significantly behind its rapidly shifting racial profile: in 2014 only about 7.5% of police officers were African-American, and almost all elected officials were white. Meanwhile the gender balance has changed just as rapidly, with Ferguson displaying the highest number of "missing black men" in the US: only 60 black men for every 100 women; thus more than 1 in 3 black men absent, presumed either dead or behind bars.*

A further influx to Ferguson—and specifically Canfield Green, the apartment complex in the southeast where Michael Brown lived and died—came from another mass demolition of housing stock: neighboring Kinloch, a much older African American neighborhood, had also been suffering from the general dynamics of declining population and high crime until much of the area was razed to make way for an expansion of Lambert–St. Louis International Airport. While Kinloch and Ferguson may together form a continuous picture of racialization, urban decay and brutalization at the hands of planners and developers, viewed at other scales it is the polarizations that start to appear: a couple of kilometers from Ferguson's southern perimeter lies the small townlet of Bellerive. Bordering on the campus of the University of Missouri–St. Louis, Bellerive has a median family income of around $100,000.

Indeed, Ferguson itself remains relatively integrated by the standards of St. Louis County, with a quite prosperous white island around South Florissant Road. Both crime and poverty are lower than in neighboring suburbs like Jennings and Berkeley. But it is a suburb in transition. If in the 1960s and 70s the racial divisions of St. Louis County were largely carved out by public policy, as well as semi-public restrictive covenants, in the 1990s and 2000s they tended to follow a more discrete and spontaneous pattern of real estate valuations. Like Sanford, Florida, where George Zimmerman had gunned down Trayvon Martin two and a half years earlier—setting in train the beginnings of a national wave of activism—Ferguson was impacted heavily by the recent foreclosure crisis. More than half the

---

* The national average for whites is 99 men for 100 women, 83 for blacks. Wolfers et al., "1.5 Million Missing Black Men," *New York Times*, 20 April 2015.

new mortgages in North St. Louis County from 2004 to 2007 were subprime, and in Ferguson by 2010 one in 11 homes were in fore-closure. Between 2009 and 2013 North County homes lost a third of their value. Landlords and investment companies bought up under-water properties and rented to minorities. White flight was now turn-ing into a stampede.

Because property taxes are linked to valuations, the Ferguson city government had to look elsewhere for funding. Between 2004 and 2011 court fines netted $1.2 million, or around 10% of the city's rev-enue. By 2013 this figure had doubled to $2.6 million, or a fifth of all revenues. The city's annual budget report attributed this to a "more concentrated focus on traffic enforcement." In that year the Fergu-son Municipal Court disposed of 24,532 warrants and 12,018 cases, or about 3 warrants and 1.5 cases per household. A Department of Justice report would soon reveal that these had been far from evenly distributed across the population:

> African Americans account for 85% of vehicle stops, 90% of citations, and 93% of arrests made by FPD officers, despite comprising only 67% of Ferguson's population. [They] are 68% less likely than others to have their cases dismissed by the court [and] 50% more likely to have their cases lead to an arrest warrant.*

In high poverty areas like Canfield Green, non-payment of fines could easily lead to further fines as well as jail time, and the re-port found that "arrest warrants were used almost exclusively for the purpose of compelling payment through the threat of incarcer-ation." Here the disappearance of white—and the destruction of black—wealth had led to a mutation in the form of the local state: revenue collected not through consensual taxation but by outright vi-olent plunder.

---

* "Investigation of the Ferguson Police Department," United States Department of Justice, Civil Rights Division, 4 March 2015. The very existence of a DoJ report taking notice of these issues in Ferguson is itself an outcome of the struggles that happened in large part because of them.

2.

On August 9, 2014, police left Michael Brown dead, and in a pool of blood, for four and a half hours, whilst "securing the crime scene," or so they later explained. With Brown lying still on the tarmac, a large angry crowd gathered in Canfield Green, as residents poured out of surrounding apartments. Cops reported gunfire and chants of "kill the police." "Hands up, don't shoot" and "We are Michael Brown" would soon be added to the chorus, while someone set a dumpster on fire; signs already that an anti-police riot was in the offing.

At a daytime vigil the next day, 10 August 2014, a black leader of the County government tried to calm the mounting unrest, but was shouted down. Members of the New Black Panther Party chanted "Black Power" and berated "that devil rap music." As day tilted into evening, the large, restive crowd met with massive police presence—a conventional proto-riot scenario. Confrontations ensued: a cop car and a TV van attacked; shops looted; a QuikTrip gas station the first thing aflame. This acted as a beacon, drawing more people out. The scorched forecourt of this place would become a central gathering point for protests over the coming weeks. And rather than the mythically random object of "mob rage," it was a deliberately selected target: rumor had it that staff had called the cops on Brown, accusing him of shoplifting. The QuikTrip was followed by some riot standards: parked vehicles set alight; looting on West Florissant Avenue—plus a little festivity, music playing, people handing out hot dogs. The cops backed off for hours, leaving that odd sort of pseudo-liberated space that can appear in the midst of a riot.

As the eyes of the nation turned to watch, people joined in on social media with the #IfTheyGunnedMeDown hashtag, mocking the media selection of the most gangsta possible victim portraits. Activists from St. Louis—some of whom had been involved in a spontaneous march the year before, through the city's downtown, in response to the acquittal of George Zimmerman—began to descend on the suburb. Meanwhile standard mechanisms sprung into action: on 11 August the FBI opened a civil rights investigation into Brown's shooting, while NAACP President Cornell William Brooks flew into Ferguson, calling for an end to violence. President Obama intervened the next day with a statement offering condolences to the Brown family and asking for people to calm down. In response to Trayvon's death his rhetoric had been characterized by tensions between racial particularity and the universality of national citizenship, tensions which registered a constitutive contradiction of American society. Faced with an immediate wave of rioting, it was predictable which way these would now be resolved: Obama eschewed any racial identification with Brown or his family, in favor of "the broader American community."

But the rioting rolled on over days; action necessarily diffuse in this suburban landscape, police lines straining to span subdivisions. Away from the front lines strip malls were looted while carnivalesque refrains lingered in the air: protesters piling onto slow-driving cars, blasting hip-hop, an odd sort of ghost riding. In altercations between cops and protesters the latter sometimes threw rocks or Molotovs. But they were also often hands-up, shouting "don't shoot." In retrospect, this may look like an early instance of the theatrics of this wave of struggle, and it would soon become a familiar meme. But it was also apparently a spontaneous response to the immediate situation, right after Brown's shooting, before the media-savvy activists rolled into town at the end of the month—for it had an immediate referent, not only symbolically, in Brown himself, but also practically, as protesters confronted the diverse toolkit of the American state: SWAT teams, tear gas, rubber bullets, pepper balls, flash grenades, beanbag rounds, smoke bombs, armored trucks. The nation was aghast as images scrolled across screens of this military hardware, of a cop saying "Bring it, you fucking animals"— coverage that police attempted at points to shut down.

Social contestation in the US has long faced much greater threat of physical violence than in other comparable countries—indeed, those protesting in Ferguson would also at points be shot at with live ammunition by unidentified gunmen, and sometimes get hit. (This is surely one reason why such contestation often seems markedly muted, given conditions.) Police violence against unarmed black people was thus not a simple *content* of these protests, an issue for them to merely carry along, like any other demand. It was also implicated in the nature of the protests themselves, where everyone out on the streets those days was a potential Mike Brown. There was, we might say, a peculiar possibility for movement unification presenting itself here, a unity one step from the graveyard, given by the equality that the latter offers; a unity of the potentially killable. Hands up, don't shoot. And as the country looked on, this performance of absolute vulnerability communicated something powerful; something with which police were ill-equipped to deal: Will you even deny that I am a living body?

Such messages, broadcast on the national stage, seemed to pose a threat to police legitimacy, and raised practical questions about the continuing management of the Ferguson unrest. Criticism of the militarized policing came even from the midst of the state—albeit its libertarian wing.* On the 14th the Highway Patrol—a state police force, less implicated in the immediate locality, with a much higher ratio of black officers and a distinctly non-militaristic style—was ordered in as an alternative, softer approach with a view to easing tensions, apparently with some success. In the evening hours, a captain even walked with a large peaceful demonstration. At "an emotional meeting at a church," clergy members were despairing at "the seemingly uncontrollable nature of the protest movement and the flare-ups of violence that older people in the group abhorred."† Meanwhile, Canfield Green turned into a block party.

After five days of protests often violently dispersed, the name of Brown's killer, Darren Wilson, was finally announced, along with a report that Brown had stolen a pack of cigarillos from Ferguson Market & Liquor—not the QuikTrip gas station—the morning of his death. The timing of this identification of criminality was probably tactical; it was soon followed by an admission that Wilson had not stopped Brown for this reason. That night, Ferguson Market & Liquor received similarly pointed treatment to the QuikTrip: it was looted. The next day a state of emergency and curfew was declared. There were now a small but significant number of guns on the streets, often fired

---

* Senator Rand Paul, "We Must Demilitarize the Police," *Time*, 14 August 2014.
† Julie Bosman, "Lack of Leadership and a Generational Split Hinder Protests in Ferguson," *New York Times*, 16 August 2014.

into the air, and police were getting increasingly nervous. On 12 August Mya Aaten-White, great-granddaughter of local jazz singer Mae Wheeler, was shot whilst leaving a protest; the bullet pierced her skull but missed her brain, lodging in her sinus cavity. She survived and refused to cooperate with police investigations.

While some came in from neighboring areas, those out on the streets in the early days remained predominantly local residents.* But a mass of creepers was already climbing over Ferguson's surface, forming vegetal tangles, trying to grasp some masonry: Christian mimes, prayer and rap circles, wingnut preachers, the Revolutionary Communist Party, "people who would walk between the riot cops and the crowd just saying 'Jesus' over and over again"; a generalized recruitment fair.† Bloods and Crips were out, participating in confrontations with cops as well as apparently protecting some stores from looters. Nation of Islam members too took to the streets attempting to guard shops, arguing that women should leave. Others called for peace in the name of a new Civil Rights Movement. Jesse Jackson was booed and asked to leave a local community demonstration when he took the opportunity to ask for donations to his church. "African-American civic leaders" in St. Louis were said to be "frustrated by their inability to guide the protesters." A rift seemed to be opening.‡

This riot could easily have remained a local affair like those in Cincinnati 2001, Oakland 2009 or Flatbush the year before. Yet it happened to coincide with a high point in the national wave of "black lives matter" activism that had started right after the killing of Trayvon Martin in 2012, and it managed to shake free of local mediators, opening up a space for others to interpret and represent it at will. Soon social media–organized busloads of activists descended on Missouri from around the country—Occupy and Anonymous apparently identities at play here, plus a scattering of anarchists. In

---

* Solid statistics on participation seem to be unavailable at present, but arrest figures chime with logical readings of the events: in its first phase, Ferguson was clearly a community anti-police riot, and its social character may thus be judged in part by using the place itself as a proxy. Ann O'Neill, "Who was arrested in Ferguson?," CNN, 23 August 2015.

† Various, "Reflections on the Ferguson Uprising," *Rolling Thunder* #12, spring 2015.

‡ Bosman, "Lack of Leadership and a Generational Split."

the following month "Freedom Rides"—another Civil Rights reference—were organized under the Black Lives Matter banner: it was
at this point that this really emerged in its own right as a prominent
identity within these movements. Ferguson was mutating from a ter-
rain of community riots into a national center for activism. Key figures began to emerge, often identified by their number of Twitter
followers: some local, like Johnetta Elzie ("Netta") and Ashley Yates;
others who had made the pilgrimage, like DeRay McKesson from
Minneapolis.*

3.

In retrospect, Black Lives Matter can be viewed as two movements:
media-savvy activists and proletarian rioters, for the most part divided both socially and geographically. But in Ferguson's aftermath
this divide was spanned by a shared sense of urgency, by the diverse
resonances of a hashtag; by developing institutional bridges, and perhaps above all by the legacy of the Civil Rights Movement itself, with
its ability to conjure black unity. The similarities were many: "black
lives matter" evoking the older slogan "I am a man,"† the faith and
religious rhetoric of many activists, the tactics of nonviolent civil
disobedience and media visibility—contrasted with the far more
opaque riots, not to mention the direct involvement of Civil Rights
organizations and veterans themselves.

The key to this encounter is the simple fact that the historic gains
of the Civil Rights Movement failed to improve the lives of most
black Americans. Today racial disparities in income, wealth, schooling, unemployment and infant mortality are as high as ever. Segregation persists. Lynching and second class citizenship have been
replaced by mass incarceration. The fight against a New Jim Crow
would thus seem to require the kind of movement that overthrew the

---

* For profiles of the new activists, see "The Disruptors," CNN, 4 August 2015.

† The iconic photo of men carrying signs reading "I am a man" is of striking garbage
workers in Memphis, 1968. That slogan can in turn be linked back to the 18th-century
abolitionist slogan "am I not a man and a brother?," which was echoed by Sojourner
Truth's "ain't I a woman?."

Old. But something fundamental has changed and therefore troubles this project: a small fraction of African Americans reaped significant benefits from the end of *de jure* discrimination. In 1960, 1 in 17 black Americans were in the top quintile of earners; today that number is 1 in 10. Inequality in wealth and income has risen significantly among African Americans, such that today it is much higher than among whites.*

For some Marxists, the participation of the black middle class in anti-racist movements is seen as a sign of their limited, class-collaborationist character. When such people become leaders it is often assumed they will attend only to their own interests, and betray the black proletariat.† It is true, as such critics point out, that the institutional and political legacy of Civil Rights has more or less been monopolized by wealthier blacks. But the intergenerational transmission of wealth is less assured for African Americans, whose historical exclusion from real estate markets has meant that middle income earners typically possess much less wealth than white households in the same income range. As a result, those born into middle income families are more likely than whites to make less money than their parents.‡ Downward mobility was amplified by the recent crisis, which negatively affected black wealth much more than white.§

When speaking about the new black middle class one must therefore be aware that this term conflates distinct layers: (1) those who made it into stable blue-collar or public sector professions, and who

---

* A simple measure is the ratio of top to bottom income quintiles within the black population. In 1966 this was 8.4 (the richest 20% blacks had about 8 times the income of the bottom 20%); by 1996 it had doubled to 17. The corresponding figures for whites were 6.2 and 10. Cecilia Conrad et al., *African Americans in the US Economy* (Rowman and Littlefield 2006), pp. 120–24.

† See, e.g., Adolph Reed Jr., "Black Particularity Reconsidered," *Telos* 39, 1979.

‡ Of those born into the bottom quintile, over 90% of both blacks and whites earned more than their parents, but only 66% of blacks born in the second quintile surpass their parents' income, compared with 89% of whites. Pew Trusts, "Pursuing the American Dream: Economic mobility across generations," 9 July 2012.

§ From 2005 to 2009, the average black household's wealth fell by more than half, to $5,677, while white household wealth fell only 16% to $113,149. Rakesh Kochhar et al, "20 to 1: Wealth Gaps Rise to Record Highs Between Whites, Blacks and Hispanics," Pew Social & Demographic Trends 2011.

thus achieved a little housing equity, but who generally live close to the ghetto, are a paycheck away from bankruptcy, and got screwed by the subprime crisis; and (2) a smaller petit-bourgeois and bourgeois layer that made it into middle-management positions or operated their own companies, who moved into their own elite suburbs, and who are now able to reproduce their class position.

Many of the new activist leaders fall into one or another of these layers.* This in itself is nothing new. The old Civil Rights leaders also tended to come from the "black elite." Yet that elite was relatively closer to the black proletariat in income and wealth, and was condemned by Jim Crow to live alongside them and share their fate. It consisted of religious and political leaders, as well as professionals, shopkeepers, and manufacturers who monopolized racially segmented markets—the "ghetto bourgeoisie." Although many helped to build Jim Crow segregation, acting as "race managers," they also had an interest in overcoming the barriers that denied them and their children access to the best schools and careers, and thus in the Civil Rights Movement they adopted the role of "race leaders," taking it as their task to "raise up" the race as a whole.

The new activists distinguish themselves from the previous generation along technological, intersectional and organizational lines. They are suspicious of top-down organizing models and charismatic male leaders. But this is less a rejection of leadership per se than a reflection of the fact that—in an age of social media niches—almost anyone can now stake a claim to race leadership, to broker some imaginary constituency. They strain against the hierarchical structures of traditional NGOs, although many are staff members thereof. They want to shake off these stultifying mediations in a way that aligns them with the younger, more dynamic Ferguson rioters, and social media seems to give them that chance.

---

* Alicia Garza, cofounder of the Black Lives Matter network, grew up in predominantly white Marin County, CA, where the median household income is over $100,000. DeRay McKesson, by contrast, grew up in a poor neighborhood of Baltimore. Yet he earned a six-figure salary as the director of human capital for the Minneapolis School District, where he developed a reputation for ruthlessness in firing teachers. Jay Caspian Kang, "Our Demand Is Simple: Stop Killing Us," *New York Times*, 4 May 2015.

But despite their good intentions and radical self-image, and despite the real unity that Ferguson seemed to offer, differences between the new generation of race leaders and the previous one only reinforce the gap between the activists and those they hope to represent. Those differences can be described along three axes:

Firstly, most of the activists are college-educated. And unlike the previous generation they have not been restricted to all-black colleges. This doesn't mean they are guaranteed well-paid jobs, far from it. But it does mean that they have a cultural experience to which very few people from poor neighborhoods in Ferguson or Baltimore have access: they have interacted with many white people who are not paid to control them, and they will typically have had some experience of the trepid, cautious dance of campus-based identity politics, as well as the (often unwanted) advances of "white allies." Thus although their activism isn't always directed at white liberals, their social and technical abilities in this respect often exceed those of skilled media-manipulators like Al Sharpton.

Secondly, unlike the previous generation, many of them did not themselves grow up in the ghetto. This is perhaps the single biggest legacy of the Civil Rights Movement: the ability to move to the suburbs, for those who could afford it. In 1970, 58% of the black middle class lived in poor majority-black neighborhoods; today the same percentage live in wealthier majority-white neighborhoods, mostly in the suburbs.* This means that they have much less personal experience of crime. Of course, they still experience racist policing, are stopped by cops far more than whites and are subject to all manner of humiliations and indignities, but they are much less likely to be thrown in jail or killed.† Indeed the likelihood of ending up in jail has fallen steadily for the black middle class since the 1970s even as it has skyrocketed for the poor, both black and white.‡

---

* Patrick Sharkey, "Spatial segmentation and the black middle class," *American Journal of Sociology* 119, no. 4, 2014.

† Karyn Lacy describes the "exclusionary boundary work" with which the black middle class distinguishes itself from the black poor in the eyes of white authority figures. *Blue Chip Black: Race, Class, and Status in the New Black Middle Class* (UC Press 2007).

‡ Western and Pettit show that in 2008 the incarceration rate for college-educated black men was six times lower than the rate for poor whites who failed to graduate

Finally, and perhaps most significantly, activism is for them, un-like the previous generation, in many cases a professional option. Today an expectation of "race leadership" is no longer part of the upbringing of the black elite. Identification with the victims of po-lice violence is generally a matter of elective sympathy among those who choose to become activists, and of course many do not make that choice.* But for those who do, traditional civil service jobs and voluntary work have been replaced by career opportunities in a pro-fessionalized nonprofit sector. These jobs are often temporary, al-lowing college graduates to "give back" before moving on to better things. DeRay McKesson, before he became the face of the new activ-ism, had been an ambassador for Teach for America (TFA), an orga-nization that recruits elite college graduates to spend two years teach-ing in poor inner-city schools, often as part of a strategy to promote charter schools and bust local teachers' unions. In general the "com-munity organizing" NGOs, whether they are primarily religious or political, are often funded by large foundations such as Ford, Rock-efeller and George Soros' Open Society. An integral aspect of the privatization of the American welfare state, they can also function as "astroturf" for groups like TFA and the Democrats.

Thus, in the aftermath of Ferguson, along with the influx of activ-ists from around the country there came an influx of dollars. Whilst existing nonprofits competed to recruit local activists, foundations competed to fund new nonprofits, picking winners.† Netta was ini-tially recruited by Amnesty International, and she and DeRay, along with another TFA organizer, Brittney Packet, would set up Campaign Zero with backing from Open Society. Subsequently DeRay gave up his six-figure salary to "focus on activism full time." He is currently

high school. Bruce Western and Becky Pettit, "Incarceration and Social Inequality," *Dædalus* (Summer 2010), 8–19.

* On the gap between proletarian and middle class black identity, see Ytasha L. Wo-mack, *Post Black: How a New Generation Is Redefining African American Identity* (Chi-cago Review Press 2010); Touré, *Who's Afraid of Post-Blackness?: What It Means to Be Black Now* (Free Press 2011).

† The Open Society Foundation invested $2.5 million in Ferguson "community groups." See "Healing the Wounds in Ferguson and Staten Island," Open Society Foundations blog, 19 December 2014.

running for mayor of Baltimore and his campaign has received donations from prominent figures in Wall Street and Silicon Valley.* Most
local activists were not so lucky. Many lost their jobs and became de-
pendent on small, crowdfunded donations. Meanwhile at least 12 of
those arrested during the rioting are still in jail, either serving time
or awaiting trial.

4.

Three weeks before Darren Wilson emptied his gun into an unarmed
Mike Brown, Eric Garner, 43, had been killed in Staten Island, New
York City, strangled by police officer Daniel Pantaleo.† Garner's dying words "I can't breathe" were caught on camera, and they quickly
took their place alongside "hands up, don't shoot" as a key slogan of
the nascent movement. Indeed, over the following months, events
would sometimes move in close parallel between America's largest
city and the small Midwestern town. On 18 August Missouri Governor Jay Nixon called in the National Guard to enforce the curfew.
Two days later Attorney General Eric Holder traveled to Ferguson,
where he met with residents and Brown's family. In nearby Clay-
ton, a grand jury began hearing evidence to determine whether Wilson should be charged. On 23 August at least 2,500 turned out for a
Staten Island Garner demonstration, led by Sharpton, with chants of
"I can't breathe," and "hands up, don't shoot," picking up the meme
from Ferguson. A group called Justice League NYC, affiliated with
Harry Belafonte, demanded the firing of Officer Pantaleo and the ap-
pointment of a special prosecutor. The next day, Brown's funeral in
St. Louis was attended by 4,500, including not only the ubiquitous
Sharpton and Jackson, and Trayvon Martin's family, but also White
House representatives, Martin Luther King III, and a helping of ce-

---

* On the subsequent trajectory of DeRay and other activists, see John Clegg, "Black
Representation After Ferguson," *The Brooklyn Rail*, 3 May 2016.
† Garner apparently sold "loosies" — individual cigarettes purchased in neighboring
states where taxes were lower — and had already been arrested multiple times in 2014
for this minor misdemeanor. For the cops this was part of the "broken windows" policing strategy made famous by the NYPD. "Beyond the Chokehold: The Path to Eric Garner's Death," *New York Times*, 13 June 2015.

lebrities: Spike Lee, Diddy, and Snoop Dogg. In the name of Brown's parents, Sharpton's eulogy disparaged rioting:

> Michael Brown does not want to be remembered for a riot. He wants to be remembered as the one who made America deal with how we are going to police in the United States.

But these were, of course, not mutually exclusive, as the history of riot-driven reform testifies. While riots generally consolidate reaction against a movement—with the usual pundits baying for punitive measures, while others jostle to conjure from the events a more reasonable, law-abiding "community" with themselves at its head—they also tend to shake the state into remedial action. Only days later the Justice Department announced an inquiry into policing in Ferguson. Shortly after, large-scale reforms to Ferguson's political and legal institutions were announced. By the end of September the Ferguson police chief had publicly apologized to the Brown family, who were also invited to the Congressional Black Caucus convention, where Obama spoke on race. From the single national community invoked against the immediate impact of rioting, he now ceded significant ground to the particularity of racial questions, speaking of the "unfinished work" of Civil Rights, while simultaneously presenting this as an issue for "most Americans."

Unrest was still ongoing through September, overstretching Ferguson's police force, who would soon be replaced again, this time by St. Louis County police. With the thickets of organizations and professional activists on the ground, other, more theatrical and non-violent forms of action were now tending to replace the community riot, such as the 6 October interruption of a St. Louis classical concert with the old Depression-era class struggle hymn "Which side are you on?" On the same day a federal judge ruled on the side of peaceful activists and against police, over whether demonstrations could be required to "keep moving." Meanwhile, Eric Holder announced a general Department of Justice review of police tactics, and from 9 October Senate hearings began on the question of militarized policing. Ferguson actions stretched on through October, under the aegis of many different groups, including "Hands Up United," which had been formed locally after Brown's death, while more protesters rolled in from around the country.

In mid-November, as the Grand Jury decision on Brown's killer drew near, Missouri Governor Jay Nixon had once again declared a state of emergency, bringing in the National Guard in anticipation of the usual non-indictment and a new round of rioting.* On 24 November these expectations were fulfilled. As the non-indictment was announced, Michael Brown's mother was caught on camera yelling "They're wrong! Everybody wants me to be calm. Do you know how those bullets hit my son?" As she broke down in grief, her partner, wearing a shirt with "I am Mike Brown" written down the back, hugged and supported her for a while, before turning to the crowd, clearly boiling over with anger, to yell repeatedly "burn this bitch down!"; if Mike Brown's life mattered little to the state, it might at least be made to. As looting and gunshots rattled around the Ferguson and St. Louis area, protests ignited in New York, Sanford, Cleveland, Los Angeles, Seattle, Washington and on—reportedly 170 cities, many using the tactic of obstructing traffic. After a "die-in" and roving traffic-blocking in the perennial activist hotspot of Oakland, riots spread, with looting, fires set, windows smashed. In the midst of the national unrest, church groups made interventions criticizing the Grand Jury decision and supporting peaceful demonstrations. Ferguson churches brought a newly religious twist to activist "safe spaces" discourses, offering themselves as "sacred spaces" for the protection of demonstrators.

In the following days, as the National Guard presence in Ferguson swelled, demonstrations were ongoing across the country—and beyond. Outside a thoroughly bulwarked US Embassy in London, around 5,000 assembled in the dank autumn evening of 27 November for a Black Lives Matter demonstration, before this precipitated

---

* Grand Juries play a filtering role in relation to normal court proceedings, determining in secret whether criminal charges should be brought. They are led by a prosecutor, and the defense presents no case. The lack of accountability here makes them a preferred option in these sorts of circumstances. Normally the absence of defense increases the likelihood of indictment, but if the prosecutor who leads the jury is reluctant to indict (due to institutional ties with the police) then non-indictments are more or less guaranteed, and can always be blamed on the Grand Jury itself.

in a roving "hands up, don't shoot" action down Oxford Street and confrontations with cops in Parliament Square—an event that drew links between Brown and Tottenham's Mark Duggan, whose own death had ignited England's 2011 riot wave.* In cities across Canada, too, there were Ferguson solidarity actions. On 1 December Obama invited "civil rights activists" to the White House to talk, while the St. Louis Rams associated themselves with the Brown cause, walking onto the field hands-up.

Then on 3 December 2014 came the second Grand Jury non-indictment in just over a week: the officer whose chokehold had killed Eric Garner, in full vision of the country at large, predictably cleared of wrongdoing. Cops, of course, are almost never charged for such things, and are even less likely to be convicted, in the US or elsewhere; the executors of state violence cannot literally be held to the same standards as the citizenry they police, even though their credibility depends upon the impression that they are. Due process will be performed, stretched out if possible until anger has subsided, until the inevitable exoneration; only in the most blatant or extreme cases will individual officers be sacrificed on the altar of the police force's general legitimacy. Nonetheless, it seems in some ways remarkable that such petrol would be poured with such timing, on fires that were already raging.†

The following day thousands protested in New York City, with roving demonstrations blocking roads, around the Staten Island site of the killing, along the length of Manhattan, chanting "I can't breathe. I can't breathe." Die-ins happened in Grand Central Station, mirrored on the other side of the country in the Bay Area. Significant actions were happening almost every day now, typically called on Facebook or Twitter, with groups blocking traffic in one corner of a city receiving live updates of groups in many other areas, sometimes run-

---

* For an account of the Duggan case, and the riot wave that followed it, see "A Rising Tide Lifts All Boats," *Endnotes* 3, September 2013.

† The prosecutor who supervised the Grand Jury investigation, Daniel Donovan, was subsequently elected to represent Staten Island, a borough heavily populated with police officers, in the United States Congress. The city later settled a wrongful-death claim by paying $5.9 million to Garner's family.

ning into them with great delight. In the coastal cities the recent experience of Occupy lent a certain facility to spontaneous demonstration. Police appeared overwhelmed, but in many cases they had been instructed to hold back. More victims of police violence at this point would only fan the flames.

V.

On April 12, 2015, Freddie Gray's spine was severed at the neck when Baltimore cops took him for a "rough ride" in a police van.* During his subsequent days of coma, before his 19 April death, demonstrations had already started in front of the Western District police station. On 25 April Black Lives Matter protests hit downtown Baltimore, bringing the first signs of unrest to come. The 27 April funeral, like Brown's, was attended by thousands, including White House representatives, the Garner family, "civil rights leaders," etc. A confrontation between cops and teenagers outside Baltimore's Mondawmin Mall was the trigger event for the massive rioting that would engulf Baltimore for days, causing an estimated $9m of damage to property. Tweets declared "all out war between kids and police" and "straight communist savage."† A familiar riot-script followed: calls for calm and condemnations of "thugs," allocating blame to a selfish minority and upholding peaceful protest in contrast; the National Guard called in; a curfew announced; mass gatherings to clean up the riot area; a disciplinarian parent puffed up into a national heroine after being caught on camera giving her rioting child a clip around the ear; suggestions that gangs were behind it all . . .

Yet in Baltimore, gangs seem to have performed the exact opposite function to that claimed early on. Police had issued warnings of an anti-cop alliance between Bloods, Crips and the Black Guerilla

---

* "Rough ride": a police technique for inflicting violence on arrestees indirectly, through the movements of a vehicle, thus removing them from the culpability of more direct aggression. Manny Fernandez, "Freddie Gray's Injury and the Police 'Rough Ride,'" *New York Times*, 30 April 2015.
† *The 2015 Baltimore Uprising: A Teen Epistolary* (Research and Destroy, New York City 2015).

Family. But it was soon revealed that the truce, brokered by the Nation of Islam, was in fact to suppress the riots. Bloods and Crips leaders released a video statement asking for calm and peaceful protest in the area, and joined with police and clergy to enforce the curfew. On 28 April news cameras recorded gang members dispersing "would-be troublemakers" at the Security Square Mall.

The similarities between Baltimore and St. Louis are striking. Both have been shrinking for decades as a result of deindustrialization, with roughly half the inner city below the poverty line. Both were epicenters of state-mandated segregation up to the 1970s, and subprime lending in the 2000s.* And while in most US cities crime rates have fallen sharply since their 1990s peak, in St. Louis and Baltimore they have stayed high, with both consistently in the top ten for violent crime and homicide. Yet while traditional black suburbs of St. Louis, such as Kinloch, have been gutted, those in Baltimore have thrived and proliferated. Situated at the nexus of the tri-state sprawl of Maryland, Virginia and DC, Baltimore's suburbs contain the largest concentration of black wealth in the US. Prince George's County is the richest majority black county in the country, the quintessential black middle class suburb, and its police force has a special reputation for brutality. In his most recent memoir Ta-Nehisi Coates cites his discovery of this fact as the source of his disillusionment with black nationalism. Coates' fellow student at Howard University, Prince Jones, was killed by a black P.G. County officer who mistook him for a burglary suspect. At the time Coates devoted an article to the questions of race and class raised by this killing:

> Usually, police brutality is framed as a racial issue: Rodney King suffering at the hands of a racist white Los Angeles Police Department or more recently, an unarmed Timothy Thomas, gunned down by a white Cincinnati cop. But in more and more communities, the police doing the brutalizing are African Americans, supervised by African-Ameri-

---

* Baltimore was the first city to adopt a residential segregation ordinance (in 1910). Richard Rothstein, "From Ferguson to Baltimore," Economic Policy Institute, 29 April 2015.

can police chiefs, and answerable to African-American mayors and city councils. *

In trying to explain why so few showed up for a Sharpton-led march in the wake of the Jones shooting, Coates pointed out that "affluent black residents are just as likely as white ones to think the victims of police brutality have it coming."

For decades these suburbs have incubated a black political establishment: federal representatives, state senators, lieutenant governors, aldermen, police commissioners. This is another legacy of Civil Rights.† It meant that Baltimore was the first American riot to be waged against a largely black power structure. This was in marked contrast to Ferguson, and it raised a significant problem for simplistic attempts to attribute black deaths to police racism: after all, three of the six cops accused of killing Gray were black.‡ It seemed, that is, that events were starting to force issues of class onto the agenda.

As FBI drones circled the skies over Baltimore, the day after Gray's funeral, Obama gave his statement, interrupting a summit with Shinzo Abe. This seemed markedly less scripted than those hitherto, stepping gingerly from phrase to phrase, balancing statements of support for police with those for the Gray family; noting that peaceful demonstrations never get as much attention as riots; fumbling a description of rioters as "protesters" — before recognizing the faux pas and quickly swapping in "criminals," then escalating and overcompensating with a racializing "thugs"; linking Baltimore to Ferguson and locating the ongoing chain of events in "a slow-rolling crisis" that had been "going on for decades"; calling on police unions not to

---

* Ta-Nehisi Coates, "Black and Blue: Why does America's richest black suburb have some of the country's most brutal cops?," *Washington Monthly,* June 2001.

† In 1970 there were 54 black legislators in the US. By 2000 there were 610. Most are in state houses, but the Black Caucus has become a powerful force in Congress, with over 40 members.

‡ 44% of Baltimore's police are black, compared to 60% of its population, but the wider metropolitan area from which police are recruited is 30% black. See Jeremy Ashkenas, "The Race Gap in America's Police Departments," *New York Times,* 8 April 2015.

close ranks and to acknowledge that "this is not good for police."

But most notably, the race contradiction which had described the polar tensions of Obama's rhetoric now receded into the background, while the problem over which "we as a country have to do some soul searching" became specifically one of poor blacks, impoverished communities, the absence of formal employment and its replacement with the illicit economy, cops called in merely to contain the problems of the ghetto; this was the *real* problem, though a hard one to solve politically. Presidential hopeful Hillary Clinton too was falling over herself to express an understanding of core social issues at play in these struggles.* Even the conservative *Washington Times* declared Baltimore's problem to be a matter of class, not race, and spoke sympathetically of how "residents in poorer neighborhoods feel targeted by a police force that treats them unfairly."† The contrast with the 1960s was striking: where ultra-liberal President Johnson once saw black riots as a communist plot, now the entire political class seemed to agree with the rioters' grievances: black lives did indeed matter, and yes, ghetto conditions and incarceration were problems.

The surprising degree of elite acceptance here might perhaps be attributed to the very different possibilities facing these two Civil Rights Movements, old and new. Where the first threatened substantially transformative social and political effects, challenging structures of racial oppression that dated back to Reconstruction's defeat, and brought the prospect of dethroning some political elites along the way, the new politics of black unity seemed to be kicking at an open door that led nowhere. Where the first could offer the prospect of incorporation of at least some parts of the black population into a growing economy, the new movement faced a stagnant economy with diminishing opportunities even for many of those lucky enough to have already avoided the ghetto, let alone those stuck in it.‡ Aspira-

---

* Hillary Clinton, "It's time to end the era of mass incarceration," 29 April 2015.

† Kellan Howell, "Baltimore riots sparked not by race but by class tensions between police, poor," *Washington Times*, 29 April 2015.

‡ See "A Statement from a Comrade and Baltimore Native About the Uprising" on sic journal.org.

tions to solve these problems were good American pipe dreams, easily acceptable precisely because it was hard to see what reform might actually be addressed to them beyond anodyne steps such as requiring more police to wear bodycams.

The contrast between Ferguson and Baltimore is testament to the enduring power of black political leaders—together with those of churches and gangs—to contain uprisings. In Ferguson, where there was only a minimal infrastructure of black political representation, the initial week-long uprising was repeated several times, each time politicizing new swaths of black youth, turning the small and hitherto obscure town into a national center for the new activism. By contrast, black elites in Baltimore moved quickly to quell unrest by indicting the police officers involved in Freddie Gray's death, winning State's Attorney Marilyn J. Mosby accolades, and shrouding the streets of Baltimore with a pall of silence, interrupted only by panics about a "Ferguson effect" on the city's crime rate. The first judgment on a police officer in the Gray case came in May of 2016. He was predictably exonerated.

The existing black elite is willing to embrace the "New Jim Crow" rhetoric as long as it funnels activists into NGOs and helps to consolidate votes—but always within a frame of paternalism and respectability, sprinkled with Moynihan-style invocations of the dysfunctional black family. Here initiatives focus on such things as mentoring to improve individual prospects, thus sidestepping social problems. Meanwhile churches function both as substitutes for the welfare state and as organs of community representation—roles they have proved willing to embrace and affirm in the context of this movement.* But it is probably significant that the word "thug" was first deployed here by those same elites—and Obama. While people across the spectrum of black American society and beyond could easily affirm that all those lives from Trayvon Martin onwards certainly did matter, what could they say to rioters from Baltimore's ghettos? Could the bonds of racial solidarity that were stretched across the

---

* See Antonia Blumberg and Carol Kuruvilla, "How The Black Lives Matter Movement Changed The Church," *Huffington Post*, 8 August 2015.

class divide still hold when the stigma of criminality pushed itself to the fore?

6.

The question of "black criminality" is overdetermined by decades of liberal vs. conservative acrimony, dating back to Daniel Patrick Moynihan's 1965 lament over the state of the "Negro family." Approximately three distinct sets of diagnoses and prescriptions stake out the rhetorical perimeter of this triangular debate. Conservatives condemn cultural pathologies and a lack of stable two-parent families, seeing this as the source of high crime in black neighborhoods; the solutions thus become promotion of religious observance and black fatherhood, paired with condemnation of rap music. Liberals defend rappers and single mothers from patriarchal conservatives, and condemn racist cops who exaggerate black criminality by over-policing black neighborhoods; thus the solution becomes police reform and fighting racism. Finally, social democrats will agree with conservatives that black crime is real but point to structural factors such as high unemployment and poverty, themselves driven in part by present and past racism; the solution thus becomes a Marshall Plan for the ghetto.

Many in the black middle class are skeptical of liberal denials of black criminality; many have family members or friends who have been affected by crime. Often open to structural arguments, they are also tired of waiting for social democratic panaceas which seem ever less likely. Noting their own capacities for relative advancement, it's easy for them to contrast the condition of the black poor to the supposed success of other racialized immigrant groups. They are thus drawn to conservative conclusions: there must be something wrong with their culture, their sexual mores, and so on. This is not just a matter of the Bill Cosbys and Ben Carsons. It is the position of influential liberal academics like William Julius Wilson and Orlando Patterson. It has also increasingly become the position of many supposed radicals: Al Sharpton raging against black youth culture and its "sagging pants" at 2013's National Action to Realize the Dream March; Cornel West decrying the "nihilism" within black culture and identifying religion as a solution.* This is what Black Lives Matter activists mean when they object to "the politics of respectability."

Such objections are, of course, essentially correct: it is stupid to blame crime on culture.† Michelle Alexander's *New Jim Crow* is a key reference point for these activists. Alexander points to racial disparities in drug-related incarceration: blacks and whites use drugs at similar rates, but blacks are arrested far more often, and sometimes receive longer sentences for the same offense, with the implication that these disparities are the work of racist cops and judges. Such liberal responses to conservative arguments tend, however, to come with a blind spot. By concentrating on low-level drug offenders—who even many conservatives agree shouldn't be serving time—Alexander avoids some thorny issues. Among prisoners, those classified as violent offenders outnumber drug offenders by more than 2 to 1, and the racial disproportion among them is as high.‡ But with violent crimes it is hard to deny that black people are both victims and perpetrators at much higher rates.§ Here the explanations of the social democrats are basically right, even if their solutions look implausible: black people are much more likely to live in urban ghettos, faced with far higher levels of material deprivation than whites.

With their endemic violence, these places are the real basis for the high "black-on-black crime" statistics that conservatives like to trot out as evidence that responsibility for the violence to which black people are subjected lies with black communities themselves. Understandably reacting against such arguments, liberals have pointed out

---

* Stephen Steinberg, "The Liberal Retreat From Race," *New Politics*, vol. 5, no. 1, summer 1994.

† For contemporary evidence of the structural determinants of crime see Ruth Peterson and Krivo Lauren, "Segregated Spatial Locations, Race-Ethnic Composition, and Neighborhood Violent Crime," *Annals of the American Academy*, no. 623, 2009.

‡ Drug offenders make up a much higher proportion of federal prisoners, but only 6% of prisoners are in federal prisons. See Forman Jr., "Racial Critiques of Mass Incarceration."

§ If we look only at homicides (generally the most reliable data), from 1980 to 2008 blacks have been 6–10 times more likely than whites to be victims and perpetrators. Alexia Cooper and Erica Smith, "Homicide Trends in the United States, 1980–2008," Bureau of Justice Statistics, 2010, p. 32.

similarities between intra-racial murder rates: 84% for whites and 93% for blacks.* This seems a polemically effective point: shouldn't white communities thus take more responsibility for "white-on-white crime" too? But again, something is being obscured: according to the Bureau of Justice Statistics, black people kill each other 8 times more often.

It is not necessary to accept the rhetorical logic by which acknowledging this appears a concession to conservative moralizing. Aren't high crime rates to be expected in the most unequal society in the developed world? And isn't it entirely predictable that violent crime should be concentrated in urban areas where forms of employment are prevalent that do not enjoy legal protections, and which therefore must often be backed up with a capacity for direct force? Arguments that avoid such things often involve implicit appeals to an unrealistic notion of innocence, and therefore seem to have the perverse effect of reinforcing the stigma of crime; here the critics of "respectability politics" reproduce its founding premise.†

While the prospect of the underlying problem being solved through a gigantic Marshall Plan for the ghetto looks like the most forlorn of hopes, many policy proposals from Black Lives Matter activists merely amount to some version of "more black cops." The history of police reform in places like Baltimore, where the police and "civilian review boards" have long mirrored the faces of the wider population, clearly demonstrates the insufficiency of these responses. But those who make the more radical claim that the demand should be less rather than *better* policing are in some ways just as out of touch.‡ The troubling fact—often cited by the conservative right, but no less true for that reason—is that it is precisely in the poorest black neighborhoods that we often find the strongest support for tougher policing. When Sharpton, in his eulogy for Brown,

---

* Jamelle Bouie, "The Trayvon Martin Killing and the Myth of Black-on-Black Crime," *Daily Beast*, 15 July 2013.

† Indeed, in questioning the reality of crime, liberals suggest that the most dispossessed are obediently acquiescing to their condition.

‡ See Alex Vitale, "We Don't Just Need Nicer Cops: We Need Fewer Cops," *The Nation*, 4 December 2014.

railed against the abject blackness of the gangster and the thug, some of the activists were horrified, but his message was warmly received by many of the Ferguson residents present. This is because Sharpton was appealing to a version of "respectability politics" that has roots in the ghetto. Ta-Nahesi Coates, who grew up in West Baltimore, has acknowledged that many residents "were more likely to ask for police support than to complain about brutality." This is not because they especially loved cops, but because they had no other recourse: while the "safety" of white America was in "schools, portfolios, and skyscrapers," theirs was in "men with guns who could only view us with the same contempt as the society that sent them."*

In this precarious world one must survive with little help, and any accident or run of bad luck can result in losing everything. It is no surprise that people get sick or turn to crime when they fall down and can't get back up. The police are there to ensure that those who have fallen don't create further disturbances, and to haul them away to prison if they do. People who are thereby snared are not just those nabbed by the cops, but people—not angels—caught in the vectors of a spreading social disintegration. At the same time, broader populations—fearful of looking down—develop their own cop mentalities. This gives the lie to anti-police slogans that present the police as an imposition on the community, that hinge on assumptions that these communities would do just fine if the police stopped interfering: where community and society are themselves in states of decay, the police offers itself as a stand-in; bringing a semblance of order to lives that no longer matter to capital.

For much the same reason, it is more or less impossible for the state to resolve the problem by changing the fundamental character of the police. A full-scale reform that did away with the present function of the police as repressive, last-resort social mediation would require a revival of the social democratic project. But with burgeoning levels of debts, states lack the key to that door. Meanwhile the softer reforms around which Black Lives Matter activists can unite with a

---

* Coates, *Between the World and Me* (Spiegel & Grau 2015), p. 85. Coates further describes this as "raging against the crime in your ghetto, because you are powerless before the great crime of history that brought the ghettos to be."

bipartisan political elite—things like decarceration for low-level drug offenders and "justice reinvestment" in community policing—only raise the prospect of a more surgically targeted version of the carceral state. The brutal policing of black America is a forewarning about the global future of a humanity made economically surplus to capital. Escaping from that future will require the discovery of new modes of unified action, beyond the separations.

7.

Drawing in people from across a vast span of American society under the heading of "black," to protest over issues deeply entwined with racializing structures, this wave of struggles has displayed a peculiar capacity to unite diverse socio-economic strata. Blackness as a unifying term carries a certain weight when set against the orientationless groping towards unity of other recent struggles such as Occupy, which foundered in the process of trying to compose a coherent movement from its "99%." But while political composition has tended to present itself as a fundamental, unsolvable riddle for such movements, they have not been compositionally static. In the global wave of 2011–12, there was a tendency to produce glimpses of possible new unities as the worse-off entered and transformed protests initiated by the better-off: occupations initiated by students or educated professionals over time attracted growing numbers of the homeless and destitute; university demonstrations over fee hikes gradually brought out kids who would never have gone to university in the first place. Later, the Ukraine's Maidan protests, kicked off by pro-European liberals and far-right nationalists, mutated into encampments of dispossessed workers. In England, such modulations terminated with the crescendo of the 2011 riots, as the racialized poor brought their anti-police fury to the streets.*

If the riddle of composition, for movements like Occupy, had stemmed from the lack of any already-existing common identity, blackness seemed perhaps to offer one. Early activists within this

---

* See "A Rising Tide Lifts All Boats" and "The Holding Pattern" in *Endnotes*, 3 September 2013.

wave had consciously sought to solve Occupy's "whiteness" problem, hoping this would lead to a broader-based movement. In the event, Black Lives Matter was able to attract many more of the poor and excluded. But it was also able to draw a surprising degree of support from celebrity and political circles. From Beyoncé and Jay-Z's bailing-out of Ferguson and Baltimore protesters, to Prince's post-Baltimore "rally4peace," to Snoop Dogg's associations with the Brown and Davis families; from Barack Obama's personal identifications with the victims of racialized violence to Hillary Clinton's careful alignment with decarceration activists—these struggles managed to secure a level of symbolic endorsement from the upper echelons of American society that would have been unimaginable for the French riots of 2005, or the English ones of 2011.

This kind of vertical integration of diverse social strata is a commonplace of American history, in which the racial bonds among whites have always been stretched over even greater spans. Slave owner and yeoman farmer, postbellum landlord and poor white sharecropper, WASP industrialist and Irish immigrant had even less in common than black political elites have today with the predominantly poor victims of racial violence. Yet the yeoman joined slave patrols and fought to defend slavery in the Civil War; the white sharecropper (after the brief interracial alliance of populism) would help to maintain Jim Crow segregation through lynch terror; and the Irish immigrant, though initially racialized himself, would brutally police black neighborhoods on behalf of his Protestant betters. Historically, whiteness was able to span these great vertical distances not because of some affinity of culture or kin, but because it was embodied in the American state itself. Now, however, that state was topped by someone ostensibly outside this construct. However tenuously, blackness too now seemed capable—at least in principle—of spanning comparable social distances. From the impoverished East Baltimore resident, clinging onto the edges of a fraying social fabric, to the US president: it is a rare movement that can seem to unite such diverse people behind a substantive social cause. But there's the rub. Stretched across such an unequal span, it was probably inevitable that the unity at play here would be correspondingly thin. At such extremes, postulations of a single black identity appear increasingly lacking in social content.

That blackness can seem to offer something more substantial is an effect of its peculiar construction: a social content forcefully given by its role as marker of subordinate class, but also an identitarian unity enabled by its ultimate non-correspondence with class. These poles in tension have long identified the specificity of black struggles: proletarian insurgency or "race leadership"; blackness as socio-economic curse or as culture. But as the divide between rich and poor gapes ever wider, and as the latter sink further into misery and crime, gestures at holding the two poles together must become ever emptier. To reach towards the social content one must loosen one's hold on the identity; to embrace the identity one must let go of the content. It is practically impossible to hold both at once. Is the core demand to be about police reform? Or is it to be about ameliorating ghetto conditions in which police violence is more or less the only check on other kinds? If blackness seems to offer itself as a space in which these demands might not actually be at odds, this is only by the indistinct light from the gloam of older capacities for solidarity, when the black middle class too lived in the ghetto and shared its fate; when the black working class could reasonably hope to see better days.

Though the social content of blackness appears increasingly contradictory, it is equally clear that it retains a capacity to induce dynamic mobilizations in the American population. And in its tensions there still lies an unstable if unaffirmable moment, at the social root of racializing logics, where capitalist social relations are rotting into nothing, and where the most pressing problems of surplus humanity lie. If race could present itself as the solution to one compositional riddle, conjuring a new unity, that unity itself now issues in another compositional impasse: could black elites really identify with Baltimore's marginalized poor once their rioting had set the city aflame? But now the ghetto has rediscovered its capacity to riot, and to force change by doing so, will other, larger components of America's poor—white and latino—stand idly by?

CONTRIBUTORS' NOTES

Jesse Ball is the author of fourteen books, most recently the novel *How to Set a Fire and Why*. His works have been published to acclaim in many parts of the world and translated into more than a dozen languages. He is on the faculty at the School of the Art Institute of Chicago, won the 2008 Paris Review Plimpton Prize, was long-listed for the National Book Award, and has been a fellow of the NEA, Creative Capital, and the Guggenheim Foundation.

Kyle Boelte is the author of *The Beautiful Unseen*, a book about fading memory, his brother's suicide, and San Francisco's fog. His writing has appeared in *ZYZZYVA*, *Orion Magazine*, *Full Stop*, *Adventure Journal*, and *High Country News*. He lives on the West Coast.

Molly Brodak is the author of *A Little Middle of the Night*, winner of the 2009 Iowa Poetry Prize, and three chapbooks of poetry. She held the 2011–2013 Poetry Fellowship at Emory University and currently lives in Atlanta, Georgia.

Endnotes is a journal of communist theory published by a discussion group of the same name based in Germany, the U.K., and the US.

Kendra Fortmeyer is a Pushcart Prize–winning fiction writer, a teen librarian, and the prose editor for *Broad!*, an all-women's and trans writers' literary magazine. Her work has been recognized by grants from the Elizabeth George Foundation and the Michener Center for Writers, and has appeared in *One Story, The Toast, Black Warrior Review,* and elsewhere. She received her MFA in fiction from the New Writers Project at UT Austin. She is the author of the chapbook *The Girl Who Could Only Say sex, drugs, and rock & roll.* Her debut novel is forthcoming from Little, Brown in 2017.

Mark Hitz was born and raised in Idaho. He spent ten years recording sound for documentary and reality television, and was a Michener Fellow at the University of Texas, where he won the 2014 Keene Prize for Literature. He is currently a Wallace Stegner Fellow at Stanford.

Mateo Hoke and Cate Malek began working together in 2001, while studying journalism at the University of Colorado–Boulder. Their interest in human rights journalism began on a project in which they spent eight months interviewing undocumented Mexican immigrants about their daily lives. From 2009 until 2015, Cate lived in the West Bank, where she worked as an editor and taught English at Bethlehem University. She previously worked as a newspaper reporter, receiving multiple Colorado Press Association awards. Mateo holds a master's degree from the University of California–Berkeley Graduate School of Journalism. In addition to his work in the Middle East, he has reported from the Amazon jungle and the Seychelles. His writing has received awards from the Overseas Press Club Foundation and the Knight Foundation, among others.

Dan Hoy is the author of *The Deathbed Editions* (Octopus Books, 2016) and several poetry chapbooks, including *Omegachurch* (Solar Luxuriance, 2010) and *Glory Hole* (Mal-O- Mar Editions, 2009). His work has been featured in *Triple Canopy, Action Yes, Novembre Magazine, Jubilat,* and other magazines and anthologies.

Laurel Hunt is an MFA candidate at the Michener Center for Writers at UT Austin. Her poems can be found or are forthcoming in *Pleiades; Forklift, Ohio; Salt Hill; Diagram;* and elsewhere.

Gary Indiana is a writer, playwright, filmmaker, and artist. He is the author of seven novels, including *Do Everything in the Dark* and *The Shanghai Gesture*, as well as several plays, collections of poetry and nonfiction, and essays in publications from *Art in America* to *Vice*. His most recent publication is the memoir *I Can Give You Anything But Love*.

N. R. "Sonny" Kleinfield is a reporter at the *New York Times*, where he is a member of the Metro department's investigations and projects team. His story on the death of George Bell was a finalist for the Pulitzer Prize in feature writing. He has also received the Polk Award, the Meyer Berger Award, and the Robert F. Kennedy Journalism Award. He is the author of eight nonfiction books, and has written for *Harper's*, the *Atlantic*, *Esquire*, *Rolling Stone*, and the *New York Times Magazine*.

Anna Kovatcheva was born in Sofia, Bulgaria, and holds an MFA in fiction writing from New York University. Her novella, *The White Swallow*, was selected by Aimee Bender as the winner of the 2014 Gold Line Press Fiction Chapbook Competition. Her stories have appeared in the *Kenyon Review* and the *Iowa Review*. She lives in New York City.

Sharon Lerner covers health and the environment for *The Intercept*. Her work has also appeared in the *New York Times*, *The Nation*, and the *Washington Post*, among other publications, and has received awards from The Society for Environmental Journalists, The American Public Health Association, the Women and Politics Institute, and The Newswomen's Club of New York.

Jason Little is the author of *Borb*, *Shutterbug Follies*, and *Motel Art Improvement Service*. His work-in-progess, *The Vagina*, is currently being serialized in the French magazine *Aaarg!* Jason teaches cartooning at the School of Visual Arts.

Rebecca Makkai is the Chicago-based author of the story collection *Music for Wartime*, as well as the novels *The Hundred-Year House* and *The Borrower*. Her short fiction was featured in *The Best American Short*

Stories anthology in 2008, 2009, 2010, and 2011, and appears regularly in publications such as *Harper's*, *Tin House*, and *Ploughshares*, and on public radio's *This American Life* and *Selected Shorts*. The recipient of a 2014 NEA Fellowship, Rebecca has taught at the Tin House Writers' Conference, Northwestern University, and the Iowa Writers' Workshop.

Anthony Marra is the author of *The Tsar of Love and Techno* and *A Constellation of Vital Phenomena*. "The Grozny Tourist Bureau" first appeared in *Zoetrope*, where it received the National Magazine Award for Fiction.

Michael Pollan is author of five *New York Times* bestsellers: *The Omnivore's Dilemma: A Natural History of Four Meals*, *The Botany of Desire*, *In Defense of Food*, *Food Rules*, and, mostly recently, *Cooked: A Natural History of Transformation*. In 2010 he was named one of the 100 most influential people in the world by *Time* magazine. Pollan served for many years as executive editor of *Harper's* Magazine and is now the Knight Professor of Science and Environmental Journalism at UC Berkeley. He lives in the Bay Area with his wife, the painter Judith Belzer, and their son, Isaac.

Da'Shay Portis is completing her MFA at San Francisco State University.

Ariana Reines is the author of *The Cow*, *Coeur de Lion*, *Mercury*, and the Obie-wining play *Telephone*. Her translations include *Preliminary Materials for a Theory of the Young-Girl* by Tiqqun and *The Little Black Book of Grisélidis Réal* by Jean-Luc Hennig. Her artworks, performances, and collaborations appear internationally, including *Mortal Kombat* at the Whitney Museum and *Pubic Space* at Modern Art, London.

Marilynne Robinson is the recipient of a 2012 National Humanities Medal, awarded by President Barack Obama. She is the author of *Lila*, a finalist for the National Book Award and the National Book Critics Circle Award; *Gilead*, winner of the 2005 Pulitzer Prize for Fiction and the National Book Critics Circle Award; and *Home*, winner of the Orange Prize and the Los Angeles Times Book Prize, and a finalist for the

National Book Award. Her first novel, *Housekeeping*, won the Hemingway Foundation/PEN Award. Robinson's nonfiction books include *The Givenness of Things*, *When I Was a Child I Read Books*, *Absence of Mind*, *The Death of Adam*, and *Mother Country*, which was nominated for a National Book Award. She lives in Iowa City, where she taught at the University of Iowa Writers' Workshop for twenty-five years.

Yuko Sakata's stories have appeared in the *Missouri Review*, *Zoetrope*, the *Iowa Review*, and *Vice*. Born in New York, she grew up in Hong Kong and Tokyo, and she has an MFA in creative writing from the University of Wisconsin–Madison. She currently lives in Queens with her husband and young daughter.

sam sax is a 2015 NEA Fellow and finalist for The Ruth Lilly Fellowship from the Poetry Foundation. He's a Poetry Fellow at the Michener Center for Writers, where he serves as the editor-in-chief of *Bat City Review*. He's the two-time Bay Area Grand Slam Champion and author of the chapbooks *A Guide to Undressing Your Monsters* (Button Poetry, 2014), *sad boy / detective* (Black Lawrence Press, 2015), and *All The Rage* (Sibling Rivalry Press, 2016). His poems are forthcoming in *American Poetry Review*, *Boston Review*, *Ploughshares*, *Guernica*, and *Poetry Magazine*. He's the winner of the 2016 Iowa Review Award.

Michele Scott is a writer who gardens passionately, and is involved in many peer education, restorative justice, victim impact, and spiritual groups at the Central California Women's Facility, where she is serving a life sentence without eligibility for parole.

Dana Spiotta is the author of four novels: *Innocents and Others* (2016), from which "Jelly and Jack" was excerpted; *Stone Arabia* (2011), which was a National Book Critics Circle Award Finalist in fiction; *Eat the Document* (2006), which was a finalist for the National Book Award and a recipient of the Rosenthal Foundation Award from the American Academy of Arts and Letters; and *Lightning Field* (2001). She lives in Syracuse and teaches in the Syracuse University MFA program.

Adrian Tomine was born in 1974 in Sacramento, California. He is the writer/artist of the comic book series *Optic Nerve*, as well as the books *Sleepwalk and Other Stories, Summer Blonde, Scenes from an Impending Marriage, Shortcomings,* and *New York Drawings*. His comics and illustrations have appeared in the *New York Times, McSweeney's,* and *The Paris Review,* and he is a regular contributor to *The New Yorker*. His most recent book, published by Drawn & Quarterly, is *Killing and Dying*.

Inara Verzemnieks teaches in the University of Iowa's Nonfiction Writing Program. Her writing has appeared in such publications as the *New York Times Magazine,* the *Iowa Review, Creative Nonfiction,* and *Tin House*. She is a Pushcart Prize winner, the recipient of a Rona Jaffe Writers' Award, and in her previous life as a daily newspaper reporter, she was named a finalist for the Pulitzer Prize in Feature Writing. Her first book, a memoir, is forthcoming from W. W. Norton.

David Wagoner was born in Ohio and raised in Indiana. Before moving to Washington in 1954, Wagoner attended Pennsylvania State University, where he was a member of the Naval ROTC, and received an MA in English from Indiana University. Wagoner was selected to serve as chancellor of the Academy of American Poets in 1978, replacing Robert Lowell, and he served as the editor of *Poetry Northwest* until its last issue in 2002. Known for his dedication to teaching, he was named a professor emeritus at the University of Washington.

Xuan Juliana Wang was a Wallace Stegner Fellow at Stanford University. Her short stories been published by the *Altantic, Ploughshares, The Brooklyn Rail, Gigantic,* and the *Pushcart Prize Anthology*. Born in Jiamusi, China, she resides in New York City.

THE BEST AMERICAN
NONREQUIRED READING
COMMITTEE

They say editing by committee never works, but they've never seen a committee like this. Below you will find the bios of the *Best American Nonrequired Reading (BANR)* committee. These students met on a weekly basis at McSweeney's Publishing in San Francisco, California, to select the work that ended up in this book. They were aided by a group of students in Ann Arbor, Michigan, whose bios you will also find herewith.

Laura Burns is a freshman at Huron High School in Ann Arbor, Michigan. As the first bio, she would like to welcome you to the student bios section. Her favorite color is irrelevant, favorite place in the world is Austin, Texas, favorite beverage is a banana shake. Chai lattes come in as a close second.

Samantha Cho is 15 years old and a sophomore at Huron High School. She is on the field hockey team and plays violin in her school orchestra. In her free time, she enjoys writing and reading historical fiction, and walking her dog, whom she finds historically cute.

Emilia Fernández is a junior at Lick-Wilmerding High School in San Francisco, who likes to read and sleep. In 20 years she sees herself writing novels in a cabin somewhere in the Alaskan wilderness, with several cats. And perhaps a domesticated wolf. She has not ruled out the possibility of wolf ownership.

Marcus Gee-Lim is a senior at Lowell High School in San Francisco. He almost got into a bike accident with a squirrel once. Now he looks both ways before crossing the street and avoids squirrels at all costs. They are utterly reckless creatures, in his estimation.

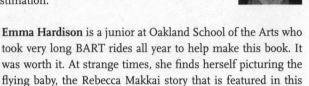

Emma Hardison is a junior at Oakland School of the Arts who took very long BART rides all year to help make this book. It was worth it. At strange times, she finds herself picturing the flying baby, the Rebecca Makkai story that is featured in this anthology. She is not sure why.

Sidney Hirschman is a junior at Lick-Wilmerding High School. They enjoy singing songs, reading books, making miniatures, pining over robots, and wearing vogue night looks to the Sunday morning farmers' market. This is their first year on the *BANR* committee.

Niki King Fredel is a freshman at New York University. She likes to take photos, read books, and listen to music. She wants to be taken seriously by other people but does not want to take herself seriously. She was formerly a student at Urban High School in San Francisco.

Sian Laing is a junior at Mission High School in San Francisco. If you need to summon Sian, simply mention the words "gymnastics" or "tea." On occasion, someone says one of these words without realizing it will automatically summon Sian. This has resulted in several uncomfortable situations.

Zoe Olson is a junior at Mission High School and this was her first year on the committee. She lives in a house full of books with her family and her cat. One day she hopes to live in a house with even more books and twice the amount of cats and a similar amount of family.

Marco Ponce graduated from George Washington High School in San Francisco this past spring. This was his fourth and final year on the committee. His motto is, and always has been: "In order to feel good you have to dress good."

A junior at Jewish Community High School in San Francisco, **Zola Rosenfeld** enjoys musical theater and rock climbing. She has been known to leave a trail of broken hearts wherever she goes, but she has also been known to pick up their pieces. She is notably tidy.

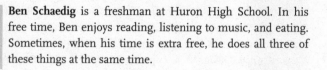

Ben Schaedig is a freshman at Huron High School. In his free time, Ben enjoys reading, listening to music, and eating. Sometimes, when his time is extra free, he does all three of these things at the same time.

Isaac Schott-Rosenfield is a senior at the Ruth Asawa School of the Arts in San Francisco. Among other things, Isaac has forgotten where he wrote down the joke he was going to use for this bio. But he did write one down, he did. It's bound to turn up sometime. These things always do.

Cynthia Van is a freshman at UC San Diego. She spent three years on the *BANR* committee, while she was a student at George Washington High School. Her interests include writing, engineering, and deer antlers, among other things. The antlers of a deer are actually considered to be more of a handicap than an advantage because of their nutritional demand. Is it just a style thing, in that case? Cynthia has wondered. This is all she can do: wonder.

Grace VanRenterghem graduated from Huron High School this past year. She was a member of the *BANR* committee for three years. The person below her is her identical twin. She enjoys having an identical twin.

Hadley VanRenterghem graduated from Ann Arbor Huron High School this past year. Like her sister, she worked on the *BANR* committee for three years. As far as she knows, she and Grace are the only identical twins in the history of *BANR*.

Annette Vergara-Tucker is a sophomore at Lick-Wilmerding High School. Most days, you will find her reading a book or spending way too much time with her best friend, Anna. As the last bio, she would like to thank you for taking the time to get to know the editors of this book. It makes her happy.

Very special thanks to Dave Eggers, Nicole Angeloro, Clara Sankey, Mark Robinson, and Jillian Tamaki. Thanks also to Adam Johnson, Daniel Handler, Mikayla McVey, Maura Reilly-Ulmanek, Elliott Eglash, Daniel Cesca, Belle Baxley, Helena Smith, Andi Winnette, Jordan Bass, Ruby Perez, Dan McKinley, Sunra Thompson, Elizabeth Hanley, Claire Boyle, Ted Gioia, Kristina Kearns, Chris Monks, Mimi Lok, Gerald Richards, Christina Perry, Kona Lai, Ashley Varady, Bita Nazarian, Jorge Garcia, María Inés Montes, Amy Popovitch, Ricardo Cruz, Kavitha Lotun, Jillian Wasick, Caroline Kangas, Molly Parent, Emma Peoples, Lauren Hall, Allyson Halpern, Amanda Loo, Alyssa Aninag, Olivia White Lopez, Jenesha de Rivera Diana Adamson, Selina Weiss, Monica Mendez, Piper Sutherland, Kate Bueler, Juliana Sloane, Rachael Reiley, Noel Ramírez, and Phyllis DeBlanche.

NOTABLE
NONREQUIRED READING
OF 2015

FATIN ABBAS
On a Morning, *Freeman's*
AAMINA AHMAD
July Sun, the *Missouri Review*
TAHMIMA ANAM
Garments, *Freeman's*

PABLO CALVI
Secret Reserves, the *Believer*
TED CONOVER
Cattle Calls, *Harper's*

PATRICK DACEY
Love, Women, the *Paris Review*
STEPHEN DUNN
Three Poems, the *Paris Review*

ALVARO ENRIGUE
El Vocho, the *Believer*

WILLIAM FINNEGAN
Off Diamond Head, *The New Yorker*

RIVKA GALCHEN
Usl at the Stadium, the *New Yorker*

JOHN GIBLER
The Disappeared, the *California Sunday Magazine*

AMANDA GOLDBLATT
The Era of Good Feelings, the *Southern Review*

SOPHIE GOLDSTEIN
The Oven, AdHouse Books

LEWIS HYDE
Forgetting Mississippi, *Tin House*

LUCY KNISLEY
Displacement, Fantagraphics

WILLIAM MALATINSKY
The Expatriates, *American Short Fiction*

THOMAS PIERCE
Tarantella, *Zoetrope*

ROBIN ROMM
What to Expect, the *Missouri Review*
Ars Parentis, *ZYZZYVA*

KATHERINE SCHIFANI
Cartography, *Epiphany*

MATTHEW SHAER
Whatsoever Things Are True, *The Atavist*

ADAM SHATZ
Magical Thinking About ISIS, the *London Review of Books*

SHUBHA SUNDER
The Footbridge, *Michigan Quarterly Review*

LISA WELLS
All Across the Desert Our Bread Is Blooming!, the *Believer*

ABOUT 826 NATIONAL

Proceeds from this book benefit youth literacy

A PERCENTAGE OF the cover price of this book goes to 826 National, a network of seven youth tutoring, writing, and publishing centers in seven cities around the country.

Since the birth of 826 National in 2002, our goal has been to assist students ages 6–18 with their writing skills while helping teachers get their classes passionate about writing. We do this with a vast army of volunteers who donate their time so we can give as much one-on-one attention as possible to the students whose writing needs it. Our mission is based on the understanding that great leaps in learning can happen with one-on-one attention, and that strong writing skills are fundamental to future success.

Through volunteer support, each of the eight 826 chapters—in San Francisco, New York, Los Angeles, Ann Arbor, Chicago, Boston, and Washington, DC—provides drop-in tutoring, class field trips, writing workshops, and in-schools programs, all free of charge, for students, classes, and schools. 826 centers are especially committed to supporting teachers, offering services and resources for English language learners, and publishing student work. Each of the 826 chapters works to produce professional-quality publications written entirely by young people, to forge relationships with teachers in order to create innovative workshops and lesson plans, to inspire students to write and appreciate the written word, and to rally thousands of enthusiastic volunteers to make it all happen. By offering all of our programming for free, we aim to serve families who cannot afford to pay for the level of personalized instruction their children receive through 826 chapters.

The demand for 826 National's services is tremendous. In 2015 we worked with more than 5,300 active volunteers and over 30,000 students nationally, hosted 674 field trips, completed 208 major in-school projects, offered 329 evening and weekend workshops, held over 1,300 after-school tutoring sessions, and produced nearly 900 student publications. At many of our centers, our field trips are fully booked almost a year in advance, teacher requests for in-school tutor support continue to rise, and the majority of our evening and weekend workshops have waitlists.

826 National volunteers are local community residents, professional writers, teachers, artists, college students, parents, bankers, lawyers, and retirees from a wide range of professions. These passionate individuals can be found at all of our centers after school, sitting side by side with our students, providing one-on-one attention. They can be found running our field trips, or helping an entire classroom of local students learn how to write a story.

Read on to learn more about each 826 National chapter, including 826 Valencia's newest outpost in San Francisco's Tenderloin District.

826 VALENCIA

Named for the street address of the building it occupies in the heart of San Francisco's Mission District, 826 Valencia opened on April 8, 2002, and consists of a writing lab, a street-front, student-friendly retail pirate store that partially funds its programs, and three satellite classrooms in local schools. 826 Valencia has developed programs that reach students at every possible opportunity—in school, after school, in the evenings, or on the weekends. Since its doors opened, over fifteen hundred volunteers—including published authors, magazine founders, SAT course instructors, documentary filmmakers, and other professionals—have donated their time to work with thousands of students.

After thirteen years of programming in San Francisco's Mission District, 826 Valencia opened a second writing and tutoring center to support San Francisco's Tenderloin neighborhood. The doors to the new center at 180 Golden Gate opened on May 19, 2016. The storefront, King Carl's Emporium, is open for business

every day. The Tenderloin is San Francisco's most densely populated neighborhood, and the home of 4,000 of the city's children. It has the second highest incidence of food stamp use in the city, with a median household income of $23,804. The 826 Valencia Tenderloin Center expects to serve at least 2,000 students a year and recruit 300 volunteers.

826 NYC

826NYC's writing center opened its doors in September 2004. Since then its programs have offered over one thousand students opportunities to improve their writing and to work side by side with hundreds of community volunteers. 826NYC has also built a satellite tutoring center, created in partnership with the Brooklyn Public Library, which has introduced library programs to an entirely new community of students. During the school year, 826NYC offers homework help and writing instruction for students 6 to 18. Tutors assist with homework in every subject and lead students in writing and reading-based enrichment activities. The center also publishes a handful of books of student writing each year.

826 LA

826LA benefits greatly from the wealth of cultural and artistic resources in the Los Angeles area. The center regularly presents a free workshop at the Armand Hammer Museum in which esteemed artists, writers, and performers teach their craft. 826LA has collaborated with the J. Paul Getty Museum to create

Community Photoworks, a months-long program that taught seventh-graders the basics of photographic composition and analysis, sent them into Los Angeles with cameras, and then helped them polish artist statements. Since opening in March 2005, 826LA has provided thousands of hours of free one-on-one writing instruction, held summer camps for English language learners, given students sportswriting training in the Lakers' press room, and published love poems written from the perspectives of leopards.

826 CHICAGO

826 Chicago opened its writing lab and after-school tutoring center in the West Town community of Chicago, in the Wicker Park neighborhood. The setting is both culturally lively and teeming with schools: within one mile, there are fifteen public schools serving more than sixteen thousand students. The center opened in December 2005 and now has over five hundred volunteers. Its programs, as at all the 826 chapters, are designed to be both challenging and enjoyable. Ultimately, the goal is to strengthen each student's power to express ideas effectively, creatively, confidently, and in his or her individual voice.

826 MICHIGAN

826 Michigan opened its doors on June 1, 2005, on South State Street in Ann Arbor. In October of 2007 the operation moved downtown, to a new and improved location on Liberty Street. This move enabled the opening of Liberty Street Robot Supply & Repair in May 2008. The shop carries everything the  robot owner might need, from positronic brains to grasping appendages to solar cells. 826 Michigan is the only 826 not named after a city because it serves students all over southeastern Michigan, hosting in-school residencies in Ypsilanti schools, and providing workshops for students in Detroit, Lincoln, and Willow Run school districts. The center also has a packed workshop schedule on site every semester, with offerings on making pop-up books, writing sonnets, creating screenplays, producing infomercials, and more.

826 BOSTON

 826 Boston provides free writing and tutoring programs for Boston students ages 6 to 18, serving more than 3,500 students. The center is located in Roxbury's Egleston Square—a culturally diverse community south of downtown that stretches into Jamaica Plain, Roxbury, and Dorchester. 826 Boston maintains a network of more than 2,500 volunteers from the Boston community—including professional writers, artists, and teachers. More than 600 volunteers regularly devote their time and talents to its programs.

826 DC

826DC opened its doors to the city's Columbia Heights neighborhood in October 2010. 826DC provides after-school tutoring, field trips, after-school workshops, in-school tutoring, help for English language learners, and assistance with the publication of student work. It also offers free admission to the Museum of Unnatural History, the center's unique storefront. In 2011, 826 DC students read their poetry before President Barack Obama.

ABOUT SCHOLARMATCH

Founded by author Dave Eggers, ScholarMatch began as a simple crowdfunding platform to help low-income students pay for college. In five short years ScholarMatch has grown into a full-service college-access organization, serving more than 500 students each year. We support students at our drop-in center, at local schools and organizations, and online through our crowdfunding platform and innovative resources like the ScholarMatcher—the first free college search tool built specifically with the needs of low-income students in mind.

Our mission is to make college possible for underserved youth by matching students with donors, resources, colleges, and professional networks. More than 80 percent of ScholarMatch students are the first in their families to go to college, and over 50 percent have family incomes of $25,000 or less. ScholarMatch students are bright, resilient young people who have overcome significant challenges, and maintain their determination to seek a better future through college.

With the support of donors, volunteers, schools, and community organizations, we ensure that college is possible for underserved students in the San Francisco Bay Area and beyond. To support a student's college journey or learn more, visit scholarmatch.org.

THE BEST AMERICAN SERIES®

FIRST, BEST, AND BEST-SELLING

The Best American Comics

The Best American Essays

The Best American Infographics

The Best American Mystery Stories

The Best American Nonrequired Reading

The Best American Science and Nature Writing

The Best American Science Fiction and Fantasy

The Best American Short Stories

The Best American Sports Writing

The Best American Travel Writing

Available in print and e-book wherever books are sold.
Visit our website: *www.hmhco.com/bestamerican*